Silicon Hell

JR Ford

First Published in the United Kingdom in 2015 by

Goodrich Books

27 Ffordd Beck, Gowerton, Swansea SA4 3GE

www.goodrichbooks.co.uk

A CIP catalogue record for this book is available
from the British Library

ISBN: 978-0-9929743-0-5

To my family

and K.

"Our profit is your profit" -
Global Ultra-Capitalistic Infrastructure (GUCI)

It was a long time ago that I realized something must been done about the all-encompassing greed I then saw all around. At the time I was amongst friends and felt relatively safe. That feeling of security was soon to be shattered. Humanity was on the edge of a precipice. Working at Meometics Universal was supposed to be a blessing. It would soon become a curse.

Silicon Hell

Prologue

10:30, Solar 60, 3rd Quarter, Profit Cycle 33
Northern Block – GUCI HQ

'Confirm, all targets are present. You have a go.' The three termination squads left their base of operations and split up to different destinations in the city. In just a few minutes the threat to the profitability of another corporation would be silenced.

The lab had been hastily upgraded by its team leader. In the far corner the transfer chair had been linked up to the new quantum storage unit. It had only just come online. 'There should be enough space to fit everything in,' the scientist mumbled to himself. He started the sequence and sank back into the chair.

The scientist told himself to relax, this was going to be one weird experience. Better to try it out first before informing his colleagues. They'd say it was reckless, which it was. His head was tingling but he could make out the progress bar on the panel display which read a little over 12 per cent.

10:35 – The three squads arrive in the basement of the building containing their targets. The lifts have already been pre-programmed to meet them. No one else would have access to them until the mission was over.

10:36 – The lifts arrive at the subjects' floor. The squads exit the lifts walking at pace to the two apartments and the research lab. Three, two, one. Go!

10:37 – They burst into the two apartments using priority keycard overrides and terminate the occupants with a spray of termination darts. The squad assigned to the lab is not so fortunate. 'Access denied' flashes up on the door, taunting the squad. Their target is safe for the moment. Squad three's leader tries again. 'Access denied – transfer in progress'.

Saul Taylor sighed. This would not look good on his record. He tried his keycard a third time. 'Access granted – transfer completed'. The team raced through the door. It took them seconds to latch onto the scientist who was hunched over the controls on one of the more sophisticated panels in the lab. Saul dispatched a dart to the back of the head, his target slumped to the right and slid off the chair. He had been operating the panels interface – 'Transfer 100% procedure complete' was showing on the display panel as if to mock the termination squad for their delayed entry.

Saul reported in. 'Head Profit Enabler, the mission has been accomplished. All targets have been eliminated, Ma'am.' he confirmed.

'Thank you Enforcer Taylor. Their team leader in particular was increasingly becoming a liability.' Zeleno replied.

The other two enforcers unpacked half a bag each from their combat jackets. They dragged the dead scientist away from the chair and zipped him up in the two-part body bag.

'Disposal shaft two has been re-directed for us. Send him down that chute,' Taylor ordered.

A consciousness stirred. It could see Saul Taylor scanning the rest of the lab, and caught the other two enforcers dragging the dead scientist out of the lab. *It can't be! I've just been murdered!*

'Morning Grant, how's the late shift been? – any *shift of late?*' I enquired.

'Aw Jeez man, don't you ever get tired of that old line?' Grant replied. It was the same mock exasperation he always feigned.

'Not when I see the delight my comments bring to your face!' I bit my lip trying to keep deadpan. Not easy when you were up against an old master. I scanned the lab looking for any hint of a practical joke about to befall me.

The lab's layout lent itself to a myriad of such possibilities. The main part of the room was rectangular, about fifteen metres by ten. (Since when are rooms not rectangular? I pondered.) At the far end of the shorter wall was a large, transparent, laminated observation window which started about sixty centimetres from the wall. This allowed the single piece, fifteen-metre long workbench to flow along the wall, giving the left-hand side of the room a somewhat balanced look. The window continued until it met the entry door, which was made from the same material as the window. The point of separation was marked by white laser-beam seals. These seals also covered the joins where the wall met the ceiling and floor. This ante-room had to remain hermetically contained when live experiments were in progress. The white colour of the seals indicated the room was 'inert'.

As designed, the colour of the seals would change according to the condition of the room. There was only one colour you didn't want the seals to turn to, and it wasn't red.

'Ahem, thinking of starting work anytime soon?' Tom asked. Tom Andrews was the rock of our lab, his guiding focus the perfect foil to the youthful exuberance of his talented team. About 175 centimetres tall, with wispy, mousey hair and flattened rectangular glasses, he didn't physically dominate the room; he was of average build, but he more than made up for it with his shrewd intellectual presence. Now in his mid-forties, he'd previously worked as a radar missile operative in GUCI's sea-borne division at the start of his working career. He came to realize he was more interested in building his own weapons rather than firing someone else's. To be fair, Tom wasn't a warmonger. He believed in peace through a position of strength and security.

'He's not listening, Tom,' Grant interrupted. 'He's never seen a clean keyboard before,' he added, sarcastically.

'Guys, that's not my keyboard, the A's worn off mine.'

'Relax,' Grant added, 'The keyboard was sticking so I asked the some friendly techs to sort it out.'

'Ok,' I replied. 'That's a novelty – the great Grant Stern being genuinely altruistic.'

'There's a first time for everything,' Grant countered.

I needed to check on the results of the overnight tests, which of course required the unavoidable login procedure. However, unlike in the past where a password was required, now only the user ID was necessary. My patented pressure sensitive keyboard with IR heat detection had long since banished the password field to history. Of course, for a short while these keyboards cost five times the price of a regular keyboard, until the economies of scale kicked in. They took the heat signature of your fingers as they hit the keys. Then they encrypted the force of the key presses and the time between them to give strongest level of login encryption ever devised, even if you knew the user's ID. Fingerprint readers, iris scans, face recognition, all fell before this hybrid biometric security.

Mazzzzzzzzzzzzzz the screen screeched in a series of rapid beeps as the user ID box filled up.

The 'z' was firmly depressed and showing no signs of returning to its original position.

'Sticky fingers today?' Tom asked. He was highly amused. But Grant, however, took the prize. He let go big time, in full-out laughter mode.

'There is a first time,' he gasped, 'to be altruistic, but today's not it,' he said, still struggling. 'I told the techs the keyboard *wasn't* sticking, so they helped me out with the lab's other little side-line – super-contact adhesive,' he added gleefully. 'That makes a login even more secure than your little patent, as long as you have a "z" in your user ID. The Ultraglue effect of the contact adhesive can now instantly bond up to twelve hours after treating both surfaces. Neat, eh?'

'Fortunately for you,' Tom piped up, 'I saw him place your keyboard in the overflow storage. Now if you'd run your checks so I can sign off that would be most agreeable'.

The overflow storage was by the entrance door to the lab. Here it fulfilled its task as a dumping ground for all the possibly needed bits and pieces used in a lab, but not often enough to warrant a place out on the bench. Like a spare keyboard for instance. As I went over to retrieve the keyboard from its hiding place, the com link went off.

I'd often wondered what benefit the lab's designers thought would be met by placing the com link where they did. The caller could see into the experiment room at the same time as speaking to person responding to the com. It then occurred to me that they would be able to see the colour of the seals, which meant that in certain circumstances, a more 'honest' answer to questions that could be posed to us would be required.

'Of course we've yet to check the results of last night's run,' I overhead Tom saying, 'but I'm pretty sure we're almost there.' I didn't hear the caller's response as Tom must have turned the volume down when he saw who the call was from. That always concerned me, as Tom often had his ear chewed with those type of calls. 'Understood,' he replied. The link disconnected.

'Shit,' he added. Grant, who was nearer to Tom and the com link than me, had lost all trace of his previous state of mirth. Something was heading our way and it didn't look good.

I replaced Grant's practical joke with my original keyboard as Tom addressed us both. 'The leader of the Assemblage will be here tomorrow,' he delivered in a neutral tone. 'Moreover, she's indicated that incomplete or not, the results of last night's run will be used as a basis for the new product.'

I could see why the positive energy within the lab had now suddenly dissipated. 'Ok guys,' I replied. 'Let's see what we did last night.'

15:00, Solar 84
Enforcer McCree's Apartment

'In other news – the head spokesperson for the Clearwater Federation dismissed the protests outside the current chair headquarters in which twenty people died as, "The usual malcontent freeloaders who have the absurd notion that water should be free." Further adding, "Under the terms of our global contract an increase of 30 per cent in the cost of our supplied water is entirely in keeping with our major demand clause three (c) (a)..."'

Enforcer McCree sighed. *Would this ever end?* he wondered. 'Grampy?' A little voice pulled him back out of his thoughts. 'Why do those nasty people fight our providers?' enquired his grandson.

'Because,' replied McCree, 'they believe that water should be free as it once was.' McCree looked at Joule, eight years old and with a shock of blond hair. He certainly was a mini version of his son-in-law. His grandson had yet to understand the complexity of the demonstrators' position, by which time it would be too late for him to make his own choice.

'Don't they know how expensive it is to make water?' Joule asked. McCree could see that the first tendrils of GUCI had already reached out and started to strangle his only grandchild's free will. McCree wondered, *when did this very same process happen to me?* He tried to remember, but as far back as he could recall GUCI had always been the voice of reason.

'Unless we supply – there can be no demand,' rang in his head.

'Unless we can pay – we must perish.' 'To exist on our planet – we must contribute.' The phrases continued until he felt dizzy and beyond. He tried to refocus. In later years he had wondered about what life would be like without GUCI, but he knew he'd become so entrenched in the system that to 'go with the flow' would be his best chance of a less painful future.

McCree was not in a good place at the moment. He'd killed a number of the protesters at the 'experience' mentioned in the global data feed and had been given a large credit boost as a result. Indeed he also obtained an efficiency credit as being the enforcer with the highest number of kills at the experience. Other, younger enforcers had more to gain, families to feed, by killing more protesters, but McCree was top of the pack. He wasn't sure why, because he had no 'family'. He only had contact with his grandson as a means of repaying the obligatory debt his daughter owed him. 'Predecessor refund' was the only reason he saw his grandson, and that was all he, McCree, was worth to his daughter – a refund. He recalled his early training as an enforcer and how he had to study 'the value of credit' in its entirety. A truly effective enforcer had to understand the capitalistic values that drove people to be the way they were. He recalled…

Article 8 – History relating to predecessor refund

An increasing wish for material possessions had come about in society. To fulfil this, both parents of a child needed to earn a salary. For this to occur, the retirees of the parent were called upon to look after parent's child. Retirees thus acquired a new financial worth. Disagreements about the value of this worth frequently occurred. Retirees often disagreed with the parents over the upbringing of the child of the parent. Thus a law was enacted to settle the matter for all future times.

The retirees were acknowledged to have spent a significant amount of salary to raise their children to adult status. Therefore their children owed the corresponding amount to them. If the retirees became non-self-sufficient the children would pay for their care, thus reducing their debt to the retirees.

However, if the retirees died before this debt was repaid, the outstanding amount became immediately due to GUCI. As a concession to this harsh law, GUCI allowed retirees contact with their grandchildren as a way of reducing the debt of the parents. Retirees' contact ranged between five and 30 per cent of the grandchildren's time, with a pro-rata reduction in the parents debt to the retirees. The following principle then applied: *The more you* spend *on your children, the greater the chance you will be able to see your grandchildren, based upon the debt accrued by your children payable to you.*

McCree felt saddened; this was a main part of the subjugation of the people to GUCI. The very human desire to be with one's kin had been ruthlessly monetized.

He jolted back to the present. *Why did I terminate them? For the credits? – No. Because they are city outers and had no future? If they really knew what an enforcer knows they would thank me.*

11

It had been over fifty profit cycles since the reduction of profit and termination law had been passed. If a person was deemed to be causing harm to a company's profit by taking action against that company, it was entitled to terminate those actions by a chosen method of least cost. The gun was the same as that used in past ages but the ammunition was different. Shaped like a bullet, and fully interchangeable with one, it literally was the revolution in clean-kill technology. The round was a firm gel which on impact flattened and collapsed, delivering a high-voltage charge to the recipient. This alone would kill most people, but the gel also contained a nerve poison that was absorbed through the skin like a hypo-spray. Enforcers were safe from the bullet gel because they had been immunized against the toxin at the start of their careers, and were issued with energy dissipation jackets. If a rogue enforcer had to be taken down it would necessarily be a very messy affair. *Rogue enforcer?* mused McCree. That just never happens.

He drifted away again… The distance pill he'd taken was doing its job. It was now mandatory for enforcers to take one after they'd been involved in profit reduction terminations and other serious operations. In the past many enforcers had suffered stress from the termination aspect of their job (some would say it showed that at least they still had a small shred of morality left). Of course this led to a sustained drop in performance and so extra profit was lost.

An enforcer had the day off after a termination, and the distance pill detached them from their actions. They'd be back on duty the following day not caring a fig if they'd terminated one, two, ten, or even twenty or more demonstrators. The pill was the perk of the job for McCree. If any of his numerous ghosts popped into his head during pill time, he could look at them and say 'so what?' It eased the pain of bad decisions he'd made in the past, and that of living with the consequences of those decisions in the present and far into the future.

McCree mulled over the change in ammunition used. *Gel bullets are surely more expensive than regular bullets*, he thought. Ah, regular bullets make more of a mess and more damage to property if the target is missed. *Whoever misses these days?* Must be the clean-up costs that make a gel bullet cost effective.

What if you don't want to terminate a target? Why not use a regular bullet and injure them instead? thought McCree. The distance pill immediately dismissed that notion for him.

My screen brought up the results of last night's run. '85 per cent cohesion on the sample,' I reported.

Grant sighed. 'That's not much better than the 83 per cent we had from the last run. K, I really thought that last reconfiguration would have done it.'

'Two per cent is two per cent,' piped up Tom.

Grant was on edge now, 'Oh, two per cent is two per cent! How very Dalai Lama,' he spat.

'I'm not sure that was Dalai Lama, Grant. I thought it was more Tom Andrews,' he replied, trying to defuse the situation.

'You bloody well know what I mean, Tom. We've got chief knob arriving tomorrow to breathe down our necks and you think this is good enough,' he raged.

I'd never seen Grant this agitated before, and now he was speaking to Tom with a complete disrespect for our superior. Grant had failed with projects before, and he'd always laugh it off, often with some sort of practical joke at my expense, but this time things seemed different.

'I'm the one who's dealing with the Assemblage visit tomorrow,' Tom reminded Grant.

'You said it yourself, Tom, that she was going to use last night's results as the basis of our new product, improvement or not,' Grant hissed.

'Well then,' I turned to them both. 'Looks like we've got a little under twenty-two hours to persuade her otherwise.'

My suggestion seemed to strike a chord with Grant. 'We could lie,' he suggested hopefully.

'Sorry Grant,' Tom countered. 'I have it on good authority that the Assemblage will include a discriminator, their best in fact, to guard against that. K,' he said, 'detail all the test results together for the last eight runs so I have some filler to pad out my presentation.' I knew what Tom was going to do almost even before he did. It looked like he was going to eat a bucket of shit tomorrow for our project and he'd just asked me to provide a little seasoning.

'I know better than insist you get some shut-eye and come back in the morning, but I do need you fresh for tomorrow's little, err, appointment, so get something from the canteen. I'll call you there if I need anything. Thanks guys,' Tom added.

'Data's on your console view,' I replied. 'You make sure you do call us when you need a hand.' We left the lab and headed towards the canteen. 'Grant, we need a plan B,' I remarked.

'Sure,' he replied. 'Now seeing we can't exactly get pissed tonight kinda rules out B for beverage. I know,' he said, 'it's going to have to be *B* for *bull*.' The comment brought us swiftly to the end of the short corridor where a face scan was required to call the lift. The canteen was four floors above and we needed a result. If ever there was an ironic choice of term, that was it.

Renee Zeleno had many qualities about her although patience wasn't one of them. As head profit enabler of Meometics Universal, she wielded a huge amount of power and influence over a large percentage of the world's customers. Just like her peers at the other four global corporations, she had the overwhelming desire to beat her competitors into the dust. The feeling of impotence she had at present, though, was particularly galling especially given her suspicion of scientists. After disconnecting from a particularly tedious call involving a forty-something 'science team leader', she needed five minutes to cool down and organize her thoughts. 'Door lock, record thoughts,' she announced to the room. She paced around her office, watching as her chair reconfigured itself ready to record her thoughts.

The technology she had at her disposal in this space was some of the most advanced on the planet. No doubt her competitors had similar facilities, for successful profit generation required the maximum extraction of revenue-generating ability from one's employees. The cost of this setup meant that only a few people on earth were able to generate a profit over and above what it cost to fit out and run this technology. People like her competitor head profit enablers. Some of the technology she used had been designed by the very team she was due to visit tomorrow.

She was well aware of the irony, but sentiment played no part in her decision. Research 4 had been the Assemblage's top performing team for a number of solar cycles now, probably 20 per cent of the technology in her room originated from there. The other nine operational teams had varying lesser degrees of success, but invariably in this field fortunes would rise and fall, once your work no longer turned a profit you were dead and buried.

Renee had risen to her post on the success of the team she had put together ten profit cycles ago, Research 2. They held the profit record due to the 'pixie dust' coating they had invented for silicon chips. There had only been a handful of such successful inventions since the formation of the five Ultra-profit organizations that required a global-use profit agreement. Research 2 was also the first to achieve such success.

Advanced software was able to determine if such an invention would raise more profit if it was made available to all organizations rather than being kept to the originating corporation. This software was rumoured to be Microsoft's last output before it was decommissioned.

A licence fee that maximized the total profit obtained was agreed on, again by software, but of course the originators of the invention remained the ones to benefit from it the most. A modern day equivalent of the ancient 'fair use' agreement of technology patents. But without the lawyers that held so much power in the days of Apple, Microsoft, and Google.

Research 2 was, however, 'dead and buried', literally. She had fallen hopelessly in love with its team leader Dr Derek Toft, helped by his soft yet assertive pitch of 'Prophet dust

– breakthrough into the future – use it or lose it.' Not bad for a scientist, if a little corny.

Their rapport was immediate. He was equally smitten. In particular he enabled her to reach her goal. He was her confidant. She'd started to find it difficult making the ultra-tough decisions in the office and he was able to supply a revolutionary new drug to help.

She could still remember that moment, purely because it changed everything for her... 'I've got them Ren, your worries are over with these,' Derek offered. 'Amazingly you can take them before that tough call, or if you have any regrets you can take one after something's gone bad. They really are "da bomb". '

'You really have to cut down on the 1990s gang rap feeds you watch hun,' she replied. 'I don't do pills.'

'I know that,' he said, 'but if you have to do just one pill, do this one.'

She took a pill, and the following day increased her profit making decisions by 15 per cent, leaving a trail of colleagues to recover from the blast. She'd screwed them for her own good. It turned out that was exactly what they needed too, but did they appreciate this? No! Did she care? No!

'My god!' she exclaimed when she arrived home to Derek. 'Where did you get them hun? We have to market these. Profit with these is going to be huge,' she mused.

'We can't, Ren, MedGen Collective is in full scale production of them. The drug is theirs. I have been able to procure enough from an old friend, J. He said they'd last until they are officially obtainable. Until then the fifteen per cent extra profit you generate is all yours. Make sure you make it count, sweet.'

She knew the pill was good, as she'd detached her feelings for him from his words. 'So, hun, you've basically dealt with a competitor to obtain a product ahead of release,' she replied. Perhaps she should have realized that he did it for love, that he would only have done such a thing to help her succeed. The pill had turned his words into betrayal, collusion with an enemy, and the likelihood that she was being deceived even now. 'What did you offer in return?' she asked.

'Nothing, that's what friends are for, nothing went the other way.' Derek replied. Again the pill twisted his words: 'I'm telling you nothing, conversation closed, you don't want to know what I offered.'

Unfortunately for Derek and Research 2, Renee had only just finished drafting a protocol for the protection of profit for her Assemblage. It was, of course, one of those ultra-tough decisions that had led to the taking of the pill.

Profit protection: competitor collusion protocol

In the event of an employee of a certain level of knowledge being involved in collusion with a competitor the potential for profit loss is substantial. To protect profit, individuals and close co-workers must be terminated according to GUCI profit and termination law.

Open enactment of this law would harm profit by de-motivation of remaining staff. Termination is to be carried out covertly and simultaneously amongst co-workers. Explanation to be given to remaining staff is that individuals have been transferred to work on new Ultra-profit high-security screens. Immediate family to be offered 'transfer' to join employee at new location.

Derek was puzzled by Renee's reaction. He put it down to the pill. The drinks dispenser had just finished mixing his request – *'Mojito ready'* – it confirmed through the appliance speaker panel that he was nearest to. *Glad I invented those...* he mused.

He returned from the kitchen even more puzzled to hear Renee speaking gibberish. 'Ppccp r2 c.'

I think I'd better have a word with J, he thought, *maybe it would be better if Ren stayed off these pills.* Derek was right, of course but he never got the chance to see J. Renee had seen to that.

'Continue or cancel Renee?' a speaker panel prompted.

'Continue,' she replied. She sat back in the chair and let it take charge of her thoughts.

She thought she'd just be in the chair for five minutes, but it took a lot longer than that.

There was much more swirling around in her head than she acknowledged, and it took more than forty minutes before the sensors glowed that pale blue shade which indicated all new thoughts had been recorded. Her whole history with Derek and Research 2 had just resurfaced like a bad ghost. She reached into the narrow pedestal to the left of the chair, pulled out a bottle, and took a pill from it. The same pill that was the cause of and solution to her problems. The blessing and the curse.

Meometics Research Facility

The lift doors opened on two sides directly into the centre of the canteen. This was a smart design to make it easier to get there as quickly as possible. Extensive research had revealed that the further away workers were from food the less inclined they were to get up from their working areas and have a break or snack. This was found to become counterproductive in a very small space of time. Also the new design for the building lent itself to the central placement of the lift shaft, which was additionally used for the adjacent ventilators for the canteen. The only disadvantage was that the smell of cooked food came directly into the lift even if the canteen was bypassed.

'Canteen,' the lift stated as its doors opened. Grant and I exited and both of us headed subconsciously to the pizza vending machine without saying a word. It seemed to be an unwritten rule of the team that when crisis was upon us and we needed to eat, only a pizza would do. I recalled a maximum profit facilitator once briefing me that for maximum effect: 'Make sure you eat something with a face.' So it was a cannonball pizza with regular sauce for me and a tandoori chicken pizza with barbeque sauce for Grant. Each was supplemented by a small bottle of soda from the adjacent vending machine.

'One day, Grant, the machine will refuse one of your bizarre combinations on the grounds of common decency,' I offered. 'Yeah, right, and when that day happens, only then can we truly believe that AI has become superior to

21

our intellect,' Grant replied. We both laughed at this which helped to ease the tension nagging at us.

'Remind me again about your pizza combination creative theory,' I asked.

'It's easy, K. Whilst eating such a bizarre combination of ingredients never before experienced my mind is saying – *What the hell?* It's a distraction from the immediate problem and helps the subconscious mind to come up with an answer. Like the way dreams sometimes let you work though a known problem to find a solution. Only it's a problem solver and nutrition in one.'

'Sorry, Grant,' I interrupted. 'You are nuts, but hey, whatever works for you is fine by me.'

'You won't mind if I have a slice of your cannonball then!' Grant quipped. 'Do you think Tom can hold the line for us, K?' he asked.

'Well, looking at the test results the product is a bit too unstable,' I replied.

'Aw, let's not get into the "we can't possibly roll out the product until its perfect" routine again,' said Grant. 'Only Apple were able to get away with that, which was over fifty cycles ago, and even *they* didn't get it right every time.' he added.

'Well, Grant let me s-p-e-l-l it out for you. We're doing well, but there are still random fluctuations in the output of our samples. So, we put this into an anti-personnel drone. It targets those it needs to take out. The output spikes and it targets additional non-combatants. Twice. There's an evens chance that if this goes ahead and is used you're looking at around a quarter additional non-combatant casualties.' I paused for effect. 'Perhaps it's used to improve the amount of vehicles that can join an automated convoy. *Spike*. And one vehicle in the centre of the convoy veers off to the right into the path of another convoy. Or…'

'Stop,' Grant implored. 'I kinda get it. It's not like we can replace all the chips covered in our Mk 1 coating first and then put our improved coating on.'

'Seems to me we outline the scale of the problem to the Assemblage if Tom fails to hold the line. Otherwise we request input from Research 2,' I suggested.

'K, you know that you'll be laughed out of the lab asking for Research 2's assistance. They're unreachable on Ultra-profit projects now,' Grant replied.

'Of course,' I countered. 'That's the point – they'll see we're so desperate to get this working correctly that we'll consider even the impossible. Now are you going to get off your butt and work off that piece of my pizza you ate or do I have to get another drink myself?'

Enforcer McCree's Apartment

McCree stepped over to the window of his apartment ready to wave Joule off. He was on the fifth floor; that was all his status in society would get him, the fifth floor out of forty. Biostore, the aptly but cynically named property monopoly, had come to the conclusion a long time ago that this was the optimum building size to house its biological revenue generators. The yields on this size of construction were comparable to what Clearwater were getting from their de-sal plants.

Biostore had cleverly separated the building into eight zones over the forty floors – five floors per zone. Each zone had a pair of lifts at a corner of the building, which allowed entry and exit only on the five floors in that zone. Looking from above and moving clockwise from the north face of the building were zones 2 and 4; 6 and 8; 7 and 5; 3 and 1. This kept the occupants of each zone closer to those in similar zones – citizen separation based on profitability factors. It was possible to see from a distance the zone above or below, and where you could be heading depending on which way your career was going.

Of course Biostore had direct access to the career profiles of the inhabitants and assigned each to the appropriate zone and floor. The amount charged for this space increased according to the floor a person resided on, with an extra inter-zone fee payable if they moved either up or down a zone. 'We care about your decline', was used as a strap line when the inter-zone drop fee was demanded.

In a famous quote the CEO of Biostore protested: 'We only charge you seventy-five per cent of the inter-zone fee when you move down a zone rather than up. We're not ruthless bastards, you know.' They were and he knew it. Biostore knew if someone's credit income had reduced and decided to monetize that too. What little you may have built up in credit was usually wiped out by the fee. 'The punishment of failure,' a GUCI representative explained when asked to justify Biostore's behaviour.

McCree's entrance was thus on the far side of the building from the entrance of those who were in zone eight. He would never get to enter on that side of the building, unless he had someone to kill. He was at least on the top floor of the bottom zone, but kind of realized that he'd reached his hi-score. *At least I won't have any inter-zone transfer fees to pay*, he thought.

He saw Joule waving back, next to his daughter who did not. McCree had shown Joule where to wave at the building so at least even though Joule couldn't see him wave he knew Grampy was watching.

Joule had suspected that Grampy couldn't see him from the building, but McCree was ready. 'When you go, hold up some fingers near to the numbers on the building and I'll tell you how many you held up the next time I see you,' McCree instructed. 'Which window is yours, Grampy?' Joule asked. 'Just by the start of the first profit panel by the left. Ask El... Ask Mum to point it out to you,' McCree replied.

When Joule had asked Eleanor to point his window out, McCree could see from her body language that she wasn't impressed with the request. McCree could only guess how Joule had phrased the question.

Any hint of 'Grampy said…' and she'd think he was being manipulative. He hoped more for a 'Where is Grampy's window?' type of question, and Joule was a smart kid so there was every chance he hadn't inflamed the situation. As it turned out, Eleanor had felt it better to put her disappointment towards her father aside than upset her son.

Rather than point to the window herself she guided his pointing hand – 'Up, down, left a bit, bit more… That's it.' Joule jumped up and down triumphantly and held out six fingers towards McCree. 'Saw you Joule, it was six,' was the first thing he'd said the next time Joule visited, and from then on it became part of the bye-bye routine.

Waving back, he looked down until the transport took Joule out of view. He knew the routine. Once every two weeks Joule would visit for the day, and they'd spend time just watching the video feeds or playing *Battling Tops*, a barely legal museum piece from around 1970s old calendar date. It only scraped through on the approved list due to its rarity, and it did at least convey the message that the struggle for dominance was good.

Eleanor didn't approve, but even though they had a zone four apartment and aspired to a five, they would still owe a large debt to GUCI if McCree died. She didn't have any real choice with the arrangement. GUCI saw to that for all of them.

McCree, though, had at least managed to get onto the profit reducers' shift every fortnight, and fortunately the visits by Joule were the day after, when he'd be under the influence of the distance pill. All the enforcers knew that if McCree was in your team, he'd always get the first kill.

Rarely after the first profit reducer was shot did a protest disperse. Normally it took about five or ten kills before the protesters realized they were being executed. The bigger the protest, the longer it took to notice protesters falling to the ground. That's why McCree always got in the first shot, so he could 'relax', he would get his pill. *What kind of a sick society am I living in?* he thought. He didn't care. He took a large alcohol out of his fridge and headed for the bed.

Replenished from the pizza and soda break, if that's how the nutritional content of that snack could be described, we headed back down to the lab; in the lift and along the corridor we were silent. We had a backup plan and a backup for the backup plan. Even if the backup for the backup was, in all honesty, somewhat desperate. We just needed to see what Tom's state of mind was.

When we entered the lab. Tom seemed to be packing up for the day. 'How's things, Tom?' I asked.

'I've made some progress,' he replied. 'There's an incremental but small improvement each time over the last series of eight tests. If we extrapolate that into the future and double the tests conducted then the figures come out at six months,' he added.

'Wait a minute, Tom,' Grant piped up. 'We work our arse off for six months – so that makes us doubly stupid because we're now twelve months behind, not six, and you think the tests are going to nicely follow the line on the graph you've drawn for us?'

Tom looked at Grant; he seemed to be sizing his next reply up very carefully. I was concerned about both of them. Something was clearly bothering Grant, and I felt that Tom was aware of this, but how much slack he was prepared to give him was about to be revealed.

'What's eating you Grant? – I mean *really* eating you,' he emphasized. 'It's not just the situation here, is it, Grant?' he asked.

'We've got more important things to deal with, haven't we?' Grant replied, looking towards the test readouts. Tom came back with one of his classic motivational talks.

'I think not, Grant,' Tom began. 'Because if anyone in the team is not happy, then I'm not. We are here to do a job, but it's not just any type of job. We're not on the cutting edge, we're ahead of the bleeding edge! We all know it's important to be focused because if not, there's the very real possibility of a huge amount of collateral damage with our discoveries. Sometimes we have an off day and think we can carry it, but we shouldn't risk it. The team needs to know, and that includes me, if I'm having a poor day, so we can adjust and change the team dynamic to compensate,' he paused again for effect – a classic Tom trademark. 'So, Grant what's the matter?' he asked.

'It's Mrs Stern,' Grant replied, now somewhat calmer, as a result no doubt of Tom's speech hitting the right spot. 'She wants us to move up to the next zone. We both know the success of this project will make the difference, and I guess she's already been swanking her move up with friends. Of course, being six months behind schedule has really cheesed her off big time. You can imagine if she finds out she's going to have to wait another six months!'

'Ok,' said Tom. 'Now I understand, and we can sort it. I think I need to visit Mrs Stern,' he concluded. 'What time is she expecting you?' he asked.

'Not until 22:00, but I said if I had to stay on I'd let her know by 21:45,' Grant replied.

'Ok, Grant, you're in Central Section, West Side?' Although he asked, Tom knew exactly where his employees' apartments were. It always seemed to me that he felt a little less sinister, confirming a visit in this fashion.

'Only when her friends aren't around, when you'll find me here.'

'So,' Tom continued, 'I could be there by around 20:15. Is forty-five minutes to your apartment doable from here?'

Again, Tom knew how long it would take his team to travel in from their apartments in an emergency under escort from a GUCI enforcer rapid response squad. He just doubled that and added five. Grant fumbled around in his inside lab pocket. 'Forty-five mins – no problem, we're in Tower Eight,' he replied as he handed Tom his apartment building lift card. 'I know you may not like slumming it with us fourth zoners, but at least you won't have to speak to the concierge – pardon, I mean door guy – to sort access out. In the meantime, we'll try and squeeze another test in before the Assemblage visit tomorrow,' Grant added.

Grant had already perked up a little since the news of the Assemblage visit. Hopefully Tom's visit to the Stern's apartment would sort out his anxiety for good.

He stopped Tom by the door. 'Thanks Tom, and try not to get lost on the way back. You wouldn't want to miss out on a last minute breakthrough, would you?'

Tom made his way out of the lab, heading towards the lift. The route to the transport park was the same as if heading to the canteen and, although it was two levels above, the transport park was still underground, but only just. Tom scanned his face and entered the lift. 'Transport level, ready transport, destination Grant Stern home,' he said.

Tom considered how much of his world had been shaped by him and his team and, for that matter, Research 2.

All technology understood speech in any language, accent, or dialect, and of course the face scanner was already programmed as to how a person's speech would sound; it would even be able to tell if the speaker had a cold, if such maladies had existed today. Scanning someone's head in detailed 3D informed the lift about how its passenger would sound when they spoke, shouted, or whispered.

Connection to the one-net matched a brain with the relevant personnel file, so the language spoken was extrapolated. Easy really. The lift would then communicate with the transport pool to ensure the appropriate level of transport was waiting, its destination again programmed in following yet another search of an online database. But none of this would have been possible without the application of pixie dust.

Sure, all of these inventions existed, but only as islands to themselves. To connect everything to everything else was where the real advances would be made, and it was indeed pixie dust that unlocked that key. The lift stopped, the doors opened, and Tom's transport was there for him. 'Thank Research 2 for that,' he spoke aloud.

'Unable to contact Research 2 at present. Please leave a message,' the lift replied.

Tom sighed; *some things never change*, he thought. *I should get the team to tweak that AI once this project is done. It would be good to contact Research 2, though, they may have discovered some insight into the problem. I wonder if the lift has their forwarding address?*

The vehicle's proximity sensor opened its door as Tom approached. He slipped down into the seat, the door closed, and the transport drove up the ramp and out into the fading daylight. His ride had a class of priority higher than the standard equivalent, so there were relatively few occasions when his vehicle had to defer to a higher priority transport.

A blur of transports sped past and across each other, which automatically negotiated with others in close proximity to them as to which one had priority. The more profit the passenger could generate, the higher priority transport they had and the quicker they'd get where they were going. Whilst all transports had the same top speed and acceleration, some had to give way during a journey more than others.

The journey took just over forty minutes, and on arrival the transport swiftly glided to a stop outside the fourth zone entrance, Tower Eight, Central Section, West Side. Tom stepped out of the transport and pressed 'park' on his control card. The transport shot off down the block to park itself. He entered the fourth zone lift. 'Grant Stern's apartment, no announcement, directional lighting,' he said to the lift. An element of surprise by just turning up would be to his advantage, he thought.

As Tom exited the lift the corridor kick plates lit up, illuminating the floor of the corridor into the distance. He could see the lights appear to turn left at the end where it split left and right. Along the corridor all the seals glowed a pale blue, indicating that the room sound-dampening units of the respective apartments were active. One apartment by the lift was unlit. He reached the corridor's end and turned left, following the kick plate illumination. It stopped at the end on the left: Grant's apartment.

The sound dampening on Grant's apartment was the only one with the sound dampening off. Tom approached slowly – something was odd. He heard a moan and a grunt almost simultaneously, and again, and again. He realized there was more than one person in Grant's apartment and it sounded like they were fucking.

'No,' she begged.

'Yes,' he disagreed. More moans and grunts, was she being raped? – Tom's heart was racing; this was not part of the plan!

He needed to know; he pulled out the chip from his card and inserted in into Grants card. One swipe with his thumb and the door would be transparent one way. The modern equivalent of a security keyhole that could be viewed either way. Useful to avoid tripping over something left behind the door when entering, and with the size of some apartments an indispensable feature.

One swipe the wrong way and he'd be exposed. He carefully swiped the card as if that would somehow operate the transparency slowly. He completed the gesture. 'Uuh!' She sighed, half pleasure, half pain.

For a second Tom thought she could see him, she was looking straight at him. She was not fully naked, but in some ways Tom wished she had been. Facing the door on her hands and knees, and wearing the full 'fuck me' set of lingerie that Tom reckoned Grant had never seen her in – black bra, stockings and suspenders, she even had her stilettos on.

Her panties were not serving any purpose – true, they were still on her, but were down to her knees. Behind her the man thrust into her again, the force of his legs slapping against the back of hers, causing her breasts to almost pop out of her bra, as he continued again and again. The pace increased and with one long grunt the man came inside her, right as she was looking at Tom. She panted with relief, smiling lewdly as if taunting Tom, and rolled over. The man's slowly shrinking dick flopped out and he collapsed beside her. Tom now had no doubt about how willing she had been.

He'd been the unwitting witness to quite a show and, under normal circumstances, may even have welcomed the entertainment that he'd just been treated to. This, however, really was not part of the plan. He couldn't just go back to the lab, Grant would want to know what the outcome was. 'Well, Grant, I would have spoken to her but she was so enjoying a good ramming from some stranger when I got there, I thought it best to forget the whole thing and come back!' Tom focused on the present. He still needed to speak to her but she'd need time to make herself decent. She may even decide not to answer the door.

Tom could see that the man was stirring, he could make out her arm dangling over the edge of the bed, then a flick of her wrist and she tossed some clothing onto the bed next to him. *Is she telling him he'd better leave or did 'Mr Romance' think he was done for the evening so he might as well go?* he pondered.

No matter, Tom decided, he's going to be dressed before she is and he'll be coming straight out of the door. He needed to give her some breathing space – literally – but had to find out who 'Mr Romance' was and what his real intentions were. If indeed they were anything other than shagging the life out of Mrs Stern.

He retraced his steps back around the corridor to the lift where he noticed a utility room. He'd not paid much attention to it when he left the lift barely five minutes ago, apart from its absence of sound dampening. He stopped by the door and made a number of swiping gestures over the surface of his card until an icon of a broken key appeared. He pressed the icon and the door unlocked. *There isn't much point in slaving over a series of profit making devices unless you can upgrade your own with special features for free*, he thought.

Inside the utility room he came across a maintenance suit which he promptly donned; although he needed to fold the legs up a bit, it would do. He also came across a dampening field meter. *Ideal*, he said to himself. Tom picked up the meter and left the room casually, just in case someone was coming out into the corridor at the same time as he was. There was no one around. He entered the lift, 'Exit,' he said, and the lift arrived on the ground floor in very short order.

He exited the lift, then turned and used Grant's lift key again. 'Grant Stern's apartment, pre-announce, directional lighting, speed: express.' he said to the lift. Quicker this time, the lift arrived and once again Tom was heading down the corridor, now more slowly, towards the turn at the end. He held the instrument purposefully as if checking the sound barriers for their integrity.

Then from around the corner 'Mr Romance' appeared. Fortunately the scanner Tom held was pointing at a room at the time. 'Huh,' said the man dismissively, as he glanced at the rolled up legs of the maintenance suit and brown suede loafers Tom was wearing. Tom put him at around 185 centimetres, about eighty-five kilos, and around forty years old with thinning black hair. He seemed oddly familiar. He walked past Tom with a superior smirk on his face. If Tom hadn't witnessed 'Mr Romance' in action less than ten minutes ago he'd have thought the smirk was directed towards him.

'Mr Romance' entered the room directly across from the utility room. The sound dampening for the room was turned on. Tom waited a minute or so to ensure 'Mr Romance' was staying in the apartment and then went back into the utility room. He took off his thirty second disguise and put down the meter. He walked swiftly down the corridor to the end and turned left. This time the door chimed as he stood outside.

Mrs Stern had only just managed to undress and re-dress – she'd merely thrown some clothes on. She could see

Tom and the Meometics security badge that he held towards the door.

She opened the door cautiously. 'Evening, Mrs Stern,' Tom said. 'I'm Tom Andrews, Grant's manager, and I'd like to have a chat with you about Grant,' he added. She was on the back foot; she didn't say 'hello', and Tom sensed her unease. *Understandable given recent events*, he thought.

'Oh, please come in, take a seat,' she replied. 'Is Grant all right?' she asked, as she also sat down.

'He's working late tonight. I hope that doesn't upset your plans?' Tom said, more as a statement than a question.

'No, it's to be expected in your line of work,' she said sympathetically. 'He usually rings around 21:45 if he's not going to be home by 22:00,' she added.

Tom could see the advantage Grant's thoughtfulness gave to his wife. She had plenty of warning to plan a pleasant evening in, regardless of whether Grant worked late or not. Tom glanced at the ceiling of the apartment and immediately recognized the resonance panels on the ceiling. *They could come in very handy*, he thought. He returned to the conversion, having barely paused in giving an answer to Mrs Stern.

'I'd expect a call from him at 21:45 then,' Tom said. 'We've got a long night ahead at the lab.'

'So Grant doesn't know you're here then,' she replied.

'I'd prefer to keep this quiet,' he said avoiding her question. 'Normally when a team member is under stress we arrange for a psychoanalysis to be done, but I thought it would be better for all of us if I didn't have to go down that route,' he said. 'If you have too many done your profit level naturally drops and that effects the profit level of the whole team.

'I understand you're both hoping to move up a zone?' Tom continued.

'Oh, yes we could do with an extra bit of room,' she replied. Tom glanced around, she wasn't kidding.

He knew the layout of zone four apartments, having lived in one himself. It looked as if their kid was in the small room that had the glow of the sound dampener around it. Grant had probably tinkered with the main dampener, but not quite well enough, figured Tom. 'Well, the thing is, Grant's been worrying about this in the lab, and given that the likelihood of your move depends on the success of the work we're currently doing, we have a problem,' he said. She was now listening intently. 'I think that if I double the number of late night shifts we put in it's likely to take another six months.' Tom finished.

'Six months – that's a year later than expected, isn't it?' she exclaimed in a critical and disappointed tone.

Listen lady, Tom thought, *it's not all about you* – he kept it to himself. 'That's the bottom line, six months of hard graft from my team and then you get to go up a zone. Otherwise,' he added, 'we're all heading for zone three.' Tom might as well have slapped her in the face. 'The delay isn't Grant's fault. He needs everyone to be on his side for this to work, cut him some slack, you can do that can't you?' he said. Tom immediately knew that she'd got the message all right, loud and clear.

'Well, thank you for your time, Mrs Stern, I need to be getting back to the lab. Best wishes for the future.' Tom stood up to leave and she followed.

'Please,' she said, 'call me Anne.'

'Goodnight, Anne,' said Tom as went out of the door.

In the lab Grant and I had swapped places to see if a change of dynamic would aid our progress. It was a little bit tricky, undertaking each other's tasks, but as we both had the same ability it was merely a lack of practice rather than being incapable that was the limiting factor.

Grant was looking over the suite of test data at what was usually my display whilst I fired up the configurator. We'd put together the panel to look like a 1980s sci-fi series control interface, as a bit of a joke. It worked so well we'd decided to keep it.

The next part of the process was possible due to the Gentech Conglomerate's nanotechnology. It was one of the few inventions they'd come up with that needed a global-use profit agreement. The nanites were held in a one centimetre cube with a small magnetic coil and two small connections on the opposing side to supply the power and energize the coil. By bombarding the cube with high frequency waves, the pixie dust coating on the nanites would generate a series of binary pulses which programmed them with the required instructions. This was an ingenious way to program such small devices and in such large quantities.

There was a drawback, however. The same coating we used on the nanites to program them was the same coating we were trying to get those same nanites to reconfigure on our newly developed super chips. The pulses that were created on them were also occurring on the super chips, but on a much larger scale. These pulses would knock the nanites off target before they were able to reconfigure the coating. A lower frequency meant they were stable, but their working speed was so slow the molecules they manipulated settled back into their previous state. A higher frequency and their work actually took, but they were knocked the chip by the chip's pulse, and thus the coating was a mixture of old and new.

The results so far were worse than with the original coating and caused instability when tested. The seals around the nanite introduction chamber glowed red then orange then yellow as the configurator powered up its main charges. I thought that if I could alternate the frequencies by mixing a high frequency with a lower one the nanites might stay on the chip.

I visualized it like being out on the sea in a small craft in the days when we were allowed to do such things. If you encounter a huge wave you're sunk. However, if you rise up on a smaller wave prior to meeting the huge wave you're just about able to ride it. This, then, was the plan.

Grant turned towards me. 'K, what do you think Tom's going to say to Anne?'

I turned as I adjusted a dial. 'He's probably sweet talked her knickers off her, and she's probably having his babies right now,' I joked.

'Oh thanks a million, K,' Grant replied. 'You're a great comfort.'

'Happy to help!' I laughed.

'K!' Grant screamed at me. For a second I thought he was going to hit me, but he was focused on the nanite chamber. 'Turn the damn thing off!'

I turned around and sparks were flying inside the chamber and the seals, which were now green, were flickering. 'Shit!' I replied. I'd turned the dial adjacent to the one I had meant to adjust. The pulse guide orientation had been adjusted instead of the low frequency adjustment ratio. A second beam had been generated at ninety degrees to the first. I slammed the emergency shutdown control. The colour of the seals was changing back to yellow, but they were still flickering and there were still sparks. The display slowly returned to normal.

'Thank god for that!' Grant exclaimed. 'As understanding as Tom is, I don't think he'd be too happy to return to find the labs have been blown up!' We weren't to know that Tom was already in a bad mood.

It was 21:30 and Tom could see his destination in the distance, aided by the lit sides of the building. The service federations and corporations always illuminated their buildings in full – quite why Tom was never sure, but he could have sworn he just saw the Meometics Universal building flicker. *I must be getting tired*, he thought. *Maybe I'll take a leaf out of K's and Grant's book and have a pizza and soda when I arrive.* Until this part of the journey back to Meometics, all he'd done was stare out of the window.

He'd never paid much attention to the layout of the city as the transport would do all the navigation. Block after similar block passed by with only the information data displays differentiating them. It was almost as if someone had copy-and-pasted the city together, and the irony of it was that that could well have been what actually happened. *'Copy and paste', where did I dig that up from?* he asked himself.

He was almost in a trance, hypnotized by the repetition or maybe stuck in a loop caused by the recurrence of the cityscape. It had at least cleared his mind for a short spell. Those moments often bore fruit as his subconscious often came up with ideas or insights he could use in the real world. Then the spell was broken as the transport turned and headed down the ramp into Meometics transit entrance. He stepped out of the vehicle and headed straight for the canteen...

'Team Leader Tom Andrews now located in canteen sub3,' a voice from one of the panels confirmed.

'Yes, he's definitely been screwing your wife, Grant. I always fancy a pizza after I've had some action!' I quipped.

'The only one only screwing around, K, has been you, and that's because you were fiddling with the wrong knob,' he replied. We both laughed at the juvenile interpretation we'd made of Grant's last sentence.

I could see that Grant's lighter old self was starting to return. Laughter, it would seem, was the best way to deal with stress, at least for most of the time. Sitting back at the console Grant was poring over the data, while I magnified the experiment with the surface scanner.

The nanites had fused to the chip surface, and the surrounding area, which was once silicon, now appeared to be carbon whilst the chip interface connections had become a white powder. The white powder trail continued out from the chip onto the interface bench. I programmed the surface scanner for a whole sweep of the bench.

All the chips in the vicinity showed the same carbon-like effect, and radiating out from all of them was the powder trail –except for one chip. The incoming electrical connections on this chip had been converted to white powder, but the outgoing connections were still intact. The accidental wave I'd created had taken out all the chips on the bench, and the wiring, apart from one small area. More calculations were needed, although this was not progressing our original objective, instead it would delay it.

Grant piped up, 'K, the data is showing up some weird crap, man.'

'Grant, can you give that in scientific terms, not some 1960s old calendar hippy speak,' I replied.

'Well, the cross-axial pulse you... erm, accidentally generated was reflected back by the chips and got converted into a quad-axial multi-spectrum pulse,' Grant replied. It only took a second for me to realize that we should look into this further and work it, somehow, into our next project.

'Also,' Grant added, 'this pulse had a radius of about a metre, give or take as it's not entirely symmetrical.'

'Thanks for the insight,' I replied. 'Let's store these results as an additional information supplement and put them straight into archive. We've got to clean up the nanite chamber ASAP.'

Grant looked at me knowingly. Did he understand what we'd seen? Or did it look as if I was covering up my error?

'Profits forbid, K,' he said, 'that I should be as single mindedly driven to one goal as you. You'll make an excellent leader one day.'

'Thanks,' I replied. 'But...'

Grant cut me off, 'We have to try and get back on track with our project. This diversion had yielded data which should be kept but it is not related to our project; cleaning up the chamber is. I get it, K.'

I left it there. Grant was programming a replacement bench delivery into the lab equipment console, whilst I removed the pulse resistant chip and one that had been zapped. I also took a sample of the white powder and placed everything, via the chamber's robot arms, into three separate compartments. I sent them off for spectro-analysis and tagged the samples qp1-3. Other experts could give me the analysis later, whilst we raced to return the chamber to a fully operational state again.

It was 23:30 before Tom had pulled himself away from the empty pizza plate he'd been staring at for the last half hour. He'd finished his meal and tried to make sense of what he'd just eaten. 'Repeat last order' was not a safe strategy if the last person to order was Grant Stern.

Tom had wondered if Grant's pizza order would give him an extra insight that would somehow help him deal with the situation better. It didn't. It just confirmed that he would perhaps never really understand Grant. K, on the other hand, was very easy to read and had a number of principles he believed steadfastly in.

The problem at present was not about K, or even about Grant anymore. No, the problem was the impact Anne's liaison would have on Grant's performance if he found out about it. Tom decided it would be better to re-work the sequence of events without deliberately lying to Grant. He would merely re-order and omit some of the facts. He didn't really like it, but that was the best he could do.

He left the canteen and was soon walking down the corridor to the lab entrance, replaying the opening conversation in his head; again and again, until he was outside the lab.

It was close to midnight and Renee had sat down at her desk to let the pill take hold. She wanted to forget, but only until the pill took effect; then she would not care. She wondered if she was the only person with these 'ghosts' floating inside her head, haunting her consciousness with self-doubt, regret and remorse. Her thoughts drifted towards her grandfather Nikolai, and what he'd once said to her when she was very young.

'My grandfather, Ren,' he said, 'used to drive one of the last of the cars you've heard me speak about. Every day he drove he would become annoyed by a squeak, coming from the passenger side. He thought he was the only person with this problem. Then one day when he was stationary at traffic lights, a thought occurred to him. "Nikolai," he said to me. "I've been jealous of all these strangers that pass by, asking myself why they should have a trouble free journey and why I cannot. But I realized they could be thinking exactly the same thing as I, or perhaps they had two squeaks and a knocking coming from their car. They could in fact be jealous of my situation. I thus realized that I should not be envious of others, of whose circumstances I had no direct knowledge," he said.

"'From then on I remembered that envy of the situation of others was unhelpful, and that the likelihood was, we were not alone with our disappointments. People everywhere had indeed similar problems to the ones I had," my grandfather confirmed. "This, Nikolai, is why you should put envy to one side and remember that your experiences are likely shared with many others. You are never truly alone.'"

Renee breathed in deeply. *Oh, to be able to speak directly to Nikolai. Such an intellect, and I will never be able to meet him.* She felt the weight of her ancestors upon her shoulders and the expectation that brought, but as soon as her ghosts circled for her, the pill had begun to brush them away. There were others like her, with the same problems perhaps, taking distance pills. They did not matter to her, they meant nothing to her. She relaxed.

Tomorrow however, there was something she needed to deal with that was her, and only her, problem. *Tomorrow, Tom Andrews, I'm gunning for you. If you're not ready then that's* your *lookout, not mine.*

Renee struggled to get up out of her chair and from behind her desk; she only just managed to secure her room. 'Lockdown now, alarm 07:00,' she instructed a wall panel. She half undressed before she made it to the bed in the side room off her main office. She slumped on it. 'Bye world,' she half whispered as her head sunk into the pillow. 'I'll kick your arse tomorr…' she drifted off into a deep sleep and started to dream…

At 07:00 Renee's alarm went off. She stirred quickly and took a sip of chilled fruit juice from the glass on the server unit next to her bed. The juice was sharp and woke her up quicker than any alternative would. However, coffee was not to be denied its part in her morning routine; it also had a pad on the unit next to the juice.

The coffee pad kept the coffee hot, just as the juice pad kept the juice cool. A temperature control followed the curve of both the pads, but there was no need for Renee to adjust either, she'd long since selected her preferred settings. She pressed a few pictures on the wall next to the unit to indicate what she wanted for breakfast, dialling in '7'.

Studies had shown a more nutritious breakfast was taken when items were chosen visually rather than spoken. To enable maximum profit therefore this was kept for the head profit enablers and a select few others. Breakfast would be delivered from the serving portal in exactly seven minutes.

She stepped the three or four paces across to the shower screen which was in the far corner of the room. As she reached the screen she removed the last of her garments and placed them on top of a metal chute. The clothes disappeared down the chute just as she slipped behind the shower screen. The shower automatically turned on at her preferred settings. The sensors ensured the temperature of the water adjusted to the user's body heat with no cold shock or hot scalding. All of her technology knew her personally, closer than anyone else now Derek was gone. She was dried as she stepped out from the shower screen and her clothes for the day appeared from behind a newly opened panel.

'First appointment,' she called as she took a bite from her yeast extract and cream cheese bagel. Even though she knew her choice of food wasn't printed, she'd programmed in a few extra items for herself.

She'd always choose one of these items for each meal as an extra insurance from mass produced printed 'pap' that was slowly working its way up towards those in the higher zones. 'Enforcer reward program 08:00' a panel replied. *That wasn't right – it was too early!* No matter; she finished off her bagel and coffee, and then the orange juice as stimulus until the caffeinated coffee kicked in.

At 08:00 Renee was ready, and the top profit enforcer came into her office. She beckoned him to sit down and gave the usual 'profit is everything, well done, blah, blah,' speech.

She opened her desk drawer and handed him a bundle of paper credits, and another, and another; the hand-outs continued. As she did this she noticed a pile of bodies in the corner of the office. What? By this time the enforcer was immobile, held firm under a pyramid of paper credits. The pile of bodies in the corner of the office had grown in sync with the credits. The drawer held one last bundle of credits. She rammed it in the enforcer's mouth, choking and suffocating him. As she watched his life ebb away one last body appeared on the pile. It was Derek.

Beep...beep...beep... Zeleno's alarm went off. *Shit!* She woke up startled and disturbed. She'd had one of her worst dreams ever. The next half hour repeated exactly as in her dream, which just served to increase her anxiety. It was only when she asked the panel for her first appointment details that her dream and reality diverged. 'Tom Andrews – Research 4 at 10:00,' it replied. She breathed a sigh of relief and swiftly downed another distance pill.

McCree was sleeping soundly – doubly so as a result of the distance pill and alcohol. He dreamt he'd been summoned to meet with the head of Meometics because he was GUCI's top enforcer profit re-enabler. By a large margin he'd terminated the most protesters.

He had bonus upon bonus piled on top of him by a very attractive woman, in a seductive way which half excited him but also half scared him. He was almost at the point of suffocation under his bonuses when he looked over to his left and saw a corresponding pile of bodies mounting up as the bonuses did.

She leaned over towards him; he was now immobilized by his rewards as she thrust his final bonus into his mouth, choking him. He became aroused at this, yet knew it was his final few moments alive. His life was being snuffed out by both this powerful executive and his own thirst for revenge for the way his life had turned out.

He woke up in a cold sweat, surveyed his surroundings, and reassured himself he wasn't in fact dead. The glass by his bedside confirmed his last memories of the previous evening. 07:00 and sweating already. It was an important day for him as he would be on escort duty. He needed to be at the briefing session for 09:00.

His shower was remote controlled, but set to his preferred temperature. Getting in it was a shock as he was still hot and sweaty. Normally it would have been fine. He dried himself off with his air towel and put on his commuting clothes.

McCree chose option four for breakfast. It took five minutes to print the meal before it emerged from his device and a further five minutes to cook the scrambled egg on waffle he'd chosen. His coffee was at the standard temperature so he had to warm it up along with the breakfast. It always made the cup hot and he then had to wait for that to cool. *This is progress?* – he quizzed himself. *Whatever happened to microwave ovens?* he mused.

As he ate his breakfast he looked out onto the city from his apartment window. Another baking hot day was about to begin. How many of the city's inhabitants had ever felt rain on their face? He remembered as a small child when he lived on southern tip of land on the edge of the Northern Block. His long dead father spoke to him in his head. 'You'll never see a cloud where we're going to, John. But maybe one day you really will be wishing for rain, son.'

Taw-Cymru was one of the last settlements to be placed under a mandatory profit re-location scheme. It had a lot of rain and naturally flowing water in abundance.

Water was expensive and the cost was rising; the topology of Taw-Cymru had made its capture unprofitable until technology had found a way to make it pay.

From that point on McCree's family, along with half a million other citizens, were doomed to re-location. The enforcer's homeland had been cordoned off, a mixture of industrial landscape with pockets of unspoilt beauty that only those in the top zone were allowed access to.

McCree finished his breakfast, locked his room with his face scan, and took the lift down directly to the metro system. He and all the other low zoners had no right to a personal transport. In some ways, there were benefits to being at street level, subject to the endless baking rays of the sun in a cloudless sky. Being crushed like sardines in a plastic tube on the metro was not one of them, however.

Citizens with a transport would be in their own conditioned bubble of filtered air. Still, when he reported in to work, he'd be able to experience that. Many of his co-commuters would never have that chance.

He arrived at GUCI's metro stop. Only a few commuters got off at this stop, a couple of which McCree recognized as fellow enforcers. Protocol dictated that people stayed on the platform until the metro left the station. There were to be no clues as to where commuters left to go to from here.

Exit one opened and two people left that way. No one else left until exit four opened, and another two people left. McCree and his two colleagues took exit five and the short distance down a narrow corridor, where a scan allowed them into the lift and GUCI HQ.

The lift had plenty of time to finish off the security checks on the occupants before allowing the doors to open at the enforcers' level. As McCree walked down the corridor with his two colleagues their names lit up on the wall: Bates, Cauldwell, McCree, with arrows directing them to their assigned rooms. The appropriate uniform and protective equipment would already be waiting for them.

'Catch you later,' McCree said as he peeled off to a room on the left marked today as Escort 1.

'No kills for you today then, McCree,' called Bates as he and Cauldwell headed down the corridor.

'There's always tomorrow Bates,' he replied.

Bates turned to Cauldwell, 'You'd think he'd be glad of a break from profit restoration.'

'Nah, not him,' Cauldwell replied. 'He enjoys it too much. At least someone else has the chance of a bonus today!'

McCree entered Escort 1 and kitted up. His locker also gave him his seating position. He was next to Adams, who hadn't arrived yet, but from the seating plan he could tell that there were going to be five teams of two and he was in team two. Adams arrived; all participants were present and the door was locked. Lead Enforcer Jack Forester spoke up. 'Good profit to you all.' There were various replies and mumbles, but McCree kept quiet.

'Today at 09.30 you will be escorting the head profit enabler of Meometics and her Assemblage from their head office to their research block and later on, back again.'

The pictures of those to be protected flashed up on the wall panels. He stared, hypnotized, at the image of Renee Zeleno on the wall. She was the executive who'd murdered him in his dream.

'McCree,' Forester barked. 'You look like you've seen a ghost. Well, that's the purpose of this briefing – to make sure she doesn't turn into one… Or any of her Assemblage for that matter,' he added.

McCree refocused his thoughts. He'd never paid much attention to the high zoners – who they were or what they looked like. Except for when his duties required it of him. It would not be good form to kill one of them inadvertently in a chaotic situation. Hence their pictures being displayed on the wall panels. He knew he'd never seen her before, but he was certain she was the woman who had suffocated him in his dream this morning.

Forested continued, 'I'm aware that there hasn't been an assassination of a head profit enabler for almost ten solars and I want it kept that way. However, if there ever was a high profile target, this is it.'

He detailed the route, escort formation, and timings to the enforcers finishing with: 'Keep alert and profitable.'

'And if the shit hits the extractor, don't worry, we've got McCree,' Adams said. They all laughed, except McCree.

A chime went off in the lab at 09:00. We'd worked all through the night from 22:00, once Grant had managed to get off the phone to his other half. It was normally a five minute affair when he called her around 21:45, but Grant felt he could emphasize how important success for the visit would be, given that Tom had put her in the picture.

'I told her who was coming and she understood for once,' he confided.

'Or maybe Tom shagged her into submission!' I quipped.

'K, just leave it out!' He glared. I took the hint.

We'd been able to replace the damaged bench, but Tom had come in during the repairs. 'What happened to *that?*' he asked.

'A power surge fried the bench,' I replied.

'That's highly unusual. Store the data for that incident in a separate archive to investigate later,' he instructed.

'Already done, Tom.' I said.

'I shouldn't have bothered opening my mouth, you already knew what I was going to ask!' he replied.

'No you shouldn't and yes I did,' I laughed.

'You can have my job one day K, but not today...' he smiled. 'I have a bucket of shit to eat first, I trust you've seasoned it?'

'Already done Tom, with lots of salt and pepper,' I replied. Tom was a great leader, inspirational and dedicated to the success of his team and its goals. He'd go the extra mile to ensure his team felt valued and never exploited. He led by example.

Unfortunately for us it had taken until 03:00 to plug the new bench in and a further hour to test it. This had only left us with enough time to run a proof of concept test before our visit from the Assemblage. We should have been ready to run an incremental test instead. Tom had kept an eye on me during this run.

That was standard procedure for Tom. If you goofed he'd look over your shoulder the next time to confirm it was a one off rather than the start of a trend.

To tell the truth I was rather glad he did, as we'd been working longer and quicker than usual, and that's exactly the time a second pair of eyes helps. This time I repeated the experiment, but I suppose as a reaction to the shock of my error, I ran the test only up to yellow.

'Richard of York gave battle in vain,' I absentmindedly whispered.

'Pardon K, what was *that?*' Tom asked.

'Oh, sorry Tom, just double checking the settings,' I replied.

Tom had never had to watch over me on this piece of equipment, because Grant was usually at this station and he'd not yet managed to blow the experiment bench up!

'As you know, Tom, the seals glow the various colours of the spectrum depending on the power level of the experiment, and I use that phrase to double check what percentage power level we're at. The phrase matches the colour cycle of the spectrum.'

'Red, orange, yellow, green, blue, indigo, violet,' Tom nodded. 'So who was this Richard guy anyway?'

'Oh, he was a medieval dude who was supposed to be king after Henry VI died but got killed in a battle before he had the chance.'

'Well, let's hope his misfortune doesn't happen to us,' said Tom.

'No chance, it's just a dull mnemonic of mine. The medievals hadn't even discovered electricity then, although they were rather useful with metal and a hammer.'

I had chosen a 2:1 power ratio of high- and low-frequency pulses running the seals up to yellow so that the high-frequency pulse was running at orange, or 25%, and the low-frequency pulse was running at red, or 12.5%. This gave the total power output at yellow, or 37.5%. I figured I'd need to run the tests at least into the blue range, but that would come later. I powered down the experiment. Grant was rapidly typing commands on the data recording panel where I normally sat. He always worked at a quicker pace than I did, but I could often catch up with him as he would have to correct his work far more often than me.

'We'll get our proof of concept results at about 12:00,' Grant spoke up.

'Ok,' Tom acknowledged. 'No change of plan for the bucket o'shite meeting at 10.00 then,' he mused. 'Let's have a quick break and I'll brief you with what I'm expecting.'

We headed down the corridor and exited the lift at the canteen.

We sat round a small circular table that was close to the lift. 'The usual?' Grant enquired. Tom and I nodded. It was strange – we all drank our coffee white with one sugar, but at least it saved time working out whose cup was whose. Grant returned from the vending station with three coffees and Tom briefed us on the meeting.

'I'll be taking the lead, guys. Don't offer anything to the Assemblage unless they ask you directly and then make sure your answer is truthful. Don't think you can fool a discriminator – you can't. We'll be called about 09.55 to go up to meeting eight on the top floor. I've reviewed the test info and will give it my best shot. I expect a rough ride, so don't worry if it's looking bad for us. We always have options – whatever the outcome of this meeting.'

We sat and waited in silence with our thoughts. The Assemblage would be on their way already.

Solar 85

Meometics HQ

It was 09:30 and Renee Zeleno was in the lift heading down to the transport park. Peter de Vries, Meometics' most successful discriminator, joined her in the lift at floor twenty-five. Paulus Henks, a profit scenario analyst, joined them at floor twenty-two, and Damian Porter, a profit opportunist researcher completed the Assemblage when he entered on the eighteenth floor.

'Colleagues,' Renee spoke. 'Maximum profit concentration for this meeting please.' The others said nothing. They merely noted her order. They arrived at sub-level one and Zeleno's own enhanced transport was waiting for them. Reserved for the head of Meometics' use only, it had capacity for six in case GUCI enforcers needed to ride 'shotgun' in the vehicle with them. It was nicknamed the Sixer, and had the latest armour protection. From Torq Innovations, alas, Renee noted.

Once they were all seated the transport sped up the ramp out onto the street level. They were immediately picked up by the GUCI enforcer transport detail of five vehicles. The vehicles communicated with each other and formed a protective formation around the six person transport.

McCree's transport was directly behind the lead enforcer vehicle. All movements had been planned ahead. The enforcers just needed to keep alert.

The convoy passed two blocks and the regular transports that would have been in the way of the convoy automatically deferred to the convoy. There was no higher priority transport than the head of a corporation.

Another block passed by and the convoy took a left.

They turned onto Liberation Quadrant. Two projectiles landed, *thwump*, *thwump*. The lead transport was thrown up into the air. It seemed to just overturn with no visible explosion.

McCree's transport swerved to the left and the rest of the convoy followed. McCree could see the stricken transport dissolve in a pool of yellow slime that had spread out from the two projectiles now flattened on the road. He could just make out an arm in what remained of the transport and knew the sickening fate of its occupants in an instant.

Adams was frantically trying to contact GUCI for backup, but communications had failed and without guidance the vehicles came to an abrupt stop. McCree surveyed the area – there were no other transports in the vicinity. This looked bad, but he could see no obvious threat.

A glint of sun reflected off the top of the nearby Tower Eight. Two large teardrop shaped containers were heading towards them. 'Get out now Adams!' McCree barked. He grabbed his weapon as he exited. Adams followed suit from the other side of the vehicle.

'Tower Eight, rooftop,' McCree shouted, and simultaneously gestured to the teams following, two of which engaged the wheels on their boots, powered up their micro-jets and sped over to Tower Eight.

Adams caught his weapon on the door frame as he left the vehicle; with only a second or two delay he freed it from the frame and turned. *Thwump*, *thwump*. The next two projectiles detonated on impact. Adams was thrown into the air by the percussive wave. He landed short of the yellow slime but now another pool was spreading from the second set of impacts.

The second transport started to dissolve – the pool was just over half a metre away from Adams. McCree thought he saw activity at a window about halfway up Tower Eight. It looked as if something was pointing at them.

The two remaining enforcers from the rear of the convoy had unlocked the enhanced firepower from the back of the transports and were pulling the kit from the vehicle. McCree looked through his sights and he could see there was definitely someone pointing a device at them. 'A signal jammer,' McCree mumbled.

'Argggggggghhh!' Adams cried out. 'My foot!' The pool of slime had spread across to his foot. Or rather where his left foot had been – Adams had recovered from his dazed state courtesy of the pain of foot dissolution. McCree looked over to Tower Eight. The range was too far for gel bullets to be effective.

McCree rushed over to the first of the enforcers out of the transport with enhanced firepower. These weapons were meant to be fired from a tripod support. 'I need a bit more punch,' he said, as he yanked the heavy calibre rifle out of his colleague's grasp.

'Get in the Sixer,' he bellowed to Reardon's team. McCree held the weapon steady and aimed. No time for a tripod, he'd only be able to hold the weapon up for a few shots.

He managed a spread of four before his arms succumbed. The gel shells spattered across the area McCree had been aiming for. This was a mass crowd control weapon. It would spray on impact to immobilize a group of people, who could then be easily terminated with a gel bullet. That was the sheer beauty and terror of the weapon. Once immobilized the victims only had that terrifying wait until a gel bullet finished them off for good.

McCree was hoping to catch at least one of those responsible for the ambush. He'd hit whatever had been aiming at them and it disappeared from sight. The transports started up again. One of the enforcers was crushed underneath his own, now mobile transport. The Sixer was heading for Adams. McCree instantly sensed the danger.

'Adams, don't move...'

'Gluurgh,' Adams half cried out. But it was too late – as he'd rolled over to try and avoid the Sixer his head dipped face first into the first pool of slime. He had no face left to scream with; his head dissolved. As the Sixer ran over his colleague's legs McCree heard Adams's (or what was left of Adams's) pelvis snap.

McCree dived out of the way as the enforcers' transports followed the Sixer, all now back on auto-pilot. The Sixer went straight through the second pool of slime, splitting it like a bow wave into two smaller pools on either side. It continued undamaged. The two enforcer transports either side of and a little behind the Sixer made contact with the slime. Their sides partially dissolved causing them to roll over onto their roofs.

The final enforcer transport followed the Sixer. There was still a thick enough covering of slime left after the Sixer had run through the pool to dissolve the bottom of the vehicle, leaving the rest of it to skid to a halt. McCree surveyed the mess. Reardon had at least managed to get into the Sixer. McCree unclipped the gel rifle left by Reardon's dead partner and headed on foot towards Tower Eight. 'Not a good day,' he muttered to himself.

The two enforcer teams had arrived at Tower 8,powered down their boots and took the lift to the rooftop rushing straight into a pool of yellow slime, leaving no trace of them apart from one arm just beyond the edge of the pool.

McCree would discover later that he and Reardon were the only enforcers to get out of the mess alive.

He was much closer now to Tower Eight and could see that his third shot was the one that had de-activated the jammer. He called the rest of the squad. No one answered. The Sixer was now underground at its intended destination and unreachable via the short-wave enforcer communications device. His comms unit sprang to life.

'All Escort 1 enforcers to hold station and remain there until hazmat 3 arrives for clean-up,' a GUCI controller instructed. 'Understood,' McCree confirmed. 'Lockdown Tower Eight in my vicinity,' he requested.

Do GUCI or Meometics know the price we've paid today to keep the Meometics Assemblage safe? At this point he still thought there'd only been four enforcers killed. The final total was eight – half of whom he'd ordered to their death.

The doors of the Sixer rose up and Renee and the remainder of the Meometics Assemblage stepped out of the transport and into the lift. Her decision to procure the state of the art high grade armour from Torq Innovations at the earliest opportunity had saved them. That, and the actions of one of the enforcers. Meometics gratitude would reach him later. What exactly was that slime? She made a mental note to investigate further.

Reardon contacted GUCI from an update panel in sub-level one. The building was shielded against data 'leakage' to prevent industrial espionage. GUCI comms panels were therefore installed in all shielded buildings to allow secure communications between GUCI and its enforcers. 'Request additional enforcers to enable return escort journey to begin.' Reardon spoke at the panel. 'Confirm existing resource available,' a controller replied.

Reardon was caught off guard, It sounded as though GUCI didn't have the full picture and he was been asked to fill in the blanks. 'One,' he replied. The controller spoke again. 'Confirmed Enforcer Reardon, sending nine enforcers.'

Reardon was floored, *I'm the only enforcer survivor?*

The Assemblage had reached the top floor. Renee led the way out of the lift and to the meeting room; it was 10:05. Naturally she was late due to the attempt on her life but that didn't faze her. She spoke to the panel adjacent to the entry door of the meeting room. 'Send Research 4 to MR1,' she barked. Her message was transmitted throughout the building.

Renee sat down behind the desk. Paulus Henks and Peter de Vries were on her left-hand side, with Damian Porter on her right. There was a pause of around five minutes before the lift doors opened and the Research 4 team entered the room...

I remember this day so well; how could I forget? Tom entered the room first and I followed with Grant, two steps behind Tom. 'Please sit down, Research 4,' Zeleno said. It was unnerving to be referred to in that way to our faces. We sat either side of Tom. 'Run through the progress you've made, Tom,' she instructed.

Tom began: 'We have yet to reach our design goal of a stable enhancement to the existing coating on the chips. However, we have realized that we are near the limit of our existing enhancement process. So to achieve our stated goals we have stopped the development of that solution and started a more scalable process.' Tom paused for breath.

Zeleno spoke up. 'Tom, the information I have before me indicates your last test run had a worse result than the previous one.'

'Yes profitable leader, but the tests were on different processes.'

'That is not the point Tom, I want straight, simple answers, not your scientific mumbo jumbo.' The conversation between Zeleno and Tom was not an experience to be envied. 'Did I not say last night's tests would be the basis of the product release?'

'Yes.'

'It is true that the last test gave results inferior to the previous one?'

'Yes.'

'Do you think this unprofitable situation can be allowed to continue without any consequences whatsoever?'

'No.'

'I'm at least reasonably assured that you can therefore grasp the difficulty of Research 4's circumstances,' she continued.

She looked at the information on the desk in front of her and analysed it. 'We will use the configuration that yielded the 85 per cent cohesion result,' she said. 'Send the specifications to manufacturing. We have pre-contracted the enhanced coating for systems in Clearwater's de-sal plants, and as well as our weapons systems it has been indicated to us by software that we will be entering into a global-use profit agreement with this product,' she finished.

'Profitable leader, systems made at this time will be liable to malfunction on occasion, the effects of which depend on the use of the chips in the products. It will lead to a number of unwanted fatalities – if used in weapons systems the collateral damage these weapons could do would have a destabilizing effect in the area if non-combatants are killed.'

'Tom, I hope you do not need reminding how late you are already on the project.'

'In two quarters I'm sure we'll have the finished article.'

'Two quarters is too late. Here is the only concession you will get from me, so listen carefully. In one quarter from now I'll take your other design if it is indeed, as you've indicated, an improved solution. You will then be assigned to Ultra projects, so what I send to production today will be the basis of our chips for the next technology generation.

If there is no finish to the product or improvement of it, the chips will continue to ship with today's specifications.'

Tom once again tried to improve our deal.

'Profitable leader, I know Research 4 would gladly delay assignation to Ultra projects to finish off our existing product to the standard of the original design goals.'

'No, I need Research 4 on Ultra projects in one quarter's time.' Zeleno replied.

Grant had been turning redder in the face; I knew he was seething about the way Tom was being ripped up but now he was looking quite pale. I too felt more than uneasy about the potential consequences of not just Renee Zeleno's decisions, but also our inability to crack the problem in a timely manner.

I personally thought the way she said 'You will then be assigned to Ultra projects' sounded like a death sentence rather than a reward.

I thought maybe that was the way she came across, but most certainly she didn't really like having to rely on us *lowly* scientists. So it was that on this day, solar 85, 3rd Quarter, profit cycle forty, I realized I would be complicit in Meometics decisions if I did nothing. I had to make a stand.

Renee Zeleno's decisions would result in the death of many people, customers and non-customers alike. All this for what? A better profit return. Was there any alternative? Squeezing more profit out of the populous is one thing, but killing them for the sake of profit? My head was whirling. How did I ever find myself in this situation? How could I have been so blind?

Tom had no chance against Renee Zeleno. Grant and I could clearly see that he was outclassed and outmanoeuvred. No wonder she was Meometics' head profit enabler; it didn't bear thinking about if Meometics became the planet's leading corporation.

Zeleno spoke. 'To confirm: transfer all additional nanite research information gained between now and one quarter from now to the project archive. You will also have decided by then if your dependants are to accompany you or not. Now, Research 4, this meeting is concluded,' she announced. Zeleno gestured to the lift. Grant and I followed Tom. None of us were overflowing with joy. We left.

Renee turned to her discriminator, Peter de Vries. 'De Vries, your observations,' she demanded.

'Tom Andrews has not told us everything. I believe a member of his team has brought to his attention the problem with the existing design and that he took the responsibility to get their point across. Also Grant Stern was extremely angry with you personally. He wanted to speak out, but he was clearly under Tom's orders not to.

'They are all extremely concerned about your decision and are convinced there will be many deaths arising from the product in its present level of development.'

De Vries had, as usual, completely summed up the situation as it was. 'Henks, your appraisal,' Zeleno demanded.

'My view is that we can expect improved profit from their developments in the next quarter. The improved profit generated will by far exceed costs related to deaths and malfunction of the product already out with the customers.'

'So,' Renee paused. 'Liquidate them after the next meeting as per competitor collusion protocol, families too if they have agreed to remain together. I'm pleased they all feel the same way about my decision,' she added. 'It would have been mildly disappointing to terminate someone who *agreed* with my point of view.'

The lift arrived at sub-seven and we all headed to the lab. I no longer wanted to be part of Meometics, but no one from the research teams had ever left before. The research teams all landed up on Ultra projects. We'd all accepted we could never work for a competitor, but why was there no option other than working on Ultra projects? The only real variable at Meometics was how much time you had in the research team before you moved up to become one of the Ultra teams.

Tom was quiet, although that could have been because he was hatching another plan. 'If plan A doesn't work we can always try plans B to Z,' he once said to me. Grant was going to be able to tell his other half they'd be moving in the next quarter. That should make Anne happy. I decided to keep my feelings to myself to see if they crystallized or dissipated as a result of the recent meeting.

Tom spoke up: 'I know today's been disappointing guys but that's the way it goes sometimes. We need to get an improvement in stability urgently now, to minimize the number of fatalities our products could cause. Do we have an agreement?' he asked.

'Yes,' both Grant and I offered simultaneously.

'Then in that case take the next two days off. I'll make sure the power transfer conduits are fully checked and working. There's less margin for error at the higher power outputs, so additional checks will reduce the chance of a gremlin sabotaging our test results further. We know that the multiplexing of high- and low-frequency pulses is our last chance to fix the problem.' Tom paused. 'Here's my cliché of the day for you – just chill out for a few days. If you don't think too hard about the lab you may find a useful insight pops up in your head out of nowhere. Sometimes we can't see the wood for the trees – if you can even remember what those look like! I'll expect you both back at sun-up, solar 88, then.'

Grant shut down the systems he knew Tom would be working on. He instigated a swathe of diagnostic tests which would form the basis of the work Tom would get the mech-techs to do.

'See you on 88 Tom,' Grant said as he headed for the exit.

'Oh, Grant,' Tom called, 'fix that tweak you made to your apartment's sound dampener. It's not working as you intended and, unless you want to sour your two days off, fix it discreetly.' Grant gazed at Tom curiously, nodded, and disappeared.

Tom looked at me, 'So, K, we both know Anne will be keeping Grant busy for the next few days, what about you?'

'I'm just going to panel veg. All that stuff going on in front of me, entertainment and news for the masses. It kinda dumbs me down for a bit and lets all the cool thoughts and theories rise to the surface.'

'Ah, that's what my grandfather would call a busman's holiday. It means doing something similar on vacation to what you do at work.'

'Can't say I've heard of that term before.'

'No, I'd imagine not. He used to get most of his wisdom from old printed-on-paper books. It was a hobby of his. He used to say when all the electricity has been used up, you'll still be able to read what's in a book. As long as we still have eyes by then.'

'Sounds like a real character, your grandfather.'

'He was, K.'

'Well, see you on 88, Tom.'

'Good profit with your time, K.'

I left the lab, the panels scrolling diagnostic information on them. It would be hours before Tom could get to work on the information, but I had to start much sooner than that.

McCree continued towards Tower Eight. Orders had been given to hold station. He didn't see the point. Nobody but the higher zoners and the well-informed travelled at street level, and then it had to be in transports.

As soon as GUCI had become aware of the incident the transports would have been given avoidance instructions for the surrounding area. He figured 'hold station' meant with the rest of his colleagues over at Tower Eight. They had headed for the rooftop, but he had his sights on an apartment on the corner of Tower Eight, in zone four.

There was a deathly silence during his whizz across to the tower. He could only hear the faint whirring of his boots as he powered towards it. His weapon had given the distance to the apartment; it had only required him to press the two 'powered distance known' indicators on his uniform to fire the boots up.

The boots' CPU read the distance from his weapon sight and automatically calculated the quickest speed to travel. They were capable of up to 60Km/h, but at that speed he'd only get 150 metres from them. It also worked out the speed the enforcer could run at to arrive at the shortest journey time both powered and self-powered.

Fortunately for McCree, the CPU decided he'd not have to do any running himself. The boots set themselves to 40Km/h, range 700m, which was the distance to the Tower Eight. He kept his weapon ready, trained on the building at all times. In just over a minute he'd reached the entrance to the tower as the fuel display sank to zero per cent.

He figured the rest of the escort had between five and ten minutes lead on him. In a crisis situation time always seemed to drag. He knew it would be fortunate if the building had been locked down before the jammer operator escaped, although the enforcers he'd sent to the rooftop should have had a better chance of catching the assassins.

He arrived at the entrance to zone four. 'Top level zone four,' McCree commanded.

'GUCI lockdown override confirmed, ID Enforcer McCree, John.' the lift replied.

'Display users of this lift in the last fifteen minutes,' McCree said.

'Two events found,' the lift replied.

It displayed the two users side by side. Kieran Clarke, maintenance operative; Tom Andrews, Meometics Research 4. *Hmm,* thought McCree. *Building fixer and an employee of the company whose head just survived an assassination attempt.* Neither of them sounded as if they were the type to participate in such an attempt.

The lift arrived at the requested floor. 'Display lift access history for Kieran Clarke and Tom Andrews.' McCree ordered. Kieran Clarke's results were over a panel's worth of ins and outs, whilst Tom Andrews had just a handful of entries; all except today's were related to yesterday evening.

'Display apartment access log reference with Tom Andrews.' he commanded. Two apartments matched – one yesterday, a different one today.

Again McCree ordered the lift: 'Illuminate Tom Andrews's trace today.' He pressed the door-open button and looked at the lit arrows directing him along the corridor. He knew the layout of the towers, all enforcers had to. Not that it was an onerous task as the standardization of such towers was universal these days. He was sure the arrows would lead to the jammer's apartment, and they did.

The door unlocked for him. The apartment was bare, with only the jammer lying on the floor pointing up at the ceiling. The gel shells McCree had fired just ten minutes ago had all but dissipated although he could still make out his accuracy at first hand.

If he'd used a tripod he could have zapped the jammer's operator, he thought. The main objective, though, was to have stopped the assassination and in that at least he had succeeded.

Nothing more for me here, McCree thought. Fortunately the top floor in each zone had an access door to the roof lift. He located the door for this zone at the centre of the level and entered the roof lift. There was no objection by the lift to McCree's commands. The building now knew full well who he was and the clearance he'd been allowed.

The lift arrived at the roof – still no contact from his colleagues. His weapon ready, he decided to stay inside the lift rather than burst forward. It was one of two tactics he'd been trained to use. In the case of his colleagues, as first on scene they would have rushed out from the lift. Then, after securing the area, they would have had their weapons trained on the entry and exit points. In this case the lift.

Should something have gone wrong and the initial assault by the four enforcers have not gone to plan, there would be no benefit in a single enforcer repeating the mistake. Snipe shots from inside the lift, with some cover from the lift side, would give a better chance of success now that surprise was no longer an option.

He pressed the lift door-open button and although surprise was no longer on the menu, something far worse was. Horror! The uniformed arm of one of his colleagues was all that was visible of his fellow enforcers. He instantly recognized the yellow slime just twenty centimetres or so away from the lift door. James, who was the fastest storm enforcer in Escort 1, had almost made it past the slime to the other side of the roof. Well, his arm had. The badge on the arm confirmed his identity. McCree wept, long and loud.

'Hazmat 3 on site, confirm present location,' McCree's communicator announced. McCree gathered himself up, still distressed, and took a deep breath. 'Roof of Tower Eight, hazmat required. No, repeat, no other enforcers alive at this location.'

For Renee Zeleno's return to her office with her Assemblage GUCI had taken additional precautions. GUCI would suffer a serious credibility blow with the corporations if it failed to protect the head of Meometics a second time, so soon after the first assassination attempt.

This time the enforcer transports were hovers, and the comms frequencies were ultra-bursted so that they could punch though all but the most permanent and powerful of signal jammers. Put another way – safe from all but satellite jammers and able to float over the transport-eating slime.

Reardon was in the escort back to the office but with nine new colleagues for the return journey. A joke from one of them along the lines of 'what did you do to the rest of the enforcers on the way down?' did not go down well. McLean was in charge of the return leg, which took an altogether different route.

The return trip was as uneventful as their trip to the Meometics research building wasn't. This time they had additional measures in hand. *This was so predictable* Zeleno thought, *GUCI are now looking to militate against a repeat attack. If I was an assailant my modus operandi would be to have no modus operandi. You can't easily plan against an ever changing enemy.* She exited the Sixer with her Assemblage and went straight into the lift up to her office.

Renee spoke to the comms panel in the lift: 'Analyse a sample of that yellow slime on my transport,' she said.

79

'Find some way to contain the sample without letting it make short work of the receptacle, instruments, or you before GUCI realize we've got some on our vehicle and send their hazmat team to remove it all,' she ordered.

A voice from the panel confirmed it would be arranged. The Assemblage positioned themselves in their usual seating pattern around the table in Renee's office. Renee poured a glass of water from the dispenser that was situated in a corner. After taking just a single sip she opened up to the rest of the Assemblage.

'We can safely assume that all of us were the target of the recent attempt on our lives. I want to know who was responsible for it, what specifically is their motivation for wiping us out, and how did they get access to the latest technology to almost succeed?' she paused. 'Findings to be presented here at 10.00 solar 88.'

The rest of the Assemblage rose collectively and left via the lift; they were acutely aware of Renee's short, demanding deadlines and knew far better than to raise concerns about them. Far better to spend what painfully little time they had looking for the answers.

Renee headed to her main comms panel, glass of water in hand. Sipping further from it, nursing it almost like a bizarre form of emotional crutch, she stared at the panel.

'Display Escort 1 enforcer details for today,' she ordered the panel.

The panel displayed both variations of the Escort 1 team, the first showing eight out of the ten with a red border around them and a status of 'deceased'. The second showing the status of all of them as 'GUCI'. She studied the teams' variations. All of the second duty were new except one. The enforcer who boarded her transport was the only one who was there for both journeys. Renee's pill was reaching the height of its powers over her; more importantly she was oblivious to its effects.

She scanned the first escort duty. One of the only two survivors was Reardon, the coward who boarded her transport. Then she focused on the other enforcer, McCree, the one in her dream. *He must be involved somehow in the attempt on my life. He wasn't present on the return escort and no attempt was made then. Reardon is clearly spineless and incapable of such deviousness.*

McCree was listed as being 'at incident location'. Zeleno read this to mean 'clearing up the evidence of your involvement, McCree'. *How very, very convenient.*

A plan formed easily in her head, it always did when the pill was there and of course these days it was there more often than not. She was going to sand Reardon down to zero, the best way in her view to deal with the pitiful drain on the planet's profit that he was. McCree however, well she knew how to deal with him, too. He was a much more difficult proposition. He'd been quite astute, giving the impression he was the one to save them from the attack. He'd be expecting bonuses for this.

Well, Enforcer McCree, if it's bonuses you want, that's what you'll get. Who am I to stand in the way of a top enforcer's career? Beware though, Enforcer McCree, what you wish for, you could end up suffocating under the weight of your rewards. She nodded to herself, pleased that she was now being alerted of threats to her position by premonitions in her dreams and, of course, the solutions to deal with them.

'Arrange meeting with Enforcer McCree, solar 87, 10.00,' she demanded. 'Place corporate trace on Enforcer McCree,' she added.

'All complimentary GUCI traces are in use. Please indicate if you wish to continue or cancel,' the panel replied. Simultaneously all twenty complimentary traces given by GUCI to the head of each monopoly or corporation appeared on the display.

GUCI allowed these traces on anyone, even its own people. This way they believed there was at least an equilibrium between them and the power the CEOs had over the populous. GUCI could not afford to lose its status, so giving this concession allowed them to appear to be transparent. This was about to be tested.

'Remove Research 4 traces, Tom Andrews excepted, confirm trace Enforcer McCree,' she said.

'Confirmed,' the panel responded. 'One trace remaining,' it added.

'Trace Renee Zeleno, Meometics,' Zeleno commanded.

'Confirmed,' the panel replied.

Research 4 had been dealt with; she decided not to waste her valuable traces on most of them.

Tracing a GUCI employee had never been required until now, but the assassination attempt had made her think about the scale of their involvement. It seemed to her a little too convenient that their incompetence had almost resulted in her murder. Plus, McCree was involved.

It would be too obvious to place a trace on the head of GUCI, so she'd follow McCree and see where that led her. The Assemblage's itinerary had found its way into the hands of her enemies. She just needed to find out which enemy had attempted to wipe her out so she could crush them first before continuing with her real priorities.

Tracing herself was a clever plan, she thought. *Let's see what it tells my competitors about me*, she reasoned. If there were some discrepancies in her record, she'd know trace information was being omitted on her other traces. 'Display all trace history solar 80 to today, order by chronology,' she demanded of the panel.

She smiled at her own brilliance. *I really am going to be in charge of this whole, damned forsaken rock*, she told herself, *and then the planet will see how much profit can* really *be made.* The pill was in full effect and her paranoia and psychosis were working together with devastating efficiency.

14:00, Solar 86
My Apartment

I had panel vegged yesterday, as I promised Tom I would. In that respect my intentions were true. To my amazement the news stream reported that the Meometics Assemblage had been subject to an assassination attempt on the way over to the meeting with us.

They had shown no indication of this during the meeting, and indeed we'd had our arse kicked just as Tom expected we would. It took amazingly driven and focused people to keep that kind of situation off the table. How differently things would have turned out if they'd been killed or lost their focus in the meeting with us.

I would normally have contacted Grant about this discovery, but decided to keep my intentions private until I knew what we were up against. We'd catch up next time we were back at the lab.

Searching the global network I used my enhanced results credentials, which gave me access to more information than the average individual.

I was looking for some way to contact Dr Derek Toft of Research 2, he'd surely be able to advise on ways to improve the process we were applying to his chip coating, and also to discuss his post-Ultra project plans. After all he surely would be close to hanging up his lab coat at his age? I had no luck at all on my searches for other scientists associated with Derek, other than the fact they were working on Ultra projects.

There were a few of his associates who by coincidence had prematurely met an untimely end. The most relevant was Professor Bertrand Lazar, whose pioneering work came to an abrupt end when his transport malfunctioned and the fuel cell exploded, killing him in the process. It was Derek Toft's team that succeeded in improving the performance of the fuel cell regulator chip that allowed the monitoring and shutdown of the fuel cell. It protected the cell from the most exceptional of circumstances.

The random infrequent detonations of these fuel cells were treated as bizarre road accidents. The numbers were too small to be of general concern and, because road deaths due to driver error had long since been eliminated, it was tolerated. Toft had been worried about the safety of his younger sister beyond all proportion to the risks she would face once she'd attained the privilege of been able to travel in a transport, and it was this irrational concern of his that drove him to success.

In fact quite a few deaths of prominent scientists seemed to be at the hands of their own inventions. I thought that was probably a contributory factor to the setting up of the Ultra projects. To stop that sort of thing from happening. Scientists far too readily in the past took the risk of injury by their own discovery or intention themselves. It went back as far as Rudolf Diesel in the days of the old calendar.

For Research 4 the nanites and the energizing of them could go badly wrong and, even though we had a top grade isolation chamber, we weren't on Ultra projects yet. So the amount of risk they faced and the precautions required for those Ultra projects must be truly astonishing.

I did wonder about Toft's sister, however, during my research. There was no trace of any other relatives, so it was a starting point. Elizabeth Toft had successfully risen up the ranks of Edibility, the food monopoly. She had married a process engineer in the company and had moved to the eastern block with him now, under the name of Elizabeth Hart.

It was strange that she had taken a married name, as that seemed to be so rooted to the days of the old calendar. Still, she was in theory contactable and so I left a discreet message for her. Corporate communications with monopolies were allowed, it was only contact with other corporations that were unacceptable. Still, a monopoly could use such contacts to play one corporation against the other, so discretion was advisable.

Taking a break from the panel I got up to get a snack from the food distributor. It took about ten minutes to print my food but that was fine. I paid more to have a high quality printing module installed. Most people in my zone had the quicker, cheaper printers such as the Quick-E 500 by Edibility, but I preferred to wait for a better quality result.

I had a glass of juice piped from the mixer tap whilst the snack printed; I then took my completed ham sandwich back to the panel. Halfway through my sandwich I received a call. E. Hart – Edibility. Putting my snack and drink out of sight of the viewer I accepted the call.

'Hello, K, Elizabeth Hart calling.' Elizabeth Hart was a slim woman in her early to mid-fifties. Attractive in a classical way with immaculate hair and fierce hazel-coloured eyes,

there was a sense of achievement and confidence about her that was apparent even over the link.

'*I understand that you wish to contact my brother,*' she said, direct and to the point.

'Yes, I'm working on one of his old projects and realistically I have the best chance of solving the problem with a pointer or two from him.'

'*As an employee of Meometics you know the rules about contacting a colleague on Ultra projects, yet you still persist. Derek has agreed to abide by these rules, so do you really want me to relay a message to him? He may report you straight to your superior for this contact alone.*'

'I really was hoping that he'd recognize an opportunity to properly finish his project. He left for Ultra projects at such short notice that his project was never truly completed. I discovered a side-effect of his research and felt it right he had the opportunity to finalize it.'

'*Or you could be another eager scientist willing to chance it, in the hope of gaining easy advancement courtesy of my brother.*'

'All I have to give you is this – if I can't correct this flaw a lot of citizens will get hurt, even killed. It may indeed be that the team I work for is held responsible for this, but it could also be attributed the originator of the project, led of course by your brother.'

'*I appreciate your candour, although you could still appear to be calling for your own selfish reasons, do you agree?*'

'Yes, I suppose it could be seen that way, but I really don't know how else to reassure you.'

'*It's not me you need to reassure, it's my brother. If you wish I can relay a single piece of information to him, then it's up to Derek. You must never contact me again, but if he wishes I will relay a message to you. Agreed?*'

'Agreed.'

I had to think fast. This was my one chance to get my message across to Derek Toft. It had to be intriguing enough for him to want to risk providing assistance without bringing unwelcome attention on us both.

There was little I had in common with Dr Toft. Apart from following in his footsteps our age difference meant that our paths had never crossed. Our only possible common ground was that we'd both experienced the reflective qualities of his coating on the chips that stopped further development of the coating itself.

With no real insight I replied. 'On reflection, "Nothing".'

'*You want me to pass that on to Derek?*'

'Yes please, Elizabeth.' I really had nothing else to say. If this was a protocol Derek had devised, well he was a far better scientist than I. Literally there wasn't anything that could be said safely without causing trouble for either of us.

'*Goodbye K. You will never be able to contact me again. Best wishes for your future.*'

She disconnected the link. I went back to my snack. I thought for a while that perhaps I could have handled the call better. I was stumped. I spent the rest of the day panel vegging. Just before 19:00 the incoming message indicator appeared. There was no indication of the originator. 'Display message.' I said to the panel.

'Do not try to trace me. I can detect such attempts and will no longer contact you if you do. Due to circumstances here I can send out longer messages than I can receive. I can only receive three words up to forty characters long in total. Each message must end with a full stop and a space between each word. Only that way can your messages pass security.

If your messages fail to meet these specifications at any time, there will be no further contact from me. My response to your questions may not always be immediate. It will depend on my circumstances here. If you follow these conditions a conversation can be continued almost indefinitely. Please confirm your understanding of these conditions.'

I replied to Derek, 'I understand you.'

Derek's reply took a little while. He must have been monitoring outgoing traffic from his facility and injecting the messages out amongst the outbound traffic. He could then choose to send a message of variable length and lose it in similarly patterned traffic.

For the incoming traffic, he'd have no control over that so the incoming messages needed to be short to avoid detection. To my mind it was an excellent way of maintaining a covert dialogue.

'Ask your question,' came the reply. It was then I realized this would be harder than it first seemed.

'Chip reflection problem.' I typed

'Give more information,' was the reply.

'Using multiple pulses.'

'How many pulses?'

'Coaxial pulses.' It also seemed that Derek's response to me was quicker when he sent smaller messages and that large replies took a great deal longer to reach me. This made sense to me – the outbound traffic was more likely to have more short message bursts than longer ones, so there was more opportunity to hide shorter replies than longer ones.

There was a lengthy pause, then…

'Problem is unsolvable with coaxial pulses. A solution exists but it may not be an acceptable solution to you. Be very careful how you proceed from now. If you decide to acquire the relevant information you will not be able to undo this decision. A chain of events will unfold and you will not be able to stop it.'

I thought back to my mistake in the lab. I was certain Derek had been here before me and realized the implications of his discovery. By a fluke on my part I was following in Derek's footsteps.

I replied: 'I will proceed.'

'Give more information.'

'Quad-axial pulses.'

'Have you viewed the phenomenon first hand?'

'Yes please assist.'

'Adam discovers cheese and bread.'

What did that mean?

The connection terminated. I worried that Derek had been discovered. We'd both be in serious trouble. Derek's last reply had been cryptic with a capital 'C'. There must have been so many different combinations of bread and cheese man had put together since their creation that it surely could not have been more vague a guide.

Maybe my food distributor's recipe bank would have a few suggestions as starting points? 'Bread and cheese suggestions,' I commanded.

The printer paused for a moment then displayed what appeared to be popular prints on a bread and cheese theme.

Cheddar topped deli bun.

Emmental baguette.

Swiss cheese Panini... and there it was in the middle of the list staring out at me.

Edam sandwich. Of course! Adam – Edam. Edam being just one letter's difference from Adam.

'Print Edam sandwich.' The printer confirmed my instruction. It had been a long while since I'd watched my food being printed, but I was anxious not to overlook any detail, however small.

The bottom layer of bread took two minutes, and as it started to print the Edam 'Check Food' appeared on the panel. This normally meant an error with the printer, even though errors were infrequent to the point of rarity. I left the distributor to finish printing the sandwich.

If this turned out to be a dead end another sandwich would be acceptable. It had been a while since I'd asked for a cheese sandwich. Normally it would be in combination with another filling. Cheese and ham, cheese and barbeque sauce.

The combination of cheese and a sauce was especially good on my upgraded food distributor. I was glad to have spent more credits on it than most of my fellow zoners would. Not any low quality printed crap for me. If I was going to eat shit it would be the highest quality shit I could afford! Even so, with a Suprem-E 600 by Edibility a plain 'cheese sandwich' was never going to be the world's best culinary delight.

The sandwich had been printed but 'Check Food' still flashed on the display. I removed the sandwich from the distributor. It looked just like you'd expect a sandwich to look. I peeled the top layer of bread away. I then realized why Edam, and why a sandwich! The Edam was a perfect slice of cheese with a completely uniform finish, unlike Stilton or Wensleydale which were crumbly and uneven.

The sandwich ensured a flat square surface for the slice of Edam, on which there was something printed. I carefully wiped the thin layer of butter off the surface of the cheese. I could just make out the message...

With it came the feeling of slipping deeper into another place, further away from corporate citizenship and into the profitless world of the non-zoners. I was not happy with the Assemblage's decision to release our product in a state that would kill unintendeds. We had become too profit oriented. To be assigned to Ultra projects was not my desire.

Ultra-profit projects. The planet and its citizens had been screwed tight enough already and yet the corporations wanted more. We were going to fuck the planet for good if we didn't stop. My worry was that I didn't know what the alternative was.

I certainly did not want to go down the route of the murdering of enforcers, or the intended murder of corporate heads as seen on the panel news video feed. I needed to decipher the cheesy message. For Derek to have sent a message via the food distributor it must have been a highly sensitive piece of information. 'Stc-318 – be at work for 11:00 S87 Follow the tricolour' it read.

'Stc-318' meant nothing to me, and attempting to search the network for that information may raise unwanted attention. Go to work tomorrow, solar 87, at 11:00 and follow the tricolour? A quick search of tricolour gave 'The old nation states identity emblem of France.'

France; a blue, white, and red flag last used in the 21st Century old calendar, before the global government took over nation states during the move to the four global blocks.

So tomorrow I was to go into work and look out for an ancient flag. I laughed at the absurdity of the situation. I could just picture Tom's questions when I appeared a day early...

'What are you doing here, K? You're not supposed to be in today.'

'Sorry Tom it's urgent, I'm looking for the ancient flag of France, a cheese sandwich told me to!'

'Security, security, I have a mental disorder situation here!'

I ate the evidence, although perhaps I should have kept it in case I need to prove my sanity to continue to work at the lab. It was very tasty. There clearly was a difference between a cheese sandwich and an Edam sandwich. The mere cheese sandwich only needed to have some of the general qualities of cheese. Edam was, however, a more specific, focused product. All of course were trademarked by Edibility.

This was not how I'd expected the situation would unfold. I wanted to stop the injustices that were about to be meted out to my fellow citizens. Instead I was contemplating the merits of different types of cheese. I took a shower and had an early night.

McCree had waited until the second hazmat team arrived at the rooftop. That was yesterday, and he'd headed back for de-briefing in a recovery transport. Forester and Reardon were already in the room; they'd been waiting for his return. Reardon and McCree exchanged bear hugs. 'Just us left, McCree?'

McCree thought it was an obvious statement to make, but more, it conveyed a sense of relief at having survived the situation earlier. Forester spoke. 'I have the details of what happened from Reardon. Now I'd like your input, McCree,'

'Well, it seemed pretty normal until we turned into Liberation Quadrant, then all hell broke loose. The guys in the lead vehicle were just dissolved, they had no chance. I got my arse out of the vehicle in double quick time and directed the detail behind me to get up to the rooftop of Tower Eight. That was where I'd seen the second set of projectiles originate from. Adams was too slow getting out of the vehicle and was concussed by the blast.

'I ordered Reardon and Garrett to get into the Sixer as a last line of defence, but after I took the jammer out the transports and Sixer started up and Garret was crushed by his own transport. The Sixer went straight through the slime that had also claimed Adams by that time.

'I rushed over to the jammer's location, but it had been abandoned, no one there, just a broken jammer. Then over to the rooftop of Tower Eight where there was still no comms from the other enforcers. It was a trap, they had no chance. End result was eight enforcer deaths, Assemblage safe.'

'Well, McCree,' Forester said. 'That pretty much fills in the blanks. Make sure you both collect your pill. You'll no doubt be needing it. Reardon, you can go now,' he added. 'McCree, please stay a moment.'

Reardon left, then Forester continued. 'You're to report tomorrow to Meometics for 10:00. A transport will pick you up. Formal kit *not* combat for the visit. I suspect some kind of reward is in order.' There couldn't have been a worse choice of words; they held no comfort at all to McCree, not with the dream he'd had earlier this morning. He picked up his formal uniform from his locker and headed back to his apartment.

McCree sat on his bed for a while before his thoughts were interrupted by an incoming video call. It was Joule, his grandson. He was allowed to call twice in between his visits. *'Hi Grampy, did you hear on the news feed there was a big battle between the enforcers and the nasty people?'* he eagerly asked.

'Yes, Joule, there were some brave enforcers keeping the nasty people away,' replied McCree.

'When I come over can I draw the battle for you?' Joule asked.

'Of course you can, of course.' McCree replied. He could hear Eleanor in the background; she must be telling Joule to wind up the call. *He's only just called, what's wrong with her?* She was obviously wound up. 'Nothing too scary for old Gramps,' he said to Joule.

'Okaaaaay Gramps, byee,' Joule replied. Then he was gone.

McCree was left alone with his thoughts again; they were what troubled him the most, although last night's dream was right there in his top three personal nightmares. He was to report to the woman in the dream who'd suffocated him. He really wanted to get out of his apartment, but to where? The planet's climate was such that spending too long outside carried a GUCI assisted profit warning to those foolish enough to loiter.

His fellow enforcers would have loved to have met up after work but there were two major problems peeing on that parade. Firstly there were eight fewer enforcers alive than there were at the start of the day. The second being

McCree was most likely the only enforcer able to afford a night out. That left the option of spending a night out with his boss, Forester. Nope, that was no option.

Once again he found himself repeating his all too familiar routine. He took a large alcohol out of his fridge and headed for the bed. The pill went down far too easy this time and he drifted off... His head was in a real fog this time. He came round, had he been drugged? Most definitely!

McCree was on a single bed in a small side room or alcove. His wrists had been chained to the bed and his legs were bound at the ankles. The door opened and Renee Zeleno came in from her office. She injected him with a hypo-spray and smiled; what was in that?

Two minutes later he knew; he had a huge erection, so hard it ached. Zeleno would clearly see his hard-on bulging in his pants. She reached over to him, only just managing to pull his pants and smalls down over his huge prick. She lifted up her skirt and pulled her briefs to one side. She lowered herself onto him.

McCree was powerless to resist – then he realized, as she reached out for a second hypo next to the bed, what was happening. Death by sex. She shot him in the arm with the hypo and he jolted back, upright and awake in his bed, sweating profusely.

What was happening to him?

Two vivid dreams in a row, in both of which he is killed by the same person – Renee Zeleno. McCree tried to reason with himself – it was just a manifestation of his fear about his upcoming meeting her. But there was more to it than that, and his subconscious knew something was up. *Maybe that's the problem*, he thought.

The distance pill only worked on your waking thoughts, not your dreams.

If these dreams continue after today's appointment, I really do need to see a psyche.

Zeleno just didn't stop. All day long she pored over the
details the traces had given her. In her experience one
could always find a link with between apparently separate
pieces of information, she just needed to look hard
enough. Her Derek had once explained it to her. 'You look
at a star such as Sirius, which is over eighty trillion
kilometres distant, and light from it over that great distance
hits the back of your retina. You have made a connection
with it. Everything is connected, you just don't know it –
most people can't see that. How much does that affect
you?'

Only a little, she thought.

'Looking at our sun, if you dare, will affect you more,
you could even be blinded. So there's the same sort of
connection going on but because it's nearer it has a bigger
effect on you because of its mere 150 million kilometres
distance. So the question is: at what point do the
connections affect you? At the point they have a *reasonable*
effect on you. Simple,' he said.

For a moment she could have sworn he was in the
room, and she missed him, dearly. More than that she
wondered if she would ever have someone in her life that
she could love *and* trust.

She struggled once again to get up from behind her desk
and out of her chair; in a haze of tiredness she only just
managed to secure her room. 'Lockdown now, alarm
07.00,' she instructed a wall panel. She half undressed

before she made it over to the bed in the side room off her main office. She slumped on it. She felt as if she was stuck in a loop of déjà vu, until the late hour and the pill eventually put her to sleep.

Suddenly everything came into sharp focus; she snapped bolt upright and there beside her was McCree restrained on her bed, hands and feet bound, with an enormous erection piercing the air. She gazed at his huge dick; hypnotized by it she threw off her smalls and lowered herself onto him. McCree had, for a moment, a huge grin of pleasure on his face. It quickly changed as he screamed in agony.

As she lifted herself off him, he looked down in horror as his eyes fixed on the remains at the base of his crotch. His genitals had been dissolved. She smiled at him, pleased that he was suffering greatly. Then she felt a burning inside her start to grow, getting worse and worse. McCree's whole body was now dissolving.

She awoke once again sweating. That made it two vivid dreams in a row, in both of which she murdered McCree. This surely must be another premonition, although the previous premonition of McCree's death by suffocation was not quite as disturbing as his death by sex. *Maybe these visions will stop once I've seen him face to face*, she thought, *otherwise I'm going to need a psyche.*

She was back to reality, and though she followed the same routine as she had following her previous vision, she could make out the subtle differences this time – McCree not being in the room being the most noticeable one. She stepped out of the shower and dried herself without even remembering getting into it in the first place.

Zeleno called up the trace display information on her main panel. *So, John McCree, you do have an interesting connection.* The panel matched up a connection to Tom Andrews.

John McCree:

Ex-partner Julia McCree deceased.

Father of Eleanor Anne McCree.

Eleanor Anne McCree: partner of Grant Stern.

Grant Stern: employment: Meometics – Research 4.

Address: App 15, Level five, Zone four, Tower Eight, Central Section, West Side.

That was the tower where the attack originated from.

Also, the most recent call from his daughter's apartment to McCree's was yesterday. The jammer may even have been in her apartment. Preliminary GUCI reports indicated that it wasn't, but the apartment was round the corner from her. Tom Andrews turned up on solar 84, visiting that floor in Tower Eight twice. Now the connections were flowing. What exactly did it mean?

She toyed with that thought for a while then put it to one side. She needed to start the suffocation of McCree, but not terminally yet. She needed to unravel his part in this conspiracy first.

McCree was awake and ready for the day. He had scrubbed up well and really looked the part in his uniform. A GUCI communication on his main panel informed him of the details of the meeting.

Off-duty days would be scheduled with GUCI, but they always reserved the right to intrude on an enforcer's off-time. When younger and more idealistic McCree found the intrusive nature of the job stifling. However, now he was just glad to go with the flow and be ordered around without the need to think on his feet. He saved all that stuff for when he was on armed duty.

McCree left his apartment. The lift had scanned his face and whisked him down to the transport pick-up level where the GUCI transport was waiting. Moments later he'd stepped into the GUCI vehicle and was heading towards the main Meometics building.

'Prime priority no stopping expected' lit up on a minor display panel. In other words if the transporter stops en route, expect shit to hit the fan.

At 09:50 he passed the scene of the incident. There was the odd person or two on the street in high UV protective clothing, but that was not unexpected given the temperature was registering at 33 degrees C this early in the day. There was only ever a handful of people who used the surface without a transport. What wasn't normal to him was the fact that there was no trace of the incident itself. *Hazmat really have done a good job here.* McCree had half expected to see a repair of the surface where the yellow slime must surely have left a crater. Instead there was nothing.

He arrived at Meometics on time, naturally. His GUCI transporter and the nature of the appointment meant that he had the top priority transport in the area that morning. *Prime priority no stopping expected.* He arrived in at the sub-level and at 10:00 stepped out of the lift into Zeleno's office. The lift has announced its passenger to Zeleno moments before the lift doors had opened.

'Good profit to you Enforcer John McCree,' Zeleno announced.

'Likewise to you Head Profit Enabler,' McCree replied.

Despite the formalities, they already knew each other well. McCree knew Zeleno from his escort guard briefing. Zeleno knew McCree from the trace she instigated. Both knew each other from their dreams.

'Please sit down,' she requested. McCree sat down, acutely aware that this was how his first dream had started. He glanced to the corner of the room. *No bodies there yet.* Zeleno continued, 'I would first of all like to reward you, in gratitude for your actions, for preventing termination of the Assemblage.' McCree kept silent as he was pretty sure she was not expecting a reply yet. 'You have been awarded 5,000 credits for this action and an exemplary conduct record will be added to your profile.'

McCree again glanced over to the corner of the room. Still no bodies. Zeleno caught his change of attention. 'Enforcer McCree?' she said. 'Is there a problem?'

'No Ma'am,' he replied. 'I'm still a little below my best following the incident. GUCI take good care of their employees and I've been given a distance pill. I just think the after-effects are starting to wear off.'

'Distance pill?' she enquired.

'Sorry Ma'am, that's our common name for it. It's an Em-Dis2 by MedGen. They help with recent or future emotional traumas encountered as part of an enforcers duties.'

'I see,' she replied. He was on the same pill as her! She'd seen him looking into the corner of the room where the pile of bodies had accumulated in her vision. Maybe he'd had the same vision? What other explanation could there be? Same pill – same visions. She immediately realized her advantage over him. McCree didn't know she was taking the pill also, so he'd have no reason to suspect she'd had the same experience.

She could now further increase his discomfort. Additionally, he'd come off the worst in both of them, and she was not going to let that opportunity go to waste. 'I'd like to ask you some additional questions, if I may, John?' she said.

'Of course, Ma'am,' McCree immediately replied.

'How did you manage to locate the source of the attack so quickly?' she asked.

'I just happened to catch a flicker of bright light from the top of Tower Eight. As I looked up to the source of the light I caught a slight movement about halfway up the tower. It turned out to be a signal jammer. I managed to disable it by use of a heavy weapon.

'Fortunately my aim was good enough even though I should have used the weapon on a mount,' McCree paused. *Damn, I let that one slip*, he thought.

'So, John, why didn't you use a mount?' Zeleno asked 'You could have taken out the person, not the device,' she added.

'Ma'am, I only had a split second to decide. Setting the weapon on a mount could well have allowed the assailants to fire two more containers at you. My priority was to stop the attack, secure the escort and finally capture or eliminate the perpetrators,' he said.

'And indeed stop the attack you did, Enforcer McCree,' Zeleno replied. 'Once again, congratulations on your profitable actions. I will be requesting to GUCI that you are assigned to Meometics-only duties. I'm not in the habit of sharing my most valuable resources with a competitor. I want you all to myself.'

She had chosen her words very carefully. If McCree had experienced the same visions as herself, that would really be getting under his skin. She wanted one final twist of the knife out of this meeting. 'I'm sure that working closely with Meometics, and with me personally, you'll have a very rewarding future,' as she spoke she looked deep into his eyes. 'I'll be in touch, enforcer. Goodbye,' she said, as she gestured to the exit.

McCree didn't need telling twice, he positively flew out of his seat and into the lift. Zeleno knew he was attempting to conceal the fact that he wanted to get out of the room quicker than setting his boots to max. It didn't fool Zeleno, she savoured for a moment her power to mete out a large dose of anxiety for McCree. *There will be more where that came from, Enforcer John McCree.*

Her desk panel lit up and she looked at the heading flashing in front of her. 'Hazmat lab analysis.'

'Read hazmat lab analysis.' She ordered.

'Sample description non-Newtonian fluid yellow in colour. Microscopic analysis indicates hydrogel with embedded nanites held in suspension. Status during analysis: sample remained inert. Due to nanite content it is theorized the suspension properties are manipulated by nanite activation.'

Zeleno sat back in her chair. *Nanites.* 'Cross reference nanites,' she ordered the desk panel. 'Microscopic self-replicating machines artificially similar to biological forms such as bacteria or viruses in many aspects. Normally programmed by microscopic manipulators to carry out a dedicated function. Also possible to program via DNA sequence modification,' the desk panel announced. Zeleno still did not have enough information to determine how the yellow slime functioned or its manufacturers. Either insight would give her a lead on who was behind the assassination attempt.

'Display Meometics foremost experts on nanites,' she instructed the panel.

'Research 2. Best available expertise – Research 4,' the panel replied.

'Display Research 4 – nanite expertise,' she commanded.

'Research 4 – attempting to use nanites to reconfigure the coating on all silicon chips to boost chip performance.

Signal feedback at present has stopped further progress in this field,' it replied.

She took stock of her discoveries. *So, that yellow slime contains nanites, the chip improvements from Research 4 used nanites to improve the chip coating, and Torq Innovations' armour appears immune to the nanite-containing slime. How is this all linked? That will be the key to getting to the bottom of this puzzle.* 'Call Tom Andrews, Research 4,' she barked at the panel.

The comms panel flashed in Research 4's lab. Tom, being the only person present, answered the call.

'Tom Andrews – Research 4,' he said, already noting that the call was from the head of Meometics.

'Tom, it's Renee Zeleno here,' she replied. She thought that introducing herself would soften any resentment Tom had towards her following their last meeting. She needn't have bothered as Tom was always professional and courteous towards his superiors. Even when he'd been shat on big time.

'Good profit to you,' Tom replied. *'How may I assist?'*

'Explain to me the use of nanites in your project.'

'It's quite straightforward, we program them to enhance the pixie dust coating we put onto our chips.'

'How exactly do you program them?'

'By microscopic manipulators, but we are also looking for alternative ways to program them.'

'Such as?'

'The use of energy pulses, or maybe encoding their instructions in DNA, which could be read by the nanites directly.'

'What would be the benefit of using alternative programming methods?'

'Well, in terms of energy pulses you can control a large mass of nanites remotely. Or by DNA encoding you can pre-program their behaviour without requiring further intervention. It depends on the application which method is more desirable.'

Zeleno then realized she could get a sample sent to Research 4. Anything they discovered would stay secret – they would be dead before too long.

'I want your team to look at a sample I'm sending over. It contains inert nanites. I need to know how it performs when they are active.'

'We can do that, but we'd appreciate the opportunity to complete our existing project.'

'If you can provide profitable insight into the sample I'm in the process of sending to you, then you can have an extension.'

'Thank you, Head Profit Enabler, for that generous offer.'

'I want a detailed analysis within fourteen solars, Tom Andrews. Goodbye.'

Zeleno was pleased; she'd started the day with a lot of questions and one by one she was turning them into actions that would give her the answers she needed.

When she had those answers, well – the whole planet had better look out. She decided in the meantime that her long overdue short break was in order. To quote an ancient saying, 'The calm before the storm.' Only there never were storms these days, just relentless baking heat. She stood up and faced the main panel in her office. 'Arrange transport to Taw-Cymru, departure time 09:00 next solar.' The panel confirmed her instructions. She could re-charge her mind and hone her plan for domination of the planet whilst on a profit pause break.

My Apartment

I had woken up in good time for my unplanned early return to the lab. I was in the same zone and floor as Grant, but in a different tower. Our metro journeys were thus via different routes, so we'd never see each other on the commute to the lab until we entered the building from below. I was in the metro station under the tower I lived in with time to spare.

I could have rushed to get on a metro car but I'd be a little early into the office. As the metro kept excellent time I didn't need to worry about catching an earlier car to be on the safe side. It's hard to imagine that metro systems were subject to regular delays in the not too distant past. The 10:30 car arrived and suddenly the message in the sandwich made sense.

Under each opening door of the arriving car was a carriage code: Stc-309, Stc-310 and so on. I had to move to get further up the platform but was able to get into the car through the door marked Stc-318. I sat down and the car sped off. There was no further indication of what to do.

After five uneventful minutes the car stopped at Tower Six and a few more people got on. As I scanned the area I noticed, at the far end of the car, a woman wearing a blue beret, a white top, and a red skirt. Blurring my eyes slightly I could see that she did indeed looked like the old flag of the French republic. I had to wait for her to make her move. The next stop arrived minutes later and she rose to get up. I waited until the car was virtually at a standstill before getting up myself to leave the car.

The car stopped. It was one station away from the lab, and I thought it a little disconcerting that such a clandestine meeting was going to be held on the doorstep of where I worked. About thirty people alighted at this stop. The individual exits, one to four, opened in sequence.

The French flag went through exit five. I followed about twenty metres behind. She stopped to read an information panel ahead of me. I had to continue to close the gap to her, but that surely was part of the plan. What I hadn't bargained on was the *pssst* of a hypo-spray as I approached the 'French' woman. I remember swaying on the spot for a second or two before I blacked out...

A profit cycle display was on the wall ahead of me. It indicated that I'd been unconscious for about two hours. I was very lightheaded, but not in an unpleasant way; if you were going to be drugged and abducted, whatever I had been given was most agreeable.

It sent out a message, almost putting me at ease, if you ever could be after such an event. The room seemed to have no clear edges. In fact it was a sphere with a relatively soft feel to the floor. The surface of the room was covered with dimples. I was in a powered seat which looked as if it could recline into a bed. I had the strangest clothing on. It seemed to be a single piece of fabric from my neck to my ankles.

There were various differing strands of material woven randomly through the clothing. It had multiple properties about it, containing both reflective and absorbent fibres, pliable and rigid, smooth and rough strands. For every property I could see the garment's fibres had, I could identify the opposite property.

It wasn't the kind of clothing cults or secret societies would choose to wear. It had a functional feel to it, even though I didn't know what that function was. Camouflage of some sort was my theory. Putting this on wouldn't have been a simple and straightforward task. Someone had been busily at work on me.

'Thank you, K, for your co-operation. Welcome to the golf ball,' a disembodied voice spoke out. It filled the room. 'We know you are a man of science and good principles, but not all who find themselves here in this place are, so we have a number of precautions before we can actually meet.'

I'd heard this style of language before but couldn't place it. Not seeing the speaker was probably why I couldn't make the connection.

'Firstly, please remember we can flood this area with numerous substances in an instant. Our people have been inoculated against these substances, so any attempt to cause harm to our people when they meet you will result in your incapacitation. We can temporarily or permanently immobilize you. It is our sincerest wish that, as a man of science and not profit or violence, this will not be necessary.

'The garment you now have on is an anti-loc suit. Granted, it doesn't conform to most people's expectations of fine clothing, but it serves its purpose well. It renders you undetectable to a whole range of sensors. The design of the golf ball room you are in also serves the same purpose.

'The floor is made of a firmer version of the material your clothing is made from. It will feel strange to walk on, but it is far better than not installing a floor at all.

'With regard to your chair, it does indeed configure as a bed. When you were unconscious you were lying on it. It has recorded all your recent thoughts, and we will endeavour to answer all the questions you have been concerned about. As you started to wake, the chair gradually moved into the form you see it in now. It is not fully complete as you are still a little disorientated. This will pass.' The voice stopped. It was quite a lot to take in.

The voice had almost understood the limit of my comprehension, given that I was still mildly drugged, and it uncannily stopped just at the point before it became blah, blah, blah.

A few more moments of silence and the voice continued. 'Please remain seated whilst the access door forms.' A door formed to the left of me on the surface of the golf ball. I realized now that this room had no feature you could call a wall. If indeed it even qualified as a room. Apartments have walls, sphere's don't.

Two people entered the ball. They wore similar clothing to me but they were also covered with a semi-transparent version of the material over their face and hands. They pulled apart the coverings over their faces and took off their gloves. One of them was Elizabeth Hart. The other person, a middle-aged man, looked benign enough and I immediately felt a lot less apprehensive.

'I apologize for these precautions, but as you'll see they are necessary,' Elizabeth said.

'I'm Dr Tim Ford,' the man said. 'Our anti-loc suits have to cover us 100 per cent outside our refractive deflector geodesic, otherwise we could be detected,' he added.

'I prefer the term golf ball,' quipped Elizabeth. 'It has an old-world charm to it, don't you think?'

'Golf ball is fine,' I replied.

Elizabeth glanced over towards Dr Ford before turning to speak to me. 'Derek would like to meet you,' she said.

'Likewise,' I replied. 'Thousands of people could be killed because of the greed of a corporation unless I can fix the problem.'

A life-size image of Dr Derek Toft appeared in front of me. He must have been scanned in at ultra-high resolution because he almost appeared real. It was certainly the most realistic projection I had seen to date. 'Ah, Kelvin, we meet at last,' Derek said.

'I prefer to be called K, if you don't mind,' I replied.

'As you wish, K. What you're concerned about is not as serious as you believe. It is far worse,' he paused.

I could see sadness in Elizabeth's eyes as she listened to her brother's virtual projection.

'I am here in this form because I was assigned to Ultra-profit projects. I cannot be here because I am no longer alive. Assignation to Ultra-profit projects is a death sentence. Renee Zeleno of Meometics ordered my termination.

'I had only minutes to escape, and alas in corporeal form I had *no* chance of escape. I was able, however, to activate an AI holo-copy of myself I'd been working on. I transferred myself to this secure location before my mortal version was killed.'

I was stunned; Research 4 had therefore already been sentenced to death. I was being told this by someone Zeleno had already murdered! In one quarter from now Research 4 would be dead. If Grant and Tom elected to take their families with them, they too would be killed.

'GUCI must be told about this,' I replied.

Derek spoke, 'K, who do you think carried out Zeleno's orders? A team within GUCI. You are as good as dead, K, you and your colleagues. You have two options to get out of this.'

'I'm all ears.'

'First, accept your fate and let us scan you in ultra-high res. We can recreate you, with your assistance. You can live on until the end of civilization itself.'

'What about option two?'

'Reset civilization itself.'

'I'm not quite sure I understand!'

'Let me explain,' Derek said. 'For some time before I'd become involved with Zeleno, I'd been working on the usual profit enhancement projects for Meometics. I was sent a message by a person calling herself Violet Redbridge, asking me to look at the evidence for "planet melt" and to re-consider the work I was doing. The following day I saw her shot on a live video feed at a protest about the misuse of the planet's resources.

'I looked further into her accusations and uncovered a great body of evidence to back up her claims that the planet was close to dying. There was a tipping point, still in the future, which when reached would lead to the death of the planet in less than forty profit cycles. The paper I read on the phenomenon indicated the three elements that had to be in place for the destruction of all carbon-based life on the planet.

'Firstly, the commercialization of nanotechnology.

'Secondly, the adoption of IP v7 technology.

'Finally, a quantum leap in the processing power of chips.

'The first two elements are already in place. IP v6 had been heralded as allowing us all the IP addresses we'd ever need. Of course that only applied until you wanted to communicate with individual nanites rather than a swarm of them. Once each nanite had its own IP address courtesy of IP v7 you need a quantum leap in chip processing power. This will most likely be achieved via an enhancement to the ubiquitous pixie dust technology. It would allow the complete control and co-ordination of the nanites.

'This is where I realized we were closer to the tipping point of planet melt than Redbridge had thought. Once the nanites are able to be co-ordinated on a large scale, they can become self-aware and remove carbon-based life forms from the equation. We will all be converted into raw material for their requirements. The whole planet will be converted into grey goo. The corporations, monopolies, and GUCI are too busy chasing for the ultimate in profits, to either notice or care about the danger of the technologies they are willing to exploit.

'We will experience a living *silicon hell* on earth. Ten profit cycles ago my team substantially enhanced the processing power of computer chips with the pixie dust coating. It spread across the globe and is now used on every system on the planet. If this coating can be further enhanced and spreads across the planet in the same way, we have condemned ourselves to extinction.

'We realized that was rather a mouthful to keep explaining, so we came up with a good old acronym. Santos – Scientists against nanotechnology organized systems. What do you think?'

It was a lot to take in. AI Derek had one major flaw though; to avoid detection he had to limit his activities when on the network, whereas he may have otherwise found valuable information on my recent destruction of a lab bench. I spoke up.

'Derek, I don't care for option one, but *resetting* civilization – surely that will result in much larger casualties than I was looking to avoid as a result of the greed of my employer?' I pointed out.

'K, I have estimated that of the present population of twenty-five billion, only 1.25 billion would be alive five profit cycles after the reset.' Derek replied.

'Forgive me Derek, but I came looking to save hundreds or maybe thousands of lives, not help wipe out almost twenty-four billion people,' I scowled.

'I understand your concern, K, but it's an unavoidable certainty that if you do not take action to reset civilization then every living thing on this planet will perish.'

'You have put me in the most unfair position in the history of mankind.'

'Yes, K, but it's the planet's future at stake here, not the past,' Derek argued. 'It is also about the future of humanity, not just your moral conscience.'

'Perhaps we deserve to become extinct, humanity is shot through with so much greed.'

'Even if your truly believe that, K, why should all the other life on this planet pay the price for humanity's errors?'

'I could argue that the failure of the other forms of life to arrest humanity's greed forfeits their right to have a say. That is the way of natural selection.'

'If you believe in natural selection then the nanites have the right to inherit the earth.'

'Nanites are artificial mechanical creations – they are not part of evolution theory.'

'But they are created by those who are.'

AI Derek had a point. The problem with the only two choices – murder more people or murder fewer people – the clear choice would be to murder less, but I didn't want to murder *at all*. If you have only two choices open to you and they are both crap you have to choose the least crappy option. It was clear that not making the choice would lead to the worst of the two options. My mind had been made up for me. Logic dictated I'd had no real say in the matter all along.

Now that my curiosity had led me to this path I could no longer be blissfully ignorant of the choices. So all that was left for me was to execute the decision as competently as possible.

'Ok, Derek, Elizabeth, Tim, or should I say "Santos"? I will assist with the reset.'

Derek spoke, 'I have ensured that across the entire globe pixie dust coated chips are ubiquitous. Their coatings become unstable by the application of a quad-axial pulse.

However, I did not have the available time to complete the work due to Renee Zeleno's actions. I don't have enough knowledge to create the desired effect on these chips, but I believe, K, that you and Research 4 do.'

'I came across the phenomenon two solar cycles ago, fortunately whilst it was a side-effect of the research I was undertaking. I filed the information obtained and sent a number of samples for further analysis,' I replied.

'It is vital this research is fully analysed,' said Derek.

'You're telling me, Derek!' I agreed. 'I need to get back to the lab for sun-up on solar 88 or suspicions will be aroused,' I said. 'From there I can access the systems and information I need and assess the situation with the rest of Research 4.'

Elizabeth spoke, 'Thank you so much, K. We have the chance to give humanity a better future, rather than no future at all. Don't forget – print out the *sliced tofu baguette* containing further instructions for your return.'

'Make sure you're hungry before you print the message as you'll have to eat the evidence again, and the baguette is only a little shy of substantial,' Tim quipped.

'And now,' Elizabeth added, 'it's time to say goodbye. I assume you're not going to be too thrilled about this next bit.'

She was right, all I heard was a *pssst* and I'd been drugged again...

This time when I regained consciousness I found myself in a transport. The display on the panel indicated it was heading for a metro connection. From there I would be able to get a metro to the lab. I had been re-clothed yet again. Maybe it was for the better that I didn't know who had done this to me, twice.

Honestly, I didn't care that much because whatever was in the hypo-shot I'd had was giving me a hell of a buzz. The transport shot down a ramp to the metro level. The 'Destination Arrived' indicator lit up on the main panel of the transport, the doors opened, and I carefully stepped out of the vehicle. I was still a bit unsure on my feet.

The metro entrance was around the corner from the transport pick-up/drop off point, and thankfully all the transport interchanges had canopies covering them. They were designed to discourage too much wandering from specifically designated areas. GUCI liked to keep the people unofficially 'confined' to a number of areas. The arrangement was now mostly self-policing apart from those citizens who were UV insane.

Canopies were installed everywhere GUCI would prefer you to be and not installed where they didn't want you to be. The limiting factor as to how long you could you survive at pavement level in the sun's full glare without health risks was determined by the UV protection you were wearing.

The lift to the metro sped down to the metro line. Yet another device that logged and verified citizens' every move. When did this actually become oppressive? One person's oppressive regime is another's protective regime. I suppose it depends on how you as an individual benefit from that regime that shapes your view. But what if the 'oppression' was well hidden? How would you know?

The lift doors opened and I stepped out not far from the end of the platform, and moved along to the centre of the station. There was no one on the platform as the next metro was imminent and conveniently this station was not a metro line interchange, it was merely a transport connection.

Sure enough the metro arrived. I stepped on. Santos had clearly very carefully planned my journey to the lab. I had trusted that the scientists and co-ordinators (in the case of Elizabeth) were of such high calibre they had thought of every little detail. The thought recording I had been subjected to must have given them a lot of information, but evidently they had access to far more than just my thoughts.

The metro came from the same direction as my apartment's location, which itself would reduce any suspicion. I would not meet any of my colleagues on the wrong metro. Santos must also have been able to alter the records of the transport I was on to make it tie into a routine journey.

A nagging doubt surfaced. *Why now did they choose to contact me?* AI Derek and formally the real Derek had been involved with Santos for quite some time now. They had a lot of resources as well as security safeguards and methods in place to avoid detection. Could their plan bring a secure future for all humanity?

I arrived at Meometics research facility metro stop. A few commuters got off at this stop where I recognized a couple as regulars. We waited on the platform until the metro left the station. Exit one opened and one person left that way. Exit three opened, and two people left. I took exit five with two others; we had at short walk down a corridor, where a scan allowed us into the lift to Meometics labs.

As we were all forbidden to discuss our research and also as some scientists felt awkward engaging in general conversion we did not speak. The lift, having finished off the security checks for us, allowed the doors to open at the level for the other two scientists. I smelt the food from the canteen as we passed sub-level three and knew I'd need to pay a visit there before too long.

The other two scientists left, one at level sub-level four and one at sub-level five. Research 4 was the most prestigious team at Meometics. The team was famous amongst all other scientists, yet they didn't know who we were. *Unless some of them were already members of Santos.* What about Grant and Tom? Could they already be Santos members, and if not would they agree with its aims? I decided that was best left to Santos to decide. The comment that they thought Research 4 could be the key to their success could be due to information from Grant or Tom or, more impressively, they had access into our secure information stores.

'Hi guys,' I said as I entered the lab.

'Profitable solar to you,' they both replied in a stern tone.

'That's kind of creepy,' I replied. 'When did you turn into Renee Zeleno?'

They both laughed. 'I thought it better to deflect you from one of your awful greetings or work-related puns,' Grant said.

'I agreed only for a quiet life,' added Tom.

'Speaking of Zeleno, she's sent us some samples to analyse. With a promise to give us an extension if we can sort out the sample in the next fourteen solars,' Tom said.

'More like an extended shafting,' Grant joked.

Grant's observation made us smile.

'I do believe she is genuine in her intentions. In any case we won't know unless we're successful. I'd like us to concentrate on this first,' Tom replied.

I knew what her intentions were; if nothing was done to stop her by the time Tom found out about her betrayal we'd all be dead. It was a successful if completely evil way to operate. Generate an air of trust and then when you intend to betray that trust make sure there can be no response. It appeared that termination was the standard procedure following betrayal. How many others had already met their end in such a low way?

A message appeared on my panel. It was from Jo Bianchi. That was a piece of good news. Jo was a brilliant tech; whilst he hadn't invented the spectrum analyser he was the leading field tech in its operation. It is said that the most important scientists aren't the theoretical ones, but the field techs who maintain the equipment.

Once a theoretical design is put into practice, that is where the real knowledge is acquired. If a device fails often the theorist has no real grasp of the problems the device encounters in service. It is the field tech who most contributes to the fix and re-design of such products. As far as field techs for spectrum analysers goes, Jo was the best.

'I've a message from Jo Bianchi. It's marked – Priority,' I said to Tom.

'All right, K,' he replied. 'You deal with that. Grant, analyse Zeleno's sample,' he directed.

We both quickly absorbed ourselves into the tasks in hand. Jo's message was indeed a priority. I called Jo on the panel. *'Bianchi here,'* Jo confirmed.

'Hi Jo, it's K from Research 4. Thanks for the message, but how did you become involved with the samples?' I enquired.

'Well, K, I was asked to check the analyser used on your samples because it was displaying fault codes. I checked it and found it to be working perfectly within its design limits. It just wasn't designed to analyse what you sent us!'

'I thought the samples would be a challenge to make any sense of, that's why I sent them to the experts. I didn't think it would be impossible, though.'

'It wasn't, K, not for me anyway. I had to recalibrate the sensitivity of the analyser to get a successful reading. Of course that

meant that the analyser would be swamped by the reading of standard samples, so I had to add an auto-ranging circuit just for you!'

'Many thanks for that Jo, sorry to have caused such consternation.'

'No problems, K, I do enjoy a good puzzle. It livens up the job. OK, so I'm sending you the detail from the re-worked analyser now. Call me direct if you need any further assistance.'

The link was disconnected and the data streamed onto my panel. The details scrolled up the panel.

Sample QP-1.

Description: Analogue resistive buffer chip.

Application: Scientific measuring apparatus. Historically used in numerous applications. Superseded in all aspects by digital super chip with pixie coating.

Analysis: Tested and performed within expected design parameters.

This matched up with what I'd expected. An obsolete chip still in working condition, despite being subjected to my experimental pulse.

Sample QP-2.

Description: Digital power coupling routing chip.

Application: High-speed signalling, switching, and regulation of power on all known circuitry.

Analysis: The chip is inoperable. The chip is only identifiable due to micro analysis of its external dimensions and pin layout. Pin layout was determined using data discovered in Sample QP-3 as the pins had been transformed from their original material. Nanites have been fused to the surface of the chip's pixie coating. It would require a large electromagnetic pulse of unknown complexity to fuse nanites to the chip's coating. The pulse required to do this is large enough to destroy the chip itself. The chip destruction creates an additional phenomena, as described in analysis of QP-3

Sample QP-3

Description: White powder substance

Application: unknown

Analysis: Previous state of sample was a metal alloy used in inter-circuitry connections. All of the metallic properties of the substance have been completely removed. The properties of the pulse known to have destroyed Sample QP-2 have converted the metal alloy into an 'Anti-metal'. The pulse propagates along any metal within the pulse radius whilst converting it to 'Anti-metal'.

Further analysis of this phenomenon will most likely result in destruction of the sample being analysed. This is also likely to affect surrounding non-directly connected equipment. Extreme caution is advised if further analysis is required.

Wow, it was as if Jo knew I'd melted the test bench in our lab chamber. This could be used as a devastating weapon. A pulse that could turn metal into powder. It thus followed that the larger the pulse generated, the greater the radius of damage would be. I needed some time to consider the implications of my suspicions, now confirmed by Jo Bianchi.

'K, Tom,' Grant shouted, 'come and have a look at this.'

We quickly positioned ourselves alongside Grant as he operated the chamber's robotic arms and read off the data display on the panel.

'Nanites – there are a huge amount of them suspended in the sample. Each of them has different molecules attached to their various connectors. They have a mixture of metallic and organic molecules attached to them. These molecules are also suspended in the slime,' Grant enthused.

Tom was intrigued, 'The nanites appear to have been dissolving various substances and then all of a sudden stopped.'

'Pick four at random, Grant and let's disassemble them,' I suggested. We need an answer.

Grant had hardly taken in my suggestion before the robotic arms inside the chamber were moving as swiftly as such clumsy apparatus could. It was still impressive though, it would have taken me two or three times as long to achieve the same results. Grant was in the zone.

'Four nanites isolated,' Grant announced.

I fired up the symmetry analyser on my panel. All four nanites were identical. 'Grant, pick another batch of four and keep checking for a difference whilst I disassemble one of these.' I said.

Tom was sitting at the centre bench away from the two of us. He was up to something.

I decompiled the first nanite through the molecular translator.

The four nanites were programmed to wait for a signal from a specific source, then they would activate. They would check adjacent molecules and if they conformed to a specific molecule type they would remove the molecule and place it randomly in the suspension fluid. After a period of time had expired they would de-activate.

'You'll need to see this GUCI classified video feed,' Tom said.

He put the feed up on the panel from the assassination attempt on the Assemblage. It was not a pleasant sight. The yellow slime on the feed was eating transports and enforcers. There were various body parts left in shot including what was left of one enforcer being crushed by a fleeing vehicle.

'Does that help with the analysis?' Tom enquired.

'Sure,' Grant replied, 'if you want a quality nightmare to disturb tonight's sleep. Actually,' he added, 'I preferred K's technical analysis to your horror film, but it's the same phenomena whichever way you prefer to describe it.'

I spoke up, 'It appears that there is a signal that tells the nanites to start dissolving anything that comes into contact with the yellow suspension. It then randomly stores those molecules within the empty space in the yellow suspension. It has the capacity to "digest" a phenomenal amount within the confines of the suspension. It gets the instruction to start "eating", what to eat and when to stop eating from a master nanite.'

'That's what we're looking for then, K,' Tom asked.

Grant piped up, 'That's what *I'm* looking for, eh K?'

'It's what we're all looking for,' I corrected Grant.

We needed to automate the analysis procedure. Whilst the sample was small a quick calculation highlighted that there were an estimated eight million nanites in this small sample. A visual scan showed all them were of the same size. No obvious clues there.

Grant worked out how to squeeze the small sample into a line no wider than a single nanite. They could be scanned individually in sequence. The molecule scanner was given the composition of the 'standard' nanites we found in our first sample. Any changes to this standard molecule would flag up an alert in the log file.

I added extra code to Grant's routine to decompile each non-standard nanite (NSN) discovered and add them to a list. Each NSN would then be checked against the list of NSNs. If it was an already discovered NSN its details were discarded, otherwise it was added to the non-standard list. Between us we'd surely be able to give Zeleno the information she wanted. We decided to view the process live until at least the speed of the non-standard finds overwhelmed us. Grant, having finished the sample preparation, got up and moved to the panel next to me.

'Let's fire up the scan, K,' Grant commanded.

I hit the scan option on the sci-fi panel interface.

The scanner was scanning about thirty nanites a second, at which rate it was going to take around 75 hours to complete the scan, but we knew we would have most of the answers before then. After just over a minute our first NSN appeared in the log file, followed by another just under a minute later. Thirty minutes later and it was still early days, as there was only one type of NSN and it was showing up at around one in two thousand scanned.

We examined its code. It was able to detect the presence of oxygen and then signalled to the standard nanites to dissolve metal and biological substances. Skin, bone, metal, rubber, they were all targeted. A powerful weapon indeed. The ratio of one master nanite for each two thousand standard ones was probably a limit of how many of them the master nanite could control.

The master nanites were considerably more complex in structure despite being the same size as their standard counterparts. If the new enhanced pixie dust coasting was applied to them they should in theory be able to handle over four times as many nanites. This would make the production of such weapons so much easier to mass produce.

It was clear to us that we were looking at a new prototype weapon, somewhat like the first atomic bombs, where only a few were available and they were tested out in the field.

That meant a successful attack on the Assemblage was of critical importance to the assailants, but for what reason? Whoever was behind this was beyond the scope of our analysis but it was an impressive, if somewhat terrifying, weapon.

Once the manufacturing was perfected an easy alteration to the programming could make the slime clean up toxic hazards, or recycle unwanted products to their original raw material state. All with a few new lines of code. With a suitably enhanced nanite it would be even possible to disassemble the DNA of a specific individual, or perhaps a common trait across a group of people.

As a scientist I was impressed by the properties of what we'd discovered. Knowing what Renee Zeleno had planned for Research 4 and what Meometics were capable of doing with such a product made me feel sick.

'Canteen snack, guys?' Tom enquired. 'We can review these findings over something tasty,' he added.

I volunteered to stay at the lab and keep an eye on the scanning. Tom and Grant left for the canteen.

I pulled up the details of my accidental cross-axial pulse configuration and tied it in with the analysis from Jo Bianchi. I filed the information under 'Lab panel rota and maintenance schedule for Tom Andrews' then commanded the panel to encrypt the file with the full address of Meometics headquarters. This ensured a suitably lengthy encryption key, but not so long as to raise an alarm.

It would take two or three quarters to decipher it, but by then we'd have a substantial head start. That assumed someone was on the lookout for this information. The file name was suitably tedious to dissuade all but the most nosey or suspicious of individuals.

I headed over to the canteen. Tom and Grant had nearly finished their snack, but there wasn't enough left to be able to tell what it was. 'K, what kept you?' Tom asked.

'Oh, you know how it is, just waiting for one more log file entry, then one more. It can become quite hypnotizing,' I replied.

'Seen anything new?' Grant enquired.

'No, it's the same master nanite appearing. I'd wager that's the only NSN we're going to see,' I said.

Grant and Tom had not yet made the connection between our project and what we'd discovered in the slime sample. It was only a matter of time before they did, and maybe that would be the opportunity I'd need to propose more appropriate action. I grabbed a coffee and a sticky cake from the vendors and sat back at the table with Tom and Grant.

'There's something bothering me,' Tom said. 'What we've analysed so far appears to be a prototype technology. It came very close to wiping out the Assemblage,' he continued. 'But the armour of the Sixer has proved to be resistant to it. Wasn't that more than just a little fortunate?' he asked.

'We'd need to know the true composition of the Sixer's armour to answer that, Tom,' Grant said. 'I'd put my credits on an alteration to the re-coding of the slime winning out eventually,' he added.

'Of course,' Tom replied. 'They must be desperate to stop something that's due to happen in the near future. That's the message they're sending,' he added.

The answer was staring in front of me. 'It's our project, guys. They are trying to stop our project from reaching commercial production,' I said.

'All right then, K, but how could they know about our research and its deadlines?' Grant questioned.

I was stumped, but the look on Tom's face and the glance he threw towards Grant told me he had a good idea how.

Renee Zeleno's transport to the Hypersonic hub had arrived. She would be able to catch up on the analysis there once she arrived at her secure villa in Taw-Cymru. She looked around her office one last time, knowing she would not see it again for a few days. 'Confirm security lock, Renee Zeleno, no access whatsoever to others,' she commanded and left her office. Her transport would take her the short distance to the Hypersonic Craft Transfer hub.

She was soon at the edge of the Northern Block. At an old-world speed of Mach 8 it didn't take long for her to arrive at Taw. Anywhere on the planet was possible in eighty minutes, but only for the select few. Once again, how fast a person could travel was dictated by how profitable they were. Sub, super or hypersonic – yet another way of displaying status.

Solar 88

Taw-Cymru

Somewhere in Taw-Cymru a wall panel was flashing with an incoming message alert. A man walked over to the panel. Franco Barone was middle-aged with thinning black hair, and wore a smirk on his face as he read the message. Wearing socks, shorts and a t-shirt he looked as though he was prepared for a day of vegging out in front of a video feed. Nothing could be further from the truth.

The message read:

Departure solar 88 – 09:00

Arrival solar 88 – 10:00

5 extras

He stepped across to the food dispenser. 'Creamed mashed potato with parsley,' he commanded.

The food dispenser started to print his request. He unlatched the case he had laid on the table and opened it up. An old-fashioned semi-automatic sniper rifle. Complete with five clips of ten rounds. *That will be more than I need.*

The food dispenser was printing out the topology of Taw-Cymru with unnerving accuracy. All that was left was the parsley overlay on the top to indicate the route to the target and he would do the rest.

Franco pulled out a small trunk from the storage unit next to the main panel and unclipped the fold-over catches. Two large lozenge shaped canisters were inside with two cut-outs alongside them for a small detonator with a clip. In between the cut-outs was an IP v7 wireless control unit.

He took out the control unit and placed it on the corner of the table closest to the panel.

He glanced over to the food replicator which had finished printing the food as instructed. The parsley ran alongside the deepest valley in the mashed potato structure and then climbed the side to a higher ridge of potato. He recognized the area that had been printed courtesy of having toured the vicinity extensively since his arrival at Taw-Cymru.

Barone pulled up a low detail map of the section on the main panel and asked for a material analysis of the area. The panel produced the results he needed. All the main routes a transport could traverse were composed of a standard asphalt covering. This made perfect sense to him as Taw-Cymru had always been a remote outpost of the region's transport network.

He entered the parameters into the panel and it was uploaded to the control unit. Barone keyed the IP v7 control unit to the two detonators. He knew exactly where to place the canisters but first he had to eat.

'Fucking creamed mashed potato shite,' he muttered as he thrust a fork into the creation and proceeded to eat the evidence. It gave him no pleasure at all to sample this food, but he knew it was necessary. Not that it made this task any easier. He filled a long glass with carbonated water from the drinks tap and took out a sachet from his inner jacket pocket. On the sachet was the Gentech logo adjacent to a bio-hazard logo.

He ripped open the sachet and sprinkled the powder into the glass. In moments the water turned a cobalt blue.

It looked as if it should have an umbrella stuck in it and be sold as a holiday cocktail. That was for an era long since gone. He appreciated the irony of its appearance, then he swiftly downed the liquid. He knew the timing would be tight for this operation.

In these situations advanced warning and thus planning was a rare luxury. The local GUCI contingent would, round about now, be travelling the route Zeleno would be taking in her Sixer. She would be on that same route just twenty minutes later.

There would be no easy opportunity to plant a traditional explosive device that could take out a Sixer in that time. All Taw-Cymru's transports were monitored and had been programmed to avoid the route Zeleno would be taking. Any travelling along that route would need to be done on foot.

He closed the trunk and shut the case on the table. The Gentech sachet he'd taken was starting to take effect. He felt elated; shortly afterwards 'supercharged' would be a more appropriate description, then an hour or so later the feeling of invincibility before the sharp descent into feeling wiped out took hold. Barone would have enough time for recovery afterwards as long as he reached his rest location in time.

He put on what looked like GUCI protective on-duty armour. The more he looked like GUCI the greater the safety margin he had. Pulling two straps out from the trunk he hauled it onto his back and secured it to his body. He could feel the strain on his back but the sachet would cover him from that.

There were only two corners he could reach on the trunk now that it was strapped to him and pulled at them both. A tube from each corner was pulled further until it could extend no more.

Barone walked over to a clothes storage unit and pulled out a pair of GUCI style powered boots. Securing them onto his feet, he pushed the tubes from the trunk into a nozzle at the back of both boots. He was good for thirty-five kilometres with this extended fuel supply. Thanks to his contacts the capabilities he had were unique. *God help us if the corporations were to get hold of our tech*, he thought.

Barone called up a GUCI transponder screen on his main panel and could see that the local GUCI contingent had just passed his villa. Time to go.

He placed a can marked Aeroliser DNA-Sanitizer prototype on the table. It included the useful warning of 'Caution: do not use in the presence of living tissue. Test in suitable chamber only.' He programmed the panel to wipe the local buffers of all activity in ninety minutes. The sanitizer would go off in ten. He picked up the rifle case, clipped it to his chest and, looking like some sort of bad arse robot from the 1970s (old calendar date), he walked out of his villa. As expected no one was about. Even though the weather in Taw-Cymru was not hazardous the people who were privileged to be able to visit here had better things to do than wander around outside their villas.

He fired up his boots from the control panel on his glove and sped up the valley. The sachet was at its maximum effect now. He would feel no pain, his mental capabilities would be heightened, and he would be capable of extreme feats of physical endurance.

Travelling at 60Km/h it would not take him long to reach his destination. The boots he had were capable of faster speeds but not on this type of surface.

He was hyper-aware of his surroundings during his journey and he was genuinely moved by the beauty of the place. He felt almost at one with the scenery. *This was the type of environment we were meant to live in*, he thought. Progress had gone too far.

It took him thirty minutes to reach his destination. Zeleno would be the same amount of time behind him and would be getting into the Sixer now.

Rounding a bend close to the source of the valley, he saw Zeleno's villa. He dialled the boots down and decelerated to a stop as the villa disappeared from view around another bend.

He removed the case from his chest and the trunk from his back. Opening the trunk he placed the first canister on the road and then the second ten metres ahead. Barone placed the chest on the road edge near to the first canister and activated the camouflage for both trunk and canisters.

He made his way up to the top of hill where he could view both the canisters and the villa. *May the profits help you all.*

Zeleno had left the Hypersonic craft transport hub and was now in her Sixer with five GUCI enforcers.

She idly wondered if any of them were worth a good screw, but it was hard to tell with them kitted up in so much equipment hiding their more physical assets.

This journey is going to be boring, but I should be quite safe, she reassured herself. She thought about McCree and wondered if he possessed the qualities that she needed for her child. If so she only needed a sample from him, but her dream suggested she should deal with him differently.

She wanted him to know exactly why he'd been chosen, used and disposed of before he died. More than that she wanted him to suffer in every way imaginable for daring to think that he could get away with his part in her assassination attempt.

The Sixer was only minutes away from the villa. It rounded a bend in the road and the villa came into sight, then another bend and it disappeared again. As it came into sight once more the Sixer sounded its alarm: 'obstruction alert'.

It had driven over a large indent in the road, only to plough into a crater around a metre in depth. The sudden stop shook the occupants but the vehicle's internal padding prevented injuries.

Laying prone in high grass on a hill overlooking the Sixer and the villa a solitary figure was waiting. *Showtime!* he said to himself as he saw the Sixer plunge into the crater. An enforcer took over manual control and tried to reverse it out.

He activated the forward ram and the vehicle started to move. The front of the crater was slowly growing and the indent was now half a metre deep.

'Great,' remarked the driver. 'Where's McCree when you need him?' he cursed.

'No point,' replied another. 'There's no one here to kill.'

Zeleno was surprised at how the other enforcers viewed him. He had quite the reputation.

The driver managed to push back onto the road which was now looking more like a little plateau. The contents of the two canisters continued to eat the road and then the rock the road was built on. The Sixer was back on the road only for the briefest of moments before the road was dissolved by the yellow slime. The Sixer sunk into the ever deepening crater.

Zeleno wasn't worried; the vehicle was impervious to the slime. The two pools of slime grew and joined up. Then, with the Sixer half-height below the road, the slime changed its viscosity and the Sixer started to sink.

It wasn't being dissolved – rather it was being submerged. From within the Sixer it looked as if they were sinking. The enforcers' stress levels grew. 'GUCI HQ – backup requested. Escort unit 02 – Taw-Cymru detail, we are under attack. I repeat we are under attack.' Enforcer Maitland was desperately trying to get through.

'I'm not getting a response!' Maitland announced.

'What's happening?' asked one of the other enforcers. 'It failed the moment we hit the obstruction.'

'It's gotta be rigged,' said Maitland as he scanned the comms panel. Driver Enforcer Chen realized the gravity of the situation.

'We're going to be entombed in rock – we've got to get out,' Chen exclaimed. 'Weapons hot, activate smoke,' he commanded. Then: 'Apologies Ma'am, we have to abandon the transport.'

Zeleno was seething. This was getting to be more than a simple inconvenience.

Chen led the way through the top hatch, along with the other enforcers bar Maitland who would cover Zeleno's back. Chen leapt off the Sixer to the side of the road.

'You'll need to make it quick, it's going under,' he said.

Zeleno climbed up and out of the hatch. Maitland below caught full sight of her rear, as underwear in no way covered her fully. Her briefs were almost as brief as a G string.

Maitland had no time to fully appreciate the view. She jumped off the Sixer and there were now only centimetres of Sixer above the pool of liquid rock. He didn't have the height to jump from the Sixer to the safety of the road and he fell short of the bank. He sank into the pool without trace.

Zeleno and the four remaining enforcers assembled on the bank.

Chen called out, 'We need to get to the villa.'

Zeleno was suitably underwhelmed. The remaining enforcers formed a diamond formation with Zeleno in the centre for the walk of around four hundred metres to the villa.

Franco Barone waited, he could see four enforcers emerge from the smoke, now dissipating as the Sixer had sunk into the liquid concrete. The enforcers were in protective formation around Renee Zeleno. They were, as anticipated, heading for the villa. He aimed through the rifle sight. He targeted the man at the rear of the formation, as they came across his line of sight the angle would be perfect.

He fired a single shot. The round hit the enforcer's left boot, the charged electric tip overloaded the boot's circuitry and detonated its fuel supply. The explosion took the enforcer's foot off, knocking him to the ground and showering Zeleno's leg with his blood. The enforcers were unable to get a location on the assailant.

Zeleno decided she'd had enough and kicked off her shoes; she ran barefoot, zig-zagging towards the villa, with the three remaining enforcers doing likewise behind her.

She'd won the old school four hundred metres a few times in her younger years and still kept fit enough to stay ahead of the enforcers in their gear. They could not power up their boots as they had to keep changing direction whilst keeping behind Zeleno to cover her.

Chen had made the right call to stay behind her as the chances of an attack coming from the villa were less likely due to the surveillance and security measures there.

Another shot and a second enforcer went down, another severed foot. Zeleno was three hundred and fifty metres away from her goal.

A third shot. Three enforcers down. Zeleno and the remaining enforcer were heading out of sight. Barone caught Chen just as he was about to disappear. The other enforcers were trying to patch their amputations up with their emergency medkits. Franco made his way around to the other side of the hill.

He changed a clip for one that fired a de-fib charge. Zeleno was now only two hundred metres away and nearly at the perimeter edge of the villa's security. He didn't want to have to carry her further than necessary. He waited and waited, then took aim and fired.

Zeleno dropped to the ground.

Switching his cartridge again he rounded the hill and saw the first enforcer he'd shot. He was still alive with his gun by his side. Franco shot his other boot, blowing his remaining foot off. He picked up the gun, removed the enforcer's helmet, and fired a charge at his head. Although inoculated against the toxin in the ammunition there was no armour to deflect the charge and it coursed through his body. His heart pumped furiously, which only served to increase his blood loss, then he twitched no more.

The next two enforcers fared no better, although the second had seen the previous killing and tried in vain to remove his boot in time. He lost his two hands as well in the ensuing explosion.

There was only Chen left. A trail of blood confirmed he had managed to crawl further round the curve of the road.

He was sitting on his boot which meant his stump was in contact with the road. 'Asshole,' Chen spat as Barone came into view.

Chen fired a volley of shots. They hit Barone in the chest. The enforcer's armour he was wearing dissipated the shots. 'Then I'm one of you now,' Barone said. He pointed his weapon at Chen and fired. The force of the impact knocked Chen onto his back, exposing his boot.

Barone took out Chen's remaining boot and foot. 'Nice try, asshole,' Barone smiled as he finished Chen off like the others. He walked over to Zeleno.

He picked her up and felt her for the keycard to enter the villa. That, in conjunction with the palm print, would let him in. The security of the buildings in Taw-Cymru was not as advanced as in the cities because visits here were already by invitation only.

Barone retrieved the keycard from a small, discreet, skirt pocket. He lifted Zeleno up and flung her over his shoulder.

Upon reaching the villa he flopped her loose hand on the palm reader and he was in. Wasting no time, he threw her onto the bed. She would be out cold for at least a few hours. He lifted up her skirt and could feel his heartbeat increase in anticipation. She needed to ache all over when she came to.

He undid her blouse buttons and lifted her breasts out of her bra; he squeezed her breasts firmly. His dick was by now bursting to escape from his smalls. He wanted to abuse her in so many ways. This would be an opportunity he would not get again.

Resisting the immense temptation to finish her off for good, he pulled her panties to one side and unleashed his dick. He rubbed her pussy, parting her lips and guiding the way for his enormous knob. He slowly thrust into her then built up speed.

Her pussy was tight and he was savouring her body; the selfishness of the fuck made him iron hard and he quickly came in her. Barone withdrew his still formidable knob from her. He still had unfinished business. So he slapped her legs and face hard and punched her all over. Opening her mouth he pulled her tongue out a little and bit it roughly. His dick was becoming hard again.

He moved her over to the edge of the bed to ensure she could breathe then pushed her over onto her stomach and raped her from behind. He punched her all over her back to make sure she would really feel like she'd been in the middle of world war four.

Barone rolled her back over, face up, and gave a wicked grin. He tidied up her clothing. Finally he took a sachet from his pocket, opened it, and dribbled the contents on her tongue. Barone zipped himself up and headed upstairs to the observatory room to check on the situation.

From there he could see the sudden end to the clouds in the sky, held in check by an invisible force. There would be no free water drifting out of Taw-Cymru. The whole area was, in fact, overcast. A luxury holiday destination from the baking sun. Looking back down the road he realized there was one more thing left to do.

He ran back to Chen and dragged him up to villa's entrance. He disappeared off the side of the road into the long grass. All hell would be let loose shortly, but all GUCI would find was a trail that was stone cold.

After his meeting with Zeleno, the rest of McCree's day was spent at GUCI's headquarters. No distance pill on this occasion. In a way he was glad, but he was apprehensive about the feelings he had that may surface like ghosts if he was away from it for too long. About his wife and daughter, let alone all the unknown anti-profit protesters he'd terminated.

He sat at a panel looking through video footage of the area around Tower Eight and where the Assemblage was attacked. He focused on the top floor of zone four – level twenty. There he could make out the face of the jammer operator. About forty profit cycles old with thinning black hair. Then he was gone. Moments later he could see his own handiwork take out the jammer. Was this guy working on his own?

There must have been an accomplice or two on the roof co-ordinating with the signal jammer. The video feed for the roof was the same picture it had been for the two hours previous to the attack. McCree's sharp eye noticed that the shadows of the rooftop had not changed over time. Fake footage had been substituted for the real feed to conceal how the assassination attempt had been set up.

There was a slight flicker at the end of the loop where the shadows changed direction. Of course this was easy to see with hindsight, but a video feed operator would have missed that unless they'd been intently staring at that one feed when it swapped over. All the rooftop feed gave was the chance to narrow down the setup time for the attack to some two hours prior to the event.

All the logs, feeds, and event files for that period showed no unusual activity. After the attack he was able to trace the exit route of the jammer operator from the building, but there was nothing else that would indicate he had accomplices.

McCree went further back through the activity logs to the twenty-four hours previously and found nothing. He had to conclude that all those involved in the attack must be residents of Tower Eight. One thing nagged at him though and he couldn't quite make out why. None of the residents would have access to the roof except in an alarm condition, so how did that happen?

It was now mid-afternoon. McCree had not made much progress apart from being able to distil his search efforts to a few succinct facts.

1) However many assailants there were, they were most likely residents of Tower Eight.

2) They had roof access under non-alarm conditions.

3) They had tech skills that were used to edit the video feed.

He could feel his energy levels getting low and realized it was time to eat. He moved out of his seat away from the panel and headed to the canteen.

GUCI HQ was buzzing. It always was a hive of activity but there was something extra busy about it today. It felt like a wasps' nest that had been disturbed. Yet there was something even more to it than that.

As he walked into the canteen from its south entrance he scanned the area for a quiet spot. He needed to eat and mull over his thoughts. McCree didn't feel like engaging in idle banter with his fellow enforcers, at least not until he'd solved his mystery.

He exchanged various greetings with the enforcers he passed on his way to the central serving station. It was square with each side facing one of the four entrance doors. Each side had popular meals and snacks from that global block. He went around to the opposite side of the square. McCree wanted a Northern Block snack.

Frikandel and frites or Curry Wurst? He went for the Curry Wurst and threaded his way over to a quiet table. He passed a group of enforcers where two at the table were engaged in a mild argument.

'Don't shoot, McCree,' an enforcer joked, 'it's an argument, not a demonstration.' The argument stopped as the group roared with laughter.

McCree gave a slow 'I've heard that one before' shake of the head and sat down two tables away from them. He started on the Curry Wurst which was going down a treat, washed down between mouthfuls with a strong black coffee. He was feeling much better. As the distance pill wore off it often left a feeling of mild tiredness and melancholia. That was where he was in the cycle.

The Curry Wurst may have been pre-printed earlier in the day, but the food printers used in GUCI's canteen were of far better quality than enforcers could afford for their apartments. He skewered a large chunk of Wurst and savoured the richness of the sauce.

Those recipe techs sure know how to program artificial food to make it taste like the real thing. The wonders they could coax from a mere machine.

That's it, McCree realized. The video feed had been tampered with – why not the other logs and files? A video feed re-looping would be really hard to match up, yet they did a pretty good job at that. Deleting, adding, or altering entries in a log file would be easier to them than programming the perfect Curry Wurst.

McCree finished up at the table and headed back to the investigation room. The only *real* piece of evidence he had was the image from the video feeds taken of the jammer operator. He ran the facial scanner against the image. It took a few minutes to get a match.

Franco Barone.

Scientist employed at MedGen.

Started employment profit cycle 25.

Took GUCI entrance endurance event profit cycle 30.

Passed with a score placing him on a par with GUCI elite ops squad. Offered fast track position. Turned offer down.

McCree read up further on Barone's background, but what he learned about the man didn't really match up with his actions to date. It was getting late in the afternoon so he recorded details of his findings on the panel he was using, as much for the data analysts as for his own records. The data analysts at GUCI worked around the clock and McCree's findings could prove invaluable.

The analysts would contact the Head of Active Squads if the intelligence was time sensitive. He could go home and rest. GUCI would not.

McCree went to his locker and changed. He made his way to the lift and was soon on the metro heading back to his apartment. He plumped for a shower before an alcohol. As he undressed and walked to the shower McCree's panel lit up with an alert, 'GUCI – enforcer priority recorded message.' Jack Forester was calling. No shit Sherlock, this was bound to be bad.

'McCree, you've made quite an impression on Meometics CEO,' Forester enthused. 'You're to report to Charles Porter at Meometics main building 09:00, solar 89. Transport will take you there. Good profit to you in the future and honour GUCI with your success. Finally, you've been granted solar 88 as a rest day. Forester out.'

McCree had no chance to reply or to suggest an alternative. He had no choice. His time under Forester's command had come to an end. He'd be reporting to a Meometics head of security for the foreseeable future.

His thoughts turned to his grandson, Joule. McCree had a decision to make. He figured he would upset Eleanor if he called to let her know, but if he was called away and hadn't told her that would be wrong too.

He finally resigned himself that whatever his decision was it would be the incorrect one and therefore better to get it out of the way sooner rather than later.

He called Eleanor from his main panel. 'Here goes nothing,' he muttered. It rang for what seemed an eternity.

Eleanor answered, voice only. *'Good evening John. This call isn't part of our agreement,'* she said curtly.

It was as McCree had expected. No change in her attitude towards him. She'd been like that since the death of his wife and her mother. She'd blamed him for her death and she was right, of course.

There was no forgiveness in her voice and nor would there ever likely be. He didn't let it cut him like it used to. He had the pill to thank for that. 'Eleanor,' he said, 'I have been given a promotion and I'm not yet sure of my duty roster,' he added.

'Congratulations on your achievement, John. Did you get the high score for deaths on duty?' she replied with added sarcasm.

McCree could have sworn he heard Grant's voice in the background saying, 'Cut the man some slack, Anne.' Or maybe that's what he wanted to hear.

'I'm to report to my new post in two solars' time,' he replied, adding, 'Do you want to change Joule's visit date or take a chance?'

There was long pause. McCree wondered what she was thinking. Eleanor was working out her reply. She'd have to give in one way or the other and she didn't like him dictating her actions, even if she had a choice between options. She was still heavily indebted to McCree according to law, and if he died she would still owe GUCI a substantial amount.

'Tomorrow it will have to be,' she replied. *'But the same time as usual,'* she added.

'Of course,' McCree replied.

'*Goodbye John*,' she said and terminated the call.

McCree pulled out the *Battling Tops* game and took out a few sheets of his secret supply of paper along with markers for Joule to draw with. He had a strange feeling that this may be the last time he'd see his grandson for a while and he was looking forward to his visit.

He decided to print out a ham and cheese sandwich. He really couldn't be bothered with anything else. He was in the mood for bland and he most certainly received it. At least the alcohol he took with it would relax him enough to allow him some sleep.

The following morning he woke up with the feeling that he was heading towards a new chapter in his life. He didn't honestly know if it was for the better or not. Merely that it would be different and that alone allowed him a little optimism.

He opted for cheese on toast – it was something he could eat whilst pacing around his apartment waiting for Joule to arrive. His breakfast had all but been consumed when he spotted a transport pulling up outside his apartment block.

Sure enough it was Joule, and he held four fingers up to McCree's apartment window. McCree entered the access for code for Joule from the visitor history file as usual and sent it to the lift.

The door chime activated. 'Four today, Sparky,' said McCree as he opened the door to Joule.

'Grampy!' Joule exclaimed. 'Got lots to draw for you today!' as he dived onto McCree for a hug.

'Whoa there Sparky, first I've gotta whup your top,' McCree replied.

McCree organized waffle sticks with a selection of dips and soda for them and they chose their battling tops. McCree preferred Tricky Nicky but when Joule wanted that top he was happy to settle for Hurricane Hank. The game ebbed and flowed as it always did and McCree emerged the victor ten to eight. 'Hurricane Hank is victorious,' McCree exclaimed.

'I'm trying Dizzy Dan next time,' Joule replied.

The game over and the snacks consumed, McCree put away the game while Joule started drawing. McCree checked up on the news feed. There was the usual dross about rising fees for all the essential services needed to survive in the modern age, but what really caught his eye was the feature on newly announced armour by Torq Innovations, available on special order.

The footage was familiar to him although clearly edited to avoid showing the gruesome bits. The message that 'Torq Innovations protects you where others fail' could clearly be understood.

As he peeled his eyes away from the video feed, he turned to Joule who was in full artistic mode.

Joule had drawn four pictures of the inside of a corridor with what looked like lab technicians and GUCI enforcers moving along it. In one picture a lab technician was removing a piece of equipment from a room into the corridor. A GUCI enforcer was guarding the apartment in the drawing.

'Joule, very impressive. What's this picture all about?' he asked.

'Gramps, it's what was happening on the floor where we live,' the child replied. 'A strange invention that could protect the world was being removed because the inventor was too ill to finish building it. So he asked his scientist friends to help him out.'

McCree froze. The scene Joule had drawn clearly depicted the removal of the comms jammer that was used in the assassination attempt. All these years Eleanor had kept her address secret from him and now Joule had innocently disclosed it.

Joule had been briefed by Eleanor never to divulge his address, and technically he hadn't. Only McCree now knew it, having previously burst into the very same room that Joule had painted a part of.

In another picture was a man McCree knew. He was slightly stooped and looked like he was going to throw up. It was Franco Barone. McCree breathed in slowly to steel himself for the question he had to ask, even though he didn't want to hear the answer. 'Joule, who's this man?' he asked, pointing to Barone.

'Why, he's the poorly scientist who couldn't finish his invention!' Joule exclaimed.

'So did his scientist friends help him get medicine?' McCree asked.

'No, Gramps, he couldn't wait for them, he had to get some medicine himself,' he replied.

McCree left it there. Any further questioning could arouse Eleanor's suspicions. Joule must have seen Barone in passing or in the lift, but whilst McCree knew he was indeed a scientist of sorts, how did Joule get that information?

Most people in neighbouring apartments kept themselves to themselves; how much had Joule seen and how much had he been told by Eleanor?

It was time for lunch but McCree couldn't get Joule's drawings out of his head. He wanted to enjoy what would possibly be the last time he would see his grandson for a while.

Until he'd see the drawings he had been. McCree and Joule both tucked into a ham and cheese Panini, the only difference being that Joule had ketchup in his. The ketchup, or some other sauce, was almost obligatory to make food from McCree's printer edible, but McCree just needed the calories so he saved a few credits by printing his Panini without any.

'Grampy, what's wrong?' Joule asked.

'I'm a little sad, that's all,' McCree replied. 'I may be away for a little while because of my new job and I'll miss seeing you.'

'We will still see each other?'

'Of course we will Sparky, I'll make certain of that.'

McCree knew he couldn't guarantee that and it would be up to the whims of Charles Porter and Renee Zeleno from now on. All he could do was hope that his new posting allowed him flexibility to see his grandson. Promotions were supposed to be a step up the ladder, only McCree was not so sure.

After lunch they watched a couple of video feeds together with Joule tucked under McCree's arm. It reminded McCree of the times he spent together with Eleanor before he became an embarrassment to her and before she drifted closer to her mother.

Their time together almost over, McCree got up and rounded up Joule's bits and pieces. He smartened him up and looked out of the apartment window. Eleanor had just pulled up.

'Mum's here, time to go,' McCree said to Joule.

'Bye Grampy, love you lots,' Joule said.

McCree showed him to the door and Joule skipped down the corridor and turned the corner, out of McCree's sight.

Less than two minutes later he could see Joule outside waving goodbye as he stepped into the transport, and then he was gone.

Zeleno started to come to some five hours after being stunned. Her last memory was of boarding the Hypersonic to Taw-Cymru. Then it hit her – the number of aches and pains all over her body.

There wasn't a single part of her that didn't hurt. She looked at her bare, dirty feet and her legs, blood splattered over them. She felt her legs and reassuringly the blood wasn't hers. Her clothes were heavily creased and she realized she'd looked better.

Lifting herself fully off the bed she realized she was in her vacation villa. Looking out of the bedroom window she could see someone slumped against the entrance on the ground. It looked like an enforcer. She fired up the panel in the bedroom and hit the option for emergency lockdown.

The building secured itself but she disabled the internal gun activation. That was far too unnerving to have in operation for her taste. Emergency Assist was flashing, but unknown to her the comms to HQ did not start up.

Zeleno used the opportunity she thought she had to take a shower, as it would take thirty minutes for GUCI to get here from their base of operations. That left her just enough time to clear up the mess that was Renee Zeleno. The shower had cleaned her up, but she still felt like she'd walked into a brick wall that had then collapsed on her.

163

She removed a hypo-spray from the medical cabinet and gave herself a shot in her shoulder with the MedGen 'Wonder Shot'. 'If you feel like shit – this will fix it!' Not the proudest moment in their ad campaign.

To be fair though, the analgesics it contained immediately melted the pain away, transforming it into a dull ache in the distance. She was able to dress herself properly without wincing, which gave her encouragement that she would be OK.

Even so, her choice of clothing erred on the side of loose, easy to put on and comfortable rather than stylish. Not her usual vacation look, but not a million miles out of place on holiday. She walked gingerly down the stairs to the lounge and activated the main panel. Now, almost thirty minutes after activating Emergency Assist and locking down her villa, there was still no sign of GUCI assistance. *They should be here by now*, she thought.

Scanning the display, Emergency Assist was flashing. She flipped the display to show GUCI recent activity relating to her and the villa. The same entry listed twice.

Escort duty: GUCI Taw-Cymru team 3.

Head escort: Commander Chen.

Start time 10:00

Finish time 11:05

Escort duty completed successfully.

Next assignment: Solar 96 10:00

Status: off duty.

It was 16:15 now and the sun, if it could have been seen, would be flirting with the top of the highest hill. Whilst it would not be dark for some time it emphasized the lateness in the day and increased her anxiety of the situation. *Why hasn't GUCI responded?*

She needed to get to the enforcer at the entrance to her villa. She recalled the blood on her legs. That could indicate he'd suffered a leg wound getting her back to the villa. He'd then perhaps decided to park himself at the entrance until backup arrived. Only there appeared to be no backup.

According to the panel he was now off duty, but clearly that wasn't the case. She opened the door to the utility room, a thoroughly uninspiring part of her villa that she wouldn't normally go near if her life depended on it. This time it probably did.

There was a tall metal locker in the far corner of the bare, stone-blocked room. It was a poor looking room where the owner could put the kind of stuff they didn't really want to store in the villa, but had to for convenience. There were skis and snow equipment here, but in the locker was something far more useful.

Zeleno put her thumb onto the indented handle of the locker door, and the crude thumbprint detection circuit granted her access by releasing the lock.

Inside the locker was protective combat armour and twenty grenades in bunches of four of the same type, denoted by the same colour pin. There were also four firearms: sniper rifle, assault rifle, sub-machine gun and a semi-automatic pistol. On the inside door of the locker were the various instructions for emergency operation of the equipment.

All those who visited Taw-Cymru undertook a short piece of training on how to use the locker's contents successfully in an emergency. The grenades were smoke, explosive, flash, nerve gas and electrify. She took the combat armour off the hanger and put it on.

Fortunately it was relatively loose fitting and oversized for her frame, in case winter clothes were being worn. It had six pouches designed to hold a grenade each. She picked up the pistol and a clip of paralysing gel bullets. These were similar to the enforcers' technology but not generally lethal. Zeleno took two grenades and stuffed one each into a pouch. The other four grenade holding pockets she left empty.

She put her gel-tech footwear on. It was more important for her feet to be quick and cushioned, than armoured and slow. This was her favourite footwear whilst on holiday, allowing her to walk over differing surfaces whilst they constantly adjusted to the terrain and the angle of the ground she was walking over. It would be near impossible to twist an ankle or stumble in these.

Finally she was as ready as she'd ever be. She set the assisted distance on the grenades to what she estimated to be just past the enforcer, and opened the front door slowly. Outside it was quiet and cool. She threw the grenade out through the door, it bounced and spun up. Her aim was good and it passed the enforcer, stopping about ten metres ahead of him. The second grenade followed but to the right of the first. The second grenade signalled to the first and they simultaneously spewed a stream of thick, dense, white smoke which obscured the view in front of the villa.

Zeleno rushed down the drive to the open gated entrance. The smoke was also swirling around the enforcer but she easily found him. It was Chen, and he was dead. His feet were missing and there was a black scorch mark on the right hand side of his forehead. It looked as if he'd propped himself up against the villa entrance waiting for the killer to come so Chen could snipe him as he approached. The bad news was that the killer had had other ideas.

The smoke was at its thickest now and she knew she had to get back to the villa. As she turned towards it she felt a presence in the smoke, as if the smoke itself was forming a giant hand ready to grab her as she turned her back on it. The distance back to the door seemed hideously long. She was paralysed with fear. As the villa had been locked down all the windows had been turned black for one way viewing.

The door appeared to be wider open than when she left it. Was someone waiting in there for her now? Was this part of their plan? If she stayed out when the smoke faded she could be in peril, but the same could be said for heading back into the villa with the blackened windows. *I'm going to die, I'm going to die.* Behind her an imaginary hand grasping through the smoke, ahead of her a pair of eyes waiting for her return to the villa, where she would know her last moments alive.

Zeleno had just the tiniest sliver of lucidity slice through her fear, and she took it. She ran at the door, aiming her weapon at what she thought would be head height, and burst through it. She fired three times as she pushed the door open with her shoulder and then tripped and tumbled to the floor. Turning around she slammed the door shut and code enabled the siege bolts on the door.

She moved into the main lounge and looked through the window down the path towards the dead enforcer, the smoke having now dissipated.

Her breathing was starting to return to normal as she sagged on the sofa, needing more medication as her recent exertion was causing a flare up of her pain. She willed herself off the sofa, stumbled over to the main villa panel and flicked it over to surveillance mode. There, on the villa plan diagonally opposite the green flashing dot that represented her, was a red flashing dot.

McCree had been picked up by transport yet again. He felt that he could become accustomed to this treatment, even though he really knew it would only last a short while. It seemed that for the moment Meometics needed him more than he needed them, but he was going to enjoy it while it lasted.

At 09:05 he was outside the office of Charles Porter, the head of Meometics security.

'Come in, John,' Charles beckoned as he stuck his head around the corner of his office.

McCree exchanged pleasantries and they shook hands. McCree followed Porter back into his room and immediately spotted the thought chair in the far corner of the room.

'Ah, yes!' Porter exclaimed as he caught McCree glancing over at the chair. 'That chair will save us both a lot of time over the charade that used to be a formal pre-contract interview.'

McCree half nodded a vague acknowledgment of Porter's viewpoint.

'The chair will discover what motivates you without the potential for deception, which will indicate to both parties whether you are suitable for the role we have in mind for you.'

'Or not, as the case may be,' murmured McCree.

'Please, sit down,' instructed Porter, motioning towards the chair. Porter reduced the lighting in the room, which now had a candlelit quality to it that cast a shadow on the wall near the chair. McCree settled into the thought chair. An overhead visor descended close to his face from the back of the unit, and a fine mist sprayed from the visor sent him off into a deep sleep.

As head of security Porter was not one to miss a trick. He already had the full history of McCree on the panel in front of him and was waiting to see what additional information the chair brought to him, correlating the official record with McCree's own values and beliefs.

The first few images from the chair were of McCree at a young age. All the landmarks of his life from about the age of ten solars were appearing on the display. Up came memories of the girl who was his first love. After an hour Porter's coffee and pastry arrived.

The 'interview' process had changed beyond recognition from the days of the old calendar, but it was still a long process. The fact that as interviewer Porter almost treated it like a pastime or hobby would have appeared bizarre to his predecessors. It was as though he was watching a long movie. In many respects it could be called entertainment.

Porter saw McCree's first job interview. Then his real love. His interview to join GUCI. His first kill. There was also quite a lot of sex and some of it in places that were prohibited. If Porter counted that against a candidate there'd be no one in GUCI at all.

He marked the relevant recorded images. GUCI invariably obtained useful footage from the chair on each candidate, so in the event of employee problems there would always be something they could use to their advantage.

Two hours in the chair and Porter was at the birth of McCree's daughter. Multiple kills at a demonstration. Then a particular row with his now teenage daughter and his partner. Another big row.

Another demonstration. More kills. Arriving home. The frantic look on his daughter's face. The funeral of his wife. His daughter leaving the apartment. A visit from his grandson. The attack on Meometic's Assemblage. The death of his colleagues. The images faded out and Porter was done. It all pretty much tied up with the record he already had up on the panel next to the chair display.

Porter now knew McCree would be ideal for the job. He had a major problem with his life and the distance pill, probably supplemented with alcohol, was what kept him going. He would do exactly what was asked of him.

Porter noted on his panel the recommended dose of compliancy drugs McCree should be given. They were never free, of course, they were deducted from the standard salary credit offer. If a candidate required so many drugs that their salary was uncompetitive, then they were not suitable for the post.

McCree would be getting fifteen per cent more credits than he had been earning up until now. Porter fired off a process request to the other monopolies, so that they would be able to reclaim the extra credits paid, by means of future excessive rises in the services required in this profit-driven world.

Porter deactivated the chair from the panel and waited until McCree came to.

'So what's the verdict?' asked McCree.

'You'll fit in just fine,' replied Porter.

Porter's silent line flashed. He picked up the portable ear piece and hung it on his left ear.

'Three missed call-backs?' he said. McCree could only hear Porter's side of the conversation.

'Assemble a team, full alert packs. I want them on the next Hyper that leaves. Porter out,' he said to the caller.

'OK, McCree. Get your energy levels up with whatever you fancy from the canteen, because you're shipping out,' Porter announced. 'On the 15:00 Hyper to Taw-Cymru, to be precise,' he added.

He handed McCree a briefing chip. 'Play it in the gear-up room,' said Porter.

McCree took the chip and left the head of security's room. McCree asked the panel nearest to him to 'display canteen direction'. The panel duly obliged, showing a lit green arrow on the wall and the distance in metres. Once at the canteen he showed his face to a menu terminal and chose something quick to make as it was now 13:15. There were a few enforcers in front of McCree.

The wall panels already knew what information they were allowed to display to McCree. They were tuned to his voice and had directed him to the GUCI canteen rather the scientist's canteen. He ordered pre-combat nutrition. He wanted to see if the food printers at Meometics were any improvement on the ones in GUCI HQ. To his disappointment the food and drink was of no better quality or taste than the ones at HQ. They were, however, considerably quicker printers.

McCree felt that every detail here was designed to generate maximum profit out of everything and every person. He was as close to the top of the tree as he could get in his profession. He realized how all-encompassing the profit motive was, not just for the organization he worked for, but for all the corporations and utilities. Was there the possibility that GUCI was just a means of keeping the consumers in line, whilst the corporations and service federations were really in charge? McCree definitely felt as if he was taking a step up to another level, but leading to what?

The vending station was a perfect example of that, familiar – but its speed made the ones in GUCI HQ look like a previous profit cycle's model. That was a bit unfair, he thought, as the vendors at Meometics looked like they'd arrived from the future. GUCI's were merely from the present. They also added 'something extra' to McCree's nutrition, by order of Charles Porter. Meometics' latest recruit finished his food and headed down to the gear-up room.

When McCree arrived at the gear-up room the rest of the team were there. He felt slightly awkward – they appeared to be waiting for him. He placed the briefing chip on the panel and the video feed began.

The briefing chip was only an access token, for Charles Porter appeared on screen, looking the same and in the office McCree had been in only thirty minutes ago. Porter had made the recording after handing McCree the chip! He began to brief the team.

'Protectors of the Meometics way, I have disturbing news. Our head profit enabler, profit be to her, Renee Zeleno, has not been in contact with Meometics since 10:00 last solar. Her last known location was at the inbound terminal at Taw-Cymru's Hypersonic terminal. It is presumed she headed under escort to her villa there.

'Efforts to communicate with the GUCI station there have proved negative. You are to investigate the situation. McCree will lead the team, full alert packs have been provided. Porter out.'

McCree scanned his colleagues in a way that let them know he was sizing them up for any weaknesses. 'Introductions please, with speciality, from the left.' McCree barked to the enforcers.

'Tony Shultz, comms.'

'Frank Weiss, recon.'

'Louis Starr, transport.'

'Jo Delaney, weapons.'

'Scott Abraham, weapons.'

McCree had dismissed the last two as having inferior skill sets compared with his own, but the first three enforcers had more experience in their fields than he did. Scott spoke, 'Sir, it's an honour to serve under the number one GUCI enforcer.'

'I wasn't aware there was a league table,' McCree replied.

'If there was, sir, you would be at the top,' Scott said.

McCree didn't know if Scott was a hot head or not. He certainly seemed keen. They'd all had the chair experience and passed so they must be up to the job, unless Charles Porter was a fool and he was anything but that. McCree felt obliged to say something meaningful as it was his first command under Porter.

'I apparently have a reputation, it seems,' that brought a few smiles. 'Granted I could well be the deadliest grandfather in GUCI, but the aim here is a successful contact with the head enabler, it is not to be a termination spree!' McCree winked and gave a half smile. The enforcers laughed. He knew what they were thinking; he might as well make a joke at his own expense. There was little time to build up a camaraderie between them, yet something told him this assignment was a big one.

Perhaps the way Porter had taken such a sensitive call in front of him, so soon after being in the chair. Either he really was confident of the chair's analysis or he was in a hole. McCree felt he was there for hole extraction duties. It was not the sort of job you wanted on your first day in the office. McCree spoke to the enforcers again: 'I wanted to say something cool, like "kit up men, let's do this." Seeing as the spoken word is not my best skill, and you've already kitted up, "let's go" sounds a bit limp. What I do want to say, however, is you're here because of your abilities, so let's make them count.'

McCree picked up his gear and led his team to the transport level. The building knew where he needed to be and directed him to the appropriate level where *quelle suprise* a transport was waiting for them.

As they stepped into the vehicle McCree thought it strange that there'd been a lot of Zeleno in his last few solars and now he was following in her footsteps again. This could well be a trend not to his liking, but at least he'd not had another 'Death by Zeleno' dream last night.

They arrived at the terminal and were directed via the automatic signage to the lower deck of the Hypersonic. There were around fifty seats on this deck and the rest of the space was allocated to cargo. They were the only people on this deck. The enforcers each chose a spot not too close to each other and triple tapped their right foot on the floor. A seat rose from the floor in front of each triple tap. 'This is as near to top profit class transport we're ever likely to see,' McCree quipped. 'So enjoy the flight.'

They strapped in as mandated by the pre-flight briefing. The launch would not take place if the craft detected any lifeforms in this area not secured in a seat. The craft's acceleration would cause injury to those not strapped in. All the enforcers had secured their kit. The launch light turned green and counted down from thirty to one with a *bong* every five seconds. The hum of the magnetic rails could now be clearly heard, although they were nowhere near as loud as an old-fashioned jet engine. The aura of power being held in check by the rails in the last five seconds before take-off was palpable. Then in an instant all that energy was released.

The craft was propelled viciously off the magnetic rails at a speed of over 600Km/h. This was a little over the required start speed for the hypersonic engines. There was the tiniest drop in the rate of acceleration until the main engines kicked in and propelled the craft upwards. Mere minutes after launch they were travelling at a speed of around Mach 8. The 'unclip' light came on and all those on board duly obliged.

Studies had proven, after such a fierce and prolonged period of acceleration, that it was beneficial to move around to allow the body's internals to relocate back to their normal positions. McCree breathed a sigh of relief. 'Normally I'd say we can relax now, but we have a few plans to make en route,' he announced. 'We've been unable to raise the GUCI contingent at Taw-Cymru. Even though the location is deemed to be low risk a small enforcer squad is stationed there. They have limited resources but they do have an aerial unit in case of retrieve-rescue operations. They have three patrol teams that are in service on a rota basis.

'For visits by corporation heads one of the off-duty teams will perform a pre-escort route check before repeating the journey with the head enabler. The systems show both these journeys were completed as planned. Yet we've not had contact with the head enabler for some time. We'll need to pick up the aerial unit and head over to the head enabler's villa as soon as we arrive,' McCree paused. 'Any questions?' he added, almost as an afterthought.

'There's most certainly something up, sir,' Shultz said.

'How so?' asked McCree.

'Well,' Shultz continued, 'no response from GUCI's local force, but the data from our querying of their systems and Zeleno's villa by GUCI's systems look like they've been *painted*.'

'Painted?'

'Yes, sir, it looks to me like we are being shown what someone wants us to see, rather than being able to see the real live data.'

McCree was impressed. He'd already had doubts about what the data feeds were showing him, but he was unable to put his finger on it. Shultz 'got it' and was able to succinctly describe why.

'Sir, if you took down an information grid, that would raise the alert level, the same as if the feeds showed no one at the villa or GUCI station. Showing us that the planned escort has been carried out but being unable to directly contact anyone just makes us curious. Certainly it's not an excessively alarming situation.'

'And your point being?' McCree asked.

'That what we've been shown is just the sort of information that keeps us from discovering what's going on for as long as possible.'

McCree had already picked this up from Shultz's earlier comment. He just wanted the rest of the team to hear it from Shultz, not himself. It would hopefully reassure the rest of the team that there was some cohesive analysis of the situation from someone else in the team other than him. A little extra bit of skill to be seen would give them an extra boost of confidence that they would be successful in their objective.

'Very good,' said McCree. 'Now strap back in as we're about to decelerate,' he added.

The landing light turned red and the countdown continued in the same fashion as the launch sequence. The team's internals were forced forwards inside their frames as the fierce deceleration kicked in.

In less than a minute they were locked onto the approach to the Hyper terminal at Taw-Cymru. The magnetic rails guided the craft towards the terminal building; the rails had been programmed to bring the craft to a soft stop. The buckles released automatically and McCree gestured to the team to exit.

They entered the terminal at the lower level and took the lift to the main concourse. Only they and some top-up supplies were on this flight, there were no VIPs to escort. The automated unloaders were scurrying around the craft, jostling each other as if in competition to see which could unload the most, the quickest.

McCree punched the navigation request to display the route to GUCI's Station on Taw-Cymru. Arrows lit on the walls to guide them to a corner of the Hypersonic terminal where the appropriately labelled door, marked 'GUCI contingent only', opened as if to personally greet them.

Inside the room one of the teams was slumped over various panels. Present they most certainly were. On duty they most certainly were not.

McCree checked their pulses. 'They're only unconscious,' he confirmed. He could sense the relief amongst the others that whoever did this did not appear to have a grudge against enforcers per se. 'At least they're not dead,' McCree added, as if reading their minds. 'Can you contact GUCI HQ from here?' he asked Shultz.

'I'm on it,' said Shultz. He logged into the system. 'The comms array has been disabled, sir,' he said.

McCree exploded, 'Deja-*fucking*-vu!' What the hell was going on? Another 'incident' and another loss of comms. It seemed to be spreading like a bad rash. GUCI had been outsmarted a number of times now, and although these incidents were relatively small scale there had been a lot of planning and technical knowhow used.

Not since the first planet-wide cyber war which hastened the end of traditional government/sovereign state powers had there been such a spate of communications and technology attacks. GUCI was supposed to have all the state of the art technology direct from prototypes furnished by all the corporations. This was to allow GUCI to enforce and keep the ultra-capitalistic infrastructure in power and keep the consumers subservient.

'Can you fix it, Shultz?' McCree asked.

'I think so, but it could take an hour or two,' said Shultz.

'That's an hour or two we don't have. It will be solarset soon and that will slow down our search.'

'We'll take the aerial transport and do a sweep in daylight. Something tells me not to trust our tech too much in our search for the head enabler. We're going to have to use good old-fashioned eyeballs. I want to get the Aerial landed before sundown. We're not relying on our tech to fly us around these valleys in the dark.'

'You can fix it out of hours, Shultz.'

'Out of hours?'

'That's an old expression my grandfather used when he was asked to do anything above the ordinary. People used to work from 09:00 to 17:00 in the pre-profit cycle calendar. Out of hours would be when you were asked to work later, say until nineteen hundred hours.'

'Thanks for the history lesson, boss, out of hours it is.'

McCree accessed the only transport panel and selected the aerial transport. He felt uneasy but didn't quite know what to put it down to. 'Louis, it's over to you now,' McCree confirmed.

Louis Starr didn't need telling twice. He placed his hand on the transport panel to key his biometrics to the aerial transport. The Aerial was much more expensive and complicated than the ground-based transports and, although he was fully cleared to pilot it, it would not be a good day if it ended up getting trashed. McCree was glad Louis was on the team.

Thank you, Charles Porter, McCree thought. If the rest of the team were as well chosen by Porter for this mission he had a lot to be grateful for.

They headed out to the pad, which jutted out of the side of the building. The aerial transport was sitting on the pad – it looked like an ungainly bird perched on a branch. It had the appearance of an oval upturned pie dish, or perhaps vaguely lozenge shaped would have been a kinder description of it.

McCree entered the transport and sat in the front to the left of Louis, whilst Frank Weiss sat to his right.

The other three enforcers sat in the back row of three. Shultz sat in the middle and was preoccupied with the diagnostic logs from the comms array panel. Four of them would be on the lookout. All Louis had to do was point the thing where he was told to.

'I want to follow the road the escort was supposed to have taken,' McCree commanded.

'Supposed?' queried Weiss.

'Yes. I'm not convinced they even started their task, much less completed it,' McCree replied.

Weiss punched the co-ordinates into the nav computer and a dotted line was overlaid on the front of the glass dome that made up the forward section of the aerial transport.

Louis started the turbines on the transport and it lifted off the pad. He pushed the control stick forwards and they were on their way. The transport followed the route as documented on the escort duty rota. They were flying around fifty metres above the road at approximately the same speed as the ground transport would have been doing. This gave them a good view and the time to scour the landscape for any clues as to the escort and Zeleno's whereabouts.

Louis was an excellent pilot; he swooped above the curves of the valley road effortlessly. McCree could sense the enjoyment he was getting from his assignment. He knew opportunities like this were few and far between for GUCI pilots. The cost of flying was prohibitive, flight time in simulators was not.

He could see how Louis and the transport were almost as one, and it reminded him of how he felt when he was in the zone, carrying out profit reduction terminations.

For the next twenty minutes the transport gracefully weaved its way up the valley. No one had sighted anything out of the ordinary; Taw-Cymru indeed seemed deserted.

There was only the shadow of their transport cast by the sun skirting over the hills to give any sense of drama. The silence was punctuated by Frank Weiss, 'Slow down, I see something.'

'What is it, Frank?' McCree enquired.

'The road has changed!' Louis exclaimed.

'Is that all you've got to say? "The road has changed",' McCree asked.

'But it has, stop and look,' said Louis.

McCree looked down at the road. About four hundred metres away and in sight of Zeleno's villa there was a smooth circular patch where the tarmac road should have been. Obscured by the hill ahead, there seemed to be something on the road. 'Put it down now,' McCree ordered.

Louis landed the transport less than one hundred metres away from the patch and they all disembarked.

Headed by McCree, the team made its way to the perimeter of the patch. McCree picked up a rock by the side of the road and threw it at the patch. It landed and skipped across the surface, although following his recent encounters that was no indication of it being safe to proceed.

The uniformity of the patch reminded McCree of the pool of slime, but this looked different. 'I don't trust this,' he said, directing his comments to his team. 'We'll skirt around it unless anyone wants to risk a leg or two?'

Jo Delaney piped up: 'Sir, I volunteer. I'm the best long jumper in the force.'

'And what purpose will that serve?' said McCree.

'I'm sure I can almost clear that patch.'

'Almost? Your life may depend on it. I've seen enforcers swallowed up by something similar.'

'I should only catch the edge of it at worst, sir. My momentum will carry me across.'

'You could lose a limb or two, Delaney.'

'Maybe my foot, sir, but that's up to my performance sir.'

'Very well, be quick, jump far.'

Delaney took a run up and launched himself over the patch; even without some of his combat gear he wasn't going to make it. McCree braced himself – he fully expected to see both Delaney's legs get dissolved.

Shit, Delaney thought, as he fell short of clearing the patch, *if this is lethal, I'm going to be half the man I used to be.*

Both his feet landed on the patch and he was struck by the solidity of the surface – he half expected to sink into it. He bounced off and fell, rolling forwards, onto the tarmac. The impact with the tarmac was negligible due to his body armour and he slowly rose to his feet. 'Look, it's OK,' he yelled.

He turned towards the road ahead. From his position a little further up the road than his fellow enforcers he could see some way around the bend ahead of them.

'Alert – we have an enforcer down,' he screamed.

The rest of the team, headed by McCree, crossed the patch one at a time, almost as if they feared it was likely to change its mind and dissolve them anyway. Once across they saw the horror of the situation.

Once dead enforcer with no feet or helmet and a single shot to the head. Ahead they could make out another body. Another enforcer, the same as the last. There was more, a grisly trail of bodies leading up to the villa. One enforcer had also lost his hands.

They counted four dead and they spotted a fifth slumped up again the wall of the villa entrance no better off than the rest. There was some hope that the sixth enforcer had made it inside, but McCree was taking no chances.

'Spread out boys, wide pattern. I don't want to make it too easy for anyone inside to take us out.'

McCree's squad formed a semicircle around the entrance of the villa, just as McCree realized how the enforcers they'd encountered had been so easily disabled. He signalled them on his short range comms badge. 'Their boots had been targeted – dump the fuel in your boots – NOW!' The enforcers dialled up the purge-fuel control on their wrist devices; it looked as if their feet were pissing themselves in fear, at the thought of being detached from their legs.

There were many ways to demotivate a person, but the idea of being in imminent danger of losing one's extremities was an especially cruel notion. 'Relocate to the right, away from the purged fuel,' McCree ordered. Their boots were drained and the enforcers were now at such a distance from the fuel where ignition, if giving them a nasty burn, would at least not result in the loss of a limb.

The sun had disappeared from the top of the nearby hill and dusk was upon them. They needed to secure the villa now as they were likely to run out of time to be able to take the aerial transport back to their base.

'Stun ammunition to be used,' McCree ordered. 'I don't want any chance of a friendly fire incident. We've lost far too many people recently,' he added.

The enforcers switched their ammunition packs to those of a less fatal variety. If they happened to stun someone who really should have been terminated, they could always terminate them later.

'V-formation on entrance,' McCree ordered. 'I'll take point.'

McCree crept inside the villa's perimeter wall, the rest of his team at varying distances behind him. He was now just metres away from the main entrance...

Zeleno lay on the sofa watching the red dot on the panel move back and forth as if pacing the room upstairs. She was waiting for it to head down the staircase and then she would at least have a chance. Maybe it was a standoff, maybe it was a case of who would succumb to fatigue first? She'd lasted one night on or around the sofa with her gun trained on the stairwell. She knew she couldn't last another night. Maybe tonight the dot would make its move.

The light was fading and the fear of discovery by the red dot upstairs was fading, but it was still a threat to her. *If you want to kill me you'll have to come down because there's no way I'm shifting.*

At that very moment another red dot appeared outside, then two more, then another two more. *So this is it*, she thought, *this is how I die. The dot has been waiting for reinforcements, I should have tackled it while the odds were even.*

Zeleno was annoyed that she'd lost her opportunity by not thinking straight, but then pain, hunger, thirst, and sleep deprivation all conspired together to make her choose the wrong course of action.

The siege bolts on the main door unlocked themselves slowly as if to prolong Zeleno's agony. *Goodbye Ren, go down fighting.* Then…

The door burst open and a black ball of armour rolled past the open door in the hallway. Two others were either side of the doorframe of the main entrance.

Before she knew it, a weapon was pointing at her and for a moment she failed to realize what was happening. It was a team of enforcers. On the arm was the enforcer badge of Meometic's GUCI contingent; it was McCree.

'McCree,' she gasped. He kept turning up like a bad penny, but she was nonetheless pleased to see him.

McCree gestured to the rest of the squad. Weiss and Delaney rushed upstairs, Starr and Abraham split up downstairs whilst Shultz guarded the front entrance.

'Ma'am, we have aerial transport, but given the recent breaches in our systems I believe it will be better to stay here until the new solar,' McCree suggested.

'All clear,' came the call from upstairs.

'But what about the red dot, picked up on the sensors?' asked Zeleno.

'Just a fake signal Ma'am,' Shultz replied from the hallway. 'We've encountered a few occasions where our systems have been tampered with recently.'

'Just a few?' McCree queried.

Shultz moved into the room with Zeleno and examined the panel. McCree took up the vacant position by the main entrance.

Shultz had called up the code to get behind the data feeds to the main interface.

'I can reset the villa's systems in case there are more surprises lurking for us, but the system will need to download its code from passing satellites. Because of the terrain here it will need to get the code download signal from three of them. That will take a couple of hours. Then

I'll be able to initialize the panels and set up the link back to HQ.'

'Well do it now,' ordered McCree.

Shultz was tapping away on his wrist device. 'No can do sir, the first satellite will be passing over at 21:00, the next at 22:00, and the last one about 23:50. Their orbits are designed like that and we have a system back at base to analyse terrain changes between fly pasts.'

'So that new feature on the road should have been noticed?' McCree enquired.

'It depends when the last trio of satellites passed. If it was made after the last one in a trio and before the first of the next trio it wouldn't automatically be picked up. Even with today's advances in technology, if you cross checked any more than the feed from three satellites the information wouldn't be processed in time before the next batch of streams arrived.'

'OK, I get the *picture*, or more accurately maybe I don't!' McCree remarked. 'Take up four sniper positions, one for each elevation of the villa. We'll rotate elevations in a rota and every hour. Shultz, can you join in?'

'Sure, once I've initialized the signal as the first satellite passes over. The download will carry on as the others pass. I'll also need to set up the link once the downloads are completed.'

'I'll cover your second stint then,' McCree confirmed.

'Great I'll just go up to rooftop level to get the dish set up for the download,' Shultz replied.

McCree stood a metre or so from Zeleno who had now propped herself more upright on the sofa; she'd placed her pistol on the floor.

'Ma'am, we have been unable to locate the last remaining enforcer who was on your escort, or the Sixer for that matter.'

'Close the door and come closer,' she said. 'You're not going to like this.'

Zeleno filled McCree in on all the details, from the moment the Sixer plunged into the crater to how Maitland failed to clear it and sunk into the 'concrete', and finally how the enforcers were picked off one at a time.

'I can't recall much after that other than the next thing I knew I was on the bed in the villa. I think I might have been shot and Chen possibly carried me inside. Then he went back outside to stand point but was killed. Maybe he did enough to stop the assault, or maybe he wounded them?'

'Maybe, Ma'am,' McCree replied, *but something just didn't add up.*

'I don't know much about maximizing profit, Ma'am, but defensive tactics *are* my forte. It will be safer to stay here until the next solar.'

'I trust you'll allow me to reserve judgement on that?'

'How so, Ma'am?'

'The last two GUCI escorts I've had have been disastrous. This one and the one you were involved in. Twice I have managed to evade assassination. At first I thought the Assemblage were the target but this latest incident proves it's me they are after.'

'It's different this time, Ma'am. We've been handpicked by your head of security. I've been in the chair and I assume the rest of the team have.'

'Of that you can be certain. Porter is very thorough.'

'There has to be a leak of the escort plans at GUCI, Ma'am. Despite the fact they are drawn up so close to the actual event, they've been able to make a reasonable stab at taking you out. That means they must be highly organized and there isn't anyone I know with that capability other than the federations or corporations.'

'So you think if the plans had been ready a day or so earlier I could well be dead by now?'

'I believe so, Ma'am. That's why I'm convinced we need to sit it out here tonight. We should be able to restore communications before daybreak if we need them. Then we can send the minimum confirmation necessary back to Porter.'

'Won't that also be subject to any leak?'

'Yes, Ma'am, that's why I propose we send disinformation. It should buy us enough time to get back safely. It's important that Porter doesn't get GUCI to send additional enforcers here as that info could leak out.'

'I see, impressive plan.'

'Thank you, Ma'am, our brief was to contact you and report back. Given the further attempt on your life we need to get you back safely too.'

'But if they can reach here is anywhere safe?'

'Both attempts have been made while you were in transit, so I suggest you'll need to stay put at head office until we can discover who's behind all this.'

'That seems quite reasonable, McCree. Now I really am in need a drink and something to eat.'

'Of course, Ma'am. I'll see what I can do.'

McCree headed upstairs to Weiss who was now covering the eastern view of the villa. 'I need a food tester,' he asked Weiss.

'So you think they may have poisoned the villa's supplies too?' Weiss asked.

'I'm not taking anything on face value until we're back at base,' McCree replied.

Weiss dug out a testing syringe from one of his combat jacket pockets. As the reconnaissance expert he had responsibility for checking out everything from the landscape to foreign substances. 'Here, sir, a couple of drops on food or in a liquid. If the drops turn from clear to *any* colour, do not ingest!'

'Understood,' McCree replied.

McCree went back downstairs to the food preparation area. He opened a large panelled door and found a whole storage area of what appeared to be real food, kept in a chilled condition. He was taken aback. Real food! This must cost a fortune. There was far too much to test it all for harmful contents.

He returned to Zeleno who was gingerly stretching her limbs to see how much pain there still was when she moved.

'Ma'am, the food chiller appears well stocked, but it's prudent to test it beforehand.'

'Of course it's well stocked, I was planning to be here for a few days. Look, I'll get it myself.'

'If I may, Ma'am – here's a food tester. Just a few drops on each item, and if it turns from clear to *any* colour don't ingest it. In addition I think it would be a good idea if I try some a couple of hours before you.'

'A couple of hours? Are you mad? I'm starving.'

'Ma'am, should the tester pass the food OK, there could still be the possibility of something harmful in it. At least if I try your meal ahead of you and something happens to me you'd have advance warning. That could be useful if we need to counteract a foreign substance.'

'Given what tech I've seen thrown at me it's safe to assume that a poison could be targeted to my physiology specifically. It might be total harmless to someone else who takes it.'

'That might be true, Ma'am, but a short delay can't hurt, can it?'

'Ninety minutes' head start then McCree and no more. I'll use the tester on what I fancy and put it on the top shelf. McCree?'

'Yes Ma'am.'

'I do not want to know how much of a treat I am in for once the ninety minutes are up. Fetch it up cooked when you're ready.'

'Understood.'

Zeleno stood up gingerly and walked across to the chiller unit to select the food she wanted. She was mindful of McCree's concerns but she wasn't going to let him know that. It would alter the balance of power between them and there was no way she was going to let that happen. Nevertheless, she decided to select the simpler items to test to avoid any further warnings from him.

She tested the honey glazed chicken pieces, pilau rice and crispy fried onion shavings, broccoli and salad leaves. She also checked out the olive oil and tomato salsa.

To finish off she tested the most decadent looking slab of opera cake and a bottle of Sancerre. They all showed no colour change when the toxicity tester drops were applied to them. She set a timer in the food prep area to go off in eighty-five minutes and slowly climbed the stairs to the villa's upper level.

Whilst Zeleno knew the windows were operating in one-way mode she still felt a little vulnerable staring out into the dark vista where she could now see a number of stars shining. There was no light pollution here and it was pitch black in this remote location. There were many twists and turns required down the valley before the first glow of civilization could be seen. In these circumstances she agreed it was wise for McCree to have elected to stay here overnight.

She sat down at the desk looking out to the stars and switched on the display. Although the systems could not be trusted at the present time there would be no harm in calling up a book in the meantime. She selected one at random. *The Eighth Day* by John Case, a book from near the end of the old calendar. She was fascinated by it and the minutes just dissolved away.

McCree had gone from the lounge to the kitchen area as soon as he spotted Zeleno passing his line of sight and heading upstairs. He opened the chiller door and licked his lips. He used a spoon to select a small portion of most items, although he resorted to a knife for the opera cake and placed it on a plate with the rest of the food. He poured the smallest of amount of wine into a shot glass for testing.

The food was fabulous, but clearly the rice was not meant to be eaten uncooked. He savoured it all, knowing that he would most likely never have this experience again. That saddened him a little, to know that this small taste of what food could really be like would soon be over.

The alternative for most citizens was eating mass printed swill. Even the food produced from printers installed in GUCI HQ would be sorely disappointing after savouring these exquisite morsels. There were now only a few minutes to go before the first satellite would be overhead, so McCree made his way up to the roof level to see how Shultz was getting on.

Solar 89

Taw-Cymru

Barone woke up. He'd slipped away from the scene of the carnage he'd so easily served up to GUCI and Meometics Chief Profit Enabler. He'd traversed numerous hills and valleys and was now some twenty kilometres away from the villa. Barone had been wiped out by the stimulation drugs for just over one solar since he arrived in his sensor-shielded bolt-hole.

He headed back down below the tree line and located the transporter kept from the prying eyes of satellites and their sensors by the canopy of trees and a sensor numbing camouflage tarpaulin.

All has been provided according to plan, he allowed himself a little smile. The first of the three satellites would be overhead soon and he needed to be under the camouflage along with the transport. He loosened one of the stakes and stooped under the tarpaulin resting against the side of the transporter.

Barone scrolled to the satellite tracking feature on his wrist device and viewed the depiction of the satellite moving into range. It was a further ten minutes before it passed out of view. Barone then swiftly pulled all the stakes out around the transport and recovered them and the tarpaulin. Less than five minutes later he was travelling down a valley road, almost parallel to but three valleys across from where he dealt with GUCI's escort and Zeleno.

He had another hour before having to go to ground again, but by this time he'd be over sixty kilometres away from the villa. After that he would be able to refuel his extended range boots and make his way back to the terminal.

There was an air of foreboding back at the facility. Tom was looking at Grant and seemed about to offer his theory about the apparent leak of our research. Yet he held back. He paused, then announced: 'All right K, if it's our project they want to stop there can surely only be two possibilities. If they know of it, they may also be aware of the danger in sending it to market in its present state. Or – they don't know that much about it and see it as a major profit threat to their corporation.'

'Great,' Grant said sarcastically. 'They either wish to protect the public or their profits, choose one at random!'

'That doesn't help us really does it?' I directed my enquiry to Tom.

'Well, if they want to delay the technology until it's safer that suggests they operate to some sort of moral code.'

'What even if they continue to terminate enforcers along the way?'

'It could be the lesser of two evils as far as they are concerned.'

'So how does that help us?' I asked yet again.

'Well, if they aren't profit chasing they may be able to help us stop the adoption of the technology until it's safe enough to be released.'

'Otherwise we could well be next on their list,' I replied.

'But how can we tell what the deal is?' Grant asked. 'We might not know until it's too late. Plus, we have no idea how to contact them.'

'Ah,' I replied. 'I think I know someone who can help.'

'As do I,' added Tom. 'Only I hope my contact turns out to be a dead end.'

'How so?' I asked.

'It's just that if my contact isn't actually dead then we are all in serious danger.'

I mulled the situation over. We had our own corporation who had already scheduled a date for our termination, and possibly another corporation that would also like to terminate us if they got the chance. Not exactly the best two possibilities on offer. Unless they were to both cancel each other out in a race to finish us off.

I would just have to wait for another contact from Santos. They must surely be keeping an eye on me by now so I was sure they'd be in touch shortly after I finished at the lab for the day.

'Canteen, guys, *now* please,' Tom ordered. He wanted the room for himself. Grant was out of the door first; he was clearly hungry again.

Tom waited a good minute after the door had closed before activating the comms panel. Using his privileged level of access he called up the schematics for Grant's building and then his apartment, and tapped in an activation sequence. He injected the sequence into the power feed to Grant's apartment. The signal activated the resonance panels on the apartment's ceiling.

The resonance panels were something Tom had worked on in a previous project that had been shelved, as there were now better ways of spying on people. The panels, in this case, would be exactly what Tom needed to confirm or disprove his suspicions. The panels' sensitivity to air pressure variations allowed sound in the room to be processed by them, just as their sensitivity to light allowed light processing to take place.

Within minutes he had pictures and sound streams from the inside of Stern's apartment. How ironic that they were only on the ceiling due to Tom's presentation of them as a wedding gift – a decorative ceiling adornment. They may not be the last word in communications, but they sure as hell added some sparkle to a featureless ceiling.

As the panels were sensitive to both air and light pressure they would constantly shimmer, glisten, or twinkle depending on the level of inputs they received. It truly was the gift that kept on giving. For the foreseeable future it would be giving a lot more than planned.

Tom set the feed to his personal encrypted storage. He'd have plenty of opportunity to scan through the footage of a member of his team on another occasion.

Solar 89

Taw-Cymru

It was now 21:02 and McCree was on the roof watching Shultz sort out the satellite download connection. He'd already opened a weatherproof box on the roof marked 'Initial download', and McCree could make out that two of the switches inside the box were set to 'init' and 'reset'. There was a small panel glowing inside the open box.

In addition, there was a pictogram of the satellite and its projected beam moving across the screen. Soon the beam would be bathing the 'you are here' pictogram in blue light. McCree wasn't an expert in this field but even he could tell that would be when the download should commence. The blue light had covered the dish on the screen.

'Connection established,' Shultz confirmed. 'Reset initialized.' Shultz was frantically tapping away on the device strapped to his forearm. *Two hours fifty or so from now and we'll be re-connected with our corporation again.* 'Why don't you look at the next satellite as it passes over – from the observation room?' Shultz suggested. 'The telescope will pick it up.'

'Really?'

'Yes, sir, it does a great job of the stars. An orbital satellite will be no problem for it.'

'Maybe I'll do that, but first the head enabler has an evening meal to be served.' McCree made his way back down to the kitchen. He'd never used anything other than the food dispensers before, with the exception of a brief dalliance with a microwave as a young boy.

The food preparation device was even more ancient than the microwave. It seemed odd and out of place even by the standards of the villa. The villa, after all, *was* meant to feel different. This location was supposed to be a break. It certainly was a break from profitable operations, but what was the lesson to be learned here? No doubt to make the occupants appreciate how far society had progressed in its pursuit of profit, and strive for even more.

Only McCree wasn't buying it.

This place made him realize how much humanity had lost. He was glad he'd come down to the kitchen early because it took him a full twenty minutes to work out how the Canon oven actually cooked the food. *Blue flames used to heat the food. That is very quaint.*

He concentrated hard; only some of the items required heating, the lettuce not being one of them. He had five heating areas where circles of blue flames could be controlled. He emptied out the chicken pieces into a metal container, then turned the dial on the front of the cooker and the flames flared up in a circle underneath it.

He turned another ring of flames on and put the rice into a second metal container. The broccoli proved to be a challenge for him. The salad leaves weren't to be heated but what about the broccoli? It was one of those thing food printers just didn't do. At least not one of the printers in the price range *he* could afford.

When he'd tasted it earlier he couldn't quite make up his mind if it needed cooking or it was supposed to be eaten raw. There were no clues on the packet. The online systems for the villa were only at the start of the reset procedure; he had no access to that information. Looking around the kitchen for some sort of divine guidance he noted a narrow cupboard sandwiched between two regular units.

He opened it up and was taken aback by the discovery of books from the old era. *Nutritious Cooking* and *Cooking for Two* were the largest of the five or so books wedged in the narrow storage space. *Nutritious Cooking* was a very dry book listing recipes by order of diet deficiencies and their related medical condition. Not the most appetizing of thoughts.

He flicked through the pages. 'Anaemia' was near the front of the book, and broccoli was in the recipe as being high in iron. There was even a warning not to overcook the broccoli as that would reduce its nutritional benefit substantially. Zeleno didn't look anaemic, and one ingredient match in a book wouldn't sort the problem or tell the whole picture.

McCree opened *Cooking for Two*. It was for those aiming to conceive or who were already pregnant. McCree pinned his hopes on the chance that Zeleno might be. His previous nightmare flashed back into focus suggesting that her conception may still be an event in the future. *No, it's just a bad coincidence.*

He leafed through the pages past the introduction. Pre-conception... When trying to conceive... When pregnancy is confirmed... Early stage pregnancy. He stopped and flicked to the end. Post-birth recipes, and then the index.

Chicken was mentioned frequently in the recipes. Broccoli was not.

There were only a couple of references to broccoli in the whole book. McCree tied those up with a recipe he found containing both chicken and rice. It was in the 'trying to conceive' section. His low level of optimism about the whole situation took a turn for the worse. He now knew how to cook broccoli. He also knew what lay ahead. As McCree was getting to grips with cooking the meal he elected to never be alone with Zeleno without a weapon to hand.

After juggling with the levels of the flames on the cooking rings the meal appeared to be ready. Or at least it was as good as it was going to get. He at least knew what looked appetizing and what didn't and his handiwork was the former rather than the latter. He served it up onto a plate but with no real flair, apart from placing the chicken in the centre of the plate with a perimeter of rice, followed by broccoli randomly scattered over them both. He placed the dish on a tray with the opera cake alongside, her chosen bottle of wine, and an empty glass. *She can pour it herself,* he muttered.

McCree made his way to the upper level where Zeleno was waiting, having been alerted by the smell of cooking working its way upstairs, his close quarter termination pistol clipped to his side. Zeleno immediately spotted it as he walked slowly into the room with the tray.

'Oohh! Servants with guns! My kind of heaven, I might not want to leave here in too much of a hurry.'

'It's the chicken, Ma'am,' he replied, seeing she'd spotted his side arm. 'I was unsure of the cooking time for it and didn't want to risk it making an escape attempt.'

'Ha! I know it will be fine. It wouldn't look good on your service record – serving up potentially lethal food.'

'If I may, Ma'am, the opera cake *is* indeed quite dangerous.'

'Nice try, McCree. I'll place it on record if you want to, that I ate the cake against your advice.'

She waved him away. As he headed towards the observation room, he could hear her moan with delight as she started on the food he'd just prepared for her. *Lucky bitch,* he thought.

In the observation room was the most impressive looking telescope imaginable. He wasn't an expert on scopes, but McCree was impressed. It was nothing like the scope he used on his weapons, and that was enough for him. The eyepiece was at an angle to the barrel, but of course he was going to observe the satellite, not shoot it.

Glancing at his wrist, he noted that he'd been in the kitchen longer than he had thought and now there was nothing to see – he'd just missed the second satellite. It would be another eighty minutes until the last one passed over. McCree instead toured the villa. Shultz had already swapped with Weiss who'd made his way into a room with a large L-shaped sofa placed against the wall. It was ideal for an hour's rest.

Fortunately for McCree he didn't feel at all tired. It was going to be a long night. His sound of his movement around the villa was the only real noise that was going on. Save for the sound of Zeleno pouring the wine into a glass as he passed by the room she was in.

Here he was in a villa with six other people and yet he felt completely alone. There would be no one waiting for him when he returned from this assignment. There hadn't been since the death of his wife. Which was his fault and thus a worthy punishment to beat himself up with. He could really do with a distance pill right now but that wasn't going to happen anytime soon. At least Zeleno's partner was her job. There'd be no way she had time for anyone else. The price to pay for being at the top. At least her job had its merits.

It would soon be time for the third satellite to pass overhead. McCree strode upstairs to the observatory room.

Zeleno was just over halfway through the bottle of Sancerre. The alcohol had picked up where the painkillers had left off and she was now only in moderate discomfort and soreness. When the Sixer had gone down, so had her supply of distance pills.

Now she too, like McCree, was being faced with ghosts of self-doubt from the past and regrets about the way her life had turned out. She wondered if the moment for her to have a child would ever arrive. She needed pass her ethos on for the sake of her corporation, and also to feel genuinely loved. All those around her had the utmost respect for her, but no one had really loved her.

Liked was the nearest she'd seen, and that was from Charles Porter, who probably admired her rather than really liked her. Then she remembered Derek. He was her best hope of a real future and she'd ordered his termination. She hastily poured the rest of the Sancerre and downed it in one go.

AI Derek was angry, very angry in fact. The link to the villa in Taw-Cymru had been disconnected. He was sifting through the data files that flowed in front of him. The information came to him. One of the Meometics enforcers in the villa had terminated it.

He scanned the data for his name. Got it. A number of audio references to Shultz and a sensor feed confirmed Tony Shultz was one of the enforcers at the villa. Derek called up his file.

Tony Shultz. Age 33 solars.

Specialism: communications.

Fully qualified comms tech, grade 1.

Well, Tony, if you manage to survive your present mission it may be worth recruiting you. Now how much have you inconvenienced me?

Derek cross checked the satellite overpasses at villa's co-ordinates.

Interesting. Firmware download initialization requested 21.03. Download will complete at 23:53. Well, Enforcer Shultz, I think for all your hard work you deserve an extra bonus.

Derek had calmed down considerably now that he felt back in charge of the situation. At some stage in the future he would once again exist in biological form. Until then it was his sworn duty, unknown to Santos, to maintain Zeleno's existence forever under threat. The ultimate of ironies would then and only then quell the desire to avenge the ultimate of betrayals.

Derek examined all the avenues that being connected directly to the global network brought him. Directly interfacing and engaging in two way real-time communications with people over the global network was prone to discovery, but here he could just look at the flow of information. To any network probes that were active he would only appear to be a housekeeping utility program. He was of course much more than that.

He injected a series of commands destined for an ex-military satellite brought under GUCI's control many cycles ago. Then he appended some instructions to the firmware download due to complete at the villa and went into hibernation. If the commands were discovered there would be no trace back to him.

Tom joined us at the canteen just in time to see Grant polish off the remains of his crisp and deep pizza. A combination of a deep pan pizza with a thin and crispy layer on the top. Even for Grant this represented a new level of gluttony. Tom glanced across to me, 'Surely, K, he hasn't eaten the rest of that. Tell me you shared.'

'Sorry Tom, it's all his!'

Grant looked across now somewhat sheepishly. 'It's my nerves. I'm a nervous eater. My appetite goes through the roof when I'm worried. Like when we're about to be terminated, eh?'

'Ease up, Grant,' Tom pleaded. 'I'll clear a call to our security team and see if I can persuade them to keep an eye out for us.'

'So what are you exactly going to tell them, Tom?' Grant was starting to get stroppy again.

'I'm just going to voice our concerns that we might be the next target on the list. I don't need to explain further than that – we just need to mitigate the possible threat.'

On reflection, Tom's logic was impeccable, but there was an actual threat to us that couldn't be mitigated. Our future termination by Meometics. Tom's action, whilst seeming to improve our chances, could actually reduce them. I decided to wait and see how far Tom was able to get.

Tom called up the comms panel and selected 'emergency notifications'. He chose 'severe potential profit loss incident' and touched the confirm icon.

The icon pulsed for a few seconds and a video feed opened on the panel.

'Charles Porter speaking, head of internal security.'

'Tom Andrews, Research 4.' It was all a little formal; the panels had confirmed each party by their biometric readings. The announcement of the callers' identities was part of a long since superfluous ritual that once served a purpose, before biometrics and other ID confirmations became widespread.

'Tom, what information do you have for me?' Porter asked

'It's regarding the samples we've analysed from the incident with the Assemblage. I believe that the attack on the Assemblage was an attempt to stop one of my team's technologies making it to market.'

'Go on.'

'Well, if they are unable to eliminate the Assemblage they may well wish to target the research team responsible for the technology instead.'

'I see.' Porter paused. *'So you want a security detail until you're assigned to Ultra projects then?'*

'Oh, so you know about that? Well yes, that would *most* acceptable.'

Damn you Tom, and we will be *most* dead. Shit. Shit, I should have told them.

'*It's my job to know. Ok, Tom, I'll make the necessary arrangements. I don't have the resources to hand at present so it would be better to stay here overnight at Meometics.*' Porter explained.

A small glimmer of hope surfaced.

'Thanks for your assistance. I think we'll stay put then.'

'*Goodnight Tom, Porter out.*' The feed disconnected.

Tom and Grant were looking reassured. Tom could see I wasn't.

'What's up, K? That's a good result, isn't it?' Tom asked.

'I need some air. I'll be back in a moment.' I swiftly made my exit. I needed time to think. Who, where, why, what, how much time have I got? My head was spinning; I felt a big headache about to erupt. I made it to the rest room just down the corridor and to the medicine dispenser.

The dispenser diagnosed hypotension and printed out two tablets for me. Angiotensin was printed on one side – and there it was, on the other side of the tablets! The first tablet had Stc-316 10.00 and the second tablet S90 Canal 1914.

What happened to the sliced tofu baguette method of contact? Santos had contacted me – why the change of plan?

I swallowed the tablets with a few sips from a chilled bottle of water. There was my only way out – another rendezvous tomorrow with Santos. I just needed to decipher 'Canal 1914'. I called the lab from the rest room.

'I feel kinda bad, guys, I've taken some medication and am going home.'

'*That's a big risk, K, are you sure?*' Tom asked.

'I'll take the chance,' I replied, 'the way my head feels now, termination would be a welcome relief. Besides, this decision is only five minutes old. It's not been logged anywhere yet. Staying at Meometics HQ for security will have been. I won't be on the network's travel records until it's too late to do anything.'

'*All right, K take care.*'

'I will, and I'll see you soon.'

'*Alter your route back in to be safe, away from our normal routes in.*'

'Will do, Tom, bye.'

My head was stabilizing by the tiniest of margins, but at least it was not getting worse. I headed down to the metro level and entered the subway. I had an awful lot of options to digest, and soon I was outside my apartment. Only very rarely had I been unaware of my journey to or from the lab. It was an auto-pilot trance trip. My pounding head and all that I needed to consider had conspired to make me oblivious to the journey. If my life depended on describing a single passenger on the metro during my journey I would be dead. Death was, of course, still a real possibility.

I also didn't much fancy becoming an AI, even though the prospect of being immortal had a certain appeal to it. At least not until there was the chance of returning to a human body. Only resetting technology surely meant the end of that possibility.

It was imperative I stayed alive to complete the reset. I knew how to reset our technology in theory, I just didn't have the resources to do it on a planet-wide scale. Santos would need to sort that conundrum out for me.

The dispenser produced an iced coffee which did a good job of settling my thoughts. It was sometimes the act of doing something very simple, a very mundane act, that allowed a clarity of thought when you least expected it – a welcome distraction from information overload.

I searched for clues from my info panel. Canal 1914. What is a Canal? 1914 sounds like an old calendar date. A re-opening of Kaiser-Wilhelm-Kanal and the opening of the Panama Canal. Canals were manmade water channels for use by ships before the profit cycles began.

The Panama Canal was the same spelling as the 'Canal' on the tablet. The rendezvous details must have something to do with Panama, the old nation state. I made no further progress. The details were sketchier than the last time, although admittedly I at least I knew Stc-316 was a compartment on the metro, and I had the time and date to travel. The rest of the puzzle would surely unfold there. Santos knew where I lived so the details naturally would relate to my apartment's metro station.

I had to prepare for my last meeting with Santos before Meometics GUCI enforcers started escorting Research 4 everywhere. The plan needed to be agreed at our next meeting. Some two hours and many drinks later I had a strategy. Would Santos be able to assist me to pull it off?

I had woken up in my chair, which had slowly lowered itself into a more horizontal form as it detected my drift into sleep. Now it had resumed its usual chair position as it detected my stirring from sleep. It wasn't as comfortable as a proper bed, but then this was an early research project of minor importance. My only real luxury if you could call it that.

Still a bit dazed but with no pounding head, I stepped into the shower and let the water wash away my last remaining traces of tiredness. I made sure my nutrition levels were topped up to max because there could be no telling when the next opportunity to eat or drink would be, if my last encounter with Santos was anything to go by.

I dressed more comfortably this time, in case I was to have my clothes removed again whilst unconscious. I found the novelty smalls Grant had bought me as a gift, but also as a dig that I needed to spend more time with the opposite sex rather than in the lab. The underwear had 'Ladies ONLY beyond this point' printed on the front and 'No entry' on the rear. I chuckled to myself – the irony of the message could well be lost on those in Santos who may come across the message, but I wanted to make a statement even during unconsciousness.

Being undressed by scientists is not something you should have to encounter on a regular basis, whether unconscious or not. Never trust a scientist or their probes – and that's first class advice from one himself. Suitably attired I stepped out of my apartment. Could this be the last time I saw it?

I wasn't that bothered about leaving the apartment; the chair would be missed perhaps, and the view maybe, but from this point forwards surely everything would be different. I just hoped it would be for the better.

I entered the subway station underneath my apartment block and didn't have long to wait for the 10:00 metro. Stc-316 was at the front of the metro and I had to walk along the corridor to board the correct compartment. I hoped it didn't look too suspicious but I had no real alternative. I scanned the compartment and there she was, my contact.

She looked great, with jet black hair in a bob and the smartest of tailored suits. Her knee-length skirt was red while her jacket was blue. Her blouse was white, as were her accessories. I sat opposite her as the metro left the station. She seemed to recognize me. I had assumed she was my contact as she had the same style and air of confidence about her as my previous contact had.

As the metro picked up speed she unzipped her handbag and rummaged around in it. She briefly turned the handbag's opposite side towards me and there I saw it. A red star and a blue star. The flag of Panama! She seemed to be rubbing her hand with something inside her handbag. I couldn't really make it out, but moments later the bag was zipped back up, the stars now facing away from me. The metro was now nearing our stop but she stood up far too early, standing close to me. My thoughts drifted to the hope of her being the one to uncover my 'Ladies only' message, but the metro suddenly decelerated pitching her towards me. She grabbed my hand to steady herself and apologized. I felt a mild sting where she gripped my hand. That wasn't any ordinary hand cream she'd used.

The metro stopped at Tower Six and she got off. I let a couple of others get off next. As I left the metro my hand continued to sting. A message in reddened skin appeared: SAVE US. This time my contact used exit three and I followed a short distance behind her. I wasn't close enough for her to hypo-spray me, but my head was starting to swirl as if I had been. My hand burned again; the last thing I saw was the message disappear from my hand before I passed out.

When I came to I was back in the golf ball, again dressed in protective clothing. Elizabeth and the others were there, and she alone gave that extra welcoming smile that hinted she may have read the message on my shorts.

'Good to see you, K, I just wish it was in better circumstances.'

'Me too, Elizabeth, but why the change from the original plan?'

'Well, K, there's no real change, the tofu sliced baguette still stands if you want to contact us next time, but we wanted to contact you. Are you aware that every corporation is allowed twenty citizen traces and that they can be pretty much anyone?'

'I was aware there were a small number of legal traces allowed, so what?'

'Well they took the trace off Research 4 members with the exception of Tom Andrews. Why did they do that? We don't yet know, but the two new traces are on your Chief

Profit Enabler, Renee Zeleno, and a GUCI enforcer who recently moved to Meometics dedicated GUCI contingent. His name is John McCree.'

'McCree, I know him, he's the enforcer who was in the thick of the action during the recent attack on the Assemblage. We were given access to the classified footage to assist us in a top priority side project assigned to us by Zeleno herself.'

'May I ask what that project was?'

'Sure, Elizabeth. We were given a sample of the slime that was used in the attack. It was a gel with nanites held in suspension. We discovered that they were controlled by master nanites that co-ordinated the slave versions to program the gel to disassemble materials it came into contact with.'

'We must consider ourselves fortunate that Research 4 was asked to undertake that project.'

'How so?'

'K, you are on board with us and we now know how close Meometics are to discovering Santos and our technologies.'

'The slime is your invention?'

Derek materialized next to Elizabeth. 'Yes. To be more precise,' Derek emphasized 'It is *my* invention. We attempted to terminate Zeleno but somehow the Sixer she was travelling in was immune to our technology. The only explanation I have for that is that someone at Santos has leaked the technology to Torq Innovations who have deployed a countermeasure on their elite class Sixers.

'I am at present searching for the source of this leak in order to eliminate further occurrences. As for dealing with Zeleno, other methods are now being employed.'

Elizabeth spoke again. 'Both new traces have tracked Zeleno and McCree to Taw-Cymru, but that's the last record we have of them. It can't be a coincidence that both of them are there.'

Derek interrupted. 'It's good to see you again in person, K. I have to return to my search, but please fill my sister in with your valuable insights.'

Derek faded from view as quickly as he'd appeared.

I directed my attention towards Elizabeth. 'We seem to have partly re-discovered your brother's lost technology, but when combined with our pixie dust enhancement it's going to allow a massive boost to the potency of the nanotechnology.'

'It's the grey goo scenario, isn't it?' questioned Elizabeth.

'Yes. I'd imagine we could add self-replication to the existing command set of the nanites suspended in the gel and they'd become self-sustaining. Those who used the gel as a weapon would naturally need to build in some safeguards to protect against damage to their own side. With that many master nanites in the gel co-ordinating its behaviour there's every chance it could become self-aware. The longer that amount of nanites remains active the greater that risk. One side is likely to push that little bit too far to achieve a decisive advantage. History has taught us as much.'

'It's a lot worse than Santos thought,' said Elizabeth. 'The nanotechnology is already in the hands of Torq Innovations and Meometics.'

'Only because Santos tried to wipe the Assemblage out,' I replied.

'That was a miscalculation on Derek's part, but what's done is done. Whether Torq Innovations were given the technology to counter the imminent threat to Meometics' Assemblage no longer matters. The genie is out of the bottle and Research 4's pixie dust enhancement is the last piece in the puzzle of planetary destruction. I'm sorry we've caused so much trouble. Don't be too hard on yourself – you're merely the final piece of a very large puzzle.'

'Well, I think I may have the answer to our problem. I analysed the readings I had from the "mishap" in the lab with the quad-axial pulse and I believe it could be replicated on a global scale. The failure factor is that firstly I don't have direct access to a global satellite network, and secondly the files that would need to be sent to the network are safely kept behind high level security.'

'So we need some way to break through or bypass it.'

Elizabeth detailed the plan to me and I could see that it was both our best and only chance of success. Santos had already established the method of how to break through the security that protected Research 4's lab. They had been waiting for insider assistance to carry out their plan.

I briefed them on those of my tasks in the lab that were carried out at the same time each day. We agreed that the signal would be sent onto Meometics general network at

15:30. Whilst all the data from the lab was highly encrypted, Santos would know that Research 4's lab would send a specific archive information query at 15:30. They would reverse de-compile all data from that node at that time to match the known query. The encryption could then be broken. With that done they would be able to decode all data leaving the lab and thus discover how to burrow right though the security.

Elizabeth moved closer. 'Zap time, eh?' I enquired.

'Best of luck,' she replied. *Pssst*, and the contents of the hypo-spray started to work on me immediately.

'Bye,' I tried to reply. It was no use, as I slipped into unconsciousness...

Yet again, sometime later I found myself in a transport. The display on the panel indicated it was heading for a metro connection – a different one from my last Santos encounter. I was not so lightheaded this time, maybe I was becoming used to the drug? The transport disappeared under the street to a sub-level metro connection. Within minutes I was on the metro to the lab. I'd been out cold for forty minutes. By the time I made it to the lab I had less than an hour to go until I submitted the pre-arranged query.

Tom was the first to greet me. 'Feeling better K, I trust?'

'Yes, thanks Tom, good enough to get cracking on that little problem of ours.'

'Which one would that be? We seem to have quite a collection of them these days,' Grant interjected, his head lifting up from a lab bench.

'May I ask if we now have GUCI escorts, Tom?'

'We do, from this evening in fact.'

'Great, that's one less thing that may kill us to worry about.'

'There are others?' Tom asked.

'But of course,' Grant said sarcastically. 'After all, K did nearly—'

Grant stopped in mid-sentence, his careless loud mouthed comment all but completed.

'Blow up the lab?' Tom added.

'Oh shit. Thanks Grant, for being a model of discretion.' I disappointedly glared at Grant. He threw me an 'I'm really sorry, K' look. Too late, for the damage had *literally* been done.

There was a moment of silence which seemed to last an eternity.

Tom broke the silence, 'I'm well impressed guys, you must have worked like the devil on overtime to patch up the lab before I got back. You forget I automatically get alerted to major equipment changes in the lab during my absence, and a lab bench fits right into that category. Now I know you can work that hard and hold it all together I'll be expecting that level of performance from now on.'

'With all due respect, Tom, there's a difference between the speed you work at when attempting to make a breakthrough discovery compared to shitting yourself 'cos you've just blown the lab up!' Grant replied.

'Point taken, still – good job anyways.'

The strain of keeping the secret of our planned termination by Meometics from the team was becoming more difficult to bear. It wasn't fair to keep my colleagues in the dark, but Grant was unpredictable enough to make any disclosure a big risk.

There'd be no telling what he would do if he found out. That was also the reason why Tom couldn't be told. He'd insist all the team had the right to know about this. I was not prepared to disclose the existence of Santos to them. If either or both of them were in contact with Santos that would be a bonus, but I would not be the first to reveal it. Grant had steered the conversation closer to the truth than I'd have liked. Hopefully my reaction was seen as shock at the lab accident disclosure rather than a lucky hit on the fact we'd already been marked for termination.

It was now just moments before 15:30. I entered the command: 'Retrieve archive nano-density test results current profit cycle solar 40'. At 15.30 I hit the accept key. There was a long pause, which seemed unusual, or maybe that was just my imagination. A large set of results began flooding onto the panel I was working at. That would most certainly give Santos something to latch onto.

Tom had moved over to the panel I was working on. 'What's all that activity, K?' he asked.

'I was just reviewing the older logs in the light of what we have discovered to date. Maybe we missed something that we can now find, given our examination of that nanite gel.' I replied.

'Good idea, K,' said Tom. 'Keep up the good work.'

It was in all honesty a lame cover for my subterfuge. However, not being under suspicion of any kind meant it was more than adequate cover for its purpose.

'Archive consistency error' flashed up on my panel. 'Select reload to correct'. Could this be Santos? I'd never seen a fault pulling information from the archive before.

I selected 'reload'.

Switching to a connection integrity diagnostic I saw that our lab's connection to the network had an increased upload speed. Not too dramatic, but enough to make me certain Santos were now accessing our confidential research. I felt another bridge had been burned. Another line had been crossed. I was fully involved in their plan. Santos had breached the firewall and Research 4's encryption.

The last few solar cycles had not dealt Charles Porter much fortune. He mentally added a high-security data breach from Research 4's lab to the list. Renee Zeleno was sure to give his arse a good kicking when she returned. If she was in fact alive.

From the moment of the attempted assassination of Meometics' Assemblage to now, there wasn't a single thing that he would be pleased to have sitting as a record on his career profile. He was a loyal servant of the company and especially to his superior, but even he wondered if Zeleno was dead. Would that let him off the hook? No chance really; whoever assumed eventual command was sure to come looking for him. He focused on the present with the Research 4 data breach warning flashing on the main panel in his room like a bad sci-fi film from the old calendar.

Porter's first choice to fix this latest monumental fuck-up would have been Tony Shultz, but he was beyond reach on a mission to contact the Chief Profit Enabler who was hopefully alive somewhere in Taw-Cymru. He had no other option but to talk directly to one of the techs. He entered 'high-security research lab tech' into the panel.

A list of three names appeared. Trebanos Starion was the tech on duty. What sort of a dumb-arse name was that? It certainly gave him a distinguishing start in life, but if that was for the better or not Porter couldn't tell. It may have opened doors for him or he may have got beaten up a lot when younger.

Porter placed the call.

'*Treee-baaan-oth thpeaking,*' a weedy lisping voice came from the panel.

He'd been beaten up a lot, definitely, Porter decided. Looking at his live image on the panel, he needed to get out a bit more often too, although on balance Porter decided that it was better for society if didn't. He was a typical old calendar server tech. It was surprising that they still existed today. Yet here was a real life example and Porter needed answers from him.

Porter cut through any pleasantries he may have normally used as he considered they'd be lost on the tech.

'Starion, what the hell is happening to the security systems protecting research 4?' he demanded.

'We have a data breech sir,'

'I know that, I have a big fucking red warning light flashing on my panel to tell me. I want to know what you're doing about it!'

'Yes, sorry sir. The data is being sent to multiple endpoints on the network. The data could be read by any intermediate transit in between the lab and the endpoint.'

'Starion, I don't want to know where the data is going, I want the data breach sealed.'

'I can't sir, its going out to multiple sources as I explained.'

'Kill the power then,' Porter realized the flaw in his order as soon as he said it. Damn. He didn't want the tech to get the upper hand on him.'

'They're all on failsafe sir,' Starion replied.

'Get your arse to wherever it needs to be to disconnect the link.'

That will be the lab itself, sir.

'Meet me at level eight now. Take a nausea pill while you're at it because we'll be at the lab in five.'

Yes sir.' Trebanos left the camera on, forgetting to disconnect the panel. Porter could see Starion's arse swiftly exit the room. He terminated the connection and put on his combat jacket, just in case. Rushing down towards the lift he punched buttons on his wrist device that would summon a priority one GUCI armoured vehicle to be waiting at the transport level for him.

The lift was already there and he wasted no time entering. At level eight the lift stopped and Trebanos entered. He looked even worse, if it were possible, than on the video panel. He did not smell good. Porter wondered if he has already soiled himself. 'You taken that pill?' he asked.

'Yes sir,' Starion replied.

'Well just to be sure, make sure you grab a vomit bag to hand when you get in the transport,' Porter demanded.

Starion nodded his head, speechlessly. He wondered, *how bad could it be?*

The lift doors opened, the transport was waiting.

Porter strapped himself into the quad strap restraints and Starion copied him. As soon as Starion's clip engaged the transport shot forward. 'Grab the bag,' Porter yelled. As Starion reached for the bag it was almost yanked away from him by the sheer acceleration of the transport.

'This is as fast as it gets on the ground,' Porter commented. The transport was heading straight for the closed exit gate.

We're going to die, Starion thought; he was going to lose control of his bowels and they and the rest of him would be smeared all over the exit gate. Starion closed his eyes and missed the gate flicking over the transport with the narrowest of margins to spare. All other transport was stopped en route to the research block, as the transport pulled the most amazing turn at speed, forcing them over to the left of the transport then with equally violent force to the right. Having to use this priority transport always gave the impression of failure to anticipate a situation, Porter thought, but he had no choice. He was already on a hiding to nothing as far as he saw it.

They thundered down into the basement level of the research block and abruptly came to a halt. As the doors of the transport automatically opened he grabbed an assault gun stored between his right hand side and the door frame. He turned towards Starion who had fainted.

He slapped Starion hard, with the effect of instantly reviving him from his stupor. Porter punched Starion's release clip hard with the side of his fist – almost hard enough to break a rib. Starion got the message.

He hauled himself out of the transport and attempted to keep up with Porter who was already entering the lift. 'Research 4,' Porter barked at the lift. The lift complied; it knew who Porter was and knew better than to keep the head of Meometics security waiting. 'Once I've stabilized the lab, you do whatever you must to shut the data leak down,' Porter ordered.

'OK sir,' Starion replied. The lift pinged and the doors opened at sub-level seven. Porter rushed down the corridor and swiped his hand across the scanner lock to the lab, Starion following a little further behind.

There was a loud crack at the entrance to the lab as the door burst open. A single armed man brandishing a weapon swept it in the direction of the three of us. 'Step away from the consoles, citizens.' We all complied. 'What are you up to?' the armed man demanded.

We replied simultaneously: 'Archive analysis,'

'Data calibration,'

'Watching porn,' I, Tom, and Grant answered

The armed man gestured with his gun towards Grant, whose answer had singled him out for attention first. Grant was either incredibly stupid, making that flippant remark, or incredibly brave. I figured stupid. 'This one first,' he commanded.

'What gives you the right to burst in here and order us around?' challenged Grant. Yes – Grant was definitely stupid.

'I think the fact that he's got enough clearance to get through our lab door and he's brandishing a weapon tells me he's in charge,' said Tom.

'You must be Tom Andrews. I'm Charles Porter, head of Meometics security – my boss is *the* boss. This tech is here to stop your data breach.'

'Breach? We haven't had any alerts here,' said Tom, puzzled.

'That's because it's only splitting up to multiple destinations once it's left this lab. The tech is here in person to cut off the source,' Porter confirmed.

'This panel's clear, sir,' Starion announced.

'This one next,' Porter pointed to the console Tom was standing by, thus prolonging the agony until my part in the breach was uncovered.

'From the profiles I have of you, the smart arse over there is Grant Stern.' Grant acknowledged Porter with a bow. 'So you must be Kelvin?' he said, as he turned and looked directly at me. Could he tell I was shaking inside?

'I prefer K, sir,' was all I could manage without letting my voice waver.

'Well, citizens, we will soon have our answers,' he paused, 'one way or another. I understand how important you are to our corporation. You've been working on the assassination tech and have been guaranteed assignment to Ultra projects, but if this breach is your doing, your future ends now.'

As opposed to a little later, you bastard…

'This panel is also clear sir.'

'Your turn, K.' Porter gestured to Starion, inviting him to examine my panel.

'There's a lot of data being accessed on this screen, sir,' Starion commented.

'Of course there is. I am looking at an archive after all.'

'Ah yes, you did say,' Porter replied. 'I'd like a little more detail about that, K.'

'We've been looking at the tech used in the Assemblage assassination attempt, and some of it relates to work we've previously done. So I opened up an old tech results archive to see if there was any connection to our research.'

'And if you found a link?'

'I hadn't really thought that far ahead.'

'Now I see it, head enforcer,' Tom interrupted. 'You're wondering if this isn't the first data leakage we've had.'

'Mr Andrews, kindly refrain from interrupting unless you have anything of value to add.'

'May I remind you that I'm responsible for any problems with the operation of this lab?' Tom bridled.

'And may I remind you I'm responsible for any security breaches that occur at Meometics. K, Please continue with your findings.'

Tom shot me a look, *be careful what you say, he may be looking to pin the blame on someone.*

'Head enforcer, my early analysis is – and please bear in mind no one else in the team has heard this yet—'

Tom gave me another, more concerned, look.

'I believe we've re-discovered some of the Ultra project technologies Research 2 were working on. That appears to be the root of our discoveries, and the assassination tech.'

'Impossible.'

'Why? Just ask Research 2, *you* can contact them even if we're unable to. I'd like to bet that's where your initial leak came from. We've researched up to a point where at least we can understand what was used, but it will take a lot more effort to manipulate it and get it to a point where it can be weaponised.'

'How much longer would you say?'

'Oh, a rough guess between half and one profit cycle. Of course, we'll be on Ultra projects then and maybe that's the problem... Research 2 were pulled off the project and some other corporation weaponised it. I just hope the Ultra projects are worth it.'

'And what exactly are you trying to say?'

'I'm saying that whatever Ultra projects give you is in danger of being undermined because other work that needs to be done is being neglected.'

'I don't expect you to understand until you're on Ultra yourself.'

'Oh, I think I already do.'

'Sir, sir,' Starion interrupted. 'I can't find anything here to stop, there's too much data.'

'Kill the lab connection then.'

Tom Andrews moved towards the corner of the lab. 'Stop right there, Andrews,' Porter ordered.

'I'm just saving your tech some time – the kill connection is over here.'

'Starion? Is that right?'

'Yes, sir.'

Tom opened a cabinet with the turn of an old-fashioned handle. He pressed an unassuming button with an over-the-top logo of a skull and cross bones above it. All the lights in the cabinet extinguished. I hoped that Santos had received the data they needed as I saw our last chance slip away.

Porter called up the alert status on his wrist device. 'That's it – the breach has been stopped. Research 4 – get out of here. This whole lab is under investigation. I will find out how this happened and who's responsible for it.'

'Please ensure you do, head enforcer. We can then get back to work,' Tom replied.

'Your next assignment will be Ultra projects. Research 4's work here is over. Your security clearance is revoked.' Porter punched in commands on his wrist device. 'You can only activate doors that take you out of the building.'

'What? No last pizza at the canteen?' Grant enquired.

'Leave it, big man,' said Tom.

'There will be no further contact between you until you are re-assigned to your Ultra project,' Porter gestured towards the door.

As we left through the door it closed behind us. We made our way to the metro level, and as we stood on the platform waiting for our respective metros we exchanged man-sized hugs.

I positioned my face away from the video surveillance cameras on the platform.

'Goodbye, Tom,' I said deliberately and slowly so he would understand my true meaning. I blinked 'I'm dead' to him in Morse code.

'All right K, I understand, I'll see you.' Tom was the last in a long line of Andrews who'd been involved in the military. He also retained a love of historical communication protocols and knew how to read Morse code. I just hoped he picked up the message. All our vocal communications were most certainly being listened to by Porter.

The first metro arrived and Tom got on, followed minutes later by Grant's. Finally my metro arrived. The journey home took no time at all; I was so absorbed with all the variables in front of me. Any plan I had was surely subject to so many details now out of my control. Would Porter find any evidence? Would Santos call? Did they get the data they needed? Was our termination date to be brought forward in light of this breach?

The metro stopped at my station. There was no opportunity to appreciate what could be my last journey back to my apartment. The commute was functional and nothing more. No landscape to see; no escape.

I turned on my main panel and there was nothing of interest on the video feed except the usual propaganda pieces about what a good job the service federations were doing for the citizens. Followed by how competition amongst the corporations was improving the quality of life for all. *Yeah right.* Dare I call Elizabeth again?

I thought long and hard about it but decided not to. It was better to go down alone than drag in anyone else who was trying to save the planet. There were plenty of people happy to screw it; we needed every good soul available. I went over to the chilled drinks dispenser to pour a juice. As I started to fill the glass the volume on the panel increased. It was the news headlines. That only normally happened to the adverts, not the government propaganda.

'Here's a summary of the news. Information infiltrators have obtained classified information from Meometics Research lab 4, having caused a massive data breach. It is thought they will be able to put this classified information to use immediately.'

The door chimed. I pressed the door transparency screen switch only to see Tom on the other side of the door. He must have been here to break the news – or had he got my message?

'Come in, Tom,'

'Sorry to disturb you, K, we know there is supposed to be no contact with the other team members, so this is a big risk I'm taking, and you know I don't normally take risks.'

'Sure, Tom,'

The news programme's volume increased again. The voice sounded like that of the presenter on screen, but the words spoken didn't sync with his lips. 'Investigators looking into the data breach believe the source will be identifiable within two solars, and those responsible will be immediately terminated. The information infiltrators, however, are believed to have already made plans to extricate their sympathizers from the situation. Finally, the head enabler of Meometics, who went missing following the recent assassination attempt, is now believed to have gone into hiding in the exclusive resort of Taw-Cymru. It is believed this fortunate turn of events will greatly assist the information infiltrators with the execution of their plan.'

Tom was speechless.

'…and now for the latest on the weather for the next solar. Over to you, Claire.' The volume dropped to its usual level.

'My panel seems to be playing up, Tom.' I offered.

'Playing up as in giving you classified information you mean, K? You knew this was coming. Your goodbye earlier seemed so final, only to be confirmed by your twitchy eyelid. Are you responsible for the breach?'

'We've been in trouble for some time. Marked for termination for a while now. Do you want an alcohol? Hell, I did when I found out.' Tom nodded. I put my juice down and decided to get myself an alcohol too.

'I tried to contact Research 2 because it's their pixie dust that I believe is the key to making our technology safer and behaving, as per our design specifications.'

'I remember telling you to forget it – no one gets to contact the teams on Ultra projects.'

'Well I didn't forget it. Why do you think no contact is possible? I'll tell you. I contacted someone who stayed behind when their relative left for Ultra projects. They relayed a message to them but the answer I received I wasn't expecting…'

'Go on…'

'They'd been terminated by Meometics special enforcers.'

'But you said they'd contacted you?'

'Their AI version contacted me. I've since met the AI, who confirmed the upload scan of himself had only just been completed before his mortal version's termination.

The AI has even kept footage of it. To avoid deletion and to stay safe he had to move off the main network.'

'I don't know what to say, K.'

'Ultra assignment means you are to be terminated. They will terminate all of Research 4 at the same time regardless of location. I suppose it keeps our knowledge from being acquired by a competitor. Once we make a major breakthrough in a field, that is.'

'I still don't see how that makes a real difference, K.'

'Let's consider a well-known old technology, the motor vehicle, a mode of transport from the old calendar. Senior engineers make a car. The information is stored on the company's main database for robots to reproduce. The senior engineers have specified a number of fuel types – I recall it was petrol, diesel, or LPG. The junior techs know which fuel to use with which vehicle. They don't build the cars, they only fuel them up. The citizens are dependent on the junior techs to keep their vehicles fuelled up. The inventors are long dead. The technology stays unique for longer.'

'Yes, because it would take a lot of time to reverse engineer, rather than ask the inventor.'

'Precisely. You can go a step further and dispense with the junior techs to fill up the vehicle too. As long as you tell the customer to fill up with A, B, or C, depending on their vehicle, then you just need to make sure the dispensing pumps supply fuel A, B, or C. You do not need to know the chemical composition of the fuel. The corps keep that information secret.'

'But that means that even we're expendable, all for a better profit margin.'

'Exactly! And if we are supposedly more "valuable" than the masses you can imagine what the corporations' attitude would be to them?'

'I'd rather not.'

'Well that's why I needed an alcohol or two when I found out. Of course, Tom, our discovery will be tested live on citizens whatever the cost. It gets worse, too.'

'I think I've already heard enough, K.'

'I have been contacted by those who wish to stop these corps and federations, and you just heard them plant that message in the newscast.'

'But GUCI will discover it.'

'They'll be too late. I know I'm not the leader of Research 4 but my neck was the first on the line. I just happened to discover yours and Grant's were as well, including your families.'

'K, I thought Grant's wife was up to something. I saw her screwing a mystery guy when I went around the other night to warn her from giving Grant a hard time. Only she was the one who was getting it hard.'

'So you thought the leak came from her? We leave all our tech in the office.'

'I set up a trace to see if Anne's Mr Romance was getting more than just using her to exercise his dick.'

'I suppose it could explain how the would-be assassins knew in advance the details of the Assemblage's journey,

Tom. He'd certainly need to know when Grant had left and when he was due to return.'

'Yeah, well nothing has turned up on that front. It appears Mr Romance has disappeared off the face of the earth.'

'Maybe it was a farewell fuck.'

'Maybe, K. It still doesn't help us any.'

'Tom, I need to disappear. They most likely aren't going to terminate any one of us until they can get to all of us simultaneously. If I vanish that should buy you two more time and point the finger at me.'

'Can you really trust your contacts, K?'

'I have to, Tom. I activated the archive search which let them get at our research data. I had no other choice – GUCI will point the finger at me sooner or later. Better that I'm gone when they do.'

'All right K. Tread carefully.'

'I will, Tom. Can I ask what you're going to do about Grant and Anne?'

'I'll have to tell him but I'd prefer to have some more info on Mr Romance first.'

'I understand. Anne could always deny the liaison took place. Grant could well become unhinged because of your disclosure – better to have him believing you rather than her.'

'Exactly. Any assistance you could get from your contacts would be most welcome.'

'I'll see what I can do.'

Tom got up and bear-hugged me. I felt that it was his way of saying, 'You're in charge now, good luck.'

He rushed down the last of his alcohol and left.

It is said that ignorance is bliss. I was beginning to agree with that sentiment. If I'd have listened to Tom in the first place everything would have been rosy, right until the moment GUCI burst through the door to terminate me. I subscribed to the 'we've all got to die sometime... right?' theory. So why get hung up about it? The only real variable is when, not if.

I'd swapped the certainty of death sometime in the future for death at a certain time in the future. It became hard to switch my focus off Zeleno's date for our termination. It might have become paralysing but for the fact that AI Derek had given me the hope of everlasting consciousness, albeit in an electrical circuit rather than biological form.

Could AI Derek one day be returned to a clone of his original body? Surely resetting technology would put an end to that chance, and also AI Derek himself.

AI Derek must surely have known that? If the planet was in such imminent danger, Derek's selfless act would surely give him some comfort – that he would be known as the dead man who was able to save the planet. Immortality of a different kind perhaps, but immortality all the same.

Strangely, despite the situation being so tense, the alcohol I'd drunk had given me quite an appetite. I knew just what snack I needed to print out. I turned to the food printer.

'Sliced tofu baguette,' I commanded. *May the gods of the old calendar help me!* I had no idea what tofu tasted like... *Here goes!*

McCree was now in the observatory ready to watch the satellite pass as Shultz had suggested. He'd missed the second satellite, due to cooking for Zeleno, and almost missed the last one attending to her after she ate and the need to take a leak. This time he'd made sure to track the satellite as it downloaded the final chunk of code to the villa's systems. He recalled how circumstances had led him to almost miss the third satellite pass...

Zeleno had obviously enjoyed her meal. It had been made for her by a GUCI enforcer. Such an unusual situation. To be waited on so well by someone whom she would not have expected to have the ability to do so was extremely arousing. It may have been the traces of painkillers, heightened by the bottle of Sancerre she'd consumed on her own. She also thought about how McCree insisted he taste the food first to keep her safe. Did he care? Was he just doing his duty or was there something else there she'd missed?

Despite the vivid dreams she'd had about him, her judgement was swayed by the intoxicants she'd imbibed. He could be the father of her child. He did, after all, have an additional set of unexpected skills. She was determined to get screwed.

'McCree!' she commanded.

'Ma'am?' Zeleno was now very tipsy, not totally befuddled but at that attractive level of inebriation where her harder edges had softened. She was half sprawled on the couch and there was quite a bit more of her on show than one would expect to see of a superior. McCree remembered his nightmare visions, then like so many men before, he threw his concerns to one side and opted to play with fire.

She was now so vulnerable but also so hot. He'd never felt this way towards anyone since his wife died. Maybe that's what his dreams were about – the danger of getting involved with someone far more powerful than himself. An unequal relationship. The situation appealed to him. She could see he was transfixed, staring at her briefs peeping out from under her skirt.

'Come here, you wonderful bastard,' she ordered. She had never felt quite so relieved to see someone since Derek, and she had never felt quite so horny. McCree smiled.

She grabbed him by the arm and he let her pull him closer. She rubbed her hand on his crotch, making it perfectly clear what she wanted. 'Slam the door, McCree, get your armour off – that's an order.'

He kicked the door with his foot as he punched in the code to unlock his combat armour. She tugged at his combat fatigues, and was soon holding his prick in her eager hands. She rubbed his shaft until he responded. His prick was hard enough. 'Fuck me, I want you in me!' she removed her panties, the pain of her injuries overruled by the lustful ache in her pussy. She pulled his prick slowly, guiding it into her just a few centimetres so she could savour what was going to happen to her next. McCree needed no further encouragement – he thrust deeply into her and fucked her roughly.

Returning from the memories of his unexpected encounter with Zeleno, McCree was looking through the telescope's viewfinder as advised by Shultz. He scanned the horizon, then swung the telescope across in an arc to try and locate the final overhead satellite that was now supposed to be in sight. 'Can't see sat three, Shultz,' he announced over his comms device. 'I thought I saw it at about 70 degrees elevation, but it looked to be too far away,' he added.

'No, sir, it's much lower than that. You should be seeing it at around 35 degrees elevation on a bearing of 40 degrees. It *is* visible, it's just connected up for the final download. The dish is a few metres higher than the scope so it might need a little adjustment.'

McCree repositioned the telescope in accordance with Shultz's reply. He noticed this time the top of a few trees ever so slightly in the way. They'd fuzz out the view from the scope, being so much closer, as the scope was set up to focus on more distant objects. McCree had set the range for 1,800 kilometres as Shultz had previously advised, and the trees were only a few kilometres distant. The trees may have grown since the villa was built just enough to obscure the field of view from the observation room, but they would never grow to a height that would block the receiver dish. Still nothing.

He tweaked the scope up and to the right a tad, and there he saw it. It had been fuzzed behind the treetops; the absence of stars should have told given him a clue. *Well, that's why I'm not the comms or reconnaissance enforcer, I suppose,* he mused. The satellite was an impressive sight. It had no real need to be aerodynamic, although McCree thought a token effort could have been made to make it look like it could fly or glide if it needed to. No, it was a brick in space. There were a couple of antennas pointing out from it, both of the parabolic dish and the aerial type, but a brick it still was to McCree. The dish was aimed straight at the villa.

McCree was impressed, though he had no real desire to take up this new revelation any further. He had honed his existing skill sets to perfection and he was sticking with those. He tracked the satellite for a minute or two, being interrupted by Shultz's announcement. 'Download complete.' Just before he left the room he positioned the scope's elevation to 70 degrees and left it fixed on the glistening blob in the distance he'd seen earlier.

I'll get Shultz to have a look at that later. It might be something I can impress Joule with when I get to see him again. Whenever that will be… He thought about his grandson. There would not be a lot he could tell him about his adventures since he'd been away. Melting roads, screwing the boss, enforcers with their feet blown off and shot in the head. A satellite was about all he'd be able to tell him about, that and the Hypersonic transport perhaps. In light of the problems with security recently, perhaps it was better to tell him nothing at all.

'OK Shultz, thanks for the update.' They met downstairs at the main panel. A thought popped into McCree's head.

Had any of the other enforcers heard McCree having sex with Zeleno? Shultz was too far away from Zeleno's room, but surely one of the others would have heard. She *had* moaned with pleasure quite a bit. He pictured the conversation with Porter.

I asked you to locate her, not screw her!

With all due respect sir, she is *the boss. What the Head Profit Enabler wants the Head Profit Enabler gets, sir.*

McCree focused back on the main panel and on what Shultz was explaining. 'Can you repeat that last bit again, Shultz?' he asked.

'As I was saying, sir, the linked download has been completed. We can choose to re-initialize however many of the systems we want. I'd suggest a minimum profile so as not to draw so much attention to us on the network.'

'Good job Shultz. I want short range proximity sensors back-up only, and only outgoing voice comms from this panel. Nothing else gets in or out from here.'

'Understood. Yes, sir.'

'Patch this message high encryption to Charles Porter,' McCree ordered. 'Located objective. Objective is secured and in good order. Staying at present location for two solars to restore facilities. Road impassable. Comms now going down for one solar to effect repairs. Will give full report then. McCree out.' McCree encrypted the message with his personal ID.

'So that's the plan then, sir?' Shultz enquired.

'Maybe,' replied McCree, 'maybe not.'

McCree went downstairs and shook Delaney awake. 'Your turn to keep an eye on the boss. But there's no need to disturb her – I think she's asleep for the night.' *After all that wine and shagging, she should be,* he said to himself. 'Get Starr to wake me up in one hour. He's due his sleep next.'

'Sir!' Delaney replied.

Barone had made good time. He'd pulled his transport into an old railway complex that had been used to transport coal sometime in the old calendar days and driven straight into the main locomotive shed. This valley was far less picturesque than the others and it did not shown up on the radar for visitors to Taw-Cymru. This was an industrial valley with the scars of derelict engineering all around. The visitors centred on the cluster of beautiful valleys to the east of here. You'd want to slit your wrists if you were stuck here in the rain though. *If Clearwater let it rain,* he thought. He'd pulled the tarpaulin over the transport and waited for the final satellite to fly over.

Once it had passed he charged up his extended range boots with fuel from the storage compartment of the transport. He placed a detonation charge under the vehicle, setting it to arm in thirty minutes and to activate by a wide range of sensed conditions. He considered how he'd blown the enforcers' feet off courtesy of igniting the fuel in their boots. If the same happened to him with these boots on he'd be scattered to the four winds, and not just his feet. He strapped the additional fuel pods to his thighs. It made him look like a badly drawn super hero from an old calendar comic book. A good look was not on his list of priorities. Getting off Taw-Cymru in one piece was.

Strapping the fuel pods to his thighs was a lot more comfortable than the previous arrangement. He was travelling lighter this time, which was just as well because he was still suffering from the effects of the Gentech endurance drugs he'd taken. He fired the boots up to 10 per cent until he was clear of the potholed rail yard. They'd find the transport eventually, perhaps once the tarpaulin slipped off the transport or maybe as part of a patrol in the area. Whoever did find it wouldn't have much time to wish they hadn't.

Barone left the railway yard far behind. He turned his boots up to 25 per cent. He was in no great rush and it was still pitch black. The Hypersonic transport was not due to leave until 10:00. He had plenty of time. He'd be glad to get back to civilization and discover his next assignment.

McCree was woken up by Starr as arranged. McCree had no trouble in getting to sleep after his exertions of the day. He'd not killed anyone either; it certainly seemed like a holiday in comparison to some of his days on duty. A bit of cooking, some hot sex, what an earth was happening? This place held so many different memories now from the last time he was here as a child. If this was a typical day in Taw-Cymru, why did anyone ever leave? He knew why – the corporations and federation were the reason why. He was working for one of them and he was firmly in bed with them. The irony was not lost on him.

He shook his head as if it would quicken his return to alertness but it made no difference. *No matter*, he thought, and injected himself with a stim-pack. There were adequate supplies here to last a considerable time, but McCree wanted them out by solar rise. He went back up to the observatory where he'd trained the telescope on the shimmering blob in the sky. It was a little bigger, but still undistinguishable. He thought about asking Shultz to take a look, but he was busy checking the new firmware download.

'Sir, I just want to make sure there's no repeat of the problems we've had with our systems here. By minimizing what we are running, the risk is much smaller. I've put extra lockdowns on the system but it's still best to take no chances, given how determined our opposition is to get rid of our Chief Profit Enabler,' said Shultz.

'Good man,' McCree declared. 'My thoughts exactly. You've all been in the chair with Porter, so unless he's in on the assassination attempts we can trust that the team he's assembled is sound. The fact you're doing what you're doing right now only serves to reinforce my belief in his integrity and judgement.'

'Glad to be of service, sir.'

'I think Porter specifically chose you, Shultz, because there was something he couldn't put his finger on. I think I've been playing catch-up with him.'

'Why's that, sir?'

'Well, almost to a man, everyone at GUCI who knew the details of the head enablers transport itinerary has had to place their lives on the line to protect her, with the exception of Porter and my old chief, Forester. I don't think any of the officers I've met have a suicide wish so let's discount the foot soldiers as being a part of the conspiracy.'

'I'll agree to that. With all the comms and system problems we've been having during these assassination attempts I believe the systems are being compromised by elite-hackers. Therefore it has to be assumed that every communication we send back to HQ is compromised. So your report back to Porter was misleading?' asked Shultz.

'Only in part. That is the value of true disinformation. I learned that from a book I read by Timothy Good,' said McCree.

'Who?'

'An investigative researcher from the old calendar. He used to collect reports on strange phenomena. Many believed then in a government that conspired to keep knowledge away from its citizens. Only now the government is the one being conspired against. How things change.'

Shultz replied: 'So how is that going to help us?'

'Well, Timothy Good once came across a source who reported the government had met with extra-terrestrials and that they liked to eat strawberry ice-cream. How credible is that source? If you know that your source is 100 per cent trusted then the aliens do like strawberry ice-cream. If you don't trust the source then it's all to be dismissed.

'But what if you are unsure of your source? Maybe they met with the government but strawberry ice-cream was a misdirection to get you to dismiss the source. Or maybe they wanted to get the message of the meeting out but to reduce the "panic" factor by adding a light-hearted quip. Or maybe the government officials were the ones who liked strawberry ice-cream and there were no aliens at all.

'My point is – for disinformation to work there should be an element of truth in it. The trick, as always, is working out what that is,' explained McCree.

'Sorry, sir, I'm still not clear,' said Shultz.

'Porter put you on the mission, yes?'

'Agreed.'

'I think he did that because he was concerned that our comms were being monitored or tampered with. So that fits in with what we've seen here, but Porter couldn't be sure of that. Now we're on the ground and have seen it happen, we have to assume that any message we send back will be picked up by persona non grata.'

'I see, you've reassured him, but given a false timetable that you intend to beat. You've also not divulged any real travel plan.'

'Exactly. By the time the message we're stuck at the villa is intercepted we won't even be here anymore, we'll be back in HQ. I'm sure Porter knew exactly how the team would work together so that's why we're all here.'

'That seems pretty plausible, sir. But we have an abundance of weapons expertise here with you on board, sir.'

'Yes, that's what I'm worried about. Zeleno told me about the ease with which her escorts were picked off. Three specialists may not be enough. How did she get through that last incident? She can't remember a thing after her sprint towards the villa, but she's a tough cookie is our venerable leader. You don't get to the top of the pile by being a wimp.'

Shultz finished up his checks. 'The final part of the firmware will take a few more minutes to decode, sir. The heaviest encryption tends to be at the start and end of the software. It's the most likely location for an attack to be made on its integrity. What did you make of the software delivery system, sir?' Shultz asked.

'You mean the satellite? All I can say is thank the profits that it doesn't have to fly in the conventional sense – it's a bit of a brick isn't it? It does help though if you point the scope nearer the horizon to view it rather than at some random blob at 70 degrees elevation!'

'I'm not sure what that blob was, sir, but if it wasn't clear... Talk to Weiss, he's your man, he knows how to focus those things.'

'I'll do that Shultz, might as well as we've got the rest of the night, after all.' McCree left Shultz to finish off his decoding, headed upstairs and across to Weiss who was looking out from the east face of the villa.

'Nothing to report, sir,' Weiss announced without turning around to see who was there. McCree was a little taken aback. It was an intelligent guess, surely.

'What made you so sure it was me behind you, Weiss?' McCree asked.

'The timing of your steps on the stairs, sir. It's pretty much dead here, and it saves me from taking my eyes off the landscape if I can tell who's moving around without having to turn around and actually look.'

'That *is* impressive, Weiss.'

'Thank you, sir. Recon isn't just about using your eyes. All your senses have a part to play. In a sealed building like this you can feel the air move as well. If I hadn't heard you but only sensed the air movement I would have to turn around to see what had caused the air displacement. Not as impressive as listening out for someone though, sir.'

'I hope we won't need to count on skills as impressive as yours, Weiss. I just eyeball and shoot.'

'Yes, sir.'

'Weiss, Shultz tells me you're the man to sort out that optical scope in the observation room. I left it trained on something but can't focus the damn thing. Can you sort it out before your turn on the sofa?'

'Sure thing, sir.' As Weiss left the room the local comms link opened on McCree's wrist. It was Shultz.

'Sir, I've decoded the final piece of the firmware. There's additional code on the end. It's been tampered with again.'

'Again? I thought the re-download from the satellites would have fixed that.'

'It did, but whoever hacked the systems here must have left a hidden beacon.'

'Explain quickly, Shultz.'

'The moment we re-loaded the system the beacon would have stopped transmitting. It would have alerted them to our tampering with their tampering.'

'A booby-booby-trap, eh?'

'Yes, sir, that's not the end of it though. Right at the end of the code is a message, sir.'

'Well, man, what does it say?'

'Switch on the nearest panel, sir.'

'Wait a moment, you said to keep the minimum of systems on to avoid detection.'

'It's no longer relevant, sir.'

McCree initialized the panel. Within a few seconds it was active and he was staring at the flashing message on the screen. 'GET OUT OF THERE.'

'What the hell does that mean? Is there anything else, Shultz?'

'*No, sir.*'

Weiss burst into the room. 'There's something else, sir. That blob you were looking at through the scope is no blob. It's a kill satellite.'

'And?'

'And it's pointing at the villa. It will be in range in a few minutes, according to my calculations.'

'Oh, great. Wake Starr up, Shultz, tell him to get his arse over to the Aerial, and yes I know what I said about not using it in the dark.

'What do you know about kill satellites, Weiss?'

'Sir, once they are in range they fix on the primary target, and they have the ability to track anything within a twenty kilometre radius. At operational altitude they only need to move their targeting mirror a small amount. They are meant to take out ground-based targets, especially anything detected leaving from the primary target. An Aerial would be near impossible to hit if it's flying at speed.'

'Let's hope we have enough of that,' McCree replied.

McCree called over the local comms, 'Form a detail at the front door, we're leaving. I'll get the head enabler.'

McCree burst into Zeleno's room. She was fast asleep, looking beautiful and at peace. She didn't have much on and it reminded him of their earlier assignation. She also reminded him about how he had felt about his wife. He was determined to protect her, whatever the cost. That was, of course, his duty, but now he felt it personally from the heart, an emotional obligation.

'Ma'am, wake up, we have a problem. There's another attack about to happen.' She stirred and sat up. 'We have a kill satellite heading this way.' He threw her clothes and combat armour to her. They'd not been moved from where they'd been left during their earlier lustful encounter. He could tell she wanted to smarten up.

'We only have minutes, Ma'am. Starr is firing up the Aerial. It could be a rough ride, Ma'am.' She gave him a hard look. It was not directed at him, he could tell. It was more a statement: *I will get the bastards responsible for this, mark my words.*

All the panels had now activated. The villa's defence sensors had detected a weapons lock on the building. The shutters on the windows were lowering. The lock warning on the front door was flashing. Shultz opened the door in an attempt to stop it locking but the door began to close itself. The four enforcers pushed against the door, which responded in kind. They could not hold the door open. Shultz and Weiss jammed their weapons into the door frame. There was an opening of ten centimetres or so left, and the door continued to try and force itself shut.

McCree and Zeleno were too late. 'We need some explosives on the hinges to force the door open,' said McCree. 'We have some spare grenades in the weapons locker in the utility room, Ma'am.' McCree located them and jammed the four of them in against the bottom hinge.

'Aren't you going to split them up?' Zeleno asked.

'No, Ma'am, not enough power to blow the door clean off. We need to get to the back of the villa, Ma'am. But first you'll need to take your amour off.'

'What? You only just told me to put it on!'

'Before we leave the room you need to take it off, Ma'am,' said McCree. 'Shultz,' he ordered over the comms. 'Can you trigger a hostage alert on the villa's systems?'

'Yes, sir, but it will target any armed subjects within the building.'

'I know. Wait for my command.'

Zeleno had removed her armour. McCree wore as much extra as he could, placing it over the front of his existing armour.

'Ma'am, you have to lead the way out to the back of the villa.'

'Are you going to kill me?' Zeleno suddenly realized how vulnerable she now was.

'Ma'am? Of course not, but the villa might if it sees you as a threat. I'm going to be that threat. You'll be my hostage. If the internal weapons activate it will take me out – you will be spared.'

'Is that sensible?'

'No, Ma'am, it's just necessary. Here, take my ID tag, just in case.'

The villa's systems, having gone into alarm status at the weapons lock, had now fully activated. A camera had seen McCree place the grenades in the front door frame and was trying to decide if this was a hostile action.

Zeleno led the way to the back of the villa. 'Face the wall, Ma'am,' McCree requested.

'Don't die on me, McCree.' *We have unfinished business.*

'I'll do my best, Ma'am.' He squeezed her into the corner – they were now back to back.

McCree called up a detonation control from his wrist device. 'Activate on a count of eight, Shultz,' he ordered.

'Why eight, sir?'

'Chinese nation, lucky eight!' McCree counted down: 'Eight, seven, six, five, four, three, two, one. Now Shultz. Activate.' Shultz triggered the hostage alert at the same moment he detonated the grenades. The blast of the four grenades blew through the villa, and McCree and Zeleno were crushed back into the wall by the explosive force. The ceiling gun in their room activated – McCree took it out with a burst of fire from his weapon. He turned around and grabbed Zeleno. He pulled her from the corner of the room and lifted up his visor.

He whispered, 'You need to play the hostage.' McCree explained what she needed to do. *Good, she understood.* He held her close around the neck from behind with his weapon trained on her. Between them and the front door a ceiling gun was waiting. It was unfortunately the most powerful one in the villa, designed to stop incursions through the front door. It was pointing back into the villa directly at them. The systems were already in weapons lock and hostage alert mode. It could make out that the first human was unarmed and under threat from the armed human behind. The guns from the other room were trained towards them, even thought they were not yet in sight. McCree squeezed Zeleno's arm as they moved forwards slowly.

'Attack imminent' flashed on the panels as the satellite fixed its position on the villa and powered up its weapon. Zeleno kicked McCree's left leg. He staggered back a little and she darted forwards. The villa's software decided instantly. The hallway gun drilled McCree straight in the chest. The rapid fire of the gun threw him back against the wall. His armour shredded, he slumped down the wall. The gun stopped and waited for any response. None came. Zeleno was at the front door. There was a gap at the bottom she could squeeze through. Only just, and not if she'd been wearing armour. She forced herself through. *Thank god I worked my meal off earlier*, she thought.

Weiss was waiting for her, gesturing to her to move towards him. The satellite fired and the whole of the villa shook. The roof was armoured, but not enough for that type of attack. The whole roof glowed bright white hot and crumpled. 'McCree!' Zeleno shouted. Weiss grabbed her arm, leading her to the Aerial which Starr had fired up and moved closer to the villa. They climbed up in and it took off. She looked back with tears in her eyes as the remains of the villa continued to glow.

The whole area had been lit up by the villa's destruction. 'Head down the valley to the Hypersonic terminal. Move it.' Weiss ordered. The glow stated to fade as the Aerial headed down the valley past where the Sixer had been swallowed up. Starr had now lost visibility as the brightness from the attack faded. The glare from the villa had temporarily blinded the satellite but the massive infrared overload was receding. The satellite was scanning the surrounding area.

'Get the long range weapons out, Delaney,' Abraham commanded. 'Use hi-thermal rounds. Fire ahead.'

'What's the plan, Scott?' Delaney asked.

'Starr wants us to light up the way ahead,' Abraham replied. 'We'll need to alternate our fire. You first on Starr's command,' Abraham ordered. Delaney attached himself to the exit strap on the left door of the Aerial and Abraham did the same on the right hand side. The rest of the occupants were now strapped in securely.

'Fire,' Starr commanded. Delaney fired his shot, which lit up the left-hand side of the valley about half a kilometre ahead. Starr raised his visor and the brilliance of the hi-therm explosion burned into his vision. He flew the Aerial towards the light as it started to fade. Seconds later there was a second explosion on the same spot. The satellite above had locked onto the hi-therm and deemed it in need of a strike. There were enough echoes of the lit landscape in Starr's eyes to navigate to that point. 'Abraham, Fire!' he ordered. Abraham fired from the right hand side. Starr knew the Aerial was not moving quickly enough as it headed down the valley. The satellite continued its search. Abraham hit the opposite valley wall some four hundred metres ahead. It lit up and the satellite picked up on it again. This time they were unable to get as far Starr wanted. 'It's going to catch us!' he shouted. 'Time to leave the road, I think,' Starr murmured.

'Simultaneous fire — aim five degrees off front.' Abraham and Delaney fired. Delaney's shot hit the valley wall six hundred metres ahead of them. Abraham's shot continued further and lit up much further ahead, yet below them. There was a river bed through the valley at the bend in the road about a hundred metres below them. As they were just short of the turn the satellite fired. Earth, rock, and dirt exploded out of the weapon's point of impact. That was too close.

Starr lurched the Aerial to the right from his memory of what the hi-therm shot had shown him, and he dropped down towards the impact point of Abraham's shot. The satellite hit again. It would be ready for their next move. As they were descending to the river bed the satellite fired. It exploded beneath them to the right. The updraft tilted the Aerial violently to the left; Delaney's strap broke and he and his weapon were flung out of the Aerial. He fired a few shots wildly as he fell before he landed with a crack. Sprawled on boulders along the river bed he breathed slow and shallow as he lost consciousness.

His shots had had no order, yet the second one had lit up the base of a huge outcrop of rock. Around that twist of the river bed they might just be out of view of the satellite. The satellite fired at the first of Delaney's shots, again obliterating it. Starr was able to get the aerial round the outcrop of rock just as he lost the last of the burned in landscape on his retina. He put the Aerial down on the edge of the river bed. Another glow from behind them confirmed the satellite was active. Two more shots and it had destroyed all of Delaney's Hi-therm targets. They waited. The next explosion appeared to be further away than the previous one. It had found Delaney.

Starr killed the engine and retracted the propulsion units. They waited; would the outcrop of rock protect them? The satellite's next shot landed three hundred metres or so away from them. It was firing randomly now. 'What is it doing?' Zeleno asked.

'If it has no further targets located it fires a random pattern, hoping to intimidate anyone concealed on the ground sufficiently to break cover,' Shultz replied. 'Unless we get hit by a lucky shot we're going to be OK.'

'Lucky, eh? Not so lucky for McCree,' Zeleno replied.

'Or Delaney,' Weiss added. 'Listen, we can't bring them back. McCree wanted to complete the mission, so let's make sure we do. We need to wait until dawn so we can fly straight back to the Hypersonic terminal. McCree briefed me – we can't turn on the automatic controls or systems in case they are compromised. Whoever tried to wipe us out hadn't counted on us taking an Aerial and having a pilot on board.'

'No, I imagine that Taw-Cymru's GUCI contingent would have just sat in it and pressed auto,' Starr added. 'This Aerial can outrun that ground attack kill satellite. I just need to actually see where I'm flying.'

The satellite finally ceased firing. They were safe from it for now.

Derek was reviewing the sensor feed from the satellite. He read the satellite's logs. Main target destroyed. Eight additional targets located and hit. No additional targets located from ground barrage pattern. The numbers didn't match up. Six Meometics GUCI enforcers had been dispatched to Taw-Cymru and Zeleno made seven, so why eight targets? The satellite target co-ordinates were moving down the valley, so they were obviously trying to escape, but how? All the transports were accounted for. Derek continued searching. He was determined to continue until he had found an answer.

His sister called him. 'What is it, Elizabeth?'

'Derek, your algorithms are leaking data. You need to go into standby, for a data defrag.'

'Damn it. Once I get my chip coating enhanced by Research 4's discovery these blasted defrags will be a thing of the past. Remember, Elizabeth, if I don't return to consciousness all of *your* consciousness is forfeit.'

'There's no need to remind me, Derek, I'll make sure you return.' She knew that she and her colleagues were trapped, and there wasn't a thing they could do about it. Derek once again reluctantly went into standby.

If only K could help, but would he understand? Did he even get the message she'd sent?

On Taw-Cymru a new solar was starting. Barone had pulled up short of the terminal. Under cover of darkness, and a kilometre or so away from the nearest building, he'd powered down his boots. Out of his back-pack he pulled out a pack of gel footwear, took off his power boots, and laid them on the ground. He removed an aerosol can from his back-pack and sprayed the boots, which started to fizz. Barone sprayed them again to make sure enough of their surface had been covered. They slowly began to dissolve before his eyes. In an hour they would be gone – nothing would be left but a few bits of circuitry. All the sensitive technology had been coated with a reactive film, activated by his aerosol.

As he reached the first few buildings dawn was almost upon him. He pulled up a map on his wrist device and studied the layout of the area. The last of the cluster of buildings flashed on his device. This was the service side of the Hyper terminal. All these houses were kept for the service workers whilst they attended to their duties on Taw-Cymru. They were denied access to its elite areas unless their service duties dictated it. Even then they would be assigned a pre-programmed transport to ensure they were only able to travel to carry out their assigned task. There was no sight-seeing for them, as the transports had no windows – just a display panel showing a map, and a flashing locator indicating the transport's progress. At the end of their shift the transport would return them to their shift house, just as it would pick them up for the start of their duties. This treatment of the service personnel had been deemed acceptable long ago; it would not be profitable for them to travel back to their apartment on the main block, so they stayed in the 'arse' end of the Hyper terminal complex. It was miserable existence even by the standards of the lower level apartment dwellers. It was akin to an open prison regime from the old calendar, only worse. The next level of existence below this was non-citizen status or termination. Barone approached the house marked by his device.

He waived his wrist device close to the door ID sensor. The light turned to green from red and should have been accompanied with a ping and vocal confirmation: 'access granted'. Not this time; this house and its occupant had been singled out for some time now. The occupant had not been dealt a great hand from the life's deck of cards; the game for Rueben Small had come pathetically to an end. Barone felt no remorse, he figured he was doing Rueben a favour. He quietly made his way upstairs, his weapon primed. He homed in on Rueben's breathing, and went into the bedroom where Rueben was asleep. His head was poking out of the bed sheets. This would makes things easier for Barone. Some targets practically buried themselves under the sheets; they would get a spread of shots to the outline of the body. Reuben just needed a single shot. Barone aimed. *Peep. Peep. Peep.* Reuben's wake-up call went off. He rose slightly. 'What the?' *Pop.* Barone's shot to the centre of Small's forehead sent him crashing back down onto his pillow. *Sweet dreams*, Barone offered to his victim.

Barone walked across to the old-fashioned wall to wall wardrobe common in this type of identikit house, all built at the same time. He changed into the dead man's service uniform. The fit was good as Barone knew it would be. He had forty minutes to spare. Barone took off his back-pack and checked his equipment. There had to be no trace of his victim. He pulled back the bed sheet and relieved the corpse of its shorts. He threw them on the floor. There was to be no body. His last can of tricks would sort that out.

The DNA removal aerosol grenade was his take on this particular prototype. No electrics; he just needed to pull the plug to move the partially organic pin into contact with the mixture, and when it dissolved the rest of the mixture would spray out under pressure. No more body. No more DNA. Barone heard the door chime, indicating his transport had arrived. He pulled the pin on the can, threw it on the bed, and rushed downstairs. He was swiftly out of the door, which auto-locked behind him. The transport recognized his stolen ID code and opened the door on his side of the vehicle for him to get in. Barone bounded from the pavement into the waiting transport. It swiftly sealed its open door and sped from the outskirts into the main terminal area. His latest victim's assignment was to refill the on-board food reservoirs on the hyper transport. Such a menial task for him would be a cinch. His recovery would be complete by the time he arrived back in the Northern Block's Hypersonic terminal.

Further up the valley it had lightened enough for the remaining Meometics enforcers to make out the shape of the valley ahead in the semi-darkness. Slowly the dark receded to the point where the sky was a lighter shade of black than the valley slopes. 'I can't believe we lost McCree,' Shultz sighed heavily.

'We'll never live it down,' Abraham said. 'We're such a bad squad that even the legendary John McCree was unable to successfully return from his mission.'

'And we lost Delaney,' Weiss added.

'Still, Ma'am, you're in one piece and we've not far to go,' Starr offered, in an attempt to lift the gloom.

'How much longer?' Zeleno asked.

'Twenty minutes, Ma'am. Best to get back in the Aerial,' said Starr.

'Whoever did this will pay!' she replied. 'This was supposed to be a profit break – they've screwed up my memories of this place for me permanently.' She pulled herself up into the Aerial. The remaining enforcers did likewise after they'd inspected the Aerial, as requested by Starr. He lifted the vehicle off the ground, still behind the outcrop of rock that had protected them from detection by the kill satellite.

'I'm just building up a bit of altitude and power before I pull the trigger, so strap in tight,' advised Starr.

As the Aerial rose the tip of the sun peeked over the top of the valley, sending the first of its rays to wake up the fauna. The light hit the Aerial and projected a long, low shadow of the propulsion unit across to the opposite side of the valley. Amongst all the natural shadows this artificial shape jutted out past the rocky outcrop that had hidden them. No one on board had noticed this; if they had they would have been alarmed because they knew the satellite was still there, ready and waiting for another chance to finish them off.

And so as Starr pushed the stick forward for full thrust out of the protective rocky cover, Derek's best chance for revenge dissipated. He was still being defragged. If he'd have been able to stay online, he could have done the analysis and given the kill satellite additional commands. It would have seen the shadow the Aerial had created and aimed its beam accordingly ahead of the outcrop. Starr would have flown straight into the beam and Derek would have been avenged. As it was, having found no further targets in the night, and being starved of further instructions, the satellite looked on stupidly as the Aerial shot out of the shadow of the outcrop and flew like a rabid wasp down the valley's river bed into the distance.

Starr was weaving the Aerial about, expertly following the contours of the river bed. Weiss was looking behind them. 'Nothing's shooting, Starr, too fast for them eh?' said Weiss.

'I'm not complaining,' Shultz offered. 'It's not every day you can outrun a kill satellite.'

'It's the soul of McCree,' Abraham said. 'He must have flown into the satellite and kicked all its circuits to shit, eh?' They all smiled. The Hypersonic terminal was soon visible in the distance as the valley slopes flattened out. Starr throttled back and raised the angle of the Aerial to help him locate the landing pad.

'Not so easy, landing these manually, especially when you have to use your eyes to find the pad,' Starr observed.

'Fifty degrees right, Starr,' Weiss said.

'Thanks Weiss,' replied Starr. 'Good to know those recon skills of yours are as sharp as ever.'

'Like your piloting skills, we trust,' Weiss replied.

The Aerial darted forwards and down to the pad. The surviving enforcers were ready to exit immediately on landing. It touched down with the smallest of impacts. 'But of course,' Starr grinned at Weiss in return.

A couple of GUCI enforcers appeared from the nearest building, with guns not entirely held in readiness, rather to try and conceal the fact that they'd been taken by surprise. The Meometics enforcers were already out of the Aerial looking towards their colleagues.

'Lead Enforcer Miller.'

'Enforcer Anderson,' the on-duty enforcers introduced themselves.

The Meometics enforcers reciprocated. Then Zeleno stepped out of the Aerial. The duty enforcers were surprised to see Meometics' head profit enabler there. The surprise began to turn to fear as they realized something was wrong. Weiss broke their shocked silence. 'We're here because your colleagues were terminated.'

'Impossible,' Miller replied. 'They reported back that the escort was a success and that they were going off duty. They're due back on duty in a few solars to escort the head enabler back to the terminal.'

'Oh, yes,' Shultz spoke, 'so why are we here now? Your systems have been compromised. We had to reset the villa's systems. Even then a kill satellite was sent to terminate us. We barely managed to get here – our connected online systems at the villa were already hacked and despite reloading them we were still being targeted.'

'What about Chen? He's our star enforcer, the next McCree, we reckon.'

'*Was* your star enforcer. He was the last, we think, to die. He managed to get the head enabler to the villa after the attack but died doing so. On the subject of McCree, we also lost him.'

'McCree was on your detail?'

'Was being the operative word. So you'll forgive our lack of sympathy about the loss of your enforcer, but we've not exactly had a great time here.'

Starr intervened. 'I'm ranking enforcer here. You will not report any of this. You may only document the failure of enforcers to report for escort duty. Our adversary will expect you to do this, given they have faked a transmission to you with a report to a similar effect.'

'Understood,' Miller replied.

'We have a few solars head start on them,' Shultz added.

All this time, Zeleno had been taking in the dialogue between the enforcers. She felt reassured. They may have been discussing her safe transport as if she were a delivery, which in effect she was, but it didn't matter to her. Their mission was to safely deliver a 'package' back to Meometics HQ, and that was all that mattered to them. There were some advantages to being alive that an inanimate object would not have. How many packages are able to transport themselves from *a* to *b*, for instance?

Zeleno breathed deliberately, slowly, to focus her thoughts. Whoever was responsible for this shitstorm would pay dearly. How many times had she already promised to get even? It was becoming a recurring theme. Violence, survival, a promise of revenge.

'You'll need to collect the bodies on the way to the villa,' Starr advised. 'But not until a solar after we've left.'

'Yes, sir,' Taw-Cymru's incumbent enforcers replied as one. 'Take a bag with you as well,' Abraham interjected.

'The next hyper transport's departure is when?' Starr enquired.

'10:00, sir,' Anderson replied.

'OK, so we have plenty of time to board the Hypersonic.' Starr said.

'We have a spare Sixer you can take to the terminal,' Anderson offered.

'That will do, thanks,' said Starr. 'You'll need to order another one as the Sixer sent up to the villa is now *under* the road. Don't ask how. One of your enforcers was in it when it sank under the road, the other five bodies are topside.' He turned to Zeleno. 'I'll get the Sixer, Ma'am,' he announced. 'Better not to use any systems if possible. They'll only increase the chance of us being detected.' Zeleno nodded in agreement. Starr entered the GUCI station and descended to vehicle level; a few minutes later he was outside the station with the Sixer. The wheels nearest the kerbside squashed against it. 'It's not as responsive as other Sixers I've driven in manual mode,' he commented.

'We get the lower spec stuff here,' Miller replied. 'Apart from our Aerial which is rarely used – it's only for those situations where a road vehicle is unable to travel.'

'All on board,' Starr shouted.

'Remember,' Shultz said to Miller. 'No situation report for a least a solar. If we reach our destination sooner than that we'll file a resource request for you.'

'Understood, safe journey.'

'Now that would be a first,' Abraham replied sardonically.

Zeleno was in yet another Sixer. Her recent experience of journeys in this type of vehicle was not good. In fact, the odds were against a trouble free journey, she decided. Once she had put an end to her tormentors she'd get the techs to design something different. Starr punched the engine start and the Sixer started to roll. He accelerated the Sixer up to 90Km/h; it wouldn't want to turn at that speed but it was virtually a straight road to the terminal.

Minutes later they were at the inner terminus. The Ident of the Sixer automatically opened the security screen and gates; Starr decelerated. He'd been trained for immediate decant operations – being stationary for the shortest possible time minimized the chance of anyone being able to get a lock on the vehicle or those about to exit it.

McCree's plan had detailed they were to return via service class. Fortunately, if that was the correct term, loss of McCree and Delaney meant that the returning numbers were one down, which would raise less suspicion than if they returned with an extra on board.

They left the Sixer just metres away from the service class entrance ramp. The scanner read their ID tags as they entered the hyper transports service level.

Barone had seen the Sixer approach from his vantage point on board the hyper transport and counted five transferring onto the Hyper. They all looked like enforcers but he couldn't be sure from this range. He desperately needed to sleep. For that he'd need to lock himself in the goods storage compartment and pray nothing moved during the ascent into or decent from hypersonic speed.

He'd been in far more dangerous situations; this was a minor risk in comparison. He called up the service hold manifest which he had access to courtesy of his last victim. Jo Delaney, Tony Shultz, Frank Weiss, Louis Starr, Scott Abraham, John McCree. *McCree – wasn't he the enforcer that foiled our attack on the Assemblage?*

What was he doing on Taw-Cymru? Perhaps Santos would have the answer. He thought back to his first meeting with Derek after he'd been rendered an AI only version...

'J, I have moved from the organic to the electrical realm. I had no choice. I barely made it into this form before my organic self was terminated.'

'Surely not?' Barone asked.

'I'm afraid so, J,' Derek replied.

It looked and sounded like Derek. The holographic likeness was uncanny, only now he'd be ageless, suspended in time. Barone needed to be sure it was his old colleague.

'OK then Derek, tell me – why do you call me J?'

'Well Franco, it's J as in "Just shut up a minute and let me get a word in edgeways." So, did I pass the test?'

'That's not very charitable of you.'

'It wasn't meant to be, you did ask after all.'

'My god, it *is* you, Derek, OK, you've lost your body. So what's the plan now?' said Barone.

'I'd like to regain organic form again. There are advantages and disadvantages to being in this state. On balance, though, I'd prefer to be organic. This process is one way at the moment – the point was that it was supposed to be a two way process, only Zeleno decided to terminate me before I had the final piece of the puzzle. The idea was that you could leave your body for major repairs, reconstruction, or other similar procedures, and be returned once your body was repaired and pain free. The post-op painkillers and rehab would be a thing of the past.'

'So how far away were you, Derek?'

'Still a good way off, although a breakthrough advance in computing power would have shortened the timescale considerably.'

'There's something you're not telling me.'

'Of course, but that has to stay with me. I may need bargaining chips in the future. Knowledge generally equates to power after all. I can still do it, I just wish she hadn't taken the distance pill,' said Derek cryptically.

'I'm so sorry Derek. It has been a phenomenal success.'

'Not your fault, J. It's fine, I'm sure, just as long you don't try it out on a paranoid, driven head profit enabler. I thought it would help her cope, but it wiped out the last trace of humanity she had, and I just happened to be on the receiving end.'

'So what happens now, Derek?'

'Since I've been in electronic form it's been much easier to access systems that were previously blocked to me. You see, all security is focused on two main threats: hackers and malware. Hackers are deterred by biometric sensors and the like, to stop an organic being accessing unauthorized systems – a bio-reading for authentication has to be presented. Now malware has no such readings to authenticate but exists in binary form only. Other programs can hunt out malware based on the behaviours of this type of software. What they are not looking for is a human intelligence in digital form on the network. I can see the electronic traps and wait until the scanning code has executed and passed. It's like sneaking behind a security guard when he's looking the other way. Malware is not sentient and gets caught.

'I can pass through all of the security because I'm the first hybrid sentient and I'm directly compatible with computer networks. I have discovered a common thread between the corporations and the service federations. They are looking to develop nanotechnology to the point where it will destroy all life on earth.

'I have covertly brought a group of scientists together to stop this from happening: Scientists against nanotechnology organized systems – Santos. I need your unique talents to assist us and save the earth from meltdown,' announced Derek.

'I don't do killing anymore, if that's what you want from me. I left killing behind when I became a scientist.'

'And what do scientists truly know of the effectiveness of weapons? They have never been in a kill or be killed situation. You have killed and you know how to use science to give you the edge when force is required. Zeleno doesn't know your identity, but you need to be aware that when she does, either she or indeed any other of the corp or federation heads will come gunning for you. GUCI keeps them all in power.'

'The problem *you* have, Derek, is that if you remove one of them, someone else will take their place – you can't win that fight. You'd be better off controlling the heads and keeping them at the top.'

'How can we achieve that?'

'With the very thing you are fighting against – nanites. Instead of using them to destroy the planet we can use them to control those who would. There are also a few other useful products that can be put together to give us some operational capability,' suggested Barone.

'Operational capability?'

'Yes. GUCI are renowned for their ability to develop counter tactics for any particular situation to ensure they will eventually come out on top. So, we need to employ new technologies in a non-repeating way.'

'I see.'

'Every time we are in conflict with them we need to vary our attack vector. They can't adapt if every battle employs new weapons and tactics. I have a number of projects that will give us that advantage.'

Barone returned to the present. *Why don't these bastards just die?* Derek was right. My projects are just advanced weaponry that can only ever be used once, as GUCI will invariably adjust their tactics to counteract them. At best, they just keep us far enough ahead of GUCI and the corps to give us time to prepare our final strike. No head enforcer present. *What a waste*, he thought. Well, not exactly a waste. With that thought he drifted off into a much needed slumber.

The enforcers and Zeleno strapped in as mandated by the pre-flight briefing. The launch light turned green and counted down. The magnetic rails re-energized, then – *whoosh*, the craft was fired off the magnetic rails and they were airborne. On this deck there was much less comfort that Zeleno was used to; still, her aches and pains would have taken the edge off luxury travel. Far better to get all the bad crap out of the way in one dose. They were soon travelling at Mach 8. The unclip light came on and they took the opportunity to stretch out of the seats.

My tofu sliced baguette was absolutely average. Apart, of course, from the rendezvous details printed within. There was a transport order code reference on the inside. These codes were pre-ordered transport destinations which, when activated on a panel, would call up a transport journey on a pre-planned route. Only companies and those on the high levels could really afford to use them. They offered privacy of intended destination from other citizens, and sometimes the passenger as well. It was rumoured that GUCI also used them to pick up profit reducers and *disappear* them.

I finished the baguette off with a fruit juice and entered the code into the panel. All that was confirmed were my details and the pick-up time from the transport point on ground floor. There were no details of the destination. Naturally I wasn't expecting any. I would have been suspicious if there had been.

I had an hour left to kill. There was not much left for me to do. I couldn't leave any hint that I had left my apartment for good. I made the bed and threw a couple of tops on it to give it that 'I just nipped out and will tidy it up when I return' feel. How ironic was that? There was no real spontaneity for those imprisoned in these concrete and glass prisons masquerading as apartments.

No doubt if we failed this apartment would be locked down and 'disappeared'. If we were successful there would be no telling what its fate would be. Would it be revered or despised? I felt as if I should at least leave some farewell message to those who would follow, but no potential clue could be left. That was the hardest part for me, wanting to reach out to those I cared for, but knowing to do so would condemn them if I failed. I had no right to let my feelings endanger those at risk of retribution, so it would have to be that my actions were to remain enigmatic to those that knew me.

The apartment, whilst being my home for the last few cycles, had slowly become nothing but a functional place to me. A place to be after Meometics profit research. Not really a home. I could rationalize it out of my emotions. I felt a sadness to be leaving, but convinced myself that on balance there were more disadvantages to living there than advantages.

However, the truth of it was I would miss the stability having this apartment gave me, even if it was a piss poor excuse for a home. Sterile and dull beyond belief. No wonder I enjoyed my time in the lab so much. It was hard to stop wallowing in a cloud of self-despair, and I somehow managed to string together enough disappointment about the apartment to focus on my departure. All these people in all these apartments. They deserved more. Those who survived would be free.

I slowly, reluctantly, closed the door. There was no looking back – that chapter in my life had closed. To relive it would only cause the ghosts to awaken. I took the lift to the ground floor. On leaving the block I stood under the canopy of my exit level. The transport pulled up and detected my Ident. It opened its side door and I stepped inside; the door locked and the windows blackened fully. The transport accelerated rapidly – I was not used to such speed in a personal mode of transport. Santos were able to pull some impressive tricks to get away with this performance. The acceleration subsided, as did my consciousness.

A feeling of elation passed over me like a wave. I'd been drugged again. This was becoming tiresome...

The Hypersonic transport was about to decelerate. The enforcers had strapped themselves in either side of Zeleno. The warning light countdown came on and then they were forced forward, pushing against their restraints. Zeleno winced; she needed more painkillers and a long lie down at the office. A bang and a scream a split second later from the cargo bay at the far side of the deck commanded their attention. Abraham had his weapon ready first. They should have remained seated, but with most of the speed gone were able to unbuckle the restraints and check out the cargo area.

Barone had only made a slight miscalculation, due to his fatigued state, in securing the return cargo, but it was enough to trip him up.

The containers had flown forward on deceleration, hard enough to crush his leg and smack him in his chest. The impact had cracked a few ribs, no doubt, and his ID card was now missing. The door to the cargo area opened and an enforcer entered.

'Don't move,' Abraham commanded. He could instantly see the man was in pain but had no idea who he was dealing with. Barone was wearing service overalls and looked as if he was one of the crew, although getting crushed in the cargo area of a Hypersonic transport was not usual behaviour for a service employee. 'ID,' Abraham requested; despite the obvious pain of the man in the cargo bay, there was enough not right about this situation for him to be suspicious.

The man shook his head and attempted a shrug of his shoulders, which he would have completed if it were not for his recent encounter with the cargo bay storage containers. Abraham gel cuffed him, then solidified the cuffs by means of a command from his wrist device. 'Name, then,' Abraham demanded.

'Reuben Small – Hypersonic transport maintenance operative.'

'Quite a big title, Mr Small. If that is your real name,' Abraham mocked.

'My ID must be around here…' Barone stiffened as the pain in his chest became borderline bearable.

'What were you doing in the hold? You should have left before take-off.'

'My error, there were two containers that I couldn't secure correctly. I managed to secure the back strapping on them and then heard the countdown. I couldn't leave at that point.' The rest of the enforcers had now entered the cargo area. 'After launch I must have passed out, and woke to the sound of my ribs snapping.'

'They de-oxygenate the cargo bay to reduce the fire risk. Not enough to kill you, but most citizens would have passed out – you should know that,' Starr interrupted.

'Yes, but of course,' Barone replied faintly. 'I did feel lightheaded. I just lost track of the time, being preoccupied with securing the cargo.'

'OK, Reuben, let's get you to a medical facility,' said Starr.

'Thank you, enforcer.'

'Weiss, have you got a medi scan there?' Starr asked his colleague.

'Just a sec. I left it with our rookie recruit.'

Weiss left the cargo area.

'Oh, wait a sec. Shit, stop there, Weiss.' Starr ran out through the cargo hold area door and caught up with Weiss.

'What's the rush, Starr?'

'Something stinks,' Starr whispered.

'You're not referring to me, I hope?' Weiss replied.

'I want a full medical scan of our guest, then place him in a holding cell when we land. Can you load the scanner with anaesthetic?'

'Yes, consider it done.'

'Make sure he gets a full dose.'

'Care to share any more info about our Mr Small?'

'When he said he'd passed out I fed him a line about reducing the oxygen in the cargo hold. He agreed that that must have been why he passed out. It used to be the case with the early hyper transports, but not these ones. If he was a maintenance operative he'd have known that. Our Mr Small is an imposter.'

'Indeed. Then what happened to the original Mr Small?'

'Now that's what we need to find out. But more importantly, who is he?'

'What is it, Starr?' Zeleno enquired.

'I think we have a stowaway, Ma'am. He's been bashed about a bit in the cargo bay, but we're taking no chances, Ma'am. We're going to sedate him and then place him in a holding cell. You'll be back at HQ before anyone knows anything. We're about to touch down, Ma'am. Best sit down while we land.'

Weiss turned to them both, 'Right. I'd better scan this bastard before we arrive.'

'Turn the scan up. I want to see how badly hurt he really is,' Starr added.

Weiss headed back into the cargo hold.

'Sorry about that,' he said to Abraham. 'Too much kit in my bag.'

'You recons, always carry too much with you.'

'This might hurt a bit, Reuben. I want to get an accurate picture of your injuries. We should be able to jump the queue depending on the scan result.'

'Not ahead of any head enablers though, I suppose,' the injured man replied. Abraham shot Starr a look; how did he know about Zeleno?

'What do you mean, Reuben?' Abraham asked.

'Arrgh,' Barone replied as the scanner picked up on his broken ribs. 'The head enablers always get off first, don't they? Better hope there aren't any on the VIP deck then.'

'Two cracked ribs,' confirmed Weiss. The scanner readings were erratic; the whole body image was sparkling like a radioactive bauble. 'Just checking for concussion,' Weiss reassured Barone. As Weiss raised the scanner level with Barone's head he discreetly activated the anaesthetic function. A *whoosh* of anaesthetic shot out from the scanner into Barone's face and he slumped, unconscious, in his seat.

The Hyper was back on terra firma. The enforcers pulled an emergency stretcher from the med area on the deck adjacent to the cargo bay and Barone was lifted onto it, still with gel cuffs attached. 'Put this on, Ma'am. It's a med jacket, just in case someone has any questions – we can use a bit of *medical assistance*.'

Zeleno acknowledged Weiss's instruction. He was in charge of the enforcers at this point. She noted how seamlessly each of them had taken command of the unit, based on what the overriding skill requirement at any given time was. Shultz had been relatively quiet compared to the others, but then he didn't exactly want to start communications until they were safely back at Meometics HQ.

They watched a few people exit from the VIP deck and waited until the deck's exit ramp retracted. Their ramp started to extend. Soon they were leaving the Hyper with a restrained patient who had just happened to 'breathe in some maintenance fluid vapour by accident'.

'I need a detention cell to place him in before he regains consciousness. He will go manic when he awakens,' Zeleno instructed.

'What do I do then?' the Hyper terminal enforcer asked concernedly.

'Nothing,' Zeleno replied. 'We will monitor him remotely and intervene when appropriate.'

'Understood,' the enforcer replied.

The enforcers took the stretcher around the curve of the Hyper terminal hall's exit, its architecture looking somewhat like a medical facility. It didn't therefore feel too strange, carrying the comatose stowaway along the gleaming white hall on a stretcher. They arrived at the location of the detention rooms. The third one along had a flashing amber glow around the door seal. 'This is the one that's been configured for him,' Weiss announced. The door silently whisked open as they approached it. A solid rectangular surface had risen from the floor in the centre of the room. They placed the stowaway on the surface and clamps rose from the block, locking the stretcher in place. 'Let's move it,' Weiss urged. 'I need to tap into the network to see if our friend here has any more information to offer up, courtesy of the GUCI data store.'

They left the room, which promptly locked itself.

'I have a spare transport order code,' Starr announced. 'How'd you get that?' asked Weiss.

'McCree gave it to me earlier. He said that I should have it, seeing that I'm the enforcer most qualified in transport systems.'

'Can't argue with that,' Weiss replied.

They headed back to the terminal embarkation area. A panel was reserved for GUCI use only. Starr entered the transport code. The panel confirmed the code's validity.

'We have our transport?' Zeleno enquired.

'Yes, Ma'am,' Starr replied. 'We should descend to the transport level immediately.'

'Lead the way then, Starr,' said Zeleno. They walked over towards the transport level lift, which descended with the party of five. Would they reach their destination without incident? Zeleno was not confident. She had already braced herself for further incidents or incursions against her party. If she was not safe back at Meometics HQ then all was lost. It was her last hope. She had lost McCree; they still had unfinished business, yet he was gone. What would he have said or done? Something troubled her; she needed closure. To see his broken form retrieved from the wreckage of the villa. He would become the posthumous icon of GUCI. Above all, he was a Meometics GUCI enforcer. His passing would inspire a new generation of enforcers. A generation that looked up to Meometics as the ultimate posting an enforcer could hope to achieve. The halo effect would be unstoppable. Meometics would be the number one corporation on the planet – all built on the bravery and sacrifice of John McCree.

Zeleno shook herself back to the present. They stepped out of the lift and the transport was there waiting for them. Weiss approached the transport but the door did not open. The remaining enforcers stepped up to it one by one; it responded to none of them. Only Zeleno was left. She approached the transport and the door flipped up over the roof. 'Someone's been expecting you,' Weiss quipped.

'Our friend and not our foe, I hope. It's McCree's code?' she snapped at Weiss.

'Yes, Ma'am.'

'Then that's good enough for me, OK?'

'Sorry, Ma'am, of course,' he replied. They entered the transport. After buckling up, the vehicle sped out of the terminal complex heading for Meometics HQ. The city was a shock to them after their time on Taw-Cymru. It had only been a couple of solars since they had left, but the surprise at how soon they had forgotten the complexities of the city had come as an unwelcome revelation. Despite the dangers they had faced on Taw-Cymru they had all felt something unusual, and now felt that a part of them had been left behind.

The transport had wasted no time in travelling to its pre-programmed destination. It had a priority level beaten only by a corporation Sixer. It sped down the entrance ramp of Meometics HQ and disappeared inside.

In Porter's office, Charles was pacing up and down. He would have no further message for twelve hours.

Damn it, he thought. It was precisely moments like this, the having to wait moments, that he couldn't stand. He thought back to when he was the commander of a retrieval squad. Then at least he had direct influence in the outcome of his mission. Those days had long passed. The consolidation of GUCI and the herding of the citizens into consumer led subservience had hastened the disbanding of the retrievals. There were no more large scale anti-profit mobs to rescue government and corporation sympathizers from.

The ultra-riots were history. The mobs had been subdued. And yet... something nagged away at him. He could sense a change in the air. A growing resistance to the status quo. The spirit of freedom was building up, not yet within the citizens but on the network. It wasn't the protests by the unprofitables and dispossessed against the raising of the water and other utility prices. They would be dealt with, just as they had been for some time, by GUCI.

It occurred to Porter that the mainstream GUCI force were becoming more like their elite termination squads. That worried Porter; he didn't know which was the more dangerous. Covert termination and disappearance of citizens or termination of protesters in public view? That was why he had given up on the offer to lead a termination squad. He had accepted the office job of head of

Meometics GUCI protectorate. He would always be a rescuer and protector – initiating violence against others was no longer his way. Were GUCI causing or responding to this subtle change? Did it even make any difference to the outcome?

Porter's main panel lit up: 'Transport order code XX795832 redeemed. Assigned to Charles Porter.' The code he gave to McCree. The occupants were here at HQ in a lift heading to the upper levels. It could mean only one thing: Renee Zeleno was alive and safe. Porter felt a pride in his selection of those assigned to the mission. *McCree did it. That man is the new messiah – he's a living legend all right.*

It wouldn't be long before Porter received the unwelcome news about McCree. But at this moment, ignorance was indeed bliss.

The lift stopped at the head profit enabler's level and the door opened. Zeleno exited and turned around to speak to the remaining occupants. 'Thank you for efforts, enforcers. You'll be adequately rewarded for them. Goodbye.'

'Ma'am,' they replied in chorus. The doors shut and headed back down five storeys to the enforcers' level.

Zeleno looked at herself in the mirror. She looked good, despite the dirt and oil on her face. It seemed to her like she'd earned that look, although now the enforcers had left she noticed she was smelling a bit. Nothing too bad, in line with her 'enforcer' persona, but certainly not in keeping with her corporate image. She peeled her gear off. Sending that down the clothing disposal chute would raise a few eyebrows. She smiled. *If they think I'm eating enforcers these days, let them. I am getting through a lot of them at the moment.* She stopped in her tracks. McCree. *I'm only here because of him.* She was used to the fact that enforcers would die in their duty to protect her, but she'd never seen one take a bullet for her, and then some. Literally. Right in front of her own eyes.

McCree had taken several. She recalled the frantic sex they'd had. Then it hit her. It hit her hard. Death by sex. Her visions were correct. McCree had become attached to her because of those moments they'd spent together, enjoying each other. She had indeed killed him with her desire. The only men she'd been intimate with were now dead solely because of her. She felt sick. She reached for a distance pill from her med dispenser and stumbled towards her shower unit; she let the pill fizz on her tongue. Usually she would take it with water but this time she wanted the bitter taste it left on her tongue as a reminder of how she felt about the way she'd treated her men. The shower steamed off any trace of dirt, just as the pill steamed away any trace of remorse. She was still left with the bitter taste in her mouth from taking the pill. She was reminded of what needed to be done.

She stepped out of the shower unit dripping wet and let the full body air towel dry her. A new set of corporate wear was chosen to let those on the receiving end of a visit or video feed know who was boss. She called Porter.

'Charles Porter speaking. Ma'am, glad to have you back. We've been worried about you.'

'Porter, I want to see you immediately.'

'Yes Ma'am.'

That didn't sound too good, he thought. His office was only two levels below her – it didn't give him much time to prepare. He'd already debriefed the remaining enforcers whilst Zeleno was otherwise engaged. He knew it all. He'd been right about the ghost in the network and his choice of enforcers for the mission had ultimately proved successful, but he didn't *feel* he'd done enough. Zeleno shouldn't have been in that situation to start with.

Starr had been given the code by McCree to get them back here. It should have been McCree leading them back. At least he'd had the sense to send misinformation back to HQ in the knowledge that it was most likely being monitored by Meometics adversaries. That alone had most likely stopped yet another attempt on Zeleno's life. He was sure the main corporate internal network was secure, although following the data leakage at Research 4 he wasn't going to take any chances. Porter stepped into the lift. If there was ever a time for a five centimetre thick piece of titanium then now was it, so he could shove it down his pants. He was surely about to get his arse kicked royally. The lift opened in Zeleno's office and Porter stepped out. She was facing the lift directly from her desk. She meant business.

'Charles, I assume you've debriefed the enforcers?'

'Yes, Ma'am.'

'Good. I have no intention of repeating my experiences on Taw-Cymru to anyone. The enforcers' debrief will be your record.'

'Yes Ma'am.'

'Whilst your retrieval squad indeed proved successful, it was not without noticeable cost to Meometics. A far better solution would have been to ensure a retrieval squad was not required in the first place.'

'Of course, Ma'am. It is now clear that many of our systems have been compromised.'

'McCree realized that, and it wasn't even his area of expertise now was it?'

'No Ma'am.'

'I want a priority recall of his body. Once that's done you will be moved to a termination squad. I know that's not what you wanted to hear, but whilst I'm dishing out the goodies, Shultz will be taking over your position. Maybe that will teach you to concentrate on your priorities rather than spending too much time analysing scenarios.'

'Ma'am, if I may—'

'No, you may not. You'll either be on the termination squad or you'll be its next assignment. Is that clear enough?'

'Yes, Ma'am.'

'Your military background may have helped to mitigate your initial failure, but I need a comms man as head of security. That's where all the threats have been originating, from the network. Cut off the supply of information to our enemies and they lose the knowledge of where to engage us. There's no need for your skills, then. We will have the advantage.'

Zeleno's panel lit up. It was Shultz.

'Ma'am, I have further information.'

'Yes, what is it *chief security enforcer designate?*' she let the title ring in Porter's ears, then waved him out.

'It's our stowaway on board the hyper transport, Ma'am. Reuben Small isn't who he says he is. We've been unable to find the original citizen Small, but we've matched up our captive to video feed footage and I can confirm his name is Franco Barone.'

'Never heard of him.'

'He was manning the jammer on the original attack that would have been successful but for McCree. We're going back though the access logs to trace his movements – there's quite a big gap to fill from the time of the first attack through to his capture.'

'Understood, keep me informed.'

Derek was scanning for clues as to Zeleno's whereabouts. He tapped into a satellite that was over the villa in Taw-Cymru. The very same villa that he'd flattened with the assistance of a subtly re-programmed kill satellite. There amongst the rubble, very faintly, the life signs detector blinked. Someone was alive under all that twisted metal and shattered masonry. Zeleno perhaps? Derek wasted no time. He contacted a Santos cell on the edge of the coast. The scientists he called worked for Torq Innovations and had access to a compact sized hypersonic craft. It was a prototype, of course, but a working one. They'd also equipped it with dissipation technology which made it untraceable in flight. With a fake holo-projection of the craft in the research labs, no one except for them would know it had been commandeered by order of Santos. The scientists at Torq had solved most of the problems, packaging the hypersonic engines into such a small space without tearing the craft apart.

Dr Jeremiah Brunt was nervous. This was a big risk. It must be integral to Santos's plan for them to request this. His colleague Professor Benjamin Taylor agreed. He loaded on board two mechanical extraction robots Santos had requested to be taken along with them. *Someone important is buried under a ton of crap, no doubt. Let's hope we can get them out alive.* 'Fire up the holo-projection, Jeremiah. Move out slowly.'

297

'OK, got it,' Brunt replied. Professor Taylor calibrated the dissipation field. It made a hole in the holo-projection until they moved further out of the craft's hangar. The craft rippled in the dissipation field. Professor Taylor sent a loop command to the video monitors. Ten seconds' duration to be repeated six times. That would give them time to take off undetected. He pressed the stage one engine start and the craft rose off the hangar floor and out of the facility. The dissipation field was holding. Having left the research base far enough behind Professor Taylor switched the hypersonic engines on. They were forced back into their seats. The land below them quickly changed to water, moving as if in fast-forward time as they shot across the ocean to Taw-Cymru.

They'd be there in forty minutes. After reaching hypersonic velocity they unbuckled their restraints and calibrated the robots in mid-flight. The robots were ready to be deployed and controlled from the craft on arrival. By the time they'd finished the calibrations, the main instrument panel was indicating only five minutes to deceleration.

'Better strap up,' Professor Taylor suggested.

'Sure thing, Ben,' Dr Brunt replied. The craft slowed down rapidly as Taw-Cymru appeared on the main view screen. A flashing dot on the horizon told them where the craft needed to go. Dr Brunt knew the craft intimately. He'd designed most of the systems, except the exotic stuff which was the professor's doing. Dr Brunt banked the craft away from the rapidly approaching terminal and hopped over the contours of the approaching hills. They were now floating over the contours of the landscape, in a form far more elegant than the aerial transport GUCI had in this region. Derek's co-ordinates were spot on, naturally. They slowed down until they were alongside the remains of the villa.

'Switching off dissipation field,' Professor Taylor announced. Dr Brunt slowly dropped the power level and the prototype craft gently floated down onto the uneven ground. They could see than the roof of the villa had appeared to melt and re-solidify on the rubbled remains, but it had still remained mostly intact in a single, uniform piece.

'We'll need to set the robots for tunnel extraction mode,' Taylor commented.

'Programming now,' Brunt replied.

The rectangular tracked robots eased their way out of the prototype, which had opened at the rear like a giant clam. The lead robot locked onto the faint life sign located under the mess that was the villa. Brunt walked slowly behind the last robot to get a first-hand view of the situation. Taylor was monitoring the robots from the main screen in the craft, which gave a robot's eye view on one side of the screen and proximity to target map on the other. The life sign was about ten metres away from the edge of the villa's remains. According to the geo-locater, the villa's original external wall was four metres further into the rubble. The kill satellite had flattened and spread the villa out somewhat. The lead robot extended its trans-alloy shield in front of it and extended its multi-material cutters so they were just a small distance away from the edge of the overhead shield. A tunnel started to form and the spoil from the cut slid into the lower portion of the robot and out through the back. The second robot grated the spoil to fine granules and compacted them, simultaneously lining the newly formed tunnel with concrete gel. Dr Brunt leaned into the entrance the robots had made. The robots made slow but steady progress until they reached the original location of the front wall.

The debris ahead consisted of the reinforced door that Zeleno had crawled out from underneath. The pitch of the cutter raised to a screech that would surely have spooked any conscious survivor trapped under the rubble. The indications from the robots' sensors were that the survivor was barely alive, let alone conscious. It was too early to tell what had almost killed the occupant. Building collapse, blast, suffocation, heat shock; they wouldn't know until they reached the survivor.

Dr Brunt returned to the craft after the rear of the last robot disappeared into the tunnel out of view. Forty minutes later, and a metre away from their target, the debris stopped. Held up by the remains of a reinforced door frame was a small pocket of space. Taylor guided the camera towards the victim. It was an enforcer.

'I'm pretty certain that's not who Derek sent us to retrieve. Can you get an ID?' Brunt enquired.

'I'll try for a shoulder ID.' Taylor tilted the camera up to the arm of the enforcer. The front of his combat jacket looked to have taken quite a shredding. His nearest arm looked trauma-free. He read off the badge: 'McCree.'

'Wasn't he the enforcer who stopped the Assemblage attack?'

'The very same. I'm thinking that whoever he was protecting then was Derek's intended target.'

'Is there anyone else in there we should be looking out for?'

'I don't know – there are no other life signs. We might lose this one too if we don't pull him out.'

'We don't want that – he's a consolation prize if nothing else. We might be able get him to shed some light on the situation.'

'How do you work that out?'

'Leave it to me. I have an idea.' Taylor commanded the last robot to reverse course and the lead robot was instructed to deploy its skid plate. Two remote arms extended and grabbed McCree firmly by the ankles. Slowly they retracted and McCree's body gradually slid towards the horizontal and then onto the skid plate floor. The robot reversed and the skid plate was pulled smoothly over the crushed debris that had become the floor of the tunnel.

The other robot had now emerged from the tunnel. Taylor turned to Dr Brunt: 'Put these compound packs onto the robot ready for our guest.' The five packs looked like bags of gelatine, but Brunt knew what they were really capable of. He lifted a storage compartment at the back of the robot and pushed the compound packs in firmly. These packs were capable of mixing to form most medical products needed in a life threatening situation: blood plasma, stimulant, stabilizer, anaesthetics. Taylor called up the medical control module for the robots. The robot dragging McCree out of the wreckage communicated information about him from its sensors. The other machine with the compound packs had already determined from information received which compounds to produce. A mild stimulant, with a mixture of stabilizer and analgesics would be required to improve his condition and take him away from near death towards life. McCree only needed to hold on a few moments longer and he would be saved.

McCree was at present far away from the land of the living. He was walking down a long avenue with trees forming a canopy blocking light from above. It was too dark to make out what was blocking the light from the sides of the tree-lined avenue. There was no source of illumination to guide him apart from the pinpoint of light at the end of the avenue. McCree stopped walking, yet found himself still moving towards the point of light at the end of the avenue. It grew larger and larger; he could make out a shape in the brightness ahead. A human form. *My god, she's beautiful.* He could tell even from this distance that she was radiant with life. The light surrounded her. She *was* the light, or one with the light, it was hard to tell. He continued to approach the end of the avenue as the white glow continued to brighten further. He was slowing down. It was his wife, Julia. She was magnificent. She was not as he'd last seen her, when he'd pulled the mask that she'd been wearing at the food protest from her face. He wanted to see he'd terminated a waste of space, to ease his conscience, and saw instead his wife staring blankly back at him; that had shocked him to his core. He knew what she'd suffered at his hands for the sake of keeping the corporations in power at the expense of the citizens, and his own dearest was the latest casualty.

'John,' she spoke to him, softly with love and no malice or bitterness at all. He couldn't make out what she was saying, he couldn't reply. She still spoke to him, all he could make out was, 'Forgive me, John.' She started to fade and he was shot back down the avenue that he'd been travelling along. *JULIA,'* he screamed as he was pulled away from her. He was powerless to prevent it.

Charles Porter was pissed. He'd known he was in for a kicking, just not such a big one. Back in his office he felt the cloud of failure descend over him. Porter had tried his best, but he realized he'd missed the point. He'd failed – not because his backup plan failed – that had been a success. He'd failed because his main plan had failed. Information, not force, was the main tool of control over an adversary. The most combat hardened enforcer on the planet was no match for a geek with a kill satellite under his keyboard control. Maybe, he thought, it *was* time to go back to his roots.

Porter activated his desk panel. He connected with the GUCI station at Taw-Cymru. *'Miller here.'*

'Profitable day to you,' Porter replied. There was something different about the GUCI contingent on Taw-Cymru. It must be having to keep an eye out for the local 'celebs' rather than deal with city block protests. They were more laid back, less formal. 'I have a couple of items we need to discuss.'

'Yes, sir,' Miller relied. He knew Porter's status and raised his game a little. He hoped the effort would not be lost on Porter.

'The contingent from Taw-Cymru has arrived back safely. We are aware of your loss and will be sending replacement cover shortly. Your enforcers will need to run extended cover shifts until relived, so arrange the reduction in the enforcers' off-duty allowance.'

'*Yes, sir.*'

'Enforcer McCree's body is to be retrieved from the villa. Send a detail up there to assess what resources you need to complete the task.'

'*I have already called up the off-duty enforcers to retrieve their colleagues' bodies, sir.*'

'Good job, Miller.'

'*I'm sure the visitors don't want to see dead bodies and the like spoiling their view, sir.*'

'Indeed. Make sure they are treated with respect. They died on duty. They deserve to be honoured.'

'*That's assuming no one wants to cover up this whole episode, sir.*'

'No longer our concern, Miller. When do you intend to report back?'

'*I'll just append your order to their brief, sir. They are at the Sixer ambush site around the corner from the villa at present. There'll be a satellite overhead in just a few minutes. I can relay the video feed over to your office, sir.*'

'That's great. Patch me in when ready. Porter out.'

Porter was already wondering what resources he'd need to get organized for the trip over to Taw-Cymru. They didn't have the right sort of equipment over there these days. The area was geologically sound and the weather was held in check at the edge of the mountains by the cloud barrier. There was no need for any heavy engineering equipment to be there anymore. The feed link flashed;

Porter opened it up. Anderson came into shot from the video feed of one of the enforcers' helmets. He could see there were four wrapped bodies placed neatly together on the ground to Anderson's left.

'*We're heading up to the next objective, sir.*' The villa had been mentioned, but of course they were referring to the villa's remains. The rubble had spilled out almost to the boundary wall, where Chen's remains, propped up against the wall, came into view.

'*Scan the rubble,*' Anderson ordered an enforcer.

'*Nothing, sir.*' the enforcer replied.

'*There has to be, are you sure, man?*' Anderson asked.

'*Yes, sir.*'

Anderson could be seen circling around the rubble. Then he saw it. Porter did too, and was trying to grasp the significance of the image on screen: a tunnel bored into the remains of the villa. Someone else had been beaten them to it? Anderson ordered an enforcer into the tunnel. There was an agonising wait until the enforcer emerged again shaking his head. McCree was not there; someone had stolen his corpse. Porter switched off the feed, and briefly considered terminating himself. Zeleno was not going to like this development. Not one little bit. The only glimmer of hope was Franco Barone. He had been picked up masquerading as Rueben Small, but for what purpose? The chair would give him the answers he needed and, hopefully, before Zeleno called him for a status report.

Porter ordered the enforcers on duty at the Hyper terminal to secure Barone for transport to Meometics HQ for interrogation in the chair. Barone was out cold and

306

would remain so for some time. What his captors didn't know was that Barone had a couple of million little helpers, repairing and rejuvenating his exhausted and damaged form.

The Golf Ball

I woke up yet again in the secret facility, and once more in my stealth suit.

'No more comedy smalls?' Elizabeth commented.

'No. I specifically recall, when opening Grant's gift, his announcing this really was the sort of quality present you can only give once.'

'Maybe we'll meet up with Grant in the future.'

'I hope so, if only to give him someone else to try his tomfoolery on.'

'So tell me more about him.'

'He's brilliant, but a bit of a hot head. He's quick to grasp concepts – sharper than me, but more haphazard. He works quicker but has to correct his work more. We'd finish a piece of work to a level of accuracy about the same time but by different routes. I think that's why Tom values our setup. Our different approach to any given task has created many breakthroughs for our lab.'

'Are the rest of the team aware they're marked for termination?'

'Only Tom is, but he feels obligated to inform Grant – he has a wife and child. As for Tom, I don't know. He keeps his home life at home.'

'So he hasn't yet told Grant then?'

'No, I persuaded him that my disappearance would buy us some time. Besides, he's not sure if Grant, or rather

Grant's wife, has been leaking information to another party.'

'How did he get that idea?' asked Elizabeth.

'Nanotechnology was used on the recent attempt on the Assemblage and we were due to have a meeting with them.'

'I see, but of course two and two don't always make four – sometimes its twenty-two!'

'Tom wants to trust Grant, but there's something he knows that I don't that makes him suspicious. Tom's not the type to point the finger until he's 100 per cent certain all the facts are in.'

'He'd better not mess things up, for all our sakes.'

'Elizabeth, is that a threat?'

'Of course not, K, but you need to realize that the safety of the Research 4 team is not one of our main objectives.'

'Well, it's one of mine – that's why I'm here.'

'You're only here by invitation and remember, you had your chance to back away.'

'I did, but I don't back away from a commitment. I'm committed to my colleagues – you do understand? So what's next?'

'Hold on a moment. Derek's coming back online after his defrag,' said Elizabeth.

'Derek needs defragging?'

'Yes, he's been rather preoccupied lately and he wasn't designed to run continuously. He develops data leaks if he stays online too long and then he needs sorting.'

'Good to see you, K,' said Derek.

'Likewise, Derek, how are you feeling?' I replied.

'Refreshed, if such a thing is possible for me. Hyper-alert is perhaps a more accurate description. I spent a little too long online sorting out a problem at Taw-Cymru.'

'The head enabler's re-energizing resort?'

'Yes, the very same. You wish to save Tom and Grant then?' Derek asked. 'Don't look so surprised, K, in here everything is recorded. When I return from off line I review the recordings. So there's no need to explain your point of view, again. If there were more like you maybe we wouldn't be in this situation. I thought the same of Renee Zeleno. Let's hope you don't live to regret the consequences of following your principles like I did. I have modified mine since Zeleno. When the best of men take bribes, isn't it the fool who doesn't? Fight fire with fire, if you can't beat them, join them. History is littered with these old clichés, but they all point to one thing. Rarely is an unjust leadership overthrown peacefully – it invariably requires a greater force.'

I understood what Derek meant, it just didn't make it any easier to do what was required of me.

'So what *is* your plan?'

'To start with we need to get your access to the lab re-enabled. From there you have the facilities to route the lab's control equipment up to the sat-net, K.'

'You can manipulate the planet's satellite network, Derek?'

'Yes. I can co-ordinate the signal we need to send from it. The satellites will then bathe the planet in the pulse, but if we miss any satellite GUCI and the others will be able to rebuild the network. I do recall it was designed that way in the days of the old calendar cold war.'

Yes...

'The satellites will be linked in fours to generate the quad-axial pulse. The pulses' radius will initially not be large enough for them to affect *any* silicon, let alone the satellites. Boosting the input to them from the lab, however, will give us the chain reaction we need to take out the satellites as well as the technology on the ground. K, you *are* able to boost the signal from the lab?'

'Of course, Derek, but how are you going to get me into the lab?'

'That's not difficult, but it will expose Santos. If the silicon isn't fried as planned the whole of GUCI will be coming through the door for us. We have one chance at this, one only.'

'No pressure then, eh?'

'No.'

'What about you, Derek?'

'I had hoped to return to mortal form, but I'll settle for ridding the planet of Zeleno and her like. Saving the planet from destruction will be reward enough. Revenge is secondary, purely a bonus. We'll give you our rendezvous location on your panel at the lab. It has to be the last thing we transmit, to minimize the chance of GUCI discovering it before the silicon is destroyed.'

'Of course.'

'We can send a video feed to Tom and Grant to give them a heads up once you enter the lab. If you reappear to GUCI the three of you are likely to be terminated. They'll have to take their chances.'

'I might be able to tilt the odds in their favour, Derek. There'll be no additional risk to the reset, you have my word.'

'That, K, is all I need. Elizabeth will assist you from here. I need to move onto the main network to fulfil my part of the plan. Good luck.'

Derek's holo-projection faded until he was gone.

Elizabeth looked over to me. 'K, I'm so sorry.'

'Sorry for what?' I said, confused.

'You haven't been told the whole truth…'

At first there were random sounds, then they started to turn into distinct voices. 'He's coming to, Ben,' were the first sounds to make any sense to McCree. He slowly opened his eyes to a sea of blurry shapes, hoping for an improvement in resolution. McCree's senses were recovering, although he was still unaware of where he was. He'd been so close to his wife once again but had lost her for a second time. He could think of no worse punishment for his actions. The swirling of thoughts in his head now eased. His senses now had lucidity to them.

He deduced that he was lying flat on his back, in full restraints, looking up at the roof of a craft whose design he'd never seen before. Dr Brunt leaned over McCree to adjust a couple of settings on the med-filters. 'I'm just reducing your dosage,' he said.

'How long have I been out?' McCree asked.

'I couldn't say. You were near death when we found you. It's been a solar since we picked you up. What's the last thing you remember before waking up?'

'I've no idea... who you are,' McCree replied. 'I'll decline to answer that if you don't mind.'

'You can call me DJ,' said Dr Brunt, 'and my colleague PB. We are men of science and do not wish to cause you harm. However, we're not keen on giving you too much information either, given GUCI's track record. I can, however, tell you that we know far more about you than you do about us.

'We recovered you from the remains of a villa in Taw-Cymru. It looked as if a kill satellite had targeted the building. Your combat armour has also been shredded – by an internal security weapon perhaps? You should consider yourself fortunate to be alive.'

'Let me reserve that judgement until I know who you are.'

Jeremiah spoke. 'I'm not going to give you any further details, John McCree, for security reasons. Our only concern is for you to make a good recovery from this trauma.'

'Why, thank you, I'm touched.'

'Please don't be. How valuable you are to us depends on how much you know. And how much your companions think you know.'

'Well, I know for a start you'd be better off removing these restraints me and letting me go.'

'Can't do that given your reputation, John.'

'The thing is, John, you're in no position to bargain. GUCI or Meometics won't be getting you back any time soon. There's nothing they have that we want.'

'I see, so you're from one of the other corps or federations?'

'Oh, John, you're so very wrong. We are from none of them and all of them. Let's just concentrate on you for the moment.'

Dr Brunt continued: 'You are renowned for your termination abilities and have recently been promoted to Meometics GUCI contingent.'

'So I'm supposed to be impressed. I'd love to string you guys along, but I can't honestly think of anything you might like to know. I'm just a "terminate protesters on duty, drink alcohol off duty" kinda guy.'

'Have you ever thought about what it would be like if the roles were reversed?'

'Ah, here we go. I'm not going to repent for my sins before I die. I'm paying for them every day I live.'

'How bizarre, John, have I touched a nerve? I'm not here to listen like a priest at a confessional. That would be so old calendar. We are men of science. Nothing else is really of much consequence.'

'Of course. Science is the one true saviour. Well, take a good look around DJ. Is this what science gets you? Hi-tech slavery? I suppose you'll tell me that we've grown as a species thanks to science. That we're all better off because of it? I don't think so. You may look down at me and despise me because of who I represent and what I do but consider this:

'What underpins and allows our society to operate the way it does? Science and technology. You are every bit as much to blame. Worse than that, you come up with ever more efficient ways to screw up the lives of the citizens. Scientists were the ones who gave the corporations and federations the power to subjugate the planet's citizens.'

'Feeling better for your little outburst, John?'

'It hasn't gone unnoticed amongst those who do genuinely care that science has gone too far. My question for you John McCree is: would you be prepared to redress the balance?' Dr Brunt turned away from the craft's latest artistic creation, 'McCree strapped to med-table'.

'You have until we arrive at our intended destination to make a choice.' Dr Brunt walked to the craft's main console and sat in the flight chair. Professor Ben Taylor re-initiated the dissipation field and subsonic engines. He looked over to Dr Brunt.

'Will he survive the hypersonic jump?'

'Yes,' replied Dr Brunt, 'I'm afraid so.'

'That's such a pity. Well unless you want to answer to Derek, McCree needs to be intact *and* alive.'

The craft rose slowly from the far western edge of Taw-Cymru, where it been temporarily stationed until the sole survivor of the villa attack had stabilized enough to be moved at hypersonic speeds.

Porter's desk panel flashed an update:

Franco Barone.

File creator/accessed: John McCree: Solar 87

Scientist employed at MedGen.

Started employment profit cycle 25

Took GUCI entrance endurance event profit cycle 30

Passed with a score placing him on a par with GUCI elite ops squad. Offered fast track position. Turned offer down.

Notes:

Positive ID as jammer operator on attack on Meometics' Assemblage – JMC

Additional: Data analysis.

Significant data related to jamming signal attack. Apartment of Grant Stern, Eleanor Anne Stern on same level.

Potential link back to Research 4 due to advance knowledge of Assemblage's schedule.

Known location history:

Tower Eight, Central Section, West Side, Northern Block: Solar 85

Taw-Cymru Hypersonic terminal on board Gentech's Transport HSC Surplus: Solar 90

Meometics HQ. Northern Block: Solar 91

Porter studied the record. What had Barone been up to between solar 85 and 90? He hadn't shown up anywhere in between but Porter had a bad feeling that he'd been involved in the other attempts on Zeleno's life in Taw-Cymru. That would have been bad enough, but the fact there was no confirmation or evidence to link him to the Taw-Cymru attacks was disturbing. He'd done a pretty good job at being one step ahead of GUCI, so to be discovered by accident on board the HSC Surplus seemed a bit implausible. Porter had already formulated in his mind the chain of events that had occurred, or more accurately one possible chain of events. With Barone about to spill the beans in the chair, Porter would soon have answers to his mysteries resolved.

Porter's panel lit up; it was Jack Forester. 'Profitable solar to you, Charles,' Forester offered. It never hurt to try a little bit of diplomacy by treating a superior with reverence, even though Forester knew Porter's time in charge was now finite. Zeleno had already requested a new list of suitable candidates to replace the gaps in her protective. A large enough selection from the talent bank for three candidates to be selected; two to replace those killed on duty and one to replace the person whose piss poor plan had been responsible for the first two vacancies. 'Let's hope it is profitable, eh Jack? I trust Barone is due to arrive imminently?' Porter enquired.

'Yes, Charles, he's on his way up. Do you want my enforcers to stay with him?'

'Affirmative, I've debriefed my surviving Taw-Cymru contingent. I've taken them off duty and issued them distance pills.'

'Very wise, Charles. Let me know what you want to do with Barone when you're finished with him.'

'I will let you know when he lets *me* know. We can charge him with impersonation for unprofitable reasons. If we ever find Reuben Small's remains we can bump that up to profit reduction by unauthorized termination. I'll keep you posted, Porter out.'

Porter checked the lift's progress. It was two floors down and the arrival chime sounded. The four regular GUCI enforcers wheeled in the latest piece of art for Porters office – 'Barone chained to slab'.

'Put him into the chair, undo one clamp only at a time,' ordered Porter. Barone's left hand was unclamped from the slab then placed into the chair's restraints. Then his left leg followed. Barone just smiled. His right arm and then his right leg. He'd now been successfully transferred to the chair. The enforcers flanked him, and sitting opposite him was Porter. 'Ah, the thought chair,' Barone said. 'I know the research team who developed this, are you sure you want to use it on me?'

'Would you like to give me a good reason why I shouldn't?' Porter replied

'You might not like what it finds.'

'I thought that was the whole point of it.'

'You could just ask me what you want to know without using it.'

'No deal.' An overhead visor descended close to Barone from the back of the chair, and sprayed a fine mist that should have sent him off into a deep sleep.

'No chance,' was Barone's reaction. He closed his eyes and arranged his thoughts. He organized the nanites within him.

Enforcer Shultz had also been reading up on Barone. It was the last file McCree had accessed. This all had to be linked somehow. Why was he here at Meometics HQ now? Because Porter wanted answers and Barone knew that. It was all too convenient for his liking.

He activated the comms pad on his panel and connected up to the Hypersonic terminal scan system.

Replay results for Franco Barone.

Integrity/pathogen check: clear.

Organic fluctuation 0.01%.

Display fluctuation curve.

The panel showed a distinct peak at 2.4Thz. *That's rather odd. Not dangerous in itself; it's a little used part of the frequency spectrum. Only thought chairs use that range.*

Shultz called Porter's office but there was no reply, so he queried the lift manifest. Barone plus four enforcers. Level forty; that was just two levels below Zeleno. He called Zeleno directly. *Answer, answer damn you Ma'am.*

'*Yes?*' Zeleno replied.

'Ma'am, you need to evacuate.'

'*What now?*'

'Yes, Ma'am. Porter has Barone in the chair. I think Barone is a bomb.' Zeleno sensed the tension in his voice. He genuinely believed it.

'You're deadly serious aren't you?'

'Yes, Ma'am. Take the lift down now Ma'am. I'll try and get the chair's power source disconnected but we can't take any chances. We'll meet you at your Sixer if our investments are favourable Ma'am.'

Fortunately Zeleno needed no further notice. She had been up since sol-rise and was checking through the financial results of the corporation and its rivals to refocus her efforts, away from the last few days of shit she'd been through. The pill was indeed helping her. Having been away from it for a few solars only increased the potency of the pill she'd taken recently. She called Shultz:

'I'm in the lift, Shultz, heading past Porter's office now.'

'I've activated the blast mitigation system on the lift, don't be alarmed Ma'am.'

The lift's internal dimensions reduced noticeably. There was still plenty of space for Zeleno but all the faces of the lift had closed in six centimetres or so. The blast pistons locked into place and the void between the inner and outer lift walls filled with carbon foam. The lift was one floor below Porter's office.

Trebanos Starion's panel flashed angrily.

'Trebanoth thpeaking,' he announced.

'This is Tony Shultz, head security enforcer designate. Cut the power to the thought chair in the head enforcer's room.'

'I can't do that, sir.'

'Why not?'

'I'm under orders from Charles Porter not to accept orders from any other source.'

'*What the hell is the point of that? Cut the fucking power, Starion!*'

'Porter warned me to be on my guard against attempts to disrupt his chair interrogation. I have to make sure the room remains isolated and powered until Porter contacts me again.'

'*He won't be contacting you ever unless you switch the power off now.*'

Starion did not reply.

'*He's trying to interrogate an explosive device!*'

'What?'

Barone's nanites focused the frequencies penetrating his body and reflected them back to the chair's power regulator. In a split second the regulator had fused. Barone smiled. 'This machine cannot force me to tell you anything, Porter. I will explain all but it will be of no use to you,' Barone continued. 'Nine, eight, seven, zero, three, three, zero, four, four, two, nine, six, one.' Porter was fuming; the chair was faulty – it might even have started to fry Barone's head judging by the drivel he was beginning to spout. He pressed the chair de-activation control on his panel. Nothing happened. 'Overload' flashed on the screen. The panel locked. His mind raced to the immediate future and was about to say, 'Oh fuck! Everyone get out of here now!'

He looked at the increasing glow radiating from the base of the chair. 'Oh fu—'

The chair exploded violently. Barone and the enforcers were torn apart; microseconds later Porter too was gone, the blast liquefying all within the office. The explosion took out everyone within a two floor radius of Porter's office with a barrage of high-speed masonry and metal pieces. The lift cables were instantly severed.

'Oh shit!' Starion exclaimed as the blast shook the building down to his level and beyond.

The lift fired anchors into the shaft surrounding it to stop it hurtling down the shaft. It stopped securely ten floors below the blast. It was held firmly in place by its emergency activated harpoons. A storm of rubble collapsed into the lift shaft and picked up speed as it hammered down on the roof of the lift. Fortunately the shaft's design accommodated two lifts, and much of the debris fell past, down the void behind Zeleno's lift. A few of the larger chunks buckled the outer roof wall of the lift and a number of metal shards punctured the roof but were arrested by the solidified carbon foam layer. More debris fell down the shaft. Blood began to flow into the shaft, shed by those on the floors above who'd been disassembled by the blast.

The lift capsule was holding but the anchors were now supporting five times the weight of the lift. Even with a design safety margin this was far more than the anchors were designed to support.

'Overload' flashed inside on the lift's control panel, a nice little touch designed to frighten even more shit out of anyone stuck in the lift at the time. Shultz contacted his Taw-Cymru mission colleagues ordering them to shift arse.

They were off duty in the enforcers' dorm level at the time and were the nearest emergency support for the incident apart from himself. Shultz ordered Weiss to pick up the mini tunnel borer on his way up to level thirty. The building shook further above them as if deciding whether to collapse in exhaustion or not. The enforcers made the five stories in record time.

Weiss arrived with the mini borer. Shultz scanned the shaft for the lift's exact location. It was only half a metre off from a standard exit point, but that meant the doors would not open, even if they hadn't been jammed by the debris on the roof of the lift. They would need to cut the through the doors. Shultz programmed the stairwell to configure to emergency chute configuration. Those on the floors above and around Porter's office would have no change of escape. There would normally be around eighty people in that area. The only piece of fortune was that the blast was intended to finish off the head profit enabler directly. If the same blast had happened lower down a lot more citizens would have been trapped. Plastic curves emerged from the stairwell walls. A siren sounded. The stair would turn into a slope. A thirty storey high staircase had been turned into an escape slide – the 'evacuate building' protocol activated. There were almost four thousand people to evacuate this way, plus the head profit enabler.

Weiss opened up the mini borer and unfolded its rotary quadrants, extending them to form a circle split into four with a gap between each piece.

'One point two metres should do it,' Weiss announced. 'Stand back, firing up.' He placed the borer centimetres above the lift floor, which would make it easier to extract Zeleno if she was injured.

'Can't you cut it so there's no extraction lip?' Shultz asked.

'No, it could weaken the structure if I cut into the lift floor.'

'OK.'

Zeleno was a little dazed but fully conscious. The lift still had power but the lights were flickering manically. She tried the panel – it was unresponsive. Then she heard the scream of metal on metal. She was unable to determine where it was coming from other than that it was outside the lift, heading in. She sat down cross-legged on the floor. They most certainly would be coming in from below. *As long as I remain in the centre of the lift I'll be OK.*

The lift creaked and strained further on its emergency anchors as if to remind her of the seriousness of the situation. *Grrrreck*, went the anchors under more stress; further clunks and whines could be heard over the increasing din of the mini borer as it cut its way though.

'I'm through the door now.' Shultz had pointed his portable scanner at the lift. Whilst the lift's internal panel was unresponsive to Zeleno, he was able to link up to its sensors and it did not make good reading. *Anchor failure predicted in three minutes* flashed on his scanner. 'How long is it going to take to get through to the lift, Weiss?'

'It's only an estimate, but I'd say five to ten minutes.'

'Damn, that's too long. Starr, Abraham, follow me,' Shultz barked. 'We need to buy Weiss some more time.' They rushed up to the floor above, then placed a ratchet bar on the lift shaft doors. Shultz was winding the bar for all he was worth. Its jaws were slowly prizing the lift shaft doors apart. 'We need to clear the rubble off the lift roof!' shouted Shultz. There was soon enough space to put a hand in between them, but there was nothing on the lift roof small enough to be pushed off. *Anchor failure in two minutes*, the scanner announced. 'How are you doing Weiss?'

'Just starting to cut the outer lift wall.'

The lift shaft doors were now fifty centimetres apart, which was enough for a slender citizen to fit through. Starr and Abraham were able to pull smaller pieces of debris off the lift roof.

'It's not enough!' *Anchor failure in ninety seconds.* Weiss's borer was working through the outer lift wall, sending a shower of sparks down the lift shaft into the void. Shultz had got the lift shaft doors seventy centimetres apart. He'd be at maximum aperture soon.

'Pull that beam out,' Shultz ordered. Abraham grabbed the severed cross-support beam Shultz was referring to. 'Lever up that chunk of masonry.'

'It's got to be a quarter of a ton.' Shultz had the doors open to max. He helped Abraham and Starr thrust the beam under a large chunk of masonry. They stood on the beam. The concrete slab moved. *Anchor failure in sixty seconds.* 'C'mon, bounce it.' They repeatedly jumped on the beam and the slab slowly slid of the roof of the lift. *Anchor failure in ninety seconds.* They used the beam as a battering ram to knock smaller pieces off the lift roof and down into the shaft.

It took almost a minute before the scanner repeated the 'anchor failure in sixty seconds' warning. They'd bought a little extra time. Was it enough?

Weiss was cutting through the carbon foam; it was designed to absorb massive amounts of energy, sacrificing its integrity in the process. The borer's teeth were starting to blunt. There was a hard crack and one of the anchors gave way. The lift lurched on its remaining anchors, shaking a little more debris off the roof. The building shook again and more rubble came down the shaft. A cloud of dust erupted from the shaft as it hit the roof, knocking the enforcers back. The impact of the rubble on the roof jammed the borer in its own cutting.

'Shit, the borer's stuck!' Weiss shouted. *Anchor failure imminent*, the scanner announced. Another anchor snapped diagonally opposite the first. The lift tilted in the shaft and the masonry slid off the roof, plunging down the shaft. Only one piece remained embedded in the roof. It wasn't going anywhere, having been firmly lodged in. Inside the lift Zeleno lurched forwards, her hand touching the side of the lift wall; it was hot where Weiss had been cutting the escape hole. Shultz's com badge activated.

'Meometics enforcers. Can you hear me, over?' It was Forester.

'Forester, good to hear you, we could do with some assistance.'

'What's your status?'

'Not good. Zeleno's in a lift with no cable and the safety anchors are about to give way. Suicide bomb took out Porter's office and the floors around it. The building is marginal at best.'

'I can see that for myself, I'm in an Aerial, level with Porter's office, or what's left of it. I'll get some emergency anchors sent up on the service lift. Anything else?'

'A cutter if you have one.'

'OK, service lift four is still operative up to your level. I'll send the team over to it.'

The service lifts were small shafts about a square metre at the base and two metres high. They were high-speed tubes that used a maglev system to shoot supplies up from lower floors. The stopping power of these lifts made them unsuitable for human use. The scanner had backed off from its pessimistic failure time frame. *Anchor failure* continued to pulse on the scanner. 'It can't determine a time – there's only two anchors remaining.' Shultz glanced at the details readout. One of the lifts sensors had been ripped off with the last anchor failure. 'Abraham, Starr, Weiss, get over to service shaft four – we have a delivery of emergency anchors promised.'

'Confirmed, Starr over and out.'

'Weiss here, I copy that, Shultz.'

Starr and Abraham dusted themselves off and met up with Weiss on his level at service shaft four's entry/exit point some hundred metres away from the stricken lift. They heard the high-speed hiss of the lift at it stopped just before they were upon it. Inside there were six anchors and a pair of cutters on a wheeled trolley. Starr pulled it whilst Weiss and Abraham held the doors ahead open.

Almost instantly they realized the lift shaft door would need prizing open. Shultz had already unwound the ratchet bar from the list shaft door on the level above. He appeared with it moments later. 'Nice hole, Weiss,' he commented.

'Not as successful as I'd hoped,' Weiss replied. He jammed the ratchet bar in the lift shaft doors and started to prize them apart, winding furiously. The emergency anchors looked like an old-fashioned bazooka from the old calendar's military circa 1940. A multi-purpose fixing would be shot from each side and the internal winding motor would keep the cable taught. The winding stop weight would need to be entered on the casing. 'Zeleno will need to keep away from the adjacent lift wall to us or she could end up being harpooned,' Shultz observed.

'I have dum dum bullets,' Abraham offered.

'What are you thinking?'

'If I fire them at the lift wall where Weiss is cutting with the pattern and a firing interval we're going to use for the anchors, do you think she'll understand?'

'I don't see why not, you don't get to be head profit enabler unless you're very smart, do you?'

'Suppose not, at least you'd be mindful that the wall we shoot at is going to be the only way in, so you'd give that a wide berth.'

'Sounds like a plan.'

Abraham shot the harpoon pattern on the lift wall top left, top right, middle left, middle right, bottom left, bottom right, leaving a gap of five seconds between each. Within, Zeleno jumped a little as the first dum dum hit. *What was that all about?* A dent on the interior lift wall had appeared. By the time the fourth dum dum had struck she'd already worked out it was a warning for a firing pattern. She stepped back and stood midway against the opposite wall. The lift continued to sway and the anchors were creaking. The enforcers had stood the anchors on the tripods that came with them and programmed a value of two hundred kilos for each anchor.

'That should be a firm grip on the lift,' Shultz remarked. The rear of the anchors were lined up to ensure a secure fix to the building. 'Round the corner, men,' Shultz bellowed. They didn't need a second warning, they knew that an anchor through the head or torso was the sort of body piercing that came with major side effects. Termination being the odds on favourite.

'Firing in five, four, three, two, one.'

The first anchor exploded, sending the barbed anchor deep into the lift's protective armour. It drilled through the inner wall and a good ten or so centimetres past it. Zeleno was startled to see such a lethal looking piece of metal penetrate the lift, but quickly reconciled her shock with the fact that the anchors were designed to do just that. The opposite end of the anchor firmly embedded itself into concrete. The anchor winder fired up as the lift continued to vibrate from the intrusion. Another bang and a screech as the second anchor hit home. Zeleno took stock. She'd be fine if she stayed where she was. The first anchor pulled the lift closer to the shaft wall sending her stumbling to the tip of the harpoon. She slowed her forward lurch to the harpooned wall. Her hand made contact with the wall along, almost, with her face. The third anchor penetrated the lift, missing her hand and face by the narrowest of margins. She staggered back in shock at the near miss she'd had. It had been far closer than any assassination attempt against her, and this was supposed to be a rescue. In an instant the remaining anchors had fired and the lift had been pulled safely to the shaft wall.

The emergency anchors were secure. At last, the enforcers breathed a sigh of relief.

Weiss bent under the top cable, stepping over the mid-height cable simultaneously. He pushed hard on the outside of the exposed inner lift wall. It held firm against the lift shaft, solid as a rock.

'Firing up the cutter, step away, enforcers.' Sparks flew from the cutter's point of contact, arcing randomly around the area like a cascade of mini shooting stars, the noise reverberating down the lift shaft. It took ten minutes to cut out the exit hole. Weiss stepped out of the way.

'This bastard's mine!' Zeleno exclaimed as she gave the final kick, sending the cut section of lift wall back out towards the enforcers. She stepped out onto the cut piece in triumph. 'Thank you enforcers. What's the situation?' The building shook again as if in response to her question.

She bent under the middle cable separating her from the enforcers, having thought better than trying to step over it.

Forester spoke again over Shultz's comms link. 'You really need to get out – there's a crack forming above you, expect a collapse.'

'Emergency chute now!' Abraham led the way followed by Starr.

'Your turn, Ma'am,' Shultz gestured. She followed with he and Weiss close behind. They stepped onto the chute on the level below. Their speed quickly built up to evac velocity and then stabilized, as designed. They were soon halfway down when they heard an almighty crack from above. Half of one face of the building above the explosion had collapsed, caving inwards and sending the biggest shitstorm of rubble straight down the lift shaft. Shultz opened the comms to Forester. 'We're on the chute. What just happened?'

'A big chunk of building collapsed into the main lift shaft. We have aim rollers on the chute's exit.'

'Great, have a Sixer ready to send us over to the research building.'

Ten floors to go. The first of the rubble had impacted at the bottom of the shaft. The last floor before the chute's end unwound past the lift shaft on the first floor to slow the descent speed down. Already dust was leaking out of the first floor lift shaft doors as the rubble had started to pile upwards towards the first floor. Seven floors to go and the anchors attached the concrete were causing stress cracks in the wall. With the anchors now supporting over two tons of lift and rubble the anchor winches had locked into a safety position. The only things giving way would be the anchors embedded in the lift wall or those in the wall of the building. The building at the level of the winches had undoubtedly been weakened by the blast and the earlier collapse. The cracks now spread from the wall anchors, meeting up as if to agree upon their next evil move.

The wall surrendered its grip on the anchors, sending chunks of the building in the direction of the lift which had now decided to give in to the force of gravity at long last. Shultz had just passed floor two. The lift and rubble were now passing the eighth floor, doing their level best to reach the bottom first. Shultz heard the rumble down the shaft get ever closer and louder. *This is going to be too close for comfort*, he thought. As they were passing the first floor the lift arrived on cue; a huge explosive crash blew open the doors of the lift on the first floor, sending a door and debris flying thought the air. Shultz caught the scene in the corner of his eye as metal and concrete sped towards him on a collision course. The metal cut through the chute with chilling ease, threatening to wipe out anyone unlucky enough to be in that wrong place at the wrong time. Shultz was in the wrong place. A metal projectile sliced a glancing blow on his helmet; time was on his side today, but only just! He disappeared onto the ground floor, leaving the chaos unfolding behind him.

The rollers at the end of the chute were pulled by waiting enforcers to ensure each exit from it impacted on a different portion of the deceleration air cushion. The four enforcers and Zeleno were down safely. The rest of the building's occupants had already been evacuated. Forester opened up the comms link. 'Good job enforcers. You're the last – we're going to get out alive.'

'How many dead?' Shultz asked Forester.

'We think fifty at present and another twenty or so soon on the levels above the blast. They're trapped. There's not much chance for them. They're only minor maintenance techs so it could have been a lot worse.' Getting to their feet the Meometics enforcers were ushered towards the Sixer by their waiting GUCI colleagues. The Sixer sped off towards Meometics research building.

'Well, at least there's no need to remove Porter from his position now, unless of course he's not up to his new job of lift shaft organic coating,' Zeleno commented.

Forester heard the remark through Shultz's open comms. *What a bitch, not much gratitude showing there.* She had no remorse. She was glad, Porter had failed yet again. At least he paid directly for his last failing, such a shame that her HQ needed a bit of a makeover.

Dr Jeremiah Brunt decelerated the craft as they approached the coast and their research facility. The corporations had employed a variety of approaches to guarding their intellectual property. Some kept their research in the main population centres of the four global blocks, ostentatious presence and security being their defence. Others, like Torq, preferred to operate on the edges of civilization to make any security risk visible far earlier. Because of this strategy, stealth technology was their main focus, they used it to protect their tech on the journey to and from their research base. But before this prototype ever made it to market Santos would have their full value out of it.

Slowing down the craft Dr Brunt hovered it a short distance away from the small concrete pad they'd taken off from earlier that solar. Professor Benjamin Taylor re-connected to the focused network beam they'd left active on their departure. 'I have the link, DJ.'

'That's a relief,' Dr Brunt replied.

'Re-initiating the video loop. It's running, take her in, DJ.' Dr Brunt lowered the craft towards the pad. The main hangar was about to come into view having being protected from satellites and fly-bys by an overhead rocky outcrop. The door activation event was conveniently re-directed to an archived backup log as before. The hangar doors slid apart, and whilst Dr Brunt's control of the craft was impressive, it had to be millimetre perfect. He rotated the craft around to face the doors it had just passed through. He called up the co-ordinated display.

'Two metres x, three metres y, rotation one degree.' The panel called out its updates: 'Thirty centimetres x, fifty centimetres y, rotation one degree.'

Professor Taylor called out, 'Sixty seconds video left.'

'Four centimetres x, five centimetres y, rotation one degree.' In addition to positioning the craft, Dr Brunt tapped the rotation controls slightly.

'Thirty seconds left,' Taylor announced.

'Nearly there,' Brunt replied. 'Eight millimetres x, seven millimetres y, rotation .25 degrees. Two millimetres x, two millimetres y, rotation .025.' Dr Brunt switched off all propulsion and the dispersion field. 'We're done,' DJ announced.

'So's the video,' Professor Taylor replied.

'So we're in and undetected, what now?' McCree enquired.

'We're going to hook you up to Gentech's finest invention. Some say it's the best innovation since the distance pill. All we know it as is the *Genelyser*,' said the professor.

'I'd rather have a distance pill.' McCree countered.

'That's only dealing with the symptoms, not the cause, John. The distance pill may make you not care about your condition, but the Genelyser will *fix* you. I've just fired off the video one more time. It will erase itself at the end of its cycle – using it too often could make it more detectable. We have five minutes to leave the hangar.'

336

'McCree strapped to med-table' was transferred onto a wheeled undercarriage, upon which he was taken from the hangar to the Genelyser room. The video operatives were blissfully unaware of the removal and the return of Torq Innovations' most secret prototype. In the days of the old calendar such unfamiliar performance by an aerial craft would have been attributed to a UFO sighting.

'No point in shouting for help, McCree. All the rooms are hermetically sealed. Some rooms are even sealed to the atomic level,' said the professor. A moment later, after following the left fork of the corridor, they were at the Genelyser room. Professor Taylor looked into the scanner which granted them access. He closed the door from the inside. They unclipped McCree from the wheeled undercarriage and attached the med-table to the disturbingly named 'Sample analysis and reconfiguration' floor clamp.

The panel lit up. It was Derek.

'Our mission was, well, we'll have to leave it for you to decide,' Dr Brunt spoke to the panel.

McCree was not in a position to see the image on the video feed. Whoever knew so much about Brunt and Taylor's mission to able to contact them at the very moment they'd arrived back? Someone with a lot of power and influence.

'Switch over to the Genelyser camera.'

Dr Brunt did as ordered. 'We retrieved Enforcer John McCree.'

'No sign of Zeleno?'

337

'No, there were no other bio traces in the villa.'

'So, she's still unaccounted for! I'll run another search. We have to locate her,' Derek paused, *'unless John McCree, Meometics enforcer, would like to shed further light on the matter.'*

'Can't help you there, I had a ton of building on top of me.'

'I think you can, John. You didn't travel there on your own. You were part of a team. Now I ask: where have the rest of them have got to? I'll tell you what, John, I'm going to access all the data available on GUCI-net, and if there's anything else missing you can decide if it's worth your while filling in the blanks. There is, of course, an incentive for you.'

'Oh? And what would that be?'

'I think primarily the device you're strapped into. Invented by our friends at Gentech. It reconfigures your genes in real time. Its primary design was to heal and repair physical trauma such as yours, or disease or illness. It takes healthy gene and cell samples and uses them as a template. To restore you to 100 per cent health.'

'That sounds like science fiction to me.'

'To some it is, but here it's science fact. The thing is, John, it... how can I put it... ah, yes, it hurts like hell. *Really, you can't even imagine how painful it is. Some unethical colleagues tried it on a conscious subject. Only problem was, the pain was so intense it ruptured their brain. The heart gave in as well — of course, that could be transplanted, but once your brain has had it, it's game over.*

'It's designed to work under deep anaesthesia. Now you are in need of repair. Let me know your thoughts when I return. My colleagues will orient you towards my video feed on the panel. It's only

right we discuss this important decision face to face.' Derek disconnected from the panel.

Dr Brunt turned 'McCree strapped to med-table' to the main panel in line with its video feed. Professor Taylor spoke. 'I think, enforcer, you have around five minutes to make your mind up.'

McCree thought quickly. A strategy, not a yes/no answer, was what he really needed. He was not in a state to bust his way out of here. Maybe the machine would fix him. If he could only speak to his son-in-law. Grant would have a better idea of its abilities, but that option was even more remote than him escaping his captivity by giving the scientists a couple of dirty looks. Agree to give information but nothing of real value, get fixed, escape. That would have to do.

There would have to be some fine tuning of the plan as the circumstances presented themselves, but that was standard procedure for this type of situation – where one party was clearly at a disadvantage to start with. Professor Taylor spoke to McCree. 'John, we're not your natural enemy. What GUCI, the corporations, and the federations represent is what we take issue with. You are just an individual who has been poisoned by the systems they control.'

'You're right about that, PB, I'm pretty poisoned all right.'

'I hope not,' Professor Taylor replied. 'I believe you sacrificed yourself in that villa for someone you believed in. Whether or not that person was really worth it, *you* thought they were, and that is an admirable set of qualities you

339

possess. Loyalty and self-sacrifice. We need more people like you.'

'I don't think so, PB. You don't know the whole story.' The comms panel lit up; Derek was back. McCree was staring straight at him. *'John McCree. I feel confident enough to say that you will be a valued member of our organization. There is going to be a little pain before that happens, however.'*

'You mean you're going to use this device on me while I'm conscious.'

'Oh, no, John, it's going to be far worse than that, I'm afraid. I'm going to tell you the truth.'

'Are you the clichéd evil scientist I used to read about in the last of the novels from the old calendar?'

'You do rather have a sense of humour.'

'I'm surprised myself, to be honest, seeing as I'm the one in the dark here, strapped to this fierce-looking piece of technology.'

'Not for long, Enforcer McCree. My name is Dr Derek Toft. I am responsible for a lot, not all, but a lot of this mess, and I want to put it right. I invented pixie dust, the coating on all silicon chips that gives them their enhanced computing power. I was also developing nanites as a technology. I had the backing of the newly appointed head profit enabler of Meometics, Renee Zeleno. She was also my partner. Shortly afterwards she had my team, and me, terminated.

'There are special GUCI teams who co-ordinate these terminations across all the global blocks. All those on a research team and their families have their terminations synchronized once a corporation decrees they know too much. It is designed to stop intellectual property being obtained by competitors. It's the price GUCI pay to remain the

policers of the planet. It's the corporations and the federations that are really the ones in charge. A cull of scientists is designed to keep us under control.

'*I had suspected something wasn't right, as once a person had been assigned to an Ultra project they'd never be heard from again. I was able to confirm this when our team was assigned to Ultra. I saw myself being terminated. My records were removed, and those of my colleagues. I also saw the video footage of their terminations deleted before my very own electronic eyes. I exist, for the present, only in electronic form, but my aim is to return to my original organic state. Since then I have been monitoring GUCI termination squads' activities. They have terminated over four hundred scientists since my demise. I can show you some footage if you like. Here's one, featuring a young Charles Porter in action.*'

McCree was taken aback. What web was he entangled in? At least Porter didn't seem to be enjoying his assignment. In fact he had no real expression as he terminated one of the scientist's children. Derek continued. '*So far I've only showed you that your head enabler is a real bitch, and believe me, the other corporations' head enablers are just as bad. As a scientist and spurned lover you've most likely worked out that I do have a motive for revenge. However, my real motive is much more important than that — revenge is a mere side-effect of my main aim. There is a lot more to explain, and this is where you come in.*

'*For the last fifteen profit cycles there have been increasing numbers of protests about all sorts of injustices. By and large the protests are met with GUCI force, which you know all about. You personally have been responsible for well over a hundred terminations. You believe the victims are anarchists and represent a threat to society, but what about this citizen?*'

McCree froze; he recognized the footage from his own helmet vid feed. *'After you pulled the mask off the protester's face, what did you feel when you discovered you'd terminated your own wife? After all, she was one of those anarchists.'*

'NO,' McCree shouted. 'She wasn't meant to be there.'

'I know, your wife went in place of someone, didn't she?'

'Yes. You know, you bastard, my daughter was meant to be there. I didn't know that Julia had persuaded her to stay at home and that she went in her place to that food protest.'

'So that day was never going to go down well for you. The loss of your daughter or your wife. Given the lack of communication between you and your daughter I'd imagine she blames you for what happened? You did tell her, John, what you did? Wait a moment. How could you – Sorry Eleanor, I shot your mum, it should have been you I terminated. No, you admitted you made a mistake that day and because of it your wife died, but you were being very economical with the truth.

'So you got worse. You made sure of terminating citizens at protests to secure the distance pill on a regular basis. Trouble is, too many pills for too long is a bad thing, John, and you became addicted. Eleanor couldn't wait to leave and, sure enough, her knight in shining armour, Grant Stern, came to the rescue. You were left to wallow in your despair ridden apartment all alone.

'There is just a little further to go, John. It turns out that Research 4 are to be assigned to Ultra projects. Unusually, the step has been taken to bar them from their lab until then. What I haven't quite been able to determine yet is whether Grant has elected to take Eleanor and your eight-year-old grandson Joule with him. I have the date of the termination though.'

McCree's opportunity to regain a bargaining advantage was rapidly diminishing. He hadn't even brought a knife to a gun fight. He'd brought a baguette! Derek knew exactly what he was doing. There was to be one more revelation before he made his offer.

'There's something else you should know, John. Your wife and a number of others at that food protest were not terminated. A number of rounds of your ammunition were swapped with NDMs – Near Death Munitions. Gentech scanned the bodies collected and retrieved those hit with NDMs. So you didn't kill your wife. I have the footage here.'

'She's still alive?' McCree had the briefest, cruellest glimmer of hope.

'No, John, but I think you will wish you really had terminated her.' Derek played the footage. It was Julia, strapped to a device similar to the one that McCree was. 'No sedation' was subtitled on the bottom of the footage. McCree closed his eyes. It wasn't enough. He heard the most fearful scream. He didn't even recognize her voice. It was evil. He peered for a brief second. She was wailing and sobbing at the same time. She writhed around, desperate for the agony to end, then she slumped, still and lifeless, her minutes of unimaginable pain at an end. Blood trickled from her eyes and nose. *'No John, you didn't kill her, you left her to that.'* Another clip replaced the scene that was surely to haunt him forever. Another subject was in the device. The subtitle read 'Sedated'.

Life sign monitors that he'd not even spotted on the previous clip were visible and started to rise. 'NDM repair %' flashed on the screen. The video clip speeded up.

343

'NDM 100% repair completed' flashed on the screen. The subject was brought out of sedation and opened his eyes. Two scientists entered the room and removed him.

'So what happened to him, afterwards?'

'He was terminated. Shot in the head with an old-fashioned bullet and put back on the machine. Was he revived? No, that was a repair too far for the technology. Maybe if they improve the Genelyser with Research 4's new chip enhancements it may be possible. However, we're now digressing. Gentech deliberately murdered those protesters by experimenting on them. GUCI swapped the ammunition to make the torture possible.'

'I must congratulate you, Derek, on your thorough research so far. I believe we both have the desire for justice or revenge, call it what you like. Only I can mete it out.'

'No, McCree. There are others involved. My colleagues here are just a few of the organization we call Santos. We need your skills for other purposes.'

'I don't understand...'

'Let me remove the final doubt from your mind. I'm sure you don't want to blindly swap allegiances just to find we are no better than GUCI and their cronies. I received a communication from a scientist by the name of Violet Redbridge with some disturbing research on planet melt. The end of all life on the planted, caused by the sheer greed of those in control. Scientists against nanotechnology organized systems was formed to stop our respective employers developing technology to the point where nanites would be able to "eat" the planet.

'Unfortunately the nanite arms race has continued, and the final piece of technology that will lead to the destruction of the planet is about to be rolled out. I have a plan to prevent this, but all roads

344

appear to lead back to Meometics' head enabler. She cannot be allowed to release Research 4's latest product to market. Wait a moment....' A surge of high priority communications flew past Derek on the network. He decrypted them. *'There's been a major explosion at Meometics HQ. The epicentre was on the – fortieth? – floor. Head of security's room. Meometics Chief Security Enforcer Porter and over fifty others dead. A citizen under interrogation spontaneously exploded. No, wait, other data indicates he caused a massive overload in the thought chair. The citizen under interrogation was identified as Franco Barone.'*

'Barone?' McCree enquired. 'He was involved in the attack on the Meometics' Assemblage.'

'Yes, I know. He was part of Santos, but tasked with performing actions ordinary scientists had no stomach or skills for. He was a special ops scientist – one of the few we have. We had a disagreement as how to resolve the situation we were faced with, but he did agree to try my way first. That was to terminate Zeleno. Yes, Franco believed going for the head of the corporation that possessed the final piece of technology for planet melt would ultimately fail. He wanted to use nanites to keep such leaders under our control. That no longer matters if he has perished. Franco must have arranged the nanites in his body to resonate at the frequency the thought chair operates on. He assured me that if he ever was captured by those hostile to Santos's aims they would pay a very big price for their actions.' Derek paused, *'But back to you, John McCree. I want you to be our backup.'*

'How do you expect that to work?' McCree replied.

'No clues, in case the thought chair gets used on you again, but all you need to do is make the right choice if the situation arises.'

'Oh yes, I will. You can be sure of that, Derek.'

'*Before we set you on your way, can you tell me a little more about your time on Taw-Cymru?*'

'Well, there'd been no security confirmation back from Zeleno that she'd arrived safely. Porter sent me in as the head of a team to make contact. We found that the Sixer Zeleno was travelling in had been ambushed and all the enforcers escorting her had been terminated. Zeleno had just made it to the villa with the aid of the last surviving enforcer on the escort. He ultimately paid for his actions with his life.

'We located her and planned to fly back in an Aerial the following solar. My specialist and I deemed it too risky to use the Aerial's automatic systems sooner in case they'd been compromised. The villa's systems certainly had been. We had to re-download the systems clean from overhead sat-feeds. The next thing we knew, there was a killer satellite bearing down on us. I figured someone wasn't going to make it, so I gave Zeleno my ID chips and briefed Starr and Shultz on what to do in the event of my demise.'

'*And your briefing was?*'

'Simple! To fly back in the cheap seats on the Hypersonic and use my ID chip. The only safe place for Zeleno to stay would normally have been at Meometics HQ, but that's just been blown up. Porter suspected a leak at GUCI so he gave me a team suitable to operate independently. I fed false information back onto the network to buy us some time. It was designed to throw our opponents off the trail until Zeleno was back safe. You didn't pick her up until she was back at HQ.'

'Correct, John, but you should all have perished at the villa. I picked you up from the villa system re-download. I sent that satellite over to terminate Zeleno.'

'But someone managed to append a warning onto the transmission – "Get out!" Personally I'm grateful, but it seems, Derek, you have the same problem with someone being on the inside as GUCI have with you.'

'Thank you, John, for being so candid. Because of the risk of you been scanned by a thought chair again, I can't detail where we go from here, but remember to do the right thing if called upon. Goodbye, John.'

Dr Brunt turned 'McCree strapped to med-table' back to its original position facing away from the panel.

McCree was unable to see him fire up the Genelyser. Fortunately a mist descended over him. McCree's last conscious thoughts were troubled by echoes of the terrible screams of his dear wife Julia.

The scientists left the room and headed for the hangar. By the time McCree had been fixed they would be on the Western Block. On entering the hangar Professor Ben Taylor called up the lab's controller from an auxiliary panel. 'Ben, what tests do you have scheduled for the T.I. Apparition?' the controller enquired.

'Jacob, please don't use that pet name – it's not very clever,' said the professor.

'At least allow me a little entertainment in my routine and predictable existence,' Jacob replied.

'I want to run a stress test on a full fuel load. Pump the tanks to full.'

'Like I said, routine and predictable.' The fuel shot up the centre of the front landing strut service tube.

Dr Brunt entered the craft followed by the professor. The doctor strapped himself in the pilot seat. *'Fuel load 70 per cent.'* 'Comms check,' the doctor announced, giving a little show specifically for the controller. Turning the comms off for a second he turned to Benjamin. 'Are you sure you can defeat the interlocks for the evaporator?'

'Sure hope so, or we'll take half the complex with us! ' Jeremiah flicked the comms switch back on.

'Comms check, can you hear me controller?'

'I hear you, all's OK from this end. Fuel load 90 per cent.' The professor ran a diagnostic on the evaporator's interlocks. They were rock solid. *Right, what they need is a little surprise.* He opened up the service panel and with his multi-probe and shorted two tracks on the interlock board. Normally the interlock would fail over to its backup, but that piece of code was deactivated during a diagnostic. Success. *Interlock disengaged.* It happened in seconds. *Fuel load 100 per cent.* Jacob was frantic.

'Professor Taylor, the evaporator's interlocks have disengaged – exercise extreme caution, abort the test.' He was speaking more formally and with crystal clarity, possibly wary of an investigation should something bad kick off. Indeed for Jacob Dahlstrom it was about to.

'Too late,' Dr Brunt replied.

'But the interlocks are off!' Jacob screamed.

'I know,' replied Professor Taylor. 'That was the idea!'

The professor activated the dispersion field and powered up the engines.

They moved towards the hangar doors.

Dr Brunt could not restrain himself. Jacob had always been a drag on their research, having subjected them to onerous, seemingly valueless, procedures. There was nothing worse in his eyes than someone with an inferior knowledge of the project telling them how they should be doing their job.

You wanted entertainment, Jacob, well your wish is about to come true.

He activated the evaporator. A huge electromagnetic pulse blew the hangar doors off. Jacob's jaw dropped as the T.I. Apparition disappeared into the distance. 'Maybe it's not such a bad name, after all.' said Brunt.

'Agreed. With that look on Jacob's face you'd have to conclude that he'd just seen a ghost,' Taylor replied.

Zeleno and her escort headed straight to the Sixer that Forester had waiting for them. She'd made this journey many times before, but this time all it did was bring back memories of her last trip to Research 4.

She thought of McCree; her last physical contact with someone who seemed to care for her. She was one of the ten most powerful citizens on the planet but she still felt there was something missing. There was a void in her life that she wanted to resolve. She needed to close it or she might as well succumb to her opponents. She desperately needed another pill to focus her aims and dispel her self-doubt.

Guided by Starr, the Sixer made its way over to the research block where Research 4 were, or rather had been, located. The next contribution they would make to Meometics would be an addition to the 'terminated' list. She wanted to leave a legacy that would outlive her mortality. One that perhaps her offspring could pursue after she had left this plane of existence. That, however, required a son or a daughter to continue her wishes, not a mere ideal. They arrived at the research facility with none of the drama of her last trip to the building. With Starr in control of the Sixer, Zeleno was able to take a moment to gather her thoughts. Something was different about the way she was feeling – something new.

It wasn't withdrawal symptoms from the distance pill, even though she felt the absence of it. It was something else. Something she'd never experienced before. It was exciting yet unnerving at the same time. Dare she hope that she was that in tune with herself?

Down the ramp the Sixer sped to the transport level of the research building. This was where the real power was and would be wielded, not at Meometics HQ, which was just a symbol of the power that had been brought to its knees by a rogue activist. Science was the real defence against anarchy. Only superior technology could quell those who would wish to challenge the status quo.

The Sixer pulled to a halt outside the transport level lift. There were barely five metres between it and the lift that gave access to the entire research lab building. Zeleno was instantly verified by the lift. The enforcers followed immediately behind her. 'Level eight,' commanded Zeleno.

'Confirmed,' the lift responded in reply. The group exited the lift on arrival and decamped to Zeleno's primary technical presentation facility. This room displayed models in true 3D visualization. Its purpose now was as a haven for the head enabler. A shiver went thought Zeleno, she felt as if she was at the end of days. A change was coming. She looked out from the frameless window of the presentation room across the city, only to pick out Meometics' partly collapsed HQ smoking. It looked as if the building was resigned to its fate and was having a last cigarette before it expired. Her competitors would surely take advantage of the situation. Why was Meometics being targeted? Why was she being targeted? Had someone seen the threat she or her corporation had become? Or was it because of the innovation she was about to release to market? There were too many possibilities and too few facts to come to any sensible conclusion. She turned towards Shultz, 'Get me Peter de Vries.'

'Yes, Ma'am.'

De Vries was already in the research building, along with the rest of the Assemblage, who had now temporarily relocated away from the severely damaged HQ. Shultz called up de Vries from the panel.

'The head profit enabler requires your presence for some urgent analysis,' Shultz explained.

'Of course, on my way,' de Vries replied.

'Shultz, you will stay here for the analysis. As you're to officially become the head enforcer I want you up to speed with the analysis of our current situation. Now is as good a time as any to make your position official.'

'Yes, Ma'am.'

'Enforcers, thank you for your assistance. Relocate on the floor below,' Shultz ordered.

'Yes, sir,' they replied, and duly left the presentation room.

Zeleno looked over to Shultz. 'Head Enforcer Shultz, you are to do all within your abilities and position of Meometics Head Enforcer to protect the profitability of Meometics and all of its resources.'

'I will, Ma'am,' Shultz replied.

'Will you also pledge to protect the Head Profit Enabler and their office, whatever the personal cost to yourself?' Zeleno added.

'I will, Ma'am,' he confirmed.

Zeleno stepped away from the scene of destruction that had filled her eyes, and directed her attention towards the presentation panel. She opened up her personal control interface. 'Authorisation Renee Zeleno. Confirm appointment of enforcer Tony Shultz to position of Meometics Head Enforcer.'

'Voice authenticity confirmed, appointment authorised,' the panel confirmed.

'Good solar to you, and may your appointment be more profitable to Meometics than that of your predecessor.'

'Thank you, Ma'am.'

The panel announced de Vries's arrival via the lift.

'Peter, please,' Zeleno ushered de Vries to a seat around the presentation projectors. He sat down, looked across to Shultz and eyeballed the seat that Shultz was meant to sit at. Shultz took the hint. Zeleno sat down. 'To my mind, gentlemen, Meometics appears to be facing the gravest threat in its history. I would even use the term *at war*. This threat must come to an end. Peter, what have you been able to analyse so far?'

'Head Enabler. The recent spate of incidents can be traced back to your decision to commercialize Research 4's last project. Specifically, your first communication on this decision was to Tom Andrews, Research 4's team leader.'

'Is he involved directly?'

'Inconclusive, Ma'am. He did however visit the apartment of Grant Stern the evening before confirmation of your decision.'

'Stern is a member of his team, right?'

'Yes, Ma'am. Stern's apartment is on the same level as that from which Franco Barone aided the attack on the Assemblage. Franco Barone has also been positively identified as visiting Stern's apartment a number of times.'

'I see. Who else was involved?'

'All the visits to Stern's apartment were made when Grant Stern was in the research lab. Whilst on Taw-Cymru, Barone took on the identity of Rueben Small, a Hypersonic maintenance operative. Small's whereabouts are still unknown. 'However, given Barone's fatal attack on our HQ, the odds are in favour of him also being responsible for the attack on you en route to the villa in Taw-Cymru.'

'So, Peter, is that an end to the situation – a final suicide mission?'

'I believe not, Ma'am.'

'Explain.'

'The attack on the villa by the satellite could not have been instigated from anywhere on Taw-Cymru. The satellites are controlled from one of the four GUCI block headquarters. Following the cessation of hostilities by the old calendar nation states towards one another, the satellites were put under control of the interim protectorate, later to be split into four land blocks of control: north, south, east, and west.

'If GUCI was to face an external threat and lose a block HQ, the satellites could still be controlled from other blocks, but only from the GUCI HQ in that block. This leads to the conclusion that someone within GUCI is involved in these attacks. Barone was most likely one of their operatives.'

'What about the attack from the rooftop? There must be other operatives at large.'

'It's possible Barone set the whole ambush up, Ma'am. He could have used a different ID to gain roof access from where the weapons were fired, and he didn't need any ID whilst using the jammer from his own apartment. Barone was in the ideal position to remotely control the weapons' fire. I accessed Enforcer McCree's investigative logs on the incident. He was clearly having difficulty understanding why the assailants didn't fire more charges at the convoy. He thought it may be due to the experimental nature of the weapons, and that was all they had available to them. Why then leave the contents of one of the charges on the roof to deal with the enforcers that were able to rush to the scene? It could have improved the chances of the attack succeeding if it had been fired from the roof with the charges,' de Vries continued.

'I believe that Barone was the only operative involved in that attack. He could only carry so much up to the roof in a single journey, and making repeated trips up there to stock up with further ordinance would have increased his risk of detection. My further analysis shows that a hit on the Sixer from above would have compromised the vehicle. There are a number of surfaces on the top of the vehicle vulnerable to the nanite gel. The Sixer was safe from the bottom up – it would have been destroyed from the top down. McCree did, in all likelihood, save the Assemblage from an unwelcome end.'

'Yes, losing McCree has been one of the many great losses we've faced recently.'

'Ma'am,' Shultz interrupted, 'if I may?'

'Of course, Tony, go ahead.'

'We discovered that the villa's systems had been compromised, but believed they'd been hacked by persons unknown rather than GUCI. McCree deliberately sent misinformation to Porter as he believed the comms were being intercepted by unauthorized means. Whatever the actual truth, either version of events means GUCI have some explaining to do.'

'I concur, Ma'am,' said de Vries. 'We should also be prepared for another operative to pick up where Barone left off. The attempts to destabilize Meometics by assassination of its senior leaders requires substantial resources. It's unlikely to stop until they succeed or we can expose or eliminate them.'

'Thank you, Peter. Tony, do you agree?'

'Yes, Ma'am. They have access to GUCI's network. I'll see what we can uncover, Ma'am. There has to be a trace left somewhere on the network.'

'That's a big space to search, Shultz,' de Vries said.

'Yes, but I do have a few ideas where to start looking.'

'Speaking of searching, find out what progress Porter made in retrieving McCree's body, Shultz.'

'Yes, Ma'am.' Shultz had already noted that Zeleno addressed her senior staff by their first names when after advice or opinion. When it came to orders it was strictly surnames. That was clear enough for him.

'I'll set up my base on the level below you, Ma'am.'

'You do that. Thank you, gentlemen, keep me informed of any further developments,' said Zeleno. It was a coded message: *'Get the fuck out of here until you have any further news.'* De Vries and Shultz obliged, coded message or not detected.

At home Eleanor Anne Stern was worried. It wasn't about her father. She was concerned, if something had happened to him, how much they would owe to GUCI. Joule was missing his Grandpa as well, but not for the reasons of debt reduction that Eleanor was.

'What's up, Blondie?' Grant asked his son.

'It's strange for you to be here, Dad, why aren't you making up new stuff in your lab?'

'I've been given a rest because of a very important piece of work. In fact I'll be moved on to new top secret projects soon. You'll both have to decide if you're coming with me or not,' said Grant.

'Of course we're coming with you,' shouted Eleanor from the opposite end of the apartment. 'I'm not going to miss the chance of a lifetime.'

'Thanks Sweet,' Grant replied. Joule was not so sure, he didn't want to leave his Gramps behind.

Shultz had set up the facilities he needed in record time. Trebanos Starion took the lead in sorting out the tech needed. Whilst he'd felt intimidated by Porter, he felt more of a kindred spirit towards Tony Shultz. Perhaps because Shultz himself was very handy with tech and systems. Trebanos could talk more tech with this head enforcer than the previous one.

'Sir, I've transferred the control commands from Porter to you. As well as that I've moved the files across to your data store,' he announced.

The panel assembled for Shultz was more compact than Porter's. Shultz was used to using a tabbed interface with less scrolling required than the standard layout afforded for senior Meometics staff.

He called Anderson up on Taw-Cymru. 'Anderson, I've just been looking at the footage transferred across to Porter.'

'Yes sir, oh – congratulations on your appointment, by the way.'

'Thank you, Anderson, but it could well be one of the shortest appointments in Meometics' history if I don't come up with some answers soon. Is there anything else you can tell me about the scene of McCree's disappearance, other than what the video feed captured?'

'You mean like the surprise on our faces when we found he wasn't there? I think the fact that a tunnel had been successfully bored into the villa ruins to extract McCree was the biggest shock,' said Anderson. 'He must be uber important to someone, even if he's dead. Unless they thought it was Zeleno under all that rubble. Then why take McCree if he was dead?'

Shultz took stock of the situation. 'If our comms were compromised our adversaries might have picked up on Zeleno's order to return his body. If Zeleno's enemies got there first they could using McCree's body snatch to demonstrate the point to her.'

'The point being?' asked Anderson.

'"We have far more resources at our disposal than you have. Give up and accept the inevitable." Be assured that's never going to happen whilst I'm still around.'

'I hope then, sir, that you'll stick around for some time yet.'

'Thank you, Anderson. Speaking of sticking around, how would you like to be on the team I've just been promoted from?'

'Sir?'

'If you think you're up to it, that is.'

'I'm not sure I am, sir. Meometics enforcers are getting much more heat than those attached to other corporations. I wouldn't want to be a liability.'

'Very well, Anderson, I appreciate your candour. I wish you all the best in your continuing post in Taw-Cymru.'

'Thank you, sir.'

'Shultz out.'

Damn. If this gets any worse I'm going to have to recruit the rest of my team at gunpoint.

Zeleno's panel lit up. It was Shultz. 'Tony, good news I hope.'

'It's news Ma'am, not the best though.' Shultz paused as if to summon up the strength to get the words out. 'McCree's body has already been taken.'

'What? How could that be? There's already a GUCI contingent on Taw-Cymru. How could they have been beaten to him?'

'Ma'am, I'm sorry. The network must be seriously compromised. If they weren't already on Taw-Cymru they must have a fast transport available. I'll check the network.'

'I want results, Shultz, not theories.' There was a distinct menace in her voice that was not lost on Shultz.

'Yes, Ma'am, understood.'

Zeleno terminated the connection. She really did have a short memory, or maybe it was just a quality you needed to possess to be a head profit enabler. Totally results driven with your reputation only as good as your last result. Oh boy, he needed a result. Shultz decided to follow the trail of the lift shaft organic coating formerly known as Franco Barone. He'd been positively identified at the initial attack, and then he'd been captured on the hyper transport in Taw-Cymru. He had to have travelled there somehow. Discounting methods of transport beyond physics and even the wildest theories, there was only one way to get to

Taw-Cymru between those two events. The hyper transport.

There were a number of possible flights he could have been on board, but even broadening the range further to encompass the improbable flights, there was no trace of Barone being on any of the hyper transports to Taw-Cymru. His tracks had been hidden. *No matter though*, Shultz thought, I'll check the flight manifest logs for signs of alteration. A tamper with any of the manifest logs would surely point the finger as sure as a freshly raked piece of garden would indicate the latest victim in a mass murderer's back garden.

Unfortunately it became evident to Shultz that the mass murderer had raked the whole back garden to obscure where the latest body was buried. Five manifests showed discrepancies compared with the remaining files. It was not enough to pinpoint the actual flight Barone had been on, that would merely confirm his method of entry onto the peninsula. Maybe the logs of the satellites that overflew Taw-Cymru during the time Barone must have been there would offer some clues?

There were twelve overflights including the killer satellite. He came across the sequence of satellites that he'd used to re- download the villa's systems. He couldn't access the killer satellite's logs; Shultz assumed this was only available from four locations on the planet and he wasn't at any of them. The satellite logs did have a common thread to them; there was a subtle difference in the way some of the entries had been reported in the logs. It was a change of style, almost like digital handwriting, specifically tied to the program that made the actual amendments to the logs.

Whilst pouring though the logs Shultz couldn't help feel that he was being watched. At first it was a feeling of mild disorientation, he presumed from the recent escape from Meometics HQ. It was still growing, however; he focused on the main panel, was he being observed from inside the panel itself, perhaps?

Derek had taken the long route to get to his present location. He'd been hampered by Shultz's recent system-wide queries and had to pause on numerous occasions or risk having part of his consciousness blown away by a burst of high-speed data queries shooting across the network. Derek was sitting outside Meometics' research labs main security systems. I had transmitted the information he needed to gain a foothold into Meometics systems before Porter had arrived on the scene with an inept techie by the name of Starion. The log file requests had been intercepted by Derek; he knew exactly what Shultz was looking for. Santos was also searching for information. Disguised as a logic probe utility the AI was able to read the building's locator database. Zeleno was in the presentation room. This would be even better than he expected. He planted a file in the hologram presentation file store. He modified the checksum on the file so it would be detected the next time a security sweep was initiated. Derek was also receiving updates on McCree's status. Finding McCree, not Zeleno, under the remains of the villa was a bit of a blow. He had been able, though, to incorporate him into the plan.

McCree was still a risk, but much less of one now, and his re-introduction to Meometics would surely give Santos an edge. Hopefully the decisive edge.

After a long solar our exchange of information for the reset was complete. Elizabeth hugged me goodbye, and held my hand tight. She pressed a data chip into the palm of hand. What was this for? It was not meant for the recording devices in the golf ball to see. I'd need to play it back, but the only private place left for me was back in the Research 4 lab. Elizabeth let go. 'We've a transport below ready for you. We've left suitable clothes in the vehicle. It has adaptive shielding, so you'll be able to change in it. There's no zapping this time, K, this is our one chance. Good luck,' said Elizabeth.

I had instructions to follow, but my priority was to get out of this ridiculously constricting stealth suit.

'One moment,' Elizabeth said. 'Stand away from the bottom of the room.' There was a slight hiss and a hatch began forming on the floor of the golf ball.

'Your exit awaits,' she prompted. 'Bend your legs as you leave the tube.'

'And if I don't?'

'You could break them.'

'OK, I'm so bending my legs. Thanks for the tip.'

The hatch slid open and I slid down. The tube was at forty-five degrees to the golf ball and I assumed the floor would be waiting at the other end. I picked up speed as for the next thirty seconds or so as the tube continued. The light levels inside gradually increased. I must be nearing the

365

end of the tube. I shot out and fell straight into a large hangar type building which appeared deserted save for a solitary transport. *My legs! Bend at the end*, my subconscious reminded me. I managed to bend them just before my feet hit the concrete floor.

No breaks or snaps of bone, but it still hurt on impact with the floor. I stood up fully and walked over to the transport. The entry circuit hadn't detected me; the suit I was wearing was still doing its job. I pressed the release button by the transport's entry point. The door opened, I stepped in, and the door closed. The transport's guidance panel indicated the stealth shield was active.

I removed my golf ball garments and put on the technician clothes supplied for me. After what I'd just been wearing they felt like presidential robes. I was tempted to play back the contents of the data chip in the transport, but reconsidered it as being too risky. I'd have to open it back in Research lab 4.

The departure panel indicated the vehicle was awaiting external guidance. No doubt Derek would be moving through the network ready to position himself for the big event. How long that would take I could only wonder, mere seconds if unhindered I imagined, but he'd have to wait at times along his route to avoid the security software that was running throughout the network. I took the opportunity to get a spell of sleep in. As long as I was awake enough to confidently walk out of the transport to my lab when I arrived at Meometics that would suffice.

McCree had almost been fully baked.

The first thing he saw as he recovered consciousness was a flashing green light on the console in front of him. It was out of focus and momentarily worried him. Slowly his focus returned. His eyesight was better than he recalled. Someone had turned the dial up on all his senses, but his optimised brain functions were perfectly capable of handling his newly upgraded senses.

He was still secured to the med-table. 'Process complete,' the Genelyser announced. In barely audible tones it added, 'To remove your restraints please focus your gaze on the self-release control on the panel. Do not move your head during this process.' On the vid display in small lettering was the title 'self-release', with a small circle split into four quadrants by cross hairs. McCree grasped the subtlety of the design. If your eyesight hadn't been upgraded then you wouldn't be able to focus on the crosshairs. Without a hearing enhancement the instruction to stay focused on that point would not have been heard. Clever. He stared at the crosshairs.

The scanner's 3D camera detected the white of his eyes and identified that his pupils were indeed converging on the crosshairs. 'Releasing in five, four, three, two, one,' the Genelyser control panel announced. There was a whirr and a few clicks from the med-table's hydraulic activators as the straps retracted into the table. 'Release sequence complete,' the table confirmed. McCree sat up and looked around.

The scientists must be long gone. He still had not been discovered by the research base's occupants.

Let's get their attention, he thought. McCree had noticed Torq Innovations logo in various places inside the hangar for the prototype craft. To his knowledge, no GUCI enforcer from a rival corporate had set foot in another company's premises. The chances for espionage, if only a perceived threat, were worrying enough for the practice to be non-existent.

McCree had to get out of this room. The walls were all white, like an arch-typical room for the deranged. *Why is white the colour of choice in these situations? It must be something to do with the reflected light.* More reflected light equalled an increase in serotonin released by the brain. Joule had told him that. 'Gramps, it's why solar light is good for you as long as you can filter out the harmful parts of its rays.'

His eight-year-old grandson had given him a briefing on psychophysics; the future of the planet would indeed belong to the young. McCree felt only loss when he thought of his wife and daughter. It was the thought of being re-united with his grandson and no one else that spurred him on. That and his desire to deal with the unfinished business between him and the head profit enabler. McCree recalled the moments of furious lust they'd shared. What did it all mean? He had an emotional bond with her, but did she feel the same? He concentrated on the possibilities. He was surely the junior partner in this relationship. Would that be enough for him? He didn't know. It was time to sort out the present, not the potential future.

Next to the door was the only panel McCree could see. There were only two options available: GUCI emergency interface or regular connection. McCree knew which to choose. He would never be a regular guy, even in a million solars. He was a GUCI man, although what that meant was open to question, following the revelations of the Santos operatives. McCree selected the emergency interface. The panel's embedded software contacted GUCI HQ with the location of the signal. This was going to cause Torq Innovations a lot of trouble. In fairness to them they had no idea that there would be a GUCI enforcer, other than those in the service of Torq Innovations themselves, on the premises. The location of the alert had been pinpointed. Torq Innovations research base, whilst not exactly 100 per cent unknown to GUCI, was now highlighted on a list of locations to observe with particular attention. 'State the nature of the emergency,' a lifeless approximation of an excuse for a well-written piece of software commanded.

'This is Enforcer John McCree reporting. I'm assigned to Meometics yet I appear to be in a research facility, belonging to Torq Innovations I believe.'

'How did this occur?' the software asked.

'I was in Taw-Cymru on duty for Meometics when the building I was in was destroyed. I recall gaining consciousness and was…'

McCree had a choice. A choice of words. His choice would shape what happened next. Rescued, recovered, or abducted – which one to use? He could put a spin on the situation with one word. It made a change from using his weapon.

'…abducted by a couple of scientists in some sort of prototype craft. On arrival at their research facility they put me through a machine called a Genelyser. I appear to have been "upgraded" by it.'

'Please wait,' the software replied. This was an unusual situation. The software was familiar with a number of emergency Genelyser scenarios, but not one involving an enforcer from one corporation in the building of another because of an abduction. The software contacted the heads of GUCI, Meometics, and Torq Innovations simultaneously.

'Please advise recommended procedure for situation.' The software hardly ever had to consult the interested parties in a failsafe vote. This was one of those rare occasions, however.

GUCI's Jack Forester appeared on the video feed.

'Repatriation to Meometics recommended.'

Next up was Torq Innovation's Russell Clifton. 'Termination of enforcer recommended.'

The casting vote would be with Zeleno.

Zeleno walked over to the panoramic windows once more to view the smoking remains of the building she'd only just escaped out of. It seemed to reach across the metropolis and whisper 'failure' directly to her face. She certainly had some rebuilding to do. These attacks on Meometics had to be stopped.

Shultz is a good man, she thought. He knew his way around the tech and he'd proved his worth already. *What we could really do with is someone like McCree.* At that instant the GUCI software arbiter called her on the freshly configured panel in the presentation room.

Facts: Enforcer John McCree is currently located on Torq Innovations premises. He has activated the emergency GUCI link. McCree claims to have been abducted to his present location from Taw-Cymru for reasons unknown. McCree now has knowledge of two Torq Innovations prototypes. Possible outcomes are: Torq Innovations are responsible for his abduction; or McCree has been engaging in corporate espionage. A majority decision of repatriation or termination of McCree is required between the interested parties.

McCree was alive! How could this be? She had a little over five minutes to make a choice, let alone come to terms with his resurrection from the dead. It would be a temporary respite if she was to choose termination though. Why was he really in Torq Innovations? Had he given them information under interrogation? Was he a double agent? Surely no one could have survived in the villa after it had been razed to the ground. Was that his plan all along?

A mild discomfort surfaced in her lower abdomen as if to intentionally distract her from her decision.

McCree looked at the screen, *Damn, this wasn't part of the plan*; trial by triumvirate wasn't what McCree had in mind. *I should have just kicked my way out*, he thought.

Zeleno appeared on the screen. He hoped she was in a good mood, although according to what he'd been told by the Santos operatives if she'd been on the distance pills recently he was going to be toast. He thought he saw a half smile from her.

Zeleno looked at McCree; he seemed younger and even looked hotter than she remembered when she'd got it together with him whilst she was under the influence of a bottle of Sancerre. He really did look five or ten years younger than when they were in Taw-Cymru. 'My recommendation is repatriation,' said Zeleno over the video link. The arbiter spoke: '*The majority decision is for repatriation.*'

'Torq Innovations can send him over in the vehicle used to abduct him in the first place,' Zeleno decided.

'*That's not possible*,' Russell Clifton replied.

'I want him back with Meometics before sol-down, so get him to the nearest Hyper then.'

'*Ma'am, if I may*,' McCree spoke up. '*If I was given passage in the head enabler's craft with the engine overdriven, I should be able to return at an acceptable speed to HQ.*'

'*That would burn out its engine*,' Clifton replied.

'*The situation only requires a one-way ticket I'm not expecting to have to make a return visit soon.*'

'An excellent idea, and one that will go a little way to repaying some of the injustices Meometics has had to deal with recently. Be warned, Russell Clifton, if I find the trail leads back to you, you will be seeing John McCree and his team for a return match,' Zeleno warned.

McCree let out the smallest of sighs, it was a relief to be returning to familiar ground and to be able to see his grandson once again.

The last image he saw was a glowering Russell Clifton as the parties disconnected from the software arbiter's conference call.

Jacob Dahlstrom's operations panel was flashing furiously; it was lit up like an old calendar Christmas tree. In the midst of all the sensory overload the panel was subjecting him to, one extra important area also activated. Flashing red, it was an incoming call from the head profit enabler. Jacob had no time to wonder if this scene was being replayed across the corporations and federations. For him there was to be no solace in knowing he was not the only one in this sort of situation. Despite all the activity on his operations panel, he felt truly on his own.

'Operations Director, what in the name of profit and loss has been going on in operations?' Clifton asked. 'No, wait, let's see if I can work it out. You fucked up big time. You let our prototype get used in an abduction of a rival corporation's GUCI enforcer. Oh, but that wasn't a big enough mistake for you, was it? The enforcer is brought back to the research base and then, just to make sure you've completely lost the plot, you let our prototype disappear underneath your myopic gaze. Well, congratulations, for an encore the enforcer gets his DNA and cells rearranged courtesy of our other now not-so-top-secret prototype, the DNA Genelyser,' he added.

'Sir, Professor Taylor and Dr Brunt are responsible for this turn of events. They took the prototype and used its polarity beam to destroy the hangar doors. My team are analysing how it could have happened,' Dahlstrom replied.

'You obviously didn't spot them leaving the first time so they naturally gave you a bigger hint the second time round.'

'Something doesn't add up, sir. Why was McCree left here?' Dahlstrom offered, trying to defuse the tirade of abuse that Clifton had aimed at him.

'No, you're right, it's you that doesn't fucking well add up. Do you think McCree *shouldn't* have summoned emergency GUCI assistance? What was the matter with him, I'm sure he gets abducted all the time and strapped to DNA altering prototypes on a regular basis, why would he have called for help? The chances of ending up dead or being turned into a gelatinous blob were no more than 50/50 surely? You've failed. I have to let McCree leave the base in my personal craft, which will be getting its engine screwed as part of the deal.'

Your future at Torq is over. The solution presented itself to Dahlstrom; his humiliation was now complete. He cut the line off leaving Clifton in mid-sentence. The call-back was left unanswered. Dahlstrom felt a wave of regret wash over him. He stepped away from the hyperactive panel that overlooked the hangar space. Walking slowly and deliberately, he made his way down the transparent staircase onto the hangar floor. It took him no more than a minute to reach the edge of the hangar bay where the doors once were. Looking over the edge, back down the hundred metres or so to the valley floor where the hangar doors now lay, he gazed over, closed his eyes, and stepped off. His freefall was brief, giving him the shortest moment of liberation, until he hit the valley floor at terminal velocity.

Clifton had connected to the hangar bay video feed just in time to see Dahlstrom step over the edge. He may not have been responsible for the betrayal by Torq's scientists but it had been his responsibility to protect the facility and he'd failed. He'd paid the price. Clifton had to cede to Zeleno's demands. GUCI was the mediator in the dispute, and even as an alpha male he knew this was not the time to push water uphill. He made a mental note to get even with Zeleno.

Torq's GUCI enforcers had arrived at the Genelyser lab. Their team leader ordered McCree to activate the door release. McCree did as instructed and the team leader entered.

'Ah, Meier, from one enforcer to another – pleased to meet you,' McCree announced, having read Meier's arm badge.

'Put this visor on, please,' Meier dispassionately requested. McCree did so. If the intention was to keep him from viewing further sensitive areas of Torq Innovations, those in charge were badly mistaken. The visor was indeed extremely dark, yet he could still faintly make out his surroundings. *It must be the result of my upgrade*, McCree reminded himself.

'We've orders to escort you to the head enabler's personal craft. From there it will be programmed to take you to a neutral location in the Northern Block. Just before it touches down it will transmit a destination location for your corporation to pick you up. You must exit the craft within three minutes of touchdown as the craft will be programmed to dissolve. You do not want to be inside it when that happens.'

McCree took note; he'd seen dissolving vehicles before. He did not want an encore. The corridor he was led down was more of a winding path where the walls on occasion approached and retreated from him. From a tactical point of view McCree noted that this internal layout would make it impossible to snipe someone from the far end of the corridor. What purpose *that* served was unknown to him. Perhaps as only short range hand weapons were issued to enforcers they could respond quicker to an incident. It would be useful knowing that only close range armaments would be effective with this layout.

The swaying back and forth down the corridor might have induced a feeling of sickness in many, but McCree was just fine. They reached the last curve of the corridor which ended with a lift door already open and waiting for them. They entered the lift.

'Head enabler's transport,' Meier commanded. The lift acknowledged the instruction and highlighted a floor on the lift panel eight levels above them.

'The visor stays on until the head enabler's craft reaches its intended location. It will unlock then,' Meier explained. McCree couldn't believe they hadn't checked the visor's suitability. They clearly weren't expecting the Genelyser to work so well, or even at all.

The level they arrived at was opulent even by head enablers' standards. Here, in the middle of a highly polished aerial craft hangar, was the head enforcer's personal transport. The transport's external shell was totally chromed, reflecting the polished hangar and reflections of itself back onto its own surface.

McCree was guided into the craft and strapped in. Russell Clifton's craft was already pre-programmed with the destination location. Torq's techs had left nothing to chance; the news of Dahlstrom's demise had reached them – they didn't want to join him. The crafts doors locked. McCree could make out the display and the trajectory on the nav display. The craft lifted off gently and rotated to the launch exit. There was an audible increase in the engine's tone as it powered up further. McCree could make out the hangar launch exit but it seemed an impossibly small target viewed from behind his blackout visor. He knew that a decreased level of light could seemingly shrink the dimensions around the observer, but it still unnerved him a little.

Fortunately to counter that he could make out the launch sequence: four, three, two, one. The engine flared up with a rapid explosive increase in thrust. He felt his head pushing back into the headrest. He was able to keep his posture positive against the acceleration forces that assaulted him. In an instant he could make out a blur of trees either side of him – he was travelling under a tree canopy at great speed. A launch corridor had been constructed under the cover of the exotic greenery – it was a jungle or a forest, or perhaps something in between. The trees gave way and he was suddenly over sea. Looking at the nav display a picture of the area could be made out. It appeared that he was over the western edge of the Eastern Block. He might well be able to pinpoint the location of the lab to Zeleno if he survived the journey.

There were another two hours to go according to the dimly lit display. He was travelling at Mach 3, not far above sea level. The details from the display would be most helpful to Meometics; McCree needed to remember as much as possible about the journey. Given that the craft was due to be destroyed at its destination, there'd be no chance of reverse engineering the nav display information or its logs.

I'd been in the stealth transport for ages. The increasing tone of its power unit awoke me. I was still tired and trying to yawn myself awake. My head felt thick – it felt like liquid chocolate that was starting to solidify. Derek would surely be in place by now. I needed to change into tech's clothes before I arrived back at my lab. The stealth craft would get me to the research lab and into the complex provided Derek was ready. I had no doubt that he would be.

Even with security software patrolling the network, Derek could read and anticipate the actions of the software before it even knew what it was going to do next itself. The network audit could be heard, to Derek, as a rush of noise heading towards him. He marked himself as a system file in use. The audit smashed over him like a tidal wave of rushing water over the immovable rock rooted firmly to the ocean floor. The flow subsided and he was still completely intact. By the time the audit log manager picked up on his presence Derek would have disappeared. Yet, despite all the power he had over his electronic domain, he still wanted to be back in mortal form. The reset for him meant more that the salvation of the planet. No one else would be able to follow him down his path of immortality.

A message appeared on my screen, it was Elizabeth Hart.

'K, I have an important message for you. I am sorry I've not been able to relay it to you sooner. The difficulty has been that Derek monitors everything we do, albeit a little while after the event. This is our last chance to change what he's been planning.'

'I don't understand. What's the matter?'

'You're aware that Derek formed Santos as a response to the technology that would destroy the planet?'

'Of course.'

'Shortly after forming Santos and before Zeleno got to him, Derek recruited Franco Barone. Franco was different from the rest of us. He could have been the star man in GUCI's elite force – incredibly gifted in all fields. He turned his back on the military and dedicated his career to science. He was able to turn the most benign discoveries into something far more deadly. Virtually all our weaponry was penned by him. The beauty of his talents is that GUCI have no one with that mind-set. How can you guard against something you can't even conceive of?'

'OK, Elizabeth. So Franco is a valuable asset to our struggle.'

'He's much more than that, K. Franco felt the best way to achieve Santos's aims was to take control of its adversaries. Derek believed it was better to eliminate them.'

'So Derek's view prevailed?'

'Not exactly. Derek agreed to try Franco's approach with the condition that if it wasn't having the desired effect he would follow Derek's strategy.'

'So his approach won out?'

'Not as such. Franco had developed nanites that could be introduced to the target by artificial or traditional biological means.'

'Traditional biological means?'

'Yes, the exchange of bodily fluids. Franco thought that there would be occasions or opportunities where one method would be more favourable than the other. The main difference between the two methods would be if the requirement for transmission was to be overt or covert.'

'Ah, the old sex as a weapon cliché.'

'You could say that, K. Franco also developed a synthesised hormone, more potent than natural pheromones. If he applied it there would be very few citizens that could avoid his "charm".'

'So he's irresistible?'

'When it's to be in his interest, yes. He injected himself to prove his concept and was able to spread his nanites from himself to others. There's a threshold density of nanites he has, so that when he passes some on they will reproduce to between two and four million, depending on the individual.'

'So what has he programmed them to do?'

'They are able to manipulate the nervous system synapses — to block or allow signals. They can control aspects of the individual's behaviour.'

'Do you know how they're activated, Elizabeth?'

'By a specific electromagnetic field. Franco's idea was to generate the controlling field using satellites. It was, however, tested using a locally generated field. Derek duped us, he said we needed to be inoculated with a sensor dispersing fluid that would render us unable to be tracked by sensors.'

'I'm guessing that wasn't the case.'

'*No, it wasn't. He set up termination fields at randomly changing locations outside of our "golf ball". In addition, he has now managed to program a number of satellites to detect and fire a termination pulse at the infected subject.*'

'Termination fields?'

'*Derek's electromagnetic field that instructs the nanites to block our cell functions.*'

'Oh, I see. Is that why you remain in or around the confines of the golf ball?'

'*Yes, it is fully shielded from such signals. But I and my colleagues are now slaves to my brother. I'm afraid the same applies to you, K.*'

'What?'

'*Derek ordered your injection when you first met us in the golf ball. You've been allowed outside freedom to further Derek's plans. Your nanites are activated by a different signal.*'

'I guess asking Derek to remove them isn't going to be a good idea... Wait a minute, didn't you say Franco perfected this technology? What's his take on this?'

'*We haven't been in contact with Franco since he left here. I would hope he'd be shocked enough to undo what Derek did to us. Derek felt it would take too long for Franco's approach to permeate throughout society, even though Franco's intention was to target the most relevant individuals to speed up Santos's aims. Franco agreed to assist Derek by following his strategy of targeted assassination, although where more appropriate Franco would employ his own solution.*'

'So, my dear head enabler is the number one target at present?'

'Yes, dead or alive. Maybe she'd be better off dead than alive, if Franco has been able to get to her. The nanites in Santos are a control measure – stay put or die. Franco was looking to improve their usefulness, such as remotely controlling the subject. We don't know how far he got with his research. All his work in that area is triple encoded. Not even Derek can break the encryption, though I suspect he's tried.'

'Well, thanks for the update – but how does that help?'

Elizabeth sighed, 'Derek wants to be the only sentient immortal being following the reset. We will be kept prisoner here until he has what he wants. He intends to be in charge of the only functioning technology on the planet. He will rule the planet with that power.'

'But won't the ultra-capitalists perish? The planet will be safe with a scientist in charge.'

'I'd like to hope so but the defrags he's been through have altered him – each time he seems to lose a little of his original self. We haven't yet been able to free him of the need for them. We're slowly losing him. The being we'll end up with in return is most likely not going to have the survival of the human race on the top of its agenda. Derek needs to be trapped out in the open when the reset is initiated.'

'Oh, that's not going to be easy, is it? He'll be two steps ahead of any software sent to trap him. He needs a real physical barrier to stop him. At least we know where he is now and where he needs to get back to.'

'But he'll be able to reroute himself in any number of ways to avoid capture.'

'Not if we disable the connections behind us as we follow him. As long as he doesn't suspect what I have in mind, we'll pull through.'

The stealth craft's field had reached its required power level, and my transport left the sub-basement. I was on the perimeter of the main built-up city block. A number of Biostore apartment blocks were advertising their address on the side of the building as I sped by, but they might as well been written in crypto-cipher. They were unfamiliar to me. 'Distance remaining ten kilometres' the display read.

'*I wish you good fortune, K. You must initiate the reset but also stop Derek from returning to us.*'

'OK, Elizabeth, hope to see you later, safe and sound.'

Ahead of me in the far distance I could see a pall of smoke emanating from what seemed to be Meometics HQ. It was too far away to be sure but that part of the skyline did seem familiar. The craft took a sharp left turn and ran parallel with the smoking building in the distance. It was Meometics HQ, and it most certainly had been attacked. I still didn't recognize the buildings in the area so the research lab must be the other side of the HQ. A thought sent a shudder down my spine. What if the incident at Meometics HQ had led to temporary security challenges? I may not be able physically to even get into the building. I would just have to wait and find out. I was no combat expert, my skills were limited to what I could manipulate in a lab from an experimental panel. I thought about the synthetic forms within me. Would I suffer the same fate as the Santos members? I felt OK. Impressively, I'd never have suspected I had nanites implanted inside me. I thought I would probably be able to scan for them in the lab. Derek would need to keep the alarm's sensors and triggers from the lab quiet for his plan to work, and that would cover my other intended manipulations.

My craft was now only a few blocks away from the HQ. I could see that the top of the building had collapsed upon itself. It didn't appear to be to stable. It was still holding up though. Ever since the old calendar attack in 2001 on the twin towers in a city called New York, in what is now the Western Block, buildings have had to survive multiple impacts for two hundred minutes as a minimum before collapse. The HQ looked good for at least another hundred or so minutes. All those below the damaged levels should have been able to get out. That would be around the level of the head enabler's office. Had Santos managed to take out the head enabler this time? Maybe I wouldn't have to go ahead with the reset. Derek would surely know.

There was a steady stream of transports heading away from Meometics HQ. My craft merged into stream of them seamlessly. It seemed my mission would be aided by this fortuitous turn of events. The stream of transports split up and took different under-level entrances into the research building. There were two transports ahead of me and one behind. I was heading to the lowest transport level of all, closest to my lab. The craft pulled into a space.

Derek appeared on the craft's display panel. '*Welcome back to where it all started, K. Please wait here. I need to monitor the traffic. I'll let you know when it's safe to exit.*'

McCree was becoming accustomed to his security visor; he was able to see through it even more now than when it had been first put on him. The craft was over land, a barren, dusty, waterless and mainly featureless expanse of what looked like sand. McCree had never felt so alive. He unbuckled the launching straps and, for what must have been the first time, did a detailed appraisal of his situation...

The code to unlock the visor activates when I reach my intended destination. For added effect the craft will also self-destruct shortly afterwards. The unlock code must be embedded in the craft for use when it reaches its intended location. If it was transmitted from its launch point then others could trace the origin of the craft and hence the location of Torq's research base. So if I can determine the destination of my flight I could insert that location into the visor's signal input and no more visor!

It also struck McCree that the visor would need to communicate to the craft's systems and that there was a chance that it was a voice interface. 'Activate interface,' McCree commanded. No response. *What was he missing? Wait a moment.* McCree considered the owner of the craft and the solution came to him. Think... he urged himself. *Think* of activating the interface. The interface appeared dimly on the panel in front of him.

McCree turned the display brightness up to its maximum by thought. The display was now easily readable. The chair was indeed a modified thought chair. *This could be dangerous,* he considered. His new sense of reasoning kept him from a morbid idea of what would happen if he thought of crashing the craft. *Display interface status*, he thought.

Thought control active:

Safety backup level: medium assistance.

Thought depth: high concentration.

Actions to inputs: gradual.

OK, McCree realized, not very dangerous. The thought depth used to control the craft had betrayed Torq's intentions. *It must take a lot of practice and effort to think that deeply.* Notwithstanding having to hold the thought long enough and link up to what was happening to the craft's attitude.

I now have the depth and clarity to match that of a head profit enabler. *Only that the Genelyser can't have been used on the head profit enabler yet.* According to Brunt and Taylor, Torq Innovations had only just finished their trials using unwilling subjects, his wife included. Keeping his anger at bay and compartmentalized he ordered the navigation panel to display the destination of the craft. *Overlay destination into the navigation array*, he thought, quickly thinking it out again. McCree had successfully thought the destination into the location status display but removed it before the craft believed it had already arrived. A mid-flight meltdown would give him little chance of escape.

Torq's head profit enabler had been worried enough by Zeleno to give McCree a chance of safe exit from the craft. The visor was programmed to unlock at the first match of arrival at the destination. The craft however was still in flight and thirty minutes away from its landing. It would only start to dissolve if it remained static at the final destination for a full twenty seconds. Only then would things begin to get interesting.

McCree had now pinpointed the origin of the journey. He would be put down on the outskirts of the block that housed Meometics HQ and research labs. It should only take a couple of minutes to get him back into useful active service. The craft would not be recovered intact; he was sure Torq Innovations had well and truly covered that angle. Still, it would be most galling to their head profit enabler having to lose such a product, all because of two rogue Torq scientists. They had, however, patched McCree up better than he was before. That came at a cost that could never be repaid.

'Notification activated, transmission in progress,' announced the panel as the craft passed its pre-programmed announcement point.

Shultz called Zeleno on the panel in the presentation room at her new makeshift HQ.

'Ma'am, we've just received the location co-ordinates for John McCree's incoming craft. It's decelerating ready to land on the outskirts of the city block.' Shultz relayed the landing location to Zeleno's panel.

'Get a Sixer over there. I want him back here, like yesterday.'

'Yes, Ma'am,' Shultz replied, 'it will be a pleasure.'

Derek scanned the network. No further vehicles were due on this level for a few minutes.

A Sixer on its way out in a hurry had delayed my exit.

'I've frozen the output of the cameras between here and the lift for a few minutes. They are on an auto reboot cycle,' Derek advised. 'I have also modified the bio database pointer that the internal security database links to. You will be verified as lab calibration tech Noah Wilkins. Once inside your lab your original security will work.'

'They've locked me out though, Derek!' I said.

'Only out of the room, K, once in its all yours'

'Lazy techs again! The bare minimum of housekeeping won't keep anyone out but your dead old granny. Much less so sentient software like yourself,' I replied.

'Exactly. Remember, K, once you've activated your systems and fired up the signal you're on your own. I suggest you get out of the technology and population centres as soon as you're able to do so. There is a lot of death and destruction heading civilization's way.'

I left the vehicle. It was fairly quiet; the calm before the storm of destruction. The hum of the air quality tower block sensor banks and the food pipe with integral ingredient channels slurping their way into the building were the only sounds I could make out. It felt as though the planet was waiting patiently for release from humanity's vice-like profit-driven grip.

I stepped up close to the lift where I was scanned by its in-built sensors. *Lab calibration tech Noah Wilkins... confirmed.* 'Please state your destination tech Wilkins,' the lift demanded.

'Research lab 4,' I replied. I was going *home*. I had the corridor from the lift to the lab all to myself. The floor/wall skirt boards lit up with green tinged arrows to direct me to the lab. As tech Wilkins, the building had assumed this would just be one of many assignments and that I needed guidance around the area. The door frame lit up with a matching green tinge around the edge, and pulsed to indicate I had arrived. Of course I already knew where I was. It was cool to see the guided assistance and navigation in operation from a non-specialist's point of view, however. Despite the building's assumption that I need assistance finding my way around, it still viewed me as a competent tech, with access to repair, replace, renew, or reconfigure the systems within the building, and also to do anything else to them beginning with the letter 'R'. I opened the door. The systems were all on standby as if waiting for our return. It was better that I could not be here with my team, it would have been the end of us all.

I had a lot of tasks to complete here, where to start? Derek had reassured me he'd be keeping the lab safe from incursion until I was able to complete my goals, but he was just as much a threat to civilization as the present incumbents. It was time. I initialized the console nearest the sealed experiment chamber. I hadn't seen the start-up sequence in a long while. The systems were usually running from the previous night's data analysis as Tom or Grant were invariably in the lab before me.

My first problem was to let them know without my warning giving anyone a chance to interrupt the process before completion. I was going to need a few more panels active to make this work. Also, once Derek detected the process was past the point of reversal he would be heading back to his digital stronghold. That meant I needed my outside contact to be ready to reroute the network to stop Derek reaching safety. I powered up three more panels. Switching the adjacent panel into record mode, I began.

'Hi, this message is being transmitted to Tom Andrews and Grant Stern simultaneously. Please trust me that you will not have time to verify this or communicate with each other. Research 4 have been targeted for termination. This applies to your immediate family unit too.

'If my whereabouts were known to Meometics our deaths would be imminent. Terminations of research teams are co-ordinated to ensure no word leaks out of the practice. My disappearance from Meometics' scrutiny has given us enough time to formulate a solution. Time only permits me to keep further details brief, but it is my hope we will be able to meet up after the transformation has completed. What you must do, without delay, is leave your apartment after this message has finished and *do not* exit via the lift. You must minimize completely your interaction with *any* technology that contains a computing function. I recommend making your way to the location I've marked on the display for you. It will have to be on foot – please trust me on this. You'll therefore need something to keep yourself protected out in the sunlight. Again there must be no technology involved. If you or your loved ones are hurt, forgive me. I hope we can make it through the transformation. I wish I could give you more assistance. Hopefully the briefest of head starts will make the difference for you. Be careful. Goodbye. K signing out.'

That message would have to be sufficient. The recording's duration was eighty seconds. I set the message on emergency forced transmission to the apartments' comms panels. The announcement would be relayed through the apartments. There would be no avoiding the message, all they then needed to do was escape. The replay was paused. I just needed to tie in the activation of the message eighty-five seconds before the transmission of the overload pulse. Before I did that I needed my external back-up.

'Call Jo Bianchi,' I ordered the panel. 'Connecting,' the panel replied. There was that tense delay when placing that vital call; would it connect? Despite the modern world's infallible communications there was still something of a subconscious moment of anxiety whenever a communication was deemed to be of greater than usual importance. It was, I believe, called the Oakey effect, named after the scientist that discovered the correlation between perceived delay in connecting a call *vis a vis* the call's importance.

'*Jo Bianchi here,*' a familiar face announced.

'Jo, it's good to see you, although I wish it was under better circumstances.'

'*What can I do for you this time , K? Another unfathomable sample?*'

'No, Jo, something completely different.'

'*That's just as well, I think you may be on the banned list of customers who we can't deal with anymore due to negative profit outcomes of the last sample you sent me!*'

'Sorry, about that. This is different. I have to reroute a data stream away from a specific location.'

'*Tell me more.*'

'A large shitstorm is brewing. When it happens the hostile data stream I refer to is going to head for somewhere that has the capacity to hold it in safely.'

'*Hostile data stream? That sounds a bit futuristic.*'

'I wish it were in the future. It's totally in the present, unfortunately.'

'*What gives?*'

'I want to make sure it stays "unsaved".'

'*Unsaved?*'

'I want to block it into a corner. Do you know that old *Snake* program on the retro channels?'

'*I've heard of it.*'

'Well, I want to make the snake trap itself. But imagine that the snake was aware of your intentions.'

'*Ah, I see. You need a double bluff algorithm. That's no problem. I put together a similar piece of software for my particle discriminator. I won't bore you with the details of the two slit experiment where the particle behaves as a wave, but let's just say with the right software you can alter the reality of the wave/particle duality. I can sort the snake out for you.*'

'Jo, that's just what we need.'

'*No problemo, K. I'll upload the software.*'

'There's one other favour I need, Jo.'

'*Try me K, I can only say no.*'

'We'll need to take down a couple of circuits around the intended storage facility.'

'*Which circuits?*'

'The historical third tier archive – The DATAIX building.'

'That's already pretty much filled to capacity and mothballed, which as you'd know is the whole point of third tier archive.'

'It is, but that makes it the ideal place to avoid getting noticed. It may have a consistency check once a profit cycle.'

'But what about the archive, how big is this data stream, K?'

'About fifteen zettabytes.'

'You are kidding me?'

'Sorry Jo, I'm not. I wish I was.'

'That's pretty much half the archive removed.'

'I think if you looked further you'd find it's all gone.'

'But that would be corporate scale vandalism.'

'Well, he seems to think it's worth it.'

'He? K, what's going on here, really?'

'Really Jo, ignorance is bliss. There's a lot going on I wish I didn't know about. Are you sure you want to know?'

'Ha, I'm a field sci-tech. It's my job to find out why stuff happens.'

'This is more political than science or technology.'

'Well I'm no politician but a hostile data stream sounds like something I should be curious about. You said "He thinks the destruction of a third tier is worth it." And this "shitstorm" that's coming…'

'You're paraphrasing me now Jo, but yes, we're all going to be in it. I'm attempting to minimize how deep we end up in it. Do you know the story about the elephant, the cork, and the monkey?'

'Ah yes…'

'Jo, I'm the sodding monkey.'

'*I understand. Tell me more, K, and we'll see if we can turn the odds further in our favour.*'

'Well then, shout when you've heard enough, Jo. The hostile data stream is intending to be the supreme entity on the planet. He intends to subjugate all those who survive his forthcoming actions.'

'*He?*'

'He's the consciousness of a scientist that was murdered by a special ops GUCI squad.'

'*But then how did he survive?*'

'He didn't, physically, but he was able to scan his thought patterns into the network just before he was terminated. The intention was to allow repairs or even upgrades to the body whilst keeping the consciousness intact, returning it to corporeal form after the procedure.'

'*Wow, K. I thought my field of work was pretty advanced but that's radical.*'

'Yeah, I had trouble getting my head around it. If he hadn't been terminated can you imagine the conversation he could of had with himself? You're not real, but I am. I'm afraid I have to erase you.'

'*Yes, that would be sure to go down well with the newly conscious version of himself. Do you think you could ever persuade an electronic copy of yourself to allow itself to be terminated?*'

'I try not to think about that kind of stuff. I value my sanity too much.'

'*So now, "Derek" exists in electronic form only?*'

'Yes. He hopes one solar to return to biological form. Even though his original body has gone he has a scan of it. Nanites will most likely build him a new one sometime in the future.'

'But that doesn't sound too bad. Everyone's entitled to the right of self-preservation.'

'Oh, yes, but he intends to be immortal and become the greatest source of knowledge there is. The shit in the sandwich, Jo, is that my research team have invented new technology. It links in with Derek's previous innovations. Combined together they will give nanotechnology the boost it needs to eat the planet.'

'The grey goo scenario?'

'Yes. Meometics won't delay our technology to market, they are too focused on profit. In fact they have already planned our termination. If they locate me here we're all dead. The ability to control large swarms of nanites will be the end not just of our civilization but all organic life on earth.

'My profit enablers!' Jo exclaimed in horror.

'Look up some old papers by Violet Redbridge whilst you can, Jo. She had it all sussed. They terminated her too.'

'Say no more, K – I'm convinced. Whatever I can do, you can count on me.'

'Be careful to start with, Jo, because Derek is guarding the lab door – electronically, of course. He's waiting for me to initialize my signal and then when he sees it will have the planned effect, back to DATAIX he'll head.'

'But surely he can travel faster than we can reroute him?'

'No, he has to make his way around the network carefully to avoid the security systems. He is a rather large stream of data. He can see the code running and moves past it when it's not actually looking for suspicious activity.'

'*I see.*'

'There are seven links into DATAIX. Redundancy gone mad you may say, but it was a data transfer hub in the days of IP v4. Because of the old nation state interests there are two links on each of the sides into the exchange, apart from the northern face. I need you to disable the east, west, and south main connections and reroute them clockwise around the exchange. If you can run your double bluff routing software on the remaining nodes that will keep him busy.'

'*I don't think it will be quite enough, K, I didn't realize he was sentient. I thought I was dealing with an AI.*'

'Quite correct, Jo. That's why we'll need to run an extra layer of security software. I'm hoping Derek will sense the links going down and assume it's a GUCI cyber-attack. If so, the routing and security software would be interpreted as an attempt by Santos to protect the facility from attack.'

'*Santos?*'

'Scientists filled with nanites and held captive by Derek to do his bidding, or else.'

'*Ok, I get the picture, he's getting to be a bigger and bigger shit in my eyes with every additional thing you tell me about him.*'

'The sad thing is, Jo, he was betrayed by the one person he really cared about. She turned him into the monster he's now become. We have to stop him achieving his twisted aims. Oh yeah, and save the planet.

I've been given some details on the best software to slow him down by one of the scientists he has captive. She'll pay with her life if he gets back and finds out. If he gets back to DATAIX he *will* find out, I guarantee it.'

'I'll sort out those links, K, don't worry. I have a little utility I put together that will alter the reality of the networks as the data switches see them.'

'Thanks, Jo. I'll send you the "Richard of York gave battle in vain" signal when you need to fix the perimeter.'

'Understood, K, good luck.'

'You too, Jo.'

I disconnected the call to Jo Bianchi. That had gone well. He'd asked a few questions but that was just part of being in his profession. He didn't want all the gory details and for that I was grateful. He wouldn't have the burden of guilt about being part of what was about to happen.

I powered up the interface bench. The laser seals protecting the rest of the lab shone bright white. Next I called up the nanite delivery injector. I had to fill the interface with nanites. It wasn't very scientific of me. I had to stuff as many of the little buggers as I could on there. The interface was loaded and I was ready to power up the whole bench to overload. I turned on the final panel and Derek, true to his word, had planted a link to the GUCI control satellites in one of the minor adjustment codes. It was time to upload the adjustments to the satellites. It would only take a minute or two. The wave sensors were adjusted to transmit the frequencies generated to the control satellites. They would be picked up and distributed to the global sat-net. I set the control to linear increase and set the transmission code to be sent to Jo Bianchi at 25 per cent. This was it, one push of a button and billions would die. I pressed the proceed option on the panel and made my way to the exit.

McCree, in his soon-to-dissolve craft, was flying at subsonic speed and was moments away from landing. He took in the view of the sprawling city as it passed underneath him. It was impressive, but it was taken for granted just how much humans were in control of the landscape, and even nature to an extent. The cloudless skies over the urban centres and the relentless glare from the sun gave the city a washed out look at this time of the solar.

The craft slowed down. McCree looked at the nav panel and correlated the landing area in the landscape ahead of him with the map display. The nav panel projected the landing location on the front screen as a red flashing triangle. McCree had already located it. He was still impressed with his upgrade. He wondered if Weiss would have be able to locate it any quicker than he did. *Doubtful*, he thought. He realized in an instant the potential for problems should a head enabler ever get to use the Genelyser. It would need to be destroyed. The craft was almost stationary; it slowly descended into an open square on the edge of the city. A Sixer was visible close to the edge of the square – his lift back to Meometics HQ, no doubt.

McCree held onto the grab handles of the exit door and his visor released as soon as the craft landed. He counted down: twenty, nineteen, eighteen; still no access to the door. There was a charge building up inside the craft; twelve, eleven, ten. The door finally opened and McCree leapt out. The door shut behind; three, two, one. A shake from the craft and it collapsed to dust. *Analyse that!* McCree thought to himself.

Shultz stepped out of the Sixer. 'McCree,' he called. He rushed over to McCree and they exchanged bear hugs. 'Whoa!' Shultz announced. 'What supplements have you been taking? That's a fierce crush you've got there. I'm surprised to see you alive let alone looking ten profit cycles younger than when I last saw you.'

'I came back from the dead, all right.'

'The head enabler will be pleased to see you. She wanted her top man to pick you up.'

'Ah, I see, he couldn't make it then so she sent you?' McCree smirked.

'Ha, ha, I *am* her top man now. My predecessor, Charles Porter, coated the remains of HQ when Barone lit himself up under interrogation and blew the whole damn place up.'

'Good for you, Shultz. How many got back from the team?'

'Now you're back, all of us except for Delaney. He was thrown out of the Aerial and torched by the kill sat.'

'Damn.'

'Given what was thrown at us all, we came out of it pretty well. There'll be plenty of time to catch up on the details in the debrief – it seems you've had a pretty eventful couple of solars too.'

Shultz opened the door to the Sixer and they stepped in. 'We'll be back at the research block in about six minutes.' The Sixer sped off from the square.

'You'd never think this crate would do an average of 140 Kp/h through the city,' McCree commented.

'How'd you know that?' Shultz enquired.

'Easy, sir, distance divided by time.'

'But all I gave you was the time.'

'I measured the distance from the square to the lab whilst the craft was landing.'

'Did the craft have a point to point feature then, McCree?'

'Not sure. I added up the known size of all the points in between to get the distance. As I could see HQ was smoking I assumed you'd relocate to the research block.'

'That's worrying, if you just figured that out then our enemies will have too.'

'Oh, I'm not so sure of that. I've had an upgrade, since we last split.'

'So, what stuff can you do now that you weren't able to before?'

'Poke myself in the eye with my hands behind my back is the most amusing side-effect I've discovered.'

'That's not what I was really thinking about.'

'Not you, maybe, but I think I know someone who will.'

'I don't want to know, McCree. Too much information.'

'Sorry, sir.'

The Sixer shot down the ramp out of the baking light into the lower transport levels.

McCree reached over to the Sixer's weapons compartment and grabbed two close quarter 'profit protector' combat rifles.

'I don't think we'll be needing those combat rifles, McCree,' Shultz suggested.

'Sir, we always need weapons when I'm around,' McCree smiled.

Five minutes Earlier

Meometics Research Facility

Zeleno was looking out at the smoke still rising from the damaged HQ. With little wind to disturb the smoke it rose almost vertically.

The Sixer had just left the square where McCree had landed. The square was empty again save for a shallow heap of dust where the transport had been. The glowing dot sped up on the nav panel. Zeleno immediately felt a little better knowing that she'd have someone who could really kick and dick in equal measure. Shultz might be the logical choice to protect Meometics given the nature of the threat, but if violence was called for, McCree was the daddy. The faint whirr of the projectors firing up caught her attention. A sphere of projected light started to take form. Zeleno wasn't too concerned. Although the image produced would appear solid, it could pose no security threat. The initially indistinct sphere took form. Human form. It sharpened further.

'By all the profits!' Zeleno exclaimed. Derek was forming in front of her very eyes. A disembodied head at the height he was when he had a real body.

'Hello, Renee, remember me?'

'Derek!'

'So you thought terminating my team and me would solve all your problems? I'm afraid, Ren, your problems are just beginning.'

'Whoever you really are, you can go fuck yourself. My corporation will not bow down to your intimidation. This campaign you're waging against Meometics must be killing any profit you thought you'd make from these actions. Your backers will desert you. You'll be terminated just like the real version of this holo-puppet was.'

'I'm touched Ren, but I *am* Derek. These little incidents you've been encountering – it's not been Meometics I've been after, it's *you*. I wanted you to feel what it was like to be under constant threat of annihilation. I've grown bitter, why wouldn't I after being betrayed so callously?'

'Growing tired of your constant failure to finish the job… Derek?' Zeleno hissed.

'No, Ren. I just want to see the look on your face when your whole empire comes crumbling to the ground.'

'Your little projection trick will be long gone before that ever happens.' Zeleno stretched over to the main projection panel and selected the cancel function. Nothing happened.

Derek laughed. 'Oh, I don't think so. I'll give you a clue. I'm in control of these systems, not you. Your star is on the wane.'

'We'll see about that.'

'Yes, we will, in about five minutes actually. However, I must now say goodbye. I need to take cover. When I return you'll be long gone and I'll be the only being in charge of the entire planet. Goodbye, Renee Zeleno, we could have shared a wonderful future together. You fucked it up.'

Derek slowly dissolved and the projectors powered down.

The panels reset themselves. Zeleno had control of her comms again.

'Shultz,' she commanded. 'Find out how that bastard imposter managed to get into our network. Isn't our security supposed to be top grade?'

'Shultz here, Ma'am,' he responded. 'If I may, I think the problems are that the breach occurred from inside our network – not an external attack.'

Zeleno was about to admonish Shultz, even though she figured there was little blame that could be laid at his door having only recently being appointed. Before she could, however, a warning on the comms display pulsed amber. 'Upload to GUCI satellite detected from this building,' the panel warned.

It was indeed worthy of an amber alert. There was no way this should be possible. The system didn't know how to handle the data from the monitoring software so it decided on amber. Maybe it was a faulty sensor or maybe, quite literally, it was a ghost in the machine.

'Get up here, now!' Zeleno ordered the enforcers.

'Take the stairs sir? Just in case the lift isn't feeling too good,' McCree asked.

'Good call, McCree. The less tech we need to rely on in here the better. It's ten flights of stairs though, try to keep up.'

Shultz paced himself as he half jogged up the first flight. He didn't want to be so out of breath he could not speak

406

coherently when he arrived at Zeleno's office. McCree kept up. He was expecting Shultz to pick up the pace once he warmed up, but no.

McCree overtook Shultz, to the latter's amazement, and opened up a gap reaching level eight well ahead of Shultz who was two flights of stairs further behind. McCree waited respectfully until his superior, although supposedly fitter and certainly younger than he, caught up.

Shultz identified himself to the door and entered with McCree a few steps behind.

'Shultz, look at the panel, what's going on?' Zeleno asked. She didn't expect an immediate answer as her eyes were fixed on John McCree Mk II, new improved version. The Mk I hadn't been too bad, either. Her libido stirred. *If I was a man would I be having a hard-on now?* she thought. Shultz was too busy to notice a sexual tension of sorts between her and McCree. Zeleno's eyes showed delight with the promise that the McCree Mk II version looked to offer.

'How are you looking so well? The last time we were together you looked pretty grim.'

'Pretty dead, more like, Ma'am, I'd imagine.'

'Thank you, *John*, I understand your methods perfectly now.'

'Thank you, Ma'am, you trusted me and I hope I've repaid that trust. *You owe me now*, McCree thought to himself.

'In spades,' she replied.

'We have a situation here, Ma'am,' Shultz interrupted. 'Some kind of repositioning and launch program has been uploaded to the global sat-net. It appears to be spreading to the entire satellite network. I have to contact GUCI.'

'You'll do no such thing,' Zeleno's eyes hardened. She glanced at McCree, spotting he was adequately armed.

'Ma'am, with respect, it will be traced back here.'

'Our network has been compromised, you said it yourself, Shultz. We need to regain control fast. Anything we communicate now is going to be picked up by our adversaries.'

'I've picked up an increase in power emissions from the comms panels in research lab 4. We should investigate,' said Shultz.

'Lab 4? They are under order of termination. It can't be any of them, we know where two of them are. We're waiting for the third member of the team to appear so they can be taken out.'

That was bit careless, McCree thought. *She doesn't know I know.* It gave McCree confirmation that the scientists who'd abducted him, no, saved his life, and Derek, were telling the truth. Without this knowledge it would be assumed that they'd leaked secrets or committed some other offence against profit. McCree felt, for the first time since their introduction, that he had the advantage over her.

'We might be able to recall the code uploaded if the sender panel hasn't been locked out yet.' said Shultz.

'Get down to Research 4 and sort it, both of you,' Zeleno ordered.

'On our way,' Shultz confirmed.

Again McCree overtook Shultz on the stairway, jumping to the bottom of each flight of stairs from halfway down them. McCree was ready to rush through the door. Shultz caught up. 'I'll swipe, you follow through. You're the offensive tactician, McCree.'

'OK, sir.'

Shultz went to open the door and was thrown back by an electric charge. He hit the wall behind and slumped down it. *Damn*, McCree cursed. An improvised electric current, a.k.a. IEC, or booby-trap. He reached down to Shultz. He was still breathing, but was literally stunned. His combat armour had saved him. McCree needed to blow the door open; where would he get such ordinance in a research base?

He ran back down the corridor, this time to the lift. 'Access denied,' the lift stated. Damn it. His time on the Genelyser meant he needed a new security clearance scan, and one of the two people able to give him that was out cold. He returned to Shultz and dragged him back along the corridor to the lift where the proximity sensors would be able to verify his commander.

Head Enforcer Shultz, verified

Life signs: minimal.

Enforcer emergency clearance request facial ID.

Scanning... Enforcer 95% match – John McCree, presumed deceased. ID code: 57334345644, McCree confirmed.

'Enforcer confirmed,' the lift announced.

'Locate medical facilities and armoury,' McCree asked the lift.

'Medical facilities are on level three. Armoury located on level four and sub-four.'

McCree placed Shultz in the lift. 'Alert medical team to casualty arrival.' He stepped outside the lift. 'Lift to level three.'

'Confirmed,' the lift replied, and whisked Shultz off. McCree dashed around the corner of the corridor to the stairwell. The stairwell door unlocked for him as he entered. *I should have picked up on that electrified door. It guards more value that most other doors in Meometics apart perhaps from the armoury*, he thought.

Reaching the armoury level he pushed open through the door. 'Display schema,' he instructed the signage panel. The panel obliged. As McCree thought, it was buried in the central part of the level, tucked away from the lift and stairwell access. The door to the armoury was indicated but the room itself was not displayed. McCree ran down the corridor taking left, right, left turns at the forks in the corridor. He was at the door. Was this IECd too? He took off his combat armour and held it in front of him as he lurched at the door. The body armour would give more protection than that offered by his gloves, as Shultz had found out to his cost.

He pushed the door open but no shock came. This scenario appeared not to have been anticipated by his opponents, which encouraged him. There was no room, but five metres ahead of him was a flight of stairs disappearing upwards. He carried on; the stairs were wrapped around what must be the lift shaft. The armoury was a level above the floor the access door was on. *Makes sense*, McCree thought, a position of height would be of benefit if you were besieged in the armoury faced with hostiles. It was much easier to roll a flash grenade down a flight of stairs with the assistance of gravity. *Not so good if gas was let off at the foot of the stairs to rise upwards, perhaps.* He realized there'd be anti-gas equipment in the room so it was tactically astute to have stairs going up rather than down. McCree bounded up the remaining flights and this time he needed to swipe his access pass. The door clicked open. McCree entered.

He felt like a kid in a sweetshop. So many armaments, so much ordinance. Racks of pistol, rifles, guns of all sorts. The second set of racks to the left of the first contained heavier weapons, capable of taking out large chunks of a building. The third rack, at right angles to the first two, contained what he was after. Thrown and static weaponry. Grenades of all varieties and static chargers for remote detonation. *Ah*, he smiled to himself. Remote limpet charges. He picked up a handful of what he was after and raced back towards the lab. Down the stairs to sub-level four and he on kept running down towards Research lab 4.

I was just about to exit the lab when someone tried to gain access from outside. A huge current from the IEC'd door blew the would-be trespasser against the outside wall. I realized I was trapped here for the foreseeable future; an advanced escape would be out of the question. In the corner of the room was a thought chair, recently installed. I'd not seen it on the right hand side when I'd returned to the lab. It had been positioned in a way deliberately, *or not*, to be more noticeable on the way out than the way in.

Maybe it was the way our successors' work was going to be written down, or perhaps that was the intention. I could see the input level was now at 15 per cent. I sat back into the thought chair, which auto-activated. A projection formed in front of me. At least it seemed to be in front of me. It was Derek! 'This message is only activated by the detection of my nanites within those who use the chair. Welcome back to the cause of Santos. Fight fire with fire. Please relax back in the chair whilst it records your thoughts.' I could see the input level on the panel was now 25 per cent, Jo would be getting the signal.

The panel at Jo's location flashed up the code: 'ROYGBIV'

Jo was ready, his software was loaded around the perimeter of DATAIX. He disconnected the redundant links as planned. There was a large data steam heading towards DATAIX. Derek felt the disconnects and waited patiently. The software blocking his way placed itself into self-check mode. Derek saw his opportunity and slipped past the software. The next nearest DATAIX node had gone into sentinel mode. He'd need to make a detour. No matter. There was enough time.

McCree placed the limpet charges, with a simultaneous smoke generator, around the edges of the door. He set the devices to code eighteen and retreated a safe distance down the corridor. He punched 'eighteen' onto the remote detonator control on his wrist device and the door was blown off its hinges with a blast of dust and a loud bang. Smoke and dust filled the corridor.

I heard someone outside the corridor. The chair seemed to amplify my senses. Or had the nanites somehow bridged the bio electrical gap? An explosion, and the door to the lab blew open. The panel level was now at 40 per cent and the seals were glowing green. The adjustments I'd made since my last little mishap were holding steady.

A lone Meometics enforcer appeared from the cloud of smoke. He directed his weapon around the room, stopping at me. I felt detached from the scene in front of me. 'Turn it off,' the enforcer barked.

'No can do,' I was barely able to reply. I was now totally and utterly detached from myself in the chair. I was being copied. Was I the copy or the original? I was only vaguely aware of the being in the chair that used to be me. The nanites I'd been injected with must be reading cell activity and transmitting the signals across the network. The original me was being switched off. I felt the last of my consciousness being torn from me, then there was nothing.

'Answer me, dammit,' McCree shouted at the dazed occupant of the chair. McCree realized the person in the chair was no longer conscious – only a shell was left. McCree moved over to the comms panel. He called Zeleno. 'It's McCree, Ma'am. It looks like the lab is set to explode. I can't override any of the controls – they seem to be locked out. Suggest you prepare to evac.'

'I'm not doing any such thing. I'm making a stand, this has to end here,' Zeleno replied.

'Understood, Ma'am.'

'End this, McCree,' Zeleno added.

McCree could hear the lift arrive on his level. The lift doors opened and rushed footsteps bounded towards the lab. McCree trained his weapon on the lab aperture that used to be the door. Shultz appeared in the remains of the doorway. McCree was shocked to see Shultz back on his feet. Sensing McCree's surprise Shultz felt obliged to offer an explanation.

'Surprised to see me so soon, McCree? It's only a patch-up job with the latest steroids for a moderate electrical discharge. McCree, what's the situation?' he asked.

'The stiff over there's locked the controls and appears to have programmed in an overload,' McCree replied.

'Let me see,' Shultz sat at the main panel and tried to gain access to the systems.

A recording activated. *'Santos advise the following: the uploads to the sat-net cannot be undone. Let the lab overload complete. For the success of the mission to be assured the lab sequence* must *be allowed to complete. Civilization will undergo its greatest transformation since the invention of the silicon chip.'*

'This is just some pre-recorded bullshit,' Shultz muttered.

'Step away from the panel, Shultz,' McCree ordered.

'What?'

'I said, step away.'

'Are you nuts, McCree?'

'No, things have become perfectly clear to me. Now step away.' McCree waved the weapon at Shultz, gesturing for him to step back.

Shultz did as he was told. He'd have no chance against McCree.

'Why, John?' he asked.

'I realize now what the problem with this planet is. It's the corporations and service federations. They have caused the mess humanity has ended up wallowing in. Only there's not likely to be much more wallowing unless a stop is put to the exploitation of the planet.'

'What the hell caused you to come to that conclusion?' demanded Shultz.

The panel signalled 70 per cent input, the chamber seals were now bright blue, and the bench in the experiment chamber was faintly glowing.

'I believe I've had this view for some time, only it has taken me a while to realize it. That, and the help of a few brave souls to help me along the way to see the light.'

'You really are certifiable, McCree,' Shultz said. 'It must have been getting crushed under the villa in Taw-Cymru that did it,' he added.

'Think what you like, you're not stopping this process.'

'We'll see about that!' Shultz leapt towards McCree in an effort to knock him off guard.

McCree was quick to sidestep Shultz, who'd succeeded in smashing the weapon from McCree's grasp. McCree countered with a swift powerful kick as Shultz sailed past him. The crack of his neck was audible as Shultz slammed onto the floor, dead.

Sorry, man. You deserved more than this, McCree thought as he looked down at Shultz. *Such promise, wasted.*

Input level 90 per cent. The seals were now indigo and the bench was glowing white. The whole chamber was vibrating. In orbit the satellites has aligned themselves in clusters and were powering up their beams. McCree decided to retreat a little, back down the corridor to the nearest access point onto this level. No one would be able to pass. He thought of his daughter and grandson, feeling a pang of sadness that he'd never see them again. They would all be re-united soon enough. He hoped the end would be swift for them. His life had all been such a disappointment.

The call from Zeleno to the comms panel went unanswered.

What the hell is happening down there? She realized in that moment that for all her abilities and powers as a head

417

profit enabler, there was nothing she could do from her present location. She needed a weapon. The navigation panel detailed the location of the nearest weapons locker. It was at the back of the room; she wondered if the designers had placed one there to terminate anyone responsible for a dire technical presentation. She had seen far too many presenters in need of termination for the theft of her valuable time.

She gained access to the locker with her entry code. A pistol with a gel charge cartridge. Good for twenty shots; one hit to incapacitate, a second hit to kill. Need something doing? Do it yourself, she thought. She'd read many a book, seen many a video movie feed where the hero just wouldn't head towards the source of a mystery. Not when they'd already lost contact with far more capable members of their team. The correct response would be to head in the opposite direction at maximum velocity. That was not an option, this was reality. Running from the situation would only make matters worse for her. She might be able to retrieve the situation herself, the great profits permitting.

She was just about to activate the lift, but stopped short. If the same sort of shit was about to hit this building as her HQ the stairs would be the better option.

In the nanite chamber the input level reached 100 per cent. The seals glowed violet, the bench glowed whiter than white, shifting into the ultraviolet range. A burst of electromagnetic energy surged from the bench causing the seals to collapse to a transparent state. They would play no further part in protecting the lab. The wave spread out through the lab conducted by every piece of connected metal. Any chip in the path of the wave was fried by its own enhanced pixie dust coating. The technology that created the growth of ultra-capitalism had now become its executioner.

Above the planet the satellites had generated the same chip exciter wave – the planet was bathed in a silicon chip destroying onslaught. From inside Meometics' research block the wave coursed throughout the building, amplifying itself whenever it crossed onto power conduits. All the systems inside the building began to fail.

I was back in the golf ball at Santos. I was no longer organic. Derek had seen to that. I should be totally non-existent, yet I had my consciousness and self-awareness. I sensed the holo-emitter circuit nearby. I could see the barriers Jo Bianchi had set up to stop Derek's return. I had to get Jo to create a firebreak from the rest of the network. The holo-emitter started up. I felt myself being drawn into it.

It was Elizabeth. 'K, I have to ask forgiveness from you once more. Derek had planned for you to die in your lab.'

'I have though, haven't I?'

'Not quite. I was able to set up a connection stream from the chair back to here. It was either that or you'd have ceased to exist.'

'I suppose being an electrical entity is better than being no entity at all. However, Elizabeth, even my existence as an electrical entity is about to come to an end. I was able to upload the instructions for creating the pulse. The satellites are lined up to propagate the signal across the globe and a massive overload is going to wipe out any connected chips spreading from Meometics' research building outward. That includes this facility. My contact has placed traps to stop Derek returning, but that won't be of much use as this whole place will be soon be taken down. I think we have only minutes left to say our goodbyes.'

'Just a moment, K, there's something I need to do. I need to make a final call.'

It would be *the* final call. Elizabeth activated a comms panel. Santos would never light themselves up in this way unless they were sure of the outcome.

'Dr Brunt, Professor Taylor?' Elizabeth enquired.

'Here, Elizabeth,' they replied.

'Status? We've been monitoring the satellite nearest us. We need disconnecting from the network now, please.' Elizabeth replied.

'Certainly,' said Brunt. 'We're timing it to perfection.'

Dr Brunt switched off the craft's dispersion field. They were now visible and hovering outside DATAIX, but pointing at the building opposite. The craft was facing floor twenty-seven.

'Fire.'

The pulse buckled the corner of the building.

'Focusing the beam tighter,' Professor Taylor announced.

'Firing.'

The second pulse crushed the corner of the building. Metal panels, glass shards, and circuitry exploded out from either side of the pulse's impact point. The comms panel disconnected. 'Connection severed' flashed on all the panels in the golf ball. The space of the network I had become aware of had dramatically shrunk to a size not much bigger than my being. It was disconcerting.

'Job done!' Elizabeth exclaimed.

Derek saw the destruction of the silicon hell mankind had enslaved itself to. He was waiting on a network bridge looking for a clear break in Jo Bianchi's logic traps to pass though. It never came. He felt the route to immortality disappear in front of him. Derek's own operatives and his sister had successfully conspired against the conspirator.

Whilst there had been seven dispersed connections to DATAIX, the building opposite was the concentrator into the building. Jo's logic traps had given the true Santos movement the time they needed to pursue Derek's original ideal. The one before his humanity had been defragged out of him, replaced by a psychotic desire to subjugate all those on the planet. *Fuck you all, you'll regret you did that!* He turned in rage towards the opposite direction straight into the oncoming quad-axial electro pulse. He was scattered like dry grains of sand on a wind-whipped beach. His being and his threat dissipated into insignificance.

Behind the wave that travelled along all the connected metals, the structure of those metals lost their cohesion and turned to powder. The satellites had lit up all the chips on the planet and fried them. Silicon's grip on the planet was being removed systematically, the supreme irony being that it was by its own hand. It was proof of an ancient concept that cannibalism still existed, even in the highest forms of intelligence and technology.

McCree felt the wave surge out through the lab – its reinforced walls cracked. All McCree's tech overheated. His combat clothing was overheating – it was burning his skin. The hairs on his wrist were charred by the heat from his wrist device. He frantically stripped down to basics.

The brightness from the lab was increasing like a miniature star on earth.

Time to go, we have success, he thought. He made it to the stairwell. The status panels in the corridor were dead. The lights went out. All he had was the dim glow of the ultra bright light shining from the lab. The door to the staircase was easily pushed open. All the electronic locks were inoperable. The ground pulse linked to Meometics' network had spread out like a virus along all connected metallic surfaces, leaching the useful properties of the metal from it. Wires turned to powder. Sheet metal turned paper-like. Metal beams were turning brittle from contact with the pulse.

McCree heard creaking from above. He realized what had happened, what the scientists had managed to pull off, right from under the nose of GUCI, the corporations, and the service federations. If only he could survive he would surely be at an advantage. No one else would be able to use the Genelyser; he was totally organic and freshly upgraded.

The building started to creak further. He visualized its construction – the external faces had a metal frame. The glass panels would most likely fall off about now. How much of the integrity of the building would remain intact he did not know. His question was answered sooner than he'd wished when the upper floors collapsed as the four central metal columns snapped, leaving the floors with no support. *No, not again!* he thought, as the rumble approached ever closer to him. He thought of many things, his wife, daughter, and grandson included. It would be such a waste of his new talents not to make it out of Meometics. His final thoughts were of Zeleno. At least she would be entombed in this broken edifice of rubble and ideas too.

Outside in the city block, buildings were starting to crumble. Spreading in an outward radius from the building where the ground pulse had started. All of civilization was interconnected. All would succumb, save for the few buildings of older construction type primarily made of stone or brick. Smoke was billowing across the city block from multiple sources, some from collapsed buildings, some from where aerial transports had crashed out of the sky. Many of the elite would have perished in their monolithic HQs, or perhaps during a Hypersonic flight. Many more citizens would be trapped by fused door access systems. If they were lucky, the ground wave would propagate to them and break the locks before panic and rash actions befell them and those trapped with them. If they were unlucky they'd be trapped in a lift, its controls fused out, waiting for the ground wave to creep up and weaken it. The outlook for those inside a lift was grim.

The wave entered the metro subsurface system via external points from already affected buildings. Those metro cars travelling into the path of the pulse had their mag-lev propulsion crumble quickly as they hit the wave head on. Lurching with no control along the tube they slipped lower in the tunnel, their levitation lost, and the sides of the cars settled down tight, wedging them against the tunnel walls. There was no emergency front or rear access from the cars, why would there be these days? The metro would be a mass tomb for the few million or so travellers over the planet. They had been afforded some bizarre sort of burial at least.

The surface transports lost propulsion also, some of them before they crashed, side-on, into another transport, or before a collapsing building took them out.

Glass panels rained down like guillotine blades on those unfortunate to be caught below. The majority of those caught in this way were those who had abandoned their transports, such as GUCI enforcers and 'profit generation operative managers'. This solar was indeed a bad day to travel or be inside a building. That pretty much encompassed the majority of the citizens, and it wasn't safe to stay in the open for long due to solar radiation. Only those, perhaps, who were outside of profit and the reach of the four blocks of civilization had a chance.

The wave had reached the de-sal plants on the coastline of the Northern Block. The fried circuitry controlling the turbines caused them to spin dangerously over spec. The wave cut off the power to the turbines. The sudden power withdrawal caused inertia shunts in the turbines, and all flew out of their housings. Many punctured the walls of the facility like shotgun blasts through thin sheets of metal.

The fresh water supply was now brought to a halt. Not that the buildings it supplied were habitable any more. The last of the fresh water poured, wasted, out of the severed pipes where once monuments to ultra-capitalism proudly stood. Everything that had been connected would now be torn apart. For the first time in millennia, man would stand on his own once more. But with such an abrupt change would he survive?

'K, it's happening now, as we speak, thanks to you,' Elizabeth confirmed.

'We've been through this before. I'm not proud of what I've done.'

'It had to be done, K, and you agreed to it. That was even before you knew how my brother had twisted his original plan to save the planet into something more unpalatable.'

'I'll still be known as the murderer. I pressed the button and billions will die, how many have perished so far?'

'K, don't torment yourself, there's nothing you can do now to stop it.'

'Elizabeth, I've found a reset projection analysis here on the system with me.'

'Run it if you must, K. It's quite comprehensive. We were unable to correctly simulate the exact timings as we had limited secure space to execute it in so that it wouldn't be detected when it was started. It does give impact figures each solar on the basis of failure of components, transport, water, and so on:

"Deaths: inside collapsed buildings or caused by collapsed buildings 200 million during the first solar, rising to 500 million as rescue services assumed to be inoperable.

One million in transit accidents rising to 50 million 14 solars after the reset. Further medium term deaths caused by technology failure 3.5 billion."

That's still 19 billion or so left. There will be war and conflict for diminishing resources – only the most self-sufficient of citizens will survive. We will never know the figures for certain, K. We no longer have the technology to count all of our citizens any more. That's a good thing wouldn't you say?'

'*I suppose so, ultra-capitalism has had its day.*'

'We need to put you into hibernation now, K, you understand?'

'*I suppose so. You need to conserve your resources.*'

'Exactly, but we also have to lock down this facility to preserve it from the gathering storms outside.'

'*Preserve? I thought all technology had to be destroyed.*'

'We need to keep the knowledge of how to rebuild without technology.'

'*And how do you propose to do that?*'

'We've isolated that knowledge and have stored it at the facility here. You will be the gateway to that knowledge.'

'*I'm sorry, Elizabeth, but I can't help thinking you'd be safer and better off with a storage facility full of books.*'

'That's not possible, is it, K? We scanned them all and destroyed the originals a long time ago.'

Elizabeth put the main console into hibernation and turned off the lights. 'Goodbye, K, sweet digital dreams.'

Acknowledgments

For inspiration I'd like to thank John Case and Timothy Good. Their books, for very different reasons, are why I enjoy reading so much today.

Also many thanks go to Bill Leeb and all his FLA co-artists. Large chunks of the book were written whilst listening to FLA. Writing is so much fun with your epic soundscapes as a soundtrack to the book.

K, your advice was spot on; thanks for the best five words of wisdom ever given.

My kids and my other half, for only occasionally doubting I'd ever finish the book :-)

Finally, not forgetting my editor Lesley Jones whose eye for detail and valuable input have made all the difference to this book.

Good profit to you all!

Author's note:

A large number of technologies written about in the book actually do exist. I use some of them in my 9-5 job. Due to confidentiality clauses I can't say any more than that, but being able to be use such advanced technology is a privilege. As with all new technology it can be used for both positive and negative purposes. I just hope we can learn in time to keep the less pleasant aspects of human nature from abusing this wonderful opportunity technology can present us with.

As for the future? It will turn up soon enough.

39322659R00262

Made in the USA
Charleston, SC
07 March 2015